THE QUARTERLANDS

DARK WATER
BOOK 4

XANTHE WALTER

For Penny
My beloved pink, sparkly girl

AUTHOR'S NOTES

Content Advisory
This book contains **mature themes and explicit sexual content.** It is intended for readers 18+ only. For detailed content information, please visit the content advisory web page for this book before reading. https://www.xanthe-walter.com/content-advisory/dark-water-book-4/

Language Note
This book uses British English spelling and grammar conventions throughout.

Quality Assurance
While this book has undergone extensive proofreading to ensure the highest quality reading experience, should you encounter any errors, please report them to my PA at XW@xanthe-walter.com for prompt correction.

Join Walter's World
Subscribe to my newsletter for exclusive content, including a FREE

spicy gay pirate novella, priority updates on new releases, giveaways, and more. Sign up here: https://geni.us/ww-bm

Chapter One
NOVEMBER 2095
Josiah

But let justice roll down like waters
And righteousness like an ever-flowing stream – Amos 5:24

Josiah woke the next morning invigorated by a new mission. Alex needed time, space, and help to heal – and he was going to give him all that and more. Maybe, one day, they could be together on equal terms without all this hanging over them, but until then, he'd do his utmost to be the friend Alex needed.

Finding Alex fast asleep when he peeked around his bedroom door, he tiptoed out of the house, leaving a note in the kitchen.

Gone to run some errands. Be back later. Call me if you want anything. J

As hard as he'd tried, Josiah knew he wasn't enough. Ted had been a good start, but what Alex needed most right now was his family. Noah might refuse a reconciliation, but Josiah knew he had to at least attempt to bring father and son together again. He called Charles first, just to make sure it wasn't a wasted journey, then set off.

There were no media outside the gate this time, and no rain, either, so he took a moment to notice the small details he'd missed last time he was here. The Orchard looked pretty in the watery autumn sun, and the golden bricks were warm and homely. But the house also exuded a shabby quality; the front garden was unkempt and the driveway covered in potholes.

Charles opened the door, looking unchanged since Josiah's last visit, even down to his sporty tracksuit. The jacket was covered in little logos; even though his moment of glory was long gone, he was clearly still a valuable sporting commodity to his sponsors.

Now he knew Alex better, Josiah searched Charles's face for a family resemblance but came up with a blank. Charles was big and blond, Alex slight and dark. Charles was handsome in a big, friendly, puppyish kind of way, but Alex, with his sharp cheekbones and deep grey eyes, was the more striking of the two brothers.

"To what do we owe this honour, Investigator Raine?" Charles asked as he shuffled slowly into the living room, holding on to his walker. "Not more questions, I hope. Please tell me you've eliminated us from your enquiries."

"More or less." Josiah inclined his head in a non-committal way.

"Goodness – we'll try to be on our best behaviour, then!" Charles laughed.

Noah Lytton was awake this time and looked a little better than on Josiah's previous visit. His face was less haggard, his eyes more alert. Josiah was struck by the difference between him and Tyler. They were the same age, but Noah could have been ten years older and Tyler ten years younger, as if they belonged to different generations entirely.

"Investigator Raine, Charles told me you were on your way." Noah stood up, less shakily than last time but still with some effort. "Here, let me shake your hand. Thank you, sir! Thank you!"

"For what?" Josiah asked, surprised. Noah's handshake was firm and heartfelt.

"Arresting George Tyler, of course! It's been all over the news. Please, sit down." Noah gestured at the threadbare sofa.

Josiah took the offered seat, and Charles plonked himself down next to him with a sigh, while Noah settled in his armchair opposite. Tea was offered and declined. The niceties over, Josiah launched straight in.

"My intention in coming here today isn't to alarm or upset you." He directed most of this to Noah – he was the one he really needed to win over. "But inevitably, you will find what I have to say distressing."

"I see." Noah's lips tightened. "I'm assuming this is about Alex, then?"

"Yes."

"What's he done now?" Noah asked wearily.

"It's less what he's done than what's been done to him, most of which, I think, you do not know," Josiah said sombrely. Now he was here, he could see how difficult this task would be. How did you tell a father that his son had been manipulated, trapped, tortured, and prostituted?

"Last time I saw Alex in person, Tyler brought him to my factory and paraded him around in an obscene costume," Noah said tightly. "I doubt there's much you can tell me that would shock me."

"Alex told me about that. You have to know he had no choice that day. Tyler used a young woman to coerce him. She'd have suffered terribly if he'd refused to do Tyler's bidding."

Noah frowned. "I didn't know that."

"Honestly, sir, there's much you don't know. Forgive me, but once Tyler's trial starts, this will become common knowledge, a talking point, freely discussed in the media. I would rather you heard it from me first."

Noah exchanged a puzzled glance with his son.

"What is it, Investigator Raine?" Charles asked anxiously. "What has Alex told you?"

"A good deal, although not, I think, everything." Josiah shot him a cool glance. There was something about Charles that irritated him, but he wasn't sure what. Was it the easy smile and vacuous charm, which Josiah perceived as hiding a certain weakness of character? Or something else, something less tangible? He turned his attention back to Noah, who he warmed to a great deal more, despite his stubbornness and the wounded pride that pervaded his every word and gesture. There was something honest about the man.

"Mr Lytton, did you know that George Tyler manipulated Alex into stealing that money from Lytton AV? That Tyler orchestrated his downfall?"

"No." Noah looked sceptical. "Why? To get back at me? But why pick Alex to do that? All he really had against us was that Isobel chose me and not him, and that was years ago!"

"Oh, George Tyler had a great deal of resentment towards the Lyttons, and it didn't begin or end with you. It started with how he perceived your family had treated his father and then himself. Yes, he hated you for stealing Isobel from him, but he saved the worst of his hatred for Alex. In his desire for revenge, he wove a very tight web around him. Alex was just a kid and – forgive me – one without the protection and support of his father. He didn't stand a chance."

Noah looked genuinely confused. "But why?"

"You know, because of that day at the factory, that your wife was having an affair with Tyler?"

Noah took a sharp intake of breath. "Please... I know, of course, but I didn't tell Charles." He looked anxiously at his eldest son, who appeared... not exactly shocked.

Josiah frowned. "Did you know about your mother's affair with Tyler, Charles?"

"Well, I suppose... yes, I did," Charles blustered. He glanced at his father, shamefaced.

"How?" Noah looked genuinely surprised.

"Tyler used to come to some of my training sessions. I saw them holding hands and even, occasionally, kissing." Charles grimaced. "Sorry, Dad. Mum said not to tell you."

"I thought you didn't know," Noah said quietly. "I didn't, until that day in my office when Tyler brought in Alex to throw it in my face. I didn't tell you because I didn't want your image of your mother tarnished. You and she were so close."

"I should have told you," Charles stammered. "But I didn't think it was important because it was all a pretence."

Josiah turned to him, startled. "What makes you say that?"

"Well, running an Olympic bid is expensive, and Tyler was sort of my unofficial sponsor."

"I gave your mother plenty of money for your training," Noah interjected, looking confused.

"Well, she said you didn't. She didn't want to ask for more in case…" Charles looked as if he was searching for the right words. "In case you decided not to support me in chasing the gold medal anymore. Mum said she'd find a way to make sure we had enough money – that's where Tyler came in."

"Isobel was using Tyler to ensure you had enough money for your training?" Josiah asked. Now it was his turn to be surprised.

"Well, yes. She was always terrible with money. Dad insisted on good record-keeping to make sure she was spending what he gave her wisely. She had to hand over all her receipts to him, and he totted everything up." That tallied with what Alex had said about how his father had made him account for every penny of his allowance while he was at university. "Mum said you weren't giving us enough, so she approached Mr Tyler. That's when their affair began," Charles explained. "She told me it didn't mean anything, that she was just using him for his money, so I didn't tell you, because it didn't seem important."

Not important? Was Charles this blasé about everything? Josiah suspected he was. He was the kind of man who liked to bumble happily through life, unbothered by details.

Noah was staring at Charles blankly. "There was more money, if she'd asked for it. I would have given her anything. I wanted you to win that gold medal every bit as much as she did. I can't believe she ever thought I didn't."

"Well, that's what she said." Charles shrugged.

This put a new spin on the affair. Had Tyler known he was being used? Or did he not care, given that at least part of his motivation in having an affair with Isobel was to get back at Noah?

"Isobel assured Tyler that she was going to leave you for him after Alex turned eighteen," Josiah continued. "That's why he hated Alex so much – she died before that could happen."

"Oh, my word," Charles exclaimed. "I didn't know that. Like I said, I thought she was just using him. I didn't know it was serious."

"We don't know that it was, for her at least," Josiah said sharply.

"However, it certainly was for him. He always loved her – maybe in part because he hated the Lyttons, and he felt you'd stolen her from him, Mr Lytton."

"I did." Noah looked skywards for a moment, as if gathering his strength. "The truth is, Isobel and George were very much in love at university. He talked about her all the time. It made me quite jealous, which I'm not proud of. I'd always been the one with everything, and now he had this beautiful girl. The moment I saw her, I fell in love. She was everything I'd ever wanted in a woman – bright, lively, funny, warm, and so pretty… and she was with George."

"The son of an IS, someone you were used to lording over," Josiah said quietly.

Noah's face reddened. "Yes. It pains me to say it, but yes. I was younger then. I hope I'm a better person now. I've had many wretched years to reflect on my shortcomings, and it's time I admitted them. In fact, it's a relief." There was a pained look on his face. "I did steal Isobel from George. I deliberately set out to win her behind his back. I took her out to fancy places, splashed my cash around and spoiled her. She'd grown up in a government work camp and never even knew her father. Her mother had to do all sorts to get by." He grimaced. "She was wise to the ways of the camp but charmingly unworldly about the normal things of life outside that environment, and I deliberately set out to impress her with my wealth. She knew she'd always be taken care of with me, whereas George – well, he had nothing except a fierce intellect and huge ambition. It could have gone either way with him; he could have ended up a billionaire or in prison. Yet, they were a good fit, a better fit than her and me. I just didn't want to see it back then."

As Noah reached out to pick up his glass of water from the coffee table, Josiah noticed that his hand was shaking.

"I'm sorry, sir. That must be a difficult thing to admit in front of your son."

"We paid a high price for my hubris," Noah said. "As a family, we paid a terrible price for making an enemy of George."

"Isobel played her part, too," Josiah pointed out. "She chose the suitor with the best prospects."

"Who can blame her, given the poverty she came from?" Noah

shrugged. "Oh, I know she loved me, but I suspect she always loved him more. No wonder he hated me." He placed his glass back on the table, his hand still trembling.

"I'm sorry, Dad," Charles murmured.

"Tyler never forgave Alex for Isobel's death," Josiah told them. "He wanted revenge, so he set him up, hiring a beautiful young woman to befriend him at university."

"What?" Charles exclaimed. "Hang on... do you mean that girl Alex was seeing on and off for a while? I met her a few times."

"You did?" Noah looked confused. "I don't remember her."

"Alex always kept her under wraps until we saw her at his graduation. He was annoyed because I brought along a camera crew to make a documentary about my paralympic bid and he didn't want to be in the spotlight again. But he was also protecting her. He didn't introduce us formally, but we saw her dancing afterwards. You might remember her because she was such a beauty. What was her name? Sally?"

"Solange," Josiah said.

"Solange... but that's the name of the girl Tyler is accused of murdering!" Charles exclaimed.

"That's right." Josiah filled them in on Alex's life with Tyler. How he was prostituted and abused, and how Solange had helped him escape and paid for it with her life. "He beat Alex so badly for trying to escape that he almost died," he told them. "She ran forward to protect him and Tyler lashed out, killing her."

Noah's face was pale, his eyes shocked, but Charles's expression interested Josiah more. He looked horrified, sickened, as if he might throw up.

"Tyler did this to Alex? He did all these evil, wicked things to him because of the accident?" he babbled almost incoherently. "All this because he told one mistake?" He reached for Noah's glass of water but fumbled it, and the glass smashed to the floor, drenching Josiah's trouser leg.

"Oh, I'm so sorry." Charles leaned forward and patted at Josiah's trousers ineffectually with his handkerchief.

"It's fine." Josiah pushed him away.

Noah's eyes were glassy. He sat looking straight ahead for a few moments. Then, finally, he turned to look at Josiah.

"Why are you here, Mr Raine?" he asked quietly. "Why did you come here to tell us this?"

"Alex is in a bad way, mentally and physically. You might remember Neil Grant? You hired him to go to university with Alex."

"How could I forget?" Noah said stonily. "Alex persuaded him to embezzle all that money."

"I rather think it was the other way around," Josiah said. "Tyler got to Neil, too. He paid him to persuade Alex to take the bait and steal the money."

"But why?" Noah asked blankly. "I gave that young man every advantage. I paid for his education. Why would he do that to Alex?"

"Because he wanted to hurt him. They'd had an affair at university, but then Alex rejected him," Josiah explained – and then, too late, he wondered just how much Noah knew about his son's sexuality.

"Alex and Neil?" On a day of shocking revelations, this was perhaps mild by comparison, but Noah looked stunned all the same. Josiah remembered reading that he was a Floodite, so maybe this was a bigger deal to him than it might be to someone else.

"Did you know that Alex is bisexual?" he asked.

"George implied he was homosexual that time he came to my office, but I knew he'd been seeing that pretty girl, so I'm not sure I believed it." Noah looked at Charles. "Did *you* know?"

"Well, yes. Alex told me and Mum years ago."

Josiah winced. There was something tone deaf about Charles.

"Was my entire family keeping secrets from me all this time? First Isobel's relationship with George, and now this!" Noah looked crushed rather than angry. "Am I such a monster that Alex couldn't tell me himself?"

"Oh no," Charles said hurriedly. "It's just you are very involved with the Floodite church and they do have quite strong views on this kind of thing."

"I *was* involved with the Floodites," Noah said in a bitter tone. "But I haven't been to church since Isobel died. My faith died with her. Not that you seem to have noticed."

"Oh! I did wonder, but I assumed it was because of your illness." Charles leaned forward and patted his father's arm gently. "Sorry, Pops. I didn't like to pry."

"You really had no idea about Neil and Alex?" Josiah asked.

"No. Like I said, Alex was seeing that young woman Charles just mentioned. Solange."

"Neil had a crush on Alex long before you sent him to spy on your son at university," Josiah explained. "Alex was using croc again, despite promising you that he wouldn't after the accident. Neil blackmailed Alex into sleeping with him as a condition for not telling you about it."

"What?" Noah looked as if this was one revelation too many.

"Neil continued to be obsessed with Alex," Josiah continued. "It was entirely one-sided – Alex didn't even like him. For years, Neil plotted to find a way for them to be together. In desperation, he abducted Alex from my house recently, injuring him quite badly. I was able to rescue him, but Neil died in the process. Ever since that night – and if I'm honest, for some time before then – Alex has been struggling. He's been through a lot, and this was the straw that broke the camel's back. That's why I'm here: to ask you to visit him."

Finally, he'd said it. He hoped he'd laid the ground work well enough that Noah would at least consider it.

"No," said Noah flatly without missing a beat, dashing those hopes instantly.

"That's an old reaction, based on your past feelings," Josiah said firmly. "Take some time to think about it. You have new information now."

"No, I just can't." Noah shook his head vehemently.

"After all I've told you about how he was targeted? How you played your part in that by sending Neil with him to university to spy on him?"

Noah made no reply. He sat staring down at his hands, clasped rigidly in his lap.

"Come now, sir," Josiah remonstrated. "You must understand that this information changes things. If you knew how brave Alex has been, how strong, holding out all this time in the hope of obtaining justice for Solange. If you understood how awful his life has been, then surely you'd forgive him."

"There's too much between us. I lost my company because of him. I lost everything because of him: Isobel, Lytton AV, my money. All gone, because of him."

"I agree, you've lost a great deal, but you could still get something back."

"What?" Noah frowned.

"Him!" Josiah exclaimed, feeling utterly exasperated. "Alex. You could get your son back."

Noah gazed at him blankly, as if this wasn't a prize he considered worth gaining.

Josiah struggled to keep control of his temper. "Listen, Alex may be a grown man, but after all he's been through, he needs his family," he said urgently. "Most of all, he needs his *father*. I was brought up in the Quarterlands, not a fancy house like this, and maybe we did things differently there, but I *knew* my father would always be there for me, no matter what. There's nothing I could have done that would have stopped him. He might have given me the sharp end of his tongue, but he'd have been there for me."

Noah's face was flushed but there was a stubborn set to his mouth. "I can see what you think of me, but you can't possibly understand what he's put this family through."

"And you don't understand what he's been through. He's shut down, at a low ebb, and I'm worried about him. He's survived so much, and I'm not sure how much more he can take. I didn't even dare to tell him that I was coming here. I didn't want to disappoint him if you said no."

"I see." Noah gazed at his hands again. "I really do, but I don't think this can be mended. There's too much water under this particular bridge."

"Then don't come." Josiah stood abruptly. "I understand that the two of you have hurt each other very much and there may need to be some robust conversations, but don't come unless you're prepared to forgive him. Alex needs a father, not a fight. Here are my details." He threw a nanocard on the coffee table. "I'll leave it up to you."

He strode to the door, feeling annoyed with both these pitiful men, locked up with each other amid the faded splendour of a life long since lost. Despite Alex's many tribulations, at least he hadn't become threadbare and diminished. He was still *vivid*, a sharp contrast to their worn-out gentility and obsession with old grudges and glories.

Pausing by the front door, he heard Charles coming up behind him, panting slightly at the effort.

"Thank you for coming and telling us all this, and thank you for giving us the opportunity to see Alex again," Charles said. "I'll come, of course – if Alex wants to see me. I mean, if he only wants to see Dad, that's fine."

"Why wouldn't he want to see you?" Josiah asked.

"In case he thinks I let him down." Charles's ruddy skin flushed a deeper shade of red. "I promised him I'd save the money to buy his contract, but I didn't."

"I see." Josiah gazed at him thoughtfully. "I'm sure Alex would like to see you, too," he said at last. "You're his brother." He might not warm to Charles, but Alex had never wavered in his love for him.

He remembered something. "One thing, Charles. Alex spoke of keeping his mother's scarf – he found it comforting. Could you bring it when you come? Or something else of hers if it can't be found?"

"Of course!" Charles brightened, looking pleased to be of some use.

"Good. Call me and let me know when," he said curtly, and then he left.

It was a relief to be out in the crisp, fresh air. There was something stifling about that place, a sense of being smothered by the weight of the past. He took a few deep breaths and climbed into his duck, glad to put The Orchard behind him.

As he drove home, he mulled over the meeting in his head. This hadn't been official business but he could never turn off his internal investigator. Something about that encounter had been off, but he couldn't put his finger on what. An inappropriate reaction? An insincere expression? Something misspoken? Whatever it was, he had the sense that he was missing a piece of a puzzle, and he usually only felt that way when digging into a case. Had something back there been material to Dacre's murder, or was it something else? He turned it over and over in his head but couldn't put his finger on it.

He put in a call to Esther. "Dacre's case," he said tersely. "I want to keep it open. I don't think we've solved it yet."

"You don't think it was Neil, then?" She sounded surprised.

"No." He didn't know why he was so sure, just that he was.

"Do you have any new evidence?"

"No, but I'll find it," he said firmly, ending the call. He turned off his nym immediately so she couldn't call back. He didn't want to answer any questions on the subject because he couldn't explain it. He just knew he was missing something, but he didn't know what.

He stopped off at the local shops and bought some chocolate, then returned home, trying to shake the unsettled feeling. Alex was up but lying on the sofa in the living room with the screen on, staring into space, as usual.

"Hey." Josiah dropped a kiss on his head. They might have agreed to take a step back from their relationship, but he still wanted Alex to feel loved.

Alex wrenched his gaze away from the fascinating spot on the wall and glanced at him. "Oh. You're back." He didn't look remotely interested.

"Yeah. I got you some chocolate." He was desperately trying to stuff calories into Alex, but it wasn't working. He ate like a bird and the weight had fallen off him. He handed Alex the bar and then went to the kitchen to make a cup of tea.

A thought occurred to him, and he brought up Charles's Olympic race on his holopad. What a different world it had been for the Lytton family back then. Charles, boyishly handsome, full of youthful vigour, smiling cheerily from his boat as he waited for the race to start. A cut to the stands, where his family were watching, tense but excited. Alex looked so young.

Their hologram images filled the room, making Josiah's heart break, for within a few weeks, this entire family would be shattered. He paused the footage and gazed at Isobel, hovering in the air in front of him. She was a beautiful woman indeed. Josiah didn't judge her; he had no idea what her life had been, or the secrets that had caused her to make the choices she had.

He resumed the race and watched as Charles strained every muscle and sinew as he rowed. He could almost feel the nation cheering him on, their first serious gold medal hope in thirty years. How exciting it must have been to be there, watching. Even knowing the outcome, he held his breath as Charles fell behind and then, from nowhere, summoned an explosive burst of energy right at the end that allowed him to win the race by a whisker.

He was interrupted by the doorbell. Pausing the holovid, he opened the front door to find Charles standing there.

"Sorry – I tried calling but your nym is offline," Charles explained apologetically. "Dad's in the duck. He wants to know if it's okay if we come in and see Alex?"

"Of course!" Glancing at the duck parked on the driveway, he saw Noah peering out anxiously. Josiah waved him in, and he climbed out of the vehicle and limped up the driveway, leaning on his stick.

Josiah offered him his arm as he came into the house and Noah took it gratefully, leaning on him while Charles shuffled in behind them.

"Thank you. I'm sorry to just turn up like this, but I knew the minute you left that I'd been a fool and I couldn't wait," Noah babbled. "Where is he?"

"In here." Josiah pushed open the living room door. He'd had no time to prepare Alex, so he hoped he'd done the right thing. "You have a visitor, Alex." He deliberately blocked the doorway so Charles couldn't follow his father into the room.

Alex turned his head lethargically, barely bothering to look up. Noah began walking as fast as he could across the room towards him.

"Dad?" It was barely more than a disbelieving whisper, but it was Noah's reaction that took Josiah by surprise. He looked down on Alex, with his bruised face, his arm in a cast, his thin body, and his pale, pinched expression, and he practically ran the rest of the way to the sofa.

"Alex! My son. My poor, darling child." Sitting down on the sofa, he wrapped his arms around his son, his hands trembling. "Alex... what have they done to you? What have we all done to you? My boy, my poor boy. Dad's here now... shh... I'm here, I'm here..."

"Dad? Daddy?" Alex clung to him, and the dam finally broke. He sobbed into his father's shoulder, letting out years of pain and suffering, crying incoherently.

Noah held him tight and rocked him back and forth all the while as if he was a small child, soothing him, whispering that his father was here and telling him that he was loved, so very loved, and he'd never let him down again.

Josiah swallowed the lump in his throat and took a step back, forcing Charles into the hallway. He closed the door to give Alex and Noah some privacy.

"You can see Alex later. Let's go into the kitchen and have some tea," he suggested. "Funnily enough, I was just watching your Olympic gold medal victory."

Charles's face lit up like a lost zone beacon. "Oh! How lovely. I haven't seen it in ages."

"Then let's go and watch it together. You can give me some behind-the-scenes commentary."

Charles was lively and enthusiastic as he talked Josiah through the race. This was his passion, the subject that interested him the most. As he spoke, Josiah felt a grudging respect for him. You didn't get to be the best at your elite sport without having a certain amount of grit and determination, so behind Charles's affable smile was surely someone of substance.

"Did you never find a special someone to share your life with?" he asked curiously, unable to turn off the investigator in him.

"There were women." Charles grinned. "Still are. But I've never felt the need to propose."

"You were very close to your mum. I suppose it's hard to find someone to measure up to such a remarkable woman," Josiah observed.

"Well, quite," Charles said softly. Then he leaned forward. "Look, I know you don't like me much, Mr Raine, and I understand why. You despise me for not saving the money to put in a bid for Alex. But you must understand that kind of money would have been far beyond me, even leaving aside the fact I wanted the operation. I simply don't make that much, even in a good year. Alex's contract is too expensive. I can barely keep The Orchard going for Dad – he refuses to move – let alone have enough money to buy the country's most expensive IS."

"At least that's honest." Josiah gave a grudging nod. "Why didn't you say so before?"

"Guilt. I knew it was too much for me, so I shouldn't have made him that promise. I just felt so terrible for him on the day he was sentenced that I wanted to give him something to hang on to, an iota of hope, however false."

"I can understand that," Josiah grunted. He liked this Charles Lytton better than the charming fool. He glanced at his watch. "They've had an hour. Would you like to see him now?"

"Oh yes." Charles beamed. "I love my brother very much, Mr Raine. I always have and I always will."

Josiah had to concede that Alex seemed equally devoted to his brother. Whatever rifts had taken place in their family, these two had never wavered in their love for each other.

He opened the living room door to see Alex and his father sitting on the sofa, talking quietly, their hands clasped.

"Hey... just checking in. Also... there's someone else who wants to see you," he said, standing aside so that Charles could shuffle in.

"Charles!" Alex got to his feet and stumbled across the room to envelop his brother in an almighty bear hug. It was the most animated Josiah had seen him in weeks. They hugged for a long time, until finally, Alex released him and they returned to the sofa together.

"Oh, before I forget." Charles reached into his pocket. "I brought you this." He pulled out a green chiffon scarf and handed it to Alex, who buried his face in it immediately and inhaled. When he looked up, his eyes were glowing. "It still smells of her. After all this time! Thank you, thank you, thank you."

"Don't thank me. When Mr Raine visited this morning, he asked me to find it and bring it." Charles beamed.

"I'll go and make some more tea, so you can reconnect as a family," Josiah said, leaving swiftly.

They stayed for several hours. Josiah had no doubt that there were some difficult conversations still to be had, but for now, they just seemed delighted to be with each other again. Laughing, they chatted only about happy memories, with Isobel never far from their reminiscences.

Eventually, it grew late, and Noah was visibly tired. "Come again, whenever you want," Josiah said, escorting them to the door. "When Alex is better, he can visit you, too." He held out his hand, but Noah brushed it aside, drawing him into an awkward hug.

"You're a good man, Mr Raine," he murmured into Josiah's ear. "And our family owes you a huge debt. I'm sorry for what I said when I first met you. I only saw the famous indiehunter, and I assumed I knew you based on that."

When they'd gone, Josiah returned to the living room to find Alex lying in his usual spot but looking completely different. He was clearly tired, but his face was relaxed and had lost that pinched expression.

"Hey, are you okay?" Josiah plonked himself down beside him.

"Yes. Thanks to you." Alex pressed a gentle kiss to his cheek. "I never thought I'd see them again. Certainly not Dad, given his health and the fact he disowned me. I have no idea how you persuaded him to visit, but it means the world to me."

"I knew it would." Josiah smiled affectionately.

Alex wrapped his arms around him and leaned in, his lips tantalisingly close. "I mean it."

Josiah pushed him away gently.

"I know you're grateful, but it came with no expectations or obligations. I care about you, Alex. Just because we've agreed to step back a bit doesn't change that. What also hasn't changed is that you need the time and space to adjust to all that's happened and find out who you are and what you want."

Alex sighed and drew back. "You're right, of course." He gave a wan smile.

"Good. Then get some rest. You look done in." Josiah deposited a firm kiss on Alex's head. Then, leaving him on the sofa, he returned to the kitchen to speak in private to Esther.

"Oh, you're talking to me again now, are you?" she asked pointedly.

"Sorry I turned off my nym. I just knew you'd ask me questions that I didn't know the answers to, and I needed time to think."

"And now?"

"Now I'm back on track. Listen, Esther, I'm going to return to the office soon, so I'll need meetings with the lawyers. We have to paint a picture to the jury of Tyler's hatred of Alex, so they understand why the events of that night unfolded the way they did, leading directly to Solange's death. We need evidence and witnesses for that, which I'm still working on."

"I'm glad to hear you're back in the ring," she said. "Not that I had any doubt you'd climb back in when you were ready. Now, what about Dacre? Are you still convinced that Grant didn't kill him?"

"Yes."

"May I ask why?"

He sighed. "I'm not sure, but I went to see Charles and Noah Lytton this morning."

"Oh?" She grimaced. "Please tell me you aren't thinking of arresting Charles Lytton too. He's a national hero."

"Don't worry, I don't think he killed Dacre, but seeing the Lyttons made me understand why I can't close the case yet. There's something I'm not seeing, Esther, about both the Lyttons and Dacre. There's a piece of the jigsaw missing in both cases. I don't think they're connected, but they're both unsolved – for now."

"Well, if anyone can find those missing pieces, it's you." She smiled. "It's good to have you back, Joe. I'll wait to hear from you."

He returned to the living room to find Alex fast asleep with his mother's scarf clutched between his fingers. Josiah reached for the blanket on the back of the sofa and gently laid it over him, heaving a sigh of relief.

He didn't kid himself that it would be this easy, or that one visit would turn Alex around and bring him out of his depression, but it was a start.

Chapter Two
APRIL 2090
Alex

Everything had changed, and yet nothing did. Tyler sent Alex back to his suite, and, bizarrely, his life resumed as normal. He spent his days working out, doing yoga, and reading, and his nights entertaining Tyler's guests. Of Tyler himself, there was no sign. Maybe now that Tyler slept with him, he was no longer interested. Alex wasn't sure whether to feel relieved about that or not. It gave him some breathing space, but it didn't help him with his mission.

The respite didn't last long. A few weeks later, Tyler had him brought up to his suite.

"I have a job for you," Tyler said, pinging a briefing document into the air. "I'm giving this one to you because you understand the importance of the floating city project."

He pointed at the diagram in front of them. Alex was familiar with the schematics of floating cities; he'd read all the books Tyler had given him and listened to him talk about his plans for them at length.

"They're the key to our entire future," Tyler said passionately. "These new floating cities are prefab. If scaled up, they're cheap to manufacture and construct and have the power to transform the world. All the refugees, the poor, the dispossessed, and homeless can be relocated onto them. We can clear out the Quarterlands cesspits and government work camps and give people a chance at a decent life, as well as freeing up actual land for agriculture in the process to make it easier to feed them."

He spoke as if he cared about those things, and maybe, in an abstract, big-picture kind of way, he did. But Alex knew his primary interest in the tech was financial. Building floating cities on an industrial scale was the next big thing, and Tyler intended to dominate the industry from the start. He'd been a big investor in Ghost Eye, but that had been a high-end venture. In order to make them viable, they had to be mass-produced, and Tyler believed he was the man to do it.

"I know you're as interested as I am in making this happen," Tyler said, leaning in, his eyes blazing with sincerity. "And this is your chance to be part of it. That's why I'm trusting this job to you and only you, Alexander."

He didn't fool himself that his role would be anything other than being Tyler's whore, so he wasn't disappointed by what came next.

Tyler pinged a holopic of a middle-aged man with bushy grey hair into the air. He wasn't in any way interesting, apart from his vivid green eyes.

"This is Rupert Walcott. He's the politician who'll be handing out the contracts to build the floating cities that will transform our future. He's also someone with certain... peccadilloes." Tyler smiled. "He's into young men and has a particular penchant for BDSM."

Alex kept his expression neutral, but his heart sank. What would Walcott want to do to him? He hoped it wouldn't be a repeat of his experiences with Harper. He was, therefore, pleasantly surprised by what Tyler said next. "He likes being dominated – the more brutally, the better – and out of all the young men at my disposal, I think you're the best suited to this job. Walcott needs someone he can talk to as well as fuck, and nobody understands the floating city project better than you."

"All the young men...?" Alex blurted.

Tyler's face creased up in a delighted smile. He always loved wrong-footing him, and it had been some time since Alex had given him the pleasure.

"Oh, you don't think you're the only young man in my stable, do you?" He laughed. "Or Marta the only woman? I have many indies in my service who perform this work for me. Did you think you were unique?" Tyler winked at him. "I need a wide cross-section of types – ages, looks, sexualities – to match the right person to the job. You've been quite a draw, obviously, because of your looks and your fame, but you're only suitable in certain circumstances, and I have a hell of a lot of people I need onside to make my business projects work." By "onside" he meant blackmailed or bribed, presumably.

"You're so naïve," Tyler sighed. "This is a normal part of being in very big business and moving in the circles I do. People expect it. Everyone is capable of being bought. You just have to find the right currency. Although..." He frowned. "There are some currencies I won't trade in." So, the man had scruples. Interesting. "I've been asked to provide children, and I could do it, too; the Quarterlands are full of underage brats who'd do anything for a hot meal and a ticket out of there. I won't trade in kids, though, however desperate they might be for an escape route."

Alex supposed, grudgingly, that that was commendable of him, but it was hard to give him much kudos for where he drew that particular line.

"If Martin Bagshaw wanted an actual boy, then...?" he asked quietly.

"He asked once – I turned him down," Tyler said abruptly. "He seems happy enough with you, and the other indie I let him have, who looks younger than he is."

If Tyler wasn't offering children, Alex was sure somebody out there would be. There were enough Quarterlands kids without strong adults in their lives to safeguard them who'd be easy prey.

"I'll do my very best to ensure Mr Walcott has a wonderful time," he said, studying the briefing document.

"I know you will. What I like about the new, improved Alexander is your work ethic. You haven't let me down since your return from Belvedere. I might have had my suspicions, but I can't deny you've performed excellent work."

Then, much to Alex's surprise, he tipped up his chin and kissed him gently on the lips. "This will be our victory, Alexander, like the Destiny ducks. Yours and mine. Our triumph. Bring me Walcott, get me that contract, and then we'll celebrate, just like we did the other day."

Alex smiled at him, hating the way his cock stirred hungrily in response to the kiss. He didn't even know if he was pretending anymore; his body seemed to want Tyler as much as his rational mind hated him.

Tyler stage-managed the seduction of his next victim with his usual finesse. First of all, there was a party where he introduced Alex to Walcott. This was subtle, a casual introduction in a room full of people. Alex soon had Walcott engrossed in a detailed conversation about floating cities. The politician knew his brief and was as evangelical about them as Tyler, although for different reasons. Like Tyler, he believed they were the answer to many of the country's most pressing problems. Unlike Tyler, he wasn't interested in them for their money-making capability. He genuinely saw them as a solution if they could be made affordable to a cash-strapped government. Money was always a problem. The world had very little of it to go around, and floating cities were expensive. The tech to build them had been possible since Pre-R days, but it was only now, so many years after the Rising, that governments had enough finance to build them on anything like the scale required.

Alex found himself liking Walcott. The man was genial and charismatic, if somewhat shambolic in appearance, with wildly uncontrollable grey hair. Yet his vivid green eyes were genuinely beautiful and gave his face a soulful quality. He spoke about his husband often and with great affection, which made Alex feel almost sorry for him.

"We've been together a long time, although there are certain things we no longer have in common," Walcott murmured. "Maybe we never did. Anyway, he's not interested in the same things as me, but I still love him."

Scenting blood, Alex went in for the kill.

"If you need someone to explore those things with, I might be interested," he murmured, handing Walcott a canape from a passing tray and holding it to the man's lips. "Eat," he ordered.

Alex was good enough at his job by now to feel the frisson passing through Walcott's body at the tone of command in his voice. For the first time since becoming Tyler's whore, he thought he might have some fun with it.

It worked. Within days, he was preparing for an intimate dinner with Tyler's new victim. Alex had asked Tyler if he could decide for himself what clothes to wear for the event, rather than rely on Andrew to provide an outfit, and, much to his surprise, Tyler had agreed.

"Baby steps," he could imagine Gideon whispering in his ear. *"This is good, but it's only a start. Tyler's trust was hard won but will be easily lost – don't squander it."*

So, he prepared meticulously for his date with Walcott.

"You're sure about this?" Tyler demanded as he surveyed the outfit Alex had selected. "It's very... subtle."

"You think I should go full-on leather queen?" Alex grinned. "All black clothes and brooding?"

"Well, we do know what he likes."

"He's not that one-dimensional. I know that from meeting him. I have plans... trust me." Alex shot Tyler a winning smile.

"I'm trying to, but this is too important to fuck up," Tyler snapped.

"I won't. I promise. I'll give him exactly what he wants. This is what I do, it's what I'm good at. You know that." Even as he said it, Alex knew he'd made a tactical mistake.

"Is that what you did to me? Gave me what I want?" Tyler's eyes were once more full of all the suspicions Alex had been trying so hard to banish.

"No, that was real. You couldn't fake how we felt flying across the lost zone in our duck," Alex told him passionately. "I was hot for you. I wanted you. I still do, if you'll let me serve you in that way again. This is about me serving you in a different way, sir. I want to make your dream of building all these floating cities come true. I can do this, I know I can."

"You'd better," Tyler said sharply.

He could feel Tyler's eyes on him later that evening, watching through the smartwall as he greeted Walcott. The outfit Alex had chosen consisted of black chinos and a soft maroon cashmere sweater. He looked stylish and sophisticated but also strong. The thin sweater hugged his toned chest and showed off every hard-won plane of his pecs and biceps. He could see Walcott drinking it in, enjoying the view. If he'd greeted the politician wearing tight black leather, he'd have scared the man off before they started. Walcott was subtler than that; he wanted a seduction, not an ambush.

Walcott was an amusing dinner guest, full of indiscreet anecdotes about his time in government, including one about the prime minister that had Alex in stitches. Over time, he'd stopped feeling guilty about his part in the eventual downfall of the people Tyler gave him to. His job was to show them a good time, and he was determined to do that. If their lives were going to be ruined by sleeping with him, he wanted that to be worth it.

After dinner, he invited Walcott back to his room. "We talked about something we might have in common," he murmured. "I'd like to show you what I mean by that."

In his room, he had an entire closet full of outfits and implements. He opened the door, letting Walcott peek inside.

"I love role-play," Alex said smoothly. "I thought we could choose some outfits and have some fun."

Walcott laughed as he held up a police officer's uniform. "Are there handcuffs to go with this?" he asked saucily.

"Of course." Alex winked, snapping one onto Walcott's wrist.

The rest of the evening was the most fun Alex had had since starting work for Tyler. Walcott was an inventive lover, and it was a breeze to go along with his suggestions. Alex had always had a good erotic imagination and he loved giving people the kind of sex they enjoyed.

He had Walcott every which way possible – handcuffed to the bed, against the wall, over a chair... The sense of power was exhilarating. Was this what Tyler got out of it, Alex wondered, one fist wrapped in Walcott's wild grey hair as he pounded into him? Only for Tyler it was real, but he was just play-acting.

Afterwards, Walcott nestled against his chest and wept.

"That was so good. I've been paying to see prostitutes," he admitted. "But they just beat me and fuck me, and it's so sterile. It's like they hate it. You made it fun, Alex. Thank you."

"It was my pleasure," Alex murmured, and he meant it.

He knew he'd done a good job, so he was confused when Tyler called him up to his suite the next day and gave him a cold glance.

"Did I screw up?" Alex asked anxiously. "Did Walcott complain about me?"

"No, he went away satisfied, and I have enough footage to ensure he's in my pocket now." Tyler gazed at him from narrowed eyes. "You were right. You knew how to play him. That is your particular skill, after all."

"I just want to do my job for you to the best of my ability to further your ambitions," Alex explained, not liking where this was going.

"Well, you succeeded. I thought he wanted it brutal, but you picked up on something else, some other yearning he had. A desire for connection that I hadn't appreciated."

"He's a human being. He's lonely. His husband isn't into him anymore, and he's afraid of his own desires," Alex said softly.

"Did you like being in control?" Tyler demanded abruptly. "It looked like you were having fun. Did you even need the blue pills?"

"Yes, of course, and I took them. Any 'fun' you saw me having was to hook Walcott for you," Alex replied, feeling a wave of despair.

He was always caught between the devil and the deep dark water with Tyler. If he did his job too well, then Tyler doubted him, and yet doing his job well was the only way he could make Tyler trust him.

He was forever walking on eggshells, trying to strategise the best way to make the man believe him, and he was so tired of it. He knew Gideon would have no sympathy with these emotions. Gideon was a Quarterlands kid with no tolerance for self-pity, so he squashed it down.

"It looked like you were enjoying your work a little too much," Tyler growled. "You were all over him."

Alex saw it, then, the way he'd seen into Walcott's psyche. He saw Tyler's jealousy, insecurity, and unquenchable desire to be the best.

Alex was so good at understanding what these men wanted and moulding himself into it. Did he even have any desires of his own, or did he exist merely as a mirror for theirs? He no longer knew.

"Everything I do is to please you," he whispered.

"Why?" Tyler demanded.

"Isn't it obvious?" Alex touched Tyler's cheek gently. "I want you again. I always want you. I wanted you every second of my time with Walcott. I kept thinking that I wanted you to do to me what I was doing to him."

"Oh, you'd like that, would you?" Tyler's eyes were dark now, and Alex knew the expression in them all too well.

"You know I would," he whispered, leaning in for a kiss.

Tyler's lips were warm and possessive, his mouth hot and hungry. He could feel Tyler's erection pressing into him and was sure they were going to take it to the bedroom... only to find Tyler's hand wrapped around his throat, pushing him away.

"No," Tyler snapped, his dark eyes glinting dangerously.

"I'm sorry, sir. Did I do something wrong?"

"I've *had* you," Tyler growled. "I wanted to have you to prove a point. I wanted you to beg, like I said you would, and you did. That's it. This is not a fucking love affair, Alexander! Did you think you could sweet-talk your way into my bed and become – what? – my boyfriend?" He laughed. "I don't fucking think so. You're a servant, an expensive one, granted, but nothing more. You did your job with Walcott well, but *if* I fuck you again, it'll be because I want to, not because you've manipulated me into it."

Alex lowered his eyes submissively. "I'm sorry, sir. I understand. I let my desire for you run away with me. My apologies." Yet he hadn't mistaken that erection. Tyler definitely still desired him, and his mixed messages spoke not so much of his need for control as his fear of losing it.

Alex pondered this as he walked back to his suite. Was that it? Was Tyler more emotionally compromised around Alex than he wanted him to know? It would make sense of his yo-yoing moods and the emotional whiplash of simply trying to please him.

He saw Walcott many times over the next few months and each

time it was a pleasure. He liked the man, and he performed his job well, not that Tyler thanked him for it. He behaved more like a jealous lover, berating Alex for his skill while all the time insisting he keep Walcott onside. It was exhausting, and Alex was wilting under the pressure. He stepped up his yoga to try and keep his emotions under control, but he hoped this particular job would soon be over.

Then, one day in early November, Andrew dressed him in a beautiful tuxedo, and he was taken by helicopter to an old manor house in the country. It was a luxury spa hotel, of the kind very few people could afford these days. He was ushered inside and taken up a flight of wood-panelled stairs to a suite, where he found Tyler waiting for him, looking sharply handsome in a dinner jacket.

"There he is! The man of the hour." Tyler broke into a round of applause and then handed him a glass of champagne.

"We're celebrating?" Alex took a sip.

"We are indeed. I'm proud to announce that I've been granted the government's contract to build dozens of floating cities. We did it!"

With a broad grin, Alex raised his glass and toasted Tyler. As he sipped on the champagne, he glanced around. The suite was grand, with a colossal four-poster bed taking centre stage. It exuded luxury, with two deep crimson velvet sofas and several large oak chests and wardrobes, giving it a cosy, old-fashioned vibe. A massive fireplace dominated one wall, with an intricately carved wooden mantle, showcasing a blazing fire. It was unusually chilly for autumn, and had even snowed briefly earlier, making the warmth from the flames even more welcome.

"Welcome to La Papillon," Tyler said, waving his arm around expansively. "One of the most exclusive hotels in the country."

"La Papillon? The butterfly?"

"That's right. The owner, Chef Richard, came from France originally," Tyler explained. "He started out in a government work camp as a refugee after one of those interminable wars in Europe – I can't remember which one. He eventually found work as an IS in a restaurant in New London and discovered he was an excellent cook. He worked hard, embraced his freedom when his contract finished, and now he owns this place. Hence the name, La Papillon."

"His life was transformed from something ugly into something beautiful," Alex murmured. "An inspiring story."

"His food is magnificent, and he's cooking just for us tonight. I've bought out the entire place. We'll have a ringside seat next to the kitchen and we can watch the genius at work. I've ordered the full tasting menu, so I hope you're hungry."

It was hard not to be swept along by Tyler's good mood. He loved showing off the history of the grand old manor house and all the luxuries it contained. Tyler, on genial good form, was almost impossible to resist, full of interesting stories which he told with his usual sharp wit.

They were taken to a rustic dining room with oak beams, and true to his word, they were the only guests there. Tyler really had bought up the entire place to reward Alex for bringing in Walcott.

Alex knew Gideon wouldn't approve, but it felt good to bask in his houder's praise, to feel relaxed and almost happy, even if only for a short time. He lived on his wits so much, his nerves constantly shredded by his need to stay in control of his emotions and keep his true nature hidden, that this was a welcome respite. Tonight, he could let go and enjoy himself, as much as was possible in the circumstances anyway.

Chef Richard was a huge man with an equally huge character, a big bear of a Frenchman. It did cross Alex's mind that Tyler might be expecting him to sleep with him, but that didn't seem to be the case. Richard was an entertaining host, talking them through every single morsel on his extensive tasting menu.

Both Alex and Tyler were naturally slim, but tonight they ate with gusto. Every mouthful was delicious – it was a gastronomic experience that lived up to every bit of the hype Tyler had given it. Alex could see why Richard had been so successful. Every time, groaning, he insisted that he couldn't eat another thing, Richard would laugh and serve up some delicious little *amuse-bouche* that he couldn't resist. It was divine.

The wine flowed freely, too, although Alex made sure he didn't drink too much. He'd noticed that Tyler was also abstemious with the alcohol. They drank enough to be pleasantly tipsy but not enough to be rip-roaring drunk. It had been so long since Alex had taken croc, or been even a little drunk, and he embraced the warm, fuzzy joy of it.

Afterwards, they rolled back to the suite, laughing and exclaiming about all the good food they'd eaten and the great time they'd had. When he stepped inside, he was surprised to find a dozen candles had been lit all around the room, while the enormous fire was still burning in the grate, casting orange shadows on the walls.

"You know..." Tyler caught Alex's hand and drew him over to a sheepskin rug in front of the fire. "I think I want to take you right here."

"This is very romantic," Alex whispered, feeling Tyler's lips brushing his hair. He wished he hadn't drunk anything now. It was hard enough keeping his wits about him when he was stone-cold sober but so much harder when he felt mellow, full of good food, and even... happy?

"I *am* a romantic," Tyler declared, and maybe he even believed it. "With the right person." Tyler looked deep into Alex's eyes. "Are you the right person, Alexander? I want to believe you are." His voice was suddenly throaty, full of longing. "I had such passion with your mother. I trusted her. She was the only person, apart from my own mother, who I *ever* trusted."

"That sounds lonely," Alex whispered, resting his hand gently on Tyler's hip. Tyler's eyes flashed with something so sad and wistful that Alex couldn't help himself. He leaned in and pressed a gentle kiss to Tyler's lips. The other man's response was electric – he wrapped his arms around him and kissed him back passionately, his tongue expertly exploring Alex's mouth. Then he pressed him down onto the rug and undressed him.

There was something so intense, so purposeful, about the way Tyler looked at him that Alex was mesmerised. Was it the soft rug beneath his bare buttocks, the romance of the candlelit room, the warmth of the fire on his skin, or the fullness in his belly making him light-headed?

Or was it Tyler's wolfish, dark-eyed gaze as he undressed him, bringing his usual laser-focussed concentration to the task, devouring him with his eyes as he worked?

Alex knew not to interfere or try to take control. He knew to allow

Tyler to always be in charge. If he did that, he was guaranteed the most exquisitely sensual sex he'd ever had.

He surrendered, giving himself up to Tyler's intense caresses and the pleasure of having such an expert lover. Tyler required so little of him. His main enjoyment in sex seemed to be to make his partner dissolve into a puddle of sexual ecstasy, and it was addictive.

Alex lost track of the time in the delicious haze of Tyler's hands on his body, Tyler's mouth on his skin, and Tyler's hard cock sliding into him. It was all too good.

When he awoke, the fire had gone out and the candles had burned down to nothing. It was a grey, dull morning, icy-blue light washing away the warm orange glow from the previous night and illuminating the room with cold precision, sweeping away the illusion of what had passed.

Alex stared at Tyler's sleeping face beside him and wondered what demon was possessing them both. The attraction was there, but hatred, distrust, and fear were there, too, on both sides. No good could come of this, and yet, he was in no position to stop it. Was he falling in love with this man? Or were they simply connected by too much history to escape?

"You're awake," Tyler murmured, jolting him out of his reverie. "Fuck, it's cold!" He stretched, then got to his feet and held out his hands. Alex took them, and let himself be pulled up then bundled into the bed. Tyler burrowed down beside him beneath the soft duvet, wrapping his arms around him and holding him close, warming them both.

It would be easier if he was a cruel lover, but he wasn't. In bed, he was superb, utterly committed to making the sex as sublime as possible, for them both.

Stockholm syndrome. Alex found the phrase reverberating around his mind. Was that what this was? He longed for an easy excuse to explain the pleasure he was taking in Tyler's embraces. It wasn't a help to know that if he wasn't enjoying it, then he'd have to feign it. It felt like a betrayal of himself, of Solange, and on some level, bizarrely, even of Gideon. He'd held out Tyler to be a monster, and yet here he was enjoying the man's caresses and going eagerly to his bed.

He almost wanted to laugh. Tyler had always claimed that *he* was the great seducer. But if he was, he'd more than met his match. Maybe that was the root of it. They were well matched, he and Tyler, and he couldn't see any way this ended other than in their own mutually assured destruction.

"Warmer now?" Tyler kissed the back of his neck and then his hands went lower. "Mmm... how do you feel about a nice morning fuck?"

Alex felt his cock rising in response to the question, and Tyler's questing hand gave it a little stroke of acknowledgement. "I can feel your answer here," Tyler whispered in his ear.

He belonged to Tyler. The man had made that clear from the moment he'd bought him, and yet, Tyler wanted his consent at every turn, demanding his pleasure along with his capitulation, and, powerless to resist, he gave it to him.

Tyler had never once taken him without his explicit consent, never once forced him. He'd always waited until he saw the light of desire in his eyes, or felt the desire in his body.

It was hard to feel he'd been raped, and yet he was choosing none of this. It was all so confusing that it was a relief to simply surrender to the undeniable enjoyment of Tyler's caresses.

They didn't leave their room for the whole weekend. Richard sent them exquisite dishes, and they dined and fucked and talked. Really talked. They loved the same things – ducks, tech, floating cities – and these were safe subjects. Alex didn't have to have his wits about him when they talked about them. They were like teenagers, barely able to take their eyes – and hands – off each other.

"The thing is," Tyler whispered as they lay on the rug again in front of another roaring fire, "you understand me, and I understand you. We share a connection, you and I."

"Yes." Alex caressed his face.

"If only I could believe it was real," Tyler said, and then he rolled over on top of Alex and pushed into him again.

"It is," Alex insisted, arching his body and moaning in pleasure as Tyler hit that sweet spot deep within.

Tyler's eyes were suddenly, unexpectedly, full of tears. Alex wiped them away tenderly, gazing up at him with every ounce of devotion he could muster. It was the first time Tyler had been so open, so vulnerable with him.

"It is," Alex repeated, moving his head to catch Tyler's lips in a deep, hungry kiss.

Everything changed after that. When they returned to Vertex Tower, Alex was installed in Tyler's bedroom and his clothes were moved into the spare room.

From then on, he went everywhere with his houder – to meetings, dinners, galas, and trips to the theatre. Tyler didn't hide him anymore. On the contrary, he seemed keen to show him off, as if he was a trophy to be paraded on his arm.

He dressed Alex in the most exquisite outfits, each one perfectly matched to the occasion. Alex had no say in them, but Andrew was kept busy fitting him for new clothes, making sure he looked every inch the perfect accessory for one of the richest and most important men in the country.

It was as if he was Tyler's partner, and Tyler was proud to show him off. Alex wondered what the media were making of this. Were they publishing photos of them together, or did Tyler have enough blackmail material to keep editors and producers quiet? Or did he *want* people to know that Alex was his lover now? He certainly made it clear they were an item, his hand resting on Alex's arse, or holding his hand, one arm wrapped possessively around his shoulders wherever they went. Nobody could doubt they were together – the heat between them was obvious.

The sex was frequent – in Tyler's office, in his duck, in the elevator, and every single room in his suite. They were hungry for each other, needing to express this passion between them whenever they could. It was their new language, and whether they were communicating love or hate, or something entirely different, it was a gnawing, necessary need that could never be entirely sated.

Tyler veered, as always, between wanting to believe Alex truly loved and desired him and a dark, hopeless despair that he was being played.

Alex, in return, wanted to believe he was still on track to perform his mission but fretted that he'd lost himself along the way, that in trying so hard to be convincing, he'd become the very thing he was pretending to be.

"If I set you free, would you marry me?" Tyler asked one day as they lay naked in bed.

Alex gazed at him hungrily. *Freedom.* His stomach somersaulted with a new hope. "Would you?" he whispered.

"Set you free or marry you?" Tyler's face twisted into an ugly snarl. "Oh, you'd like that, wouldn't you? I set you free, and then you show your true colours and reveal that this was a lie, a charade all along." He wrapped his hand around Alex's throat.

Alex lay there, completely still.

"Is this a charade?" he whispered, thrusting his hips up against Tyler, his hardness evident.

"I don't know. Fuck it, I'm tired of not knowing!" He released his hold and rolled out of the bed. "What the hell are we doing, Alexander?" he rasped wearily.

Alex wondered what reply he could possibly make. None of this was of his doing; Tyler called all the shots.

"You want to know if you can trust me, but you can't know that without actually trusting me," he said softly.

"And then it might be too late," Tyler replied bitterly.

Alex reached out and gently stroked Tyler's back. "I wish I could make you believe me."

"But you know I never can."

Tyler left in a fury, and a few hours later, Andrew entered the suite.

"You're being sent on an assignment," he said, looking as surprised as Alex felt. Tyler was nothing if not possessive, and there had been no assignments since Walcott. "Although this time you are on strict instructions *not* to sleep with the man."

That made more sense. "Who is he, and what does Mr Tyler want me to do for him?"

"It's an odd request, but it seems you made a big impact on one of Mr Tyler's guests, so he's asked if he can borrow you for a bit."

"Borrow me?" Alex raised an eyebrow. "If not to have sex, then to do what?"

"Be his muse." Andrew shrugged. "It's Elliot Dacre. He wants to make holopics of you, apparently."

"What?" Alex sat up. This was so unexpected that it was hard to wrap his head around, although some space from the torturous tightrope he walked daily with Tyler would be welcome.

"I know. Bonkers," Andrew laughed. "Come on, then, let's get you ready for your close-up, shall we?"

Chapter Three
NOVEMBER 2095
Josiah

Josiah woke up the next morning to a delicious smell. He wandered downstairs to find Alex in the kitchen, cooking as well as he could with one arm in a cast.

"Hey, what's all this?" he asked, smiling because Alex was singing as he danced around the kitchen.

"Me trying to make up for being such a shitty IS these past few weeks." Alex paused while dancing past him to press a kiss to his cheek.

Josiah grunted. "I'm glad you're feeling brighter, but pace yourself, Alex. As I said before, you're on a rollercoaster right now." He was under no illusions that this new state of mind would be permanent. Alex was like a pinball, ricocheting all over the place.

"Don't be such a grouch. Come on, it's all ready. You carry the tray into the dining room and I'll bring the tea with my free hand." He picked up the teapot awkwardly and followed Josiah into the dining room.

"Dad looked well, didn't he?" Alex babbled as they walked. "I know he's not in great health, but he looked better than I'd have expected, and Charles was so much fun. We laughed our heads off."

It would have taken a heart of stone to begrudge him the joy of his family reunion. Josiah could only imagine how it must feel to lose the people you loved most in the world and then, magically, be reunited with them again when you least expected it. He was delighted that he'd been able to give Alex such a happy experience after so many terrible ones. He just wished he could only ever give him such joy, but that was impossible. He cleared his throat.

"Uh-oh." Alex made a face.

"Yeah. Much as I've loved spending time with you, I have to get back to work."

"I understand, and you should. I'm fine now," Alex said far too brightly.

Josiah didn't contradict him because he didn't want to bring him down, but he knew Alex wasn't fine. It was impossible to undo years of damage in one day.

"Alex, I need to explain to you the reality of Tyler's trial," he said in a serious voice, reaching for his holopad. "I'm going to record our conversation, not for any reason other than to jog my memory."

"Uh... okay."

"In court, we have to present a narrative to the jury to explain why Tyler hated you so much. The entrapment by Solange, the fraud, the affair with your mother... all of it will come out. Do you understand?"

Alex was quiet for a beat, and then he nodded. "I suppose I hadn't thought about that, but yes."

"The jury will need to appreciate why he was so consumed by rage the night he lost control. We have to help them understand the nature of the vendetta Tyler conducted against you, and they'll need to be told about all the blackmail material he has, and how he prostituted you and others to get it. It'll all come out, and the media will go to town. It has all the ingredients they love, frankly – money, sex, and you."

"Fuck." Alex stared at him glumly. "I suppose I hadn't thought about what the trial would actually entail."

"I thought not," Josiah said softly. "Alex, I'm going to ask you a question, and I want an honest answer. Is there anything you haven't told me?"

Alex blinked. "What do you mean?"

"Is there anything – anything at all – that might conceivably come up in the trial that I should know about? I don't ask to pry but because we can't have anything derail this once we reach court. I must know if you've told me everything, or if there's anything you're still hiding." Alex gazed at him for a long moment, without speaking. "Alex?" Josiah prompted.

"I'm trying to think, but no, I don't think there's anything."

"You're sure?"

Alex nodded. "Absolutely."

Josiah tapped his fingers on the table thoughtfully. That was a lie, and it hurt after all they'd been through. What was it about this family and all their secrets? He supposed he shouldn't judge, given all the secrets he carried, but he'd kept them for the sake of all the people he'd rescued. What possible excuse did Alex have?

"I need you to be very sure. I can help you, however bad it is, if you just tell me. Tyler will go through your life with a fine-tooth comb, so if there's anything you've withheld, then I need to know about it, so we can prepare a response."

Alex gave a bitter snort. "Trust me, Joe, there's no new information that Tyler can use against me in the trial."

That wasn't the question Josiah had asked, and he was too good an investigator not to notice. "So there's nothing else I should know? No more skeletons lurking in the Lytton family closet?" he pressed one last time.

Alex gave a bark of laughter and shook his head. "There's nothing more I can tell you." Which also didn't answer the question.

Josiah knew that whatever the Lyttons were hiding, Alex wouldn't reveal it. He'd already told him so many deep and dark secrets, some of which painted him in a bad light, making no effort to sugar-coat any of it. So, what else could there possibly be that he would refuse to reveal it at this stage in the game?

Josiah wondered if it was worth speaking to Charles or Noah but decided to hold back on that for now, not wanting to sour their relationship with Alex so soon after being reunited.

Alex's mood had changed on a sixpence, as it tended to these days, and all the joyful energy of earlier dissipated. He looked flat and low, suddenly exhausted.

"Sorry. Wore myself out," he muttered.

His face was so white that Josiah was alarmed.

"Making breakfast was the most you've done in weeks, to say nothing of all that dancing around." He grinned. "Come on, let's get you to the other room so you can lie down."

He helped Alex into the living room where he immediately collapsed onto the sofa.

"You're so good to me. Too good," Alex muttered. "I'm sorry I've been such a shit lately, but this is me, Joe. I've always been a shit. I'm not the sweet little IS I pretended to be. I did wonder if my experiences had changed me, but I guess not."

"I don't want you to pretend. I want you to express yourself in any way that feels right, even if it means you're not very nice to be around," Josiah told him firmly. "After all you've been through, this is a necessary rebalancing. It'll take a while for you to find a way back to yourself."

"But what's the point?" Alex asked wearily. "I mean, I appreciate the chance you're giving me, but after the trial, even assuming Tyler is convicted, I'll have to put that mask back on and say, 'Yes sir, no sir,' to some shitty new houder."

"Tell me about the mask," Josiah asked. "I mean, it's impressive, but where did you learn it?"

"Belvedere." Alex gave a wan smile.

"Ah. That's one thing we haven't talked much about."

"I know."

"Was it bad? I wondered if something terrible happened to you there."

"Actually, no. It wasn't without its challenges, but for the most part, it was a respite after the awfulness of life at Tyler's."

"And you learned how to be an IS there?"

"Yes. I enjoyed that. I've always liked learning, even though I don't think I'm anyone's idea of a natural valet or butler." Alex gave a twisted grin.

"And the mask? Seems an odd thing to be on the curriculum at a training centre."

"Well, that's a whole different story." Alex sighed and closed his eyes.

Josiah let him rest for a moment, then prodded him. "We have all day."

"I thought you'd say that. Okay." Alex sat up and put a cushion behind his head. "I made a good friend at Belvedere, a man I admire and respect more than almost anyone else, except for you." He grinned.

Josiah grinned back. "Flattery will get you everywhere. Go on."

"He was a friend to me when I needed it most. He taught me how to construct the mask and gave me the tools I needed to keep myself mentally strong, my face impassive, so I wouldn't give myself away."

"The yoga and the song?" Josiah hazarded.

"That's right. It wasn't an easy thing to learn, but he was a good teacher. His name was Gideon."

"Gideon. Was he the man Tyler referred to in that meeting after the break-in? The one who died of cancer several months ago?"

"Yes."

"So, he ran Belvedere?"

"Yes. He set me up in the beginning. He befriended me without telling me who he was so he could get close to me. But if he hadn't, I wouldn't have opened up and told him about Tyler and what he'd done to Solange."

"You told him?" Josiah asked, surprised. "He knew but didn't do anything?"

"No. He was an IS too, and he wouldn't do anything to compromise his houder. He was weirdly obsessed with her." Alex shrugged. "Tyler tasked him with turning me into the perfect IS, so he did. Once he knew about my mission, he equipped me to complete it. That's how he helped me."

"And this man became your friend?" Josiah stared at Alex, perplexed.

"What?" Alex asked truculently.

"Alex, your friends are people who at best aren't honest with you but at worst have betrayed you in some way. Solange, Gideon... You speak so highly of them but they both deceived you."

"I know." Alex's mouth was set into a hard line. "I told you when we first set out for Tyler's house, weeks ago, that I wasn't sure if I could trust you, and I said that if you knew my history you'd know why. Maybe I'm a monumentally bad judge of character, or maybe I just underestimated the effort people would go to in order to trap me. All I can say is that I do view both of them as friends. I was *lonely*, Joe, and Solange and Gideon were both good to me in their own way. Besides, they were all I had." He gave a miserable shrug.

"Or all you felt you deserved," Josiah murmured.

"I don't know. I just know that I liked Gideon. You'd have liked him too. He was sharp, perceptive, and without self-pity, and he wouldn't tolerate it in others either. He forced me to pick myself up when I was at my lowest ebb and find the strength of character to go back to Tyler, act like I was the best IS in the whole bloody country, and fool him into trusting me."

"That must have been exhausting," Josiah said softly. "I have no idea how you survived those years with Tyler, having to pretend all the time to be one thing while working towards something completely different."

"It was a complicated time," Alex admitted. "I wouldn't have got through it without Gideon's tutelage. I could imagine his voice in my head whenever the going got tough. It helped me through. It hit me hard when Tyler told me Gideon had died. I wish I could have gone to his memorial service. I'm sure I cared about him more than most of the people there."

"Were you in love with him?" Josiah asked.

Alex laughed. "God, no. I wasn't his type, or he mine, which was a relief. I liked that he didn't find me attractive. He thought you were dead sexy, though."

"Me?" Josiah raised a surprised eyebrow. "How on earth did he know about me?"

"I had these photographs of you, and of Mum and Dad and Charles. I tore them out of some magazines in the rec room at Belvedere. It was soon after Peter was murdered so some gossip rag ran a piece on you. I kept them with the photo of Solange that Ted gave me after she died, the one I showed you."

"Hmm. How on earth did you keep Solange's photo a secret from Tyler?"

"I didn't. I left it behind at Belvedere."

Josiah frowned. This was one of those missing puzzle pieces that might be important. "Then how do you have it now?"

Alex took a deep breath. "I found it in my gym bag in March, after a workout. It could only have come from Gideon. I thought at the time that he was chiding me, reminding me of my mission because he thought I'd given up on it. Now I realise that he must have known he was dying, and he wanted me to have it."

"That's when you put it in the frame behind the Hudson Brink picture?"

"Yes. I couldn't risk Elliot finding it and telling Tyler that I had it. After that, I used to search for Gideon every time I went to the gym. I wanted to speak to him so badly. I loved that he still thought about me enough to find a way to get that picture to me. I used to imagine us sitting and talking." He gave a distant smile, as if he was still imagining it. "In my fantasy, he helped me rediscover my sense of purpose because I was totally stalled. I was so paranoid about giving myself away. Whenever I made the slightest attempt to fulfil my vow to Solange, it went wrong and I became more and more paralysed."

"I wonder how he got access to your gym bag?"

"It was in my locker, which was locked, but those locks aren't exactly hard to get into, and Gideon was a resourceful man."

"Of course, it might not have been Gideon who left it there for you."

"Who else could it possibly have been?" Alex looked taken aback.

"I don't know, but we can't assume. You didn't see him, did you?"

"No." Alex shook his head. "I suppose it could have been Ted, as he had the original, but he'd surely have mentioned it by now, wouldn't he?"

"I'd have thought so, yes." Josiah mused on this for a moment.

"You love it, don't you?" Alex said softly.

"What?"

"This – the problem-solving, nurdling away at cases, figuring it all out. I'm sorry I was so vile to you at the hospital. This is who you are. I'm also sorry that you've had to babysit me for the past few weeks. I know I've been rubbish company. If you want to go back to work, then you should. I can look after myself now."

"I'm still working, I just do it when you're asleep. I don't need to go back for a few more days." He didn't want to leave Alex alone just yet. He was too damaged, too fragile, and too unpredictable right now.

He spent a couple of hours going through various aspects of Alex's life with him, taking notes. Then he left Alex on the sofa napping and took his holopad into the dining room to work. Reed was providing status updates every few hours, although he still hadn't found Tyler's blackmail footage. Josiah didn't expect him to. Material that incendiary would be kept in a very secure location, and Tyler had had several days to move it somewhere Inquisitus wouldn't be able to find it. That didn't mean he was about to give up. It just meant he had to strengthen the rest of their case as much as possible – and keep looking.

It was late afternoon when the doorbell rang. Josiah answered it and found a very familiar person on the doorstep.

"Elsie? But how...? When...?"

"Don't I get a hug? I've been gone for weeks."

She walked into his arms, and he wrapped them around her small frame and held her tight. "Oh, Elsie! You have no idea how good it is to have you back!" He pushed her away with a frown. "But why *are* you back?"

"Oh, honestly, there's only so long I could hang around in that pottery driving everyone nuts." She grinned.

"I'm sure you weren't driving anyone nuts."

"I was driving *myself* nuts with nothing to do. I love Liz and those kids to death, but I missed my home, my friends, and would you believe it – I even missed you and your chaos magnet of a boyfriend."

"We're not together anymore, Elsie," he told her quietly, and then he led her into the kitchen for a quiet catch-up.

"So you set him free?" she mused over a cup of tea.

"I wouldn't go that far. That's not in my power. I simply suggested we end our relationship because I could tell his heart wasn't in it."

"But you're still in love with him." She gazed at him perceptively.

He stared down at his mug of tea, then looked up in despair. "Of course I am, although I question it all the time. Is it really love, Elsie? Or are we just trauma-bonded by what happened to Peter? Even if it *is* love, how can I be sure *who* I'm in love with? He's a wraith, Elsie, and he changes all the time. I'm not sure even he knows who he is from one second to the next. He was a damaged teenager when he was trapped in Tyler's web, and he's been struggling to get out ever since. I don't think he has a clue who he is outside of that struggle."

"That sounds tough, Joe. Then again, you never did like to make it easy for yourself." She placed a warm brown hand over his and squeezed. "Now look, I'm back now, and I can take care of this wraith while you return to work."

"Would you?" He let out a sigh of relief. "I must warn you: he's not easy to look after. His moods are volatile and change as fast as the weather."

"Joe, I used to work with the criminally insane." She laughed. "I'm sure I can handle Alex."

"Elsie, why *did* you come back? Be honest."

"I could see how things were when you and I talked," she said quietly. "I discussed it with Liz, but knowing what you'd been through, and that you were both bruised, battered, and struggling to heal, I couldn't stay away. Not when you need me so much. I used to be a nurse, remember? I know you said it might be dangerous to remain in the UK, but you're here, and I'd rather be here with you than with Liz, fretting about what's happening to you."

"Thank you." He swept her up in another big hug. "You're right. I am itching to get back to work. I don't do well cooped up in a house, and Alex isn't always easy to be with."

"I'll take care of him, then."

"You should know that Tyler is onto the Kathleen Line. I might not be able to protect you."

"Oh, darling," She laughed. "I knew that when I came back. I'm an old woman, Joe. If I die in jail, or as an IS, then so be it. But I'm like you, I have to be useful."

The look on Alex's face when he woke up and saw her convinced Josiah that he had nothing to worry about. Alex saw Elsie as part mother figure, part guardian angel. She'd been a lifeline during his escape attempt and he adored her.

He came to, saw her, and his eyes widened. Then, without saying a word, he sat up, threw his arms around her, and hugged her tight. They spent the rest of the evening talking quietly, while Josiah tapped away on his holopad.

"I don't need babysitting," Alex told her as she prepared to leave. "You don't have to come back tomorrow."

"I want to." She beamed. "I want to spend time with you and really get to know you, sweetheart."

"I'll try and be on my best behaviour, then."

"You'll do no such thing." She fixed him with a stern glare. "Just be yourself. That's all any of us wants from you right now."

"I'm not always very nice when I'm being myself. Ask Joe, he knows." He looked down, shamefaced.

Elsie smiled and patted his arm. "Honey, did Josiah ever tell you about my past?"

"You used to be a nurse?"

"Yes, a very specialist kind of nurse. I worked in a high-security psychiatric hospital for years."

"Wow, really?" Alex looked at Josiah for confirmation, and he nodded.

"Oh, yes. Our Elsie is quite the formidable lady." Josiah grinned. "Go on, tell him your favourite story, Elsie."

She laughed. "Well, I used to look after this man who'd killed a few women in a most unpleasant way. When I was first assigned to him, he gave me a look that would turn a person to stone, and he said: 'You should run, because when I get my hands on a knife, I'll cut your head off.'"

"Bloody hell! What did you do?"

"I fixed him with my sternest look, the one I used on the naughty kids at Sunday School, and I told him to pipe down because I wouldn't take any of his nonsense."

"Shit. Did he go nuts?"

"Not at all." She laughed again. "I think he was impressed. We got on ever so well after that and often had a laugh together. Perhaps because he knew I wasn't scared of him. Mind you, I always made sure to double-check he didn't have a knife. As much as he liked me, he'd have chopped my head off in a heartbeat." She smiled as Josiah held out her coat for her. "So, there's nothing you could do that'd ever scare me, Alex, trust me."

Josiah felt he was breathing easily for the first time in weeks as he drove to the office the next day. He had no qualms about leaving Alex with Elsie, and he was relieved beyond belief to be heading back to work. This was the first time in years that he'd stopped work in the middle of a case, and the investigator in him was itching to be let loose again.

There was so much to do. In addition to putting the case against Tyler together, there was still the matter of Dacre's killer, and solving the mystery at the heart of the Lytton family. He wasn't sure if the latter was relevant to either case, but something told him it was important.

It felt wonderful to be striding into the SID again, greeting colleagues and feeling his brain sliding effortlessly back into work mode. He saw his team for a catch-up in the morning and spent the afternoon with Esther, briefing the lawyers.

"Good work, Joe," she said as he left for the day. "It's good to have you back."

He spent the next few weeks forensically sifting through Alex's life to help the lawyers build their case, interviewing dozens of people in the process. He tracked down a personal stylist called Brian, aka Lorenzo, who'd once worked for Tyler.

"Tyler's a shit. I got out as soon as I could. I hated what he did to Alex," Brian said. He had a pronounced and very likely fake Italian accent, but Josiah liked him. Everyone was entitled to their harmless eccentricities, after all. "Is he okay?" Lorenzo asked, sounding genuinely concerned.

"Well… he survived," was all Josiah could reply. Brian agreed to give a statement, but his knowledge of Tyler's operation was limited.

Alex's other stylist, Andrew, was still employed as Tyler's IS. A sweet, gentle soul, he looked anxious throughout his interview and refused to give a formal statement. Josiah didn't blame him. Tyler would make his life hell if he said the wrong thing.

He spent an amusing afternoon with a colourful character called Marlon Baxter, who flirted with him outrageously without ever quite crossing a line.

"I hear we have you to blame for these god-awful holoties people are wearing these days," Josiah said on first meeting him.

"*Thank!* You have me to thank," Baxter insisted, laughing.

Josiah glanced around the exquisitely furnished house Baxter owned.

"You've done well out of them, Mr Baxter," he remarked.

"Please, call me Bax, everyone does." Bax had the most gorgeous almond-shaped green eyes that sparkled with mischief. "I know it seems like I was an overnight success, but it took years of hard work to get to the point where everyone is wearing them – except you." He shot Josiah a disapproving look. "May I ask why?"

"Can't stand 'em," Josiah admitted.

"Well, I doubt you'd be able to pull them off, anyway," Bax sniffed. "It wouldn't suit your style, which, I have to admit, is divine. Old-fashioned male elegance. You can't beat it on a man with your build." He cast an admiring glance at Josiah's charcoal tweed suit with lilac shirt and pocket square.

"You're not wearing one either," Josiah pointed out, waving a hand at Bax's skin-tight pink-and-green sweater and his flowing harem pants.

"Oh, I've moved on, darling!" Bax announced dramatically. "I'm working on a whole range of holoclothes. Soon, even you will succumb, my dear Investigator Raine."

"Much as I like talking about men's fashion – and you have no idea how much," Josiah sighed, "I'm here to talk about Alex Lytton."

"I thought so." Marlon's mood changed abruptly. "How is he? When I last saw him, I wasn't very nice to him, and I've always regretted that."

"No need. He told me all about it, and there are no hard feelings on his part."

"I was angry with him. He had so much promise, and he threw it all away."

"Also, he tried to seduce you," Josiah pointed out.

Bax threw his hands in the air. "He almost succeeded, too. He always knows which buttons to press. But there was something faded and diminished about him, something a little... desperate? I had a fiancé I adored – now my husband – and I wasn't going to throw it away for a few grubby hours with Alex Lytton, no matter how gorgeous he is."

"He was delighted that you turned him down. Tyler was trying to trap you. He used Alex to entice people into compromising positions and then held the footage over them as blackmail."

Marlon gave a sharp little gasp, his eyes flashing in shock.

"If you'd gone to bed with Alex that night, I can guarantee you wouldn't be here, living the life of your dreams right now." Josiah glanced around the impeccably furnished house with its view over the river.

"Well, that doesn't exactly restore him in my estimation," Bax murmured.

"Oh, don't blame him – this is all on Tyler. Alex was acting under the kind of extreme duress you can't begin to imagine."

"But he could have warned me."

"Not without betraying himself and a cause that is undeniably noble. Besides, he didn't need to. It seems that your moral compass steered you in the right direction that night, Bax."

Bax flushed, but he looked pleased. "Well, I'm glad you've explained his actions. I'm sorry for all the trouble he's found himself in. I'm also sorry because I said something rather mean about his art. He showed me some of his drawings that night, and I was cutting about them. I didn't mean it. He's always been a huge talent."

"He doesn't hold that against you. He was just pleased that you escaped the Tyler blackmail machine. Now, I have to ask – just how much money did you make with the invention of the holotie?" Josiah threw that question in when Bax was least expecting it. "Enough to make a bid to buy Alex's contract?"

Bax stared at him, open-mouthed. "What?"

"You and he had unfinished business. Maybe he preyed on your mind after that encounter?"

"I was angry with him. Why on earth would I want to buy him?"

"I don't know. *Did* you make a bid on him, Mr Baxter?" Josiah dropped the flirtatious banter, watching Bax's reaction carefully.

"No! I've barely given him much thought in the past few years, if you must know. I've been far too busy with the holotie, with my marriage, and... well, we're hoping to adopt a child." He looked down, smiling softly, and Josiah had no doubt this was something close to his heart. "Trust me, Alex really didn't feature in my plans for the future."

"Thank you," Josiah said, feeling inclined to believe him. "Forgive the line of questioning, but I had to be sure. By the way, too much water might have flowed under this particular bridge, but if you want to visit Alex at any time, I'm sure he'd love to see you and explain himself in person."

Bax gazed at him steadily. "I'm not sure that would be a good idea."

"Maybe not." Josiah sighed. "But please, think about it. He needs all the friends he can get right now. He's been through a lot."

"I'll think about it then," Bax murmured. "I'll always have a soft spot for Alex Lytton."

Moving on, Josiah had a long list of people whose names had been supplied by Alex, Mick, and Ted, but none of them cooperated. Why would they? Tyler was no doubt dangling his blackmail footage over their heads, and it certainly wasn't in their interests to talk.

Martin Bagshaw, Clive Hastings, Jake Harper, Hugo Purvis, Rupert Walcott... They all talked, but only to warmly praise Tyler. They all looked shocked at the idea they might have been filmed having sex with one of his indies and the footage used to blackmail them.

"Never happened, mate," Harper said, leaning back in his chair and threading his hands behind his head. "You're being lied to."

"I'm sure I am," Josiah replied coldly. "By somebody, anyway."

Harper just laughed. Josiah hated the man; of all the people who'd abused Alex, he was the one he'd feared the most.

Bagshaw was a soft-bellied man with one lazy eye that always seemed to be looking somewhere else. He refuted every accusation in a tone of outrage and informed Josiah that he was a devoted husband and family man, and it would never cross his mind to search for pretty young men to perform a certain kind of sexual fantasy for him.

And so it had gone on. Everybody agreeing on the fact that it had never happened and they definitely weren't in Tyler's pocket as a result.

Rebecca Lang came the closest to cracking under his questioning. She coloured and apologised, although she didn't specify for what. However, despite his forceful interrogation, she refused to corroborate Alex's story.

Josiah also took detailed statements from Noah and Charles, and further statements from Ted and Mick, finding everyone's impressions of Alex as contradictory as the man himself.

Alex remained the elusive heart of everything, a broken butterfly whose wings seemed to change colour the more you learned about him. Alternately bratty, loyal, moody, and kind, but always utterly impossible to pin down.

The case came together slowly, without any major breakthroughs that would guarantee a conviction. Josiah could only hope that his painstaking detective work would pay off in lieu of any new dramatic evidence.

A couple of weeks later, Josiah arranged a surprise day out for Alex and Noah.

"Where are we going?" Alex asked as they set off in Josiah's duck.

"To the seaside for the day. I thought you'd both enjoy it," Josiah replied, smiling at him. Alex's arm was on the mend and he was doing a little better.

"Thank you for inviting me along to join you," Noah said a little stiffly. "I can't drive myself anymore, so I'm reliant on Charles. But he often has speaking engagements and sponsorship events, so I'm on my own at The Orchard most of the time." There was no self-pity there, he was just giving an accurate account of his existence. "A day out is a rare treat. I do appreciate it, Mr Raine."

"Please, call me Joe, and you're welcome. Alex has been cooped up a lot too, and I thought a day out would be good for everyone. I was down this way a couple of weeks ago for work and thought how pretty it is."

Alex and his father were slowly rebuilding their relationship. There had been holochats, and Charles occasionally brought Noah to visit, but Josiah felt they needed some time together without Charles. Their conversations were often stilted, both of them aware of how fragile their bond was, and how easily it might be broken again. It was as if their relationship was a delicate vase that they passed gingerly back and forth between them, and it frustrated Josiah. Sometimes, he wanted to yell at them, bash their heads together and force the pace of their reconciliation, but he tried to remain patient. This was a complicated relationship, with eggshells everywhere. No wonder they were tiptoeing around each other. He hoped that today's excursion would help, but he knew he was taking a risk given what he had planned.

They spent a pleasant few hours by the sea. It was a sunny day, although there was a cold wind. Neither Noah nor Alex seemed to mind that – both were wrapped up warmly. Josiah could tell how much they appreciated getting away from their normal lives and doing something together. Such simple pleasures – a drive out to the coast and a short walk along the promenade, which was all Noah could manage – and yet, it was something that had been utterly impossible for them for so many years.

"I thought we'd stop at this café I know on the way home," Josiah said nonchalantly, glancing at his watch as they piled back into his duck. "Break up the journey."

An hour later, he pulled into a nondescript service station a little off the beaten track. It was more of a truck stop, as evidenced by the huge rigs on the forecourt.

Alex glanced around. "I'm sure I know this place," he said slowly.

"You do. You've been here before."

Alex turned to him, his eyes wide. "Why are we here?"

"We're meeting someone I believe you wanted to see?" Josiah smiled at him gently.

"Shit... he's here?" Alex covered his mouth with his hand.

"Yes. I interviewed him here a couple of weeks ago. I needed to take a statement from him, but he was too busy to come to Inquisitus, so I met him here. I asked if he'd agree to see you. I didn't tell you because he said he couldn't get here until five, and I wanted you to relax and enjoy the day without fretting."

"What's going on?" Noah asked. "Who are you meeting? Shall I stay in the duck?"

"No." Josiah turned in his seat to look at him. "This is someone you'll want to meet."

They climbed out of the duck, and Josiah took Noah's arm and helped him walk to the café. Alex went ahead, looking around eagerly as he entered, searching...

Josiah stopped just inside the door.

"Let's give them a moment," he murmured to Noah, and they watched as Alex let out a cry and then ran towards a man in his fifties. He was ordinary-looking, with short grey hair, balding on top, wearing a black-and-white lumberjack shirt that was stretched tightly over his bulging belly. He stood up as Alex approached and held his arms open. Alex didn't even hesitate – he went straight in for a long, heartfelt hug. Josiah felt a lump rise in the back of his throat.

"Who is that?" Noah asked, peering across the room.

"His name is Barney Bates," Josiah replied. "He's a long-distance lorry driver. He stopped and bought Alex food and gave him clothes, money, and a safe place to sleep when he escaped from Tyler."

"Then you're right. I *do* want to meet the man who helped my son when he needed it most," Noah exclaimed.

They crossed the café, and Josiah introduced Noah to Barney.

"I'm Alex's father," Noah said, sounding a little choked. They shook hands. "Thank you," Noah told him, still shaking vigorously. "Thank you for taking care of my son."

"That's okay, mate." Barney beamed at him. "I reckon he needed a dad that day and, well, to be honest, I needed a son, too, so it suited us both."

"How is your son?" Alex asked as they all sat down.

Barney's face fell. "He's still with that bastard houder up north."

"I thought he was only serving a five-year sentence?"

"Yeah, he was, but they say he's been difficult, caused them problems, and his sentence's been increased a couple of times now without a trial or nothing. Judge just rubber-stamped it. I don't think his houder ever intends to let him go. Every time his contract comes up, he makes up some shit about Robbie's behaviour and they stick more years on his contract. I think if I had the money to bribe his houder I could get him out, but I don't, although I work all the hours God sends." Barney took a gulp of his Coke. "Fuckers. Fucking IS system. Fucking hate this country. Good to see you again, Johnny... Though that's not your name, is it, lad?" He smiled at Alex. "Joe here told me who you really are."

"Yes, sorry. I couldn't risk telling you the truth. I can't tell you how much I wanted to see you again, Barney. It's been worrying me for so long. I wanted to explain... Did Joe tell you why I didn't get on that boat?"

"Nah. He said it wasn't his story to tell, but if I agreed to meet with you, he was sure you'd wanna spill. Listen, Alex, you've got nothing to explain to me. I'm sure you had your reasons."

Alex reached across the table and took Noah's hand in his. "Sorry, Dad, I haven't told you this. After I escaped from Tyler, I tried to get to the coast. I walked for days with no money and no food. Barney saw me and scooped me up. He fed me, and then he took me to the coast and arranged for a friend of his to take me to France. He gave me some cash to pay for the trip, but I never got on the boat."

"Why not?" Noah frowned.

"Because that was the day you had your first stroke," Alex said gently. "I heard about it on the radio, and I couldn't bear to leave in case you died and I never had a chance to say goodbye. So, I used the money to get to the hospital and see you."

Noah looked shaken. "I thought I heard your voice, but Charles told me I'd imagined it. I was so sure I heard you, saw you... that you'd held my hand and spoken to me. I tried to reply, but I couldn't make the words make sense."

"I thought you saw me. I knew you were trying to say something."

"You gave up your chance to escape because of me?" Noah looked profoundly moved by this revelation.

"We'd had so many cross words and I regretted them all," Alex said softly. "I'm so sorry, Dad."

"As am I. I was hurt, but I should never have disowned you. You're my son and I never stopped loving you," Noah said firmly.

"There, see, I told him so," Barney cut in. "I said his dad would never have stopped loving him. Dads don't, do we?" He beamed at Noah, who smiled back.

Josiah sat back in his chair, watching as some very old, very deep wounds started slowly healing. So often, he'd been left in despair by Alex's story, but this was one of those occasions when the best of human nature had come to the fore for a change.

They stayed to eat because Alex said this place served the best fish and chips in the country. Josiah had to concede that it was, indeed, very good, and his full belly agreed. They parted with hugs all round, nyms exchanged, and a great sense of happiness. Alex's future might still be uncertain, but one small moment in his past had been revisited and rectified.

Clearly exhausted by the long day out, Noah fell asleep in the duck on the way back. Alex rested his head on Josiah's shoulder as he drove.

"Thank you for today, Joe," he said softly. "You're a good man."

"We exist. Barney Bates is, too, as is that man asleep in the back." Josiah glanced in the mirror, smiling. "I'm sorry you've met so many shitty ones along the way, Alex, but it's my firm belief that there are more like Barney Bates in this world than George Tyler. I hope you can believe that one day."

Alex smiled, and soon he, like his father, was fast asleep. Josiah felt a great sense of peace wash over him. There had been so many sad days for Alex, but this, at least, wasn't one of them.

Chapter Four
DECEMBER 2090
Alex

Elliot Dacre lived in a big house in Crystal Palace.

"Oh, thank God! I've been in a creative funk ever since that night!" he announced when Alex was delivered to his lounge. "I've been lying awake, thinking about all the beautiful art I could make with *you* as my muse."

"I'm flattered." Alex liked Dacre. The man was a fool, anyone could see that, but he was a charming one, and after living with Tyler's changeable moods for months, it was a welcome relief to be with a less mercurial personality.

More importantly, there could be an opportunity here. Dacre's house was unlikely to be as closely guarded as Tyler's, and therefore, his movements not as monitored.

In that, he was disappointed. Tyler had sent a team of bodyguards with him, who accompanied him at all times – as much to ensure that Dacre didn't sleep with him as anything else.

Dacre was a man of many enthusiasms, all of which he talked about at length. "I love the ballet but hate the opera! All that posturing drives me nuts! I adore the human form, but when it stands there in all its portly glory with its mouth open, bombarding us with all that musical pomposity...!" He did a passable imitation, making Alex laugh, which delighted him and caused him to show off even more. It was so easy to flatter Elliot Dacre. He wasn't a suspicious man, or prone to dark and jealous moods.

Alex's arrival sent Dacre into a creative frenzy. Alex had never seen holoart being made before and had no idea about the process. It was similar to photography, but as it involved movement, Dacre wanted something choreographed that created a specific mood.

"It's a new art form. Once, people thought photographs weren't as artistic as paintings, but they were wrong. They're wrong about holoart too, and I'll prove it to them," Dacre declared passionately, positioning Alex so that he was staring up at the holocam. "No, don't look at the holocam. Look away! Pretend I'm not filming you. Oh God, yes, there it is. How do you do that?"

"Do what?" Alex asked, surprised.

"Look so elusive. The holocam loves it. I'm not surprised. It's that same quality your mother had. You know who else had it? The *Mona Lisa*."

Alex laughed. "I don't think I'm in *quite* the same league as the *Mona Lisa*!"

"No, no, no... you misunderstand. It's a certain *something* I'm looking for. You said you liked that holopic I made of Hudson Brink. Well, he's a handsome man, and everyone loves the way he looks straight at you in that picture, promising sex. He exudes it. You, on the other hand, are every bit as sexy as he is, and yet you're withholding. You offer something, but you also hold something back. You can't be known. It's maddening, it's fascinating, and so much more *interesting* than just gorgeous looks. Beauty, sexiness, can be bland, banal. You make them into something deeper, something so much *more*."

"I'm flattered, of course, but you're the one producing the art, not me. It's your skill, not mine."

All the same, Alex was taken aback when Dacre showed him the first holopic he made of him. He was sitting in a chair, gazing out of a window, then he turned, startled, as if hearing a noise. There was something haunting about the image, a sense of a private moment being intruded upon, of someone hiding, even from himself.

It was odd to see himself as others saw him, but he was delighted by how perfect his mask now was. He thought Gideon would like the piece and wished he could send it to him. Or Joe... but he tried not to think about Joe these days because he was sure he wouldn't approve of what he was doing. How could he explain to a man like Josiah Raine that he hated George Tyler with every fibre of his being but yearned for his touch at the same time? He couldn't even explain it to himself. He kept coming back to Stockholm syndrome, but that was a cop-out, and he was starting to loathe himself for enjoying sex with Tyler.

"That's it! That's the look I want to explore," Dacre said, pointing his holocam at him again. The holocam was as insatiable as Tyler's obsessive interest in him. They both wanted to own him, consume him, and make him theirs, yet found it impossible. They could put him under their looking glass, like a fly in amber, but they were never able to truly capture him. He remained forever unknowable and never quite theirs.

Alex knew that Dacre desired him. The fingers lingering on his skin, gently caressing him as he was positioned for his next picture made it all too obvious. Yet Tyler's guards watched their every move, so Dacre was forced to resist temptation.

He wasn't allowed to stay overnight at Dacre's house. He was driven there every morning and back to Vertex Tower every evening, but at least it was some respite from whatever it was he and Tyler were doing to each other. He could never be relaxed or carefree, but thankfully, he didn't have to police himself so tightly at Elliot's.

It was only when he was away from Tyler that his shattered nerves had a chance to recover. He wasn't sure how much longer he could walk the tightrope of Tyler's emotions. Dacre was light and amusing after all the intensity, and he started to breathe again.

He was, therefore, disappointed when Tyler terminated the agreement abruptly a few weeks later, wrenching him out of a shoot that Dacre had spent days setting up.

"Did you miss me?" Tyler grabbed him the second Alex was returned to his suite. His hands were everywhere, his mouth warm and demanding on Alex's mouth, and – oh, yes – the chemistry was still there, as hot and hungry as ever.

"Of course," Alex replied fiercely, pressing up against him, longing for his touch. Yes, he'd missed this, whatever *this* was. He'd missed the wild passion of the sex, the insane hatred of the lust.

"I bet that old lech salivated over you every single fucking day," Tyler breathed, the thought of someone else desiring *his* property clearly turning him on.

He ripped Alex's clothes off, pushed him over the arm of the sofa, and entered him hard. "I bet you dreamed about this when you were with that old fool. I bet you longed for it," he growled, his hands making imprints on Alex's thighs. He came with a shout and leaned over Alex for several minutes, breathing heavily, still lodged deep inside him.

Alex lay there, wondering what had just happened. This man prided himself on being in control but now seemed dangerously close to losing it. Was he finally winning this battle of wits?

"Sorry," Tyler muttered unexpectedly, stroking his back gently. He withdrew and stepped back, allowing Alex to get up.

"For what? I'm yours, you can enjoy me any way you wish," Alex murmured, but he knew why Tyler was apologising. He was upset because he hadn't demanded Alex's consent and enthusiastic participation. Tyler hadn't seduced him or bothered to arouse him – he'd simply taken him.

"I know that," Tyler said irritably. He pulled Alex towards him and kissed him gently, as if trying to make up for it. Alex returned his kisses eagerly, and that seemed to mollify him. He sat down, pulling Alex onto the sofa next to him.

"It was passionate. Hot. I enjoyed it. I love that you want me so much," Alex said, snuggling against him. He was still naked, Tyler fully dressed, as was so often the way with them, because his houder enjoyed the power imbalance that conveyed. Tyler wrapped an arm around him and kissed him.

"I missed you so much," he said fiercely. "I tried not to. I hoped that when you were away, I'd be able to forget about you, but I couldn't. It drove me nuts thinking of that silly old fool enjoying you."

"He didn't lay a finger on me," Alex assured him.

"Not enjoying you that way. Having the pleasure of your company, listening to you talk. I didn't just miss the sex – I missed *you*, Alexander." The desperation was back in Tyler's eyes. "Oh, fuck, what have you *done* to me?" he asked in despair.

Was it possible that Tyler was falling in love with him? If so, was it also possible that he might one day set him free? If only to see if he came back to him? Was there a way out of this mess after all? He'd hardly dared hope for so long, but now it flared inside him, a tiny kernel of light trying desperately to become a flame. It was dangerous, and he knew that Gideon would chide him for it, but he couldn't help himself. His life had been so awful for so long that he needed to believe that one day it would get better.

"I only want to make you happy," he said, leaning in for a kiss.

"Happy? I've never been happy." Tyler took a fistful of his hair and pulled his head back. "It's not in my nature. I just wish I didn't feel this... obsession." He spat out the word. "This is so similar to how it was with Isobel, but worse, much worse, and I don't understand why because I *have* you. I own you. You're mine in a way she would never commit to being, and yet, I still don't feel... safe."

Alex could see, if Tyler could not, that he'd replicated the same problem with him that he'd had with his mother. He wanted to own them, to trust them, to love them completely and have that returned – but he feared his feelings weren't reciprocated, and there was no way of convincing him that they were.

Tyler couldn't cope with love because he loathed being vulnerable. Now he was caught in a web of his own making. He didn't trust Alex, but he was in love with a fantasy of what they could have together.

A few days later, as they sat in the dining room eating breakfast together, Tyler received a delivery: a small white box, tied with a red bow and a gift card saying *Thank You!*

"Ah, from your friend, Dacre," Tyler said, holding up the box.

"A light box?"

"That's right. Shall we see what he's gifted me?" Tyler pressed the switch… and suddenly another Alex was in the room. Only this one was standing by an open window looking out, a non-existent wind moving in his hair. He looked so real – the render was perfect, seamless, as if he was there. Alex frowned. He didn't remember this holopic being made; he hadn't posed for it. Then he recognised it as the day Dacre had been fiddling around with the holocam, saying it wasn't working, and Alex had become so bored he'd drifted off. Now, he realised that had been a lie so that Dacre could catch him in an unguarded moment – and he had.

He remembered that he'd been daydreaming of climbing out of the open window, throwing himself into the air and flying across the water to Inquisitus and Joe. It had been a flight of fancy, but the expression of yearning in his eyes was all too real – God, how he'd longed to escape!

HoloAlex steeled his shoulders, hummed his song, and turned back to see whether Elliot had fixed the tech… and his eyes immediately and visibly became veiled, drained of personality. Gone was that brief moment of yearning, gone the desperation, hope, and despair… and in their place was… nothing. A complete emptiness. It all happened so fast that, in the moment, you'd have missed it. But Dacre, with his skilled, creative eye, had somehow burned a hole into Alex's soul and found a way to capture it.

Alex knew immediately that he was in trouble.

"So there *is* someone in there, after all," Tyler observed, his tone light and sardonic. "Yet you hide it so well. Who is *this* Alexander?" he demanded, pointing at the hologram. "What's he thinking? Feeling? Plotting?" His voice was hard and low as he spat out that last word.

"I was thinking of my mother," Alex blurted, trying desperately to find a lie that would suffice. "Wishing she was still here, that I'd done everything differently and not hurt you both so much."

"Then why hide it?" Tyler demanded. "Why pretend that *this* Alexander doesn't exist?"

"Because what I think and feel hurts people, and I don't want to be responsible for any more pain." It was the best answer he could muster.

"Hmm." Tyler gazed at him for a long moment. "I wish I could believe you." He turned back to the hologram and watched it again, gazing at it obsessively.

"You can."

"But I don't," Tyler flung back. "You showed that old fool Dacre who you really are but you hide yourself from me. There can be only one reason for that. You're lying, and you've been lying to me all along."

"I'm not." Alex was usually passive, understanding Tyler's need for control, but he was genuinely frightened now. He threw himself at his houder, pressing his body against him. "Is *this* lying?" He put Tyler's hand on his semi-hard cock, moaning. Tyler reached out as if to caress his hair – then slapped him hard across the cheek instead.

"You're a filthy little liar."

"Please! I want you. I *need* you."

Tyler slapped him again, making him fall backwards. He scrambled to get away, but Tyler pursued him like a panther, his flanks heaving, his eyes dark and deadly. He caught Alex, ripped his robe from him, and pinned him down, making him cry out.

There was blood running down his chin from his cut lip and he was acutely aware of the weight of Tyler on him as he fucked him. Tyler's breath was coming in rasping gasps, and Alex could feel the depths of his rage, hatred, hurt, and distrust.

When he was done, Tyler lay panting on top of him, his eyes still dark. For a moment, Alex was genuinely afraid. The man pinning him to the floor was lost to himself, and Alex knew what he was capable of. He'd killed Solange the last time he'd been this out of control. Was that to be his fate now? Dying on this floor to be disposed of in the same way, slung into the dark water of a lost zone, his death covered up, his body left to rot?

Slowly, the light seeped back into Tyler's eyes.

"Look what you made me do," he hissed.

"I'm sorry," Alex babbled. "I'm so sorry, sir. It was all my fault."

"I don't like the way you make me feel." Tyler withdrew, making Alex whimper with pain. He looked down on him broodingly. "I shouldn't have to deal with all your lies."

"I'm sorry," Alex whispered again.

"Good." Tyler reached down and pulled him to his feet, then surprised him by wrapping his arms around him. He was freezing cold, shivering with shock, and his body ached. Tyler stroked gentle swirls on his skin.

"Shh. Let's not do this. Let's put it behind us. I'm sorry, too, Alexander. That wasn't me."

But it was. It was the part of himself that Tyler hated, the part that had lost the one thing he craved more than anything else – control. It was also the part that had killed Solange, and now, Alex feared, would one day kill him, too.

Tyler's jealousy was well and truly roused, and his need for control escalated. He refused to let Alex out of his sight for even a second. He sat in on every business meeting, attended every event, and was by Tyler's side at all times, in bed and in life. This forced him to concentrate more deeply than ever as he tried desperately to hide his emotions so he didn't give himself away.

He decided to use Tyler's paranoia to his advantage, drinking in every single decision Tyler made, paying attention to even the smallest aspect of his vast business empire, filing away the knowledge for the day when he could hand the whole lot over to Joe to bring Tyler to justice – if that day ever came.

The weeks turned into months, and Tyler's interest in him didn't wane. If anything, it became even more intense. Being by Tyler's side night and day made it almost impossible for Alex to perform his yoga and listen to his song, and he needed his anchors now more than ever.

It was a risk, but he had no choice. He slid out of bed in the middle of the night, tiptoed down the hallway to Tyler's gym, and played his song softly as he performed his yoga moves. He watched himself in the mirror as he worked, knowing he'd failed if he could see so much as a glimmer of Alexander Lytton in the looking glass.

It became his obsession, every bit as strong as Tyler's obsession with him. He had to do this, had to keep his mask perfect, because he couldn't afford for it to slip for even a second when he was with Tyler. So, night after night, he performed this secret ritual.

Sometimes, he had to spend hours in the gym, performing his moves and listening to his song over and over again until he was sure he'd wiped away all trace of himself. Only when he was convinced that Alexander Lytton was completely obliterated did he tiptoe back to bed, hoping his absence had gone unnoticed.

One morning, Tyler seemed particularly cheerful, grinning down on him as he lay in bed.

"Get up! We have a busy day ahead. I've been waiting for this day for weeks."

He demanded that Alex dress in the clothes that made him look most like himself – or at least the self he'd been when he was free. Alex wasn't sure that he'd dress like this now, if he had the choice. He'd been younger then and a very different person.

"I want today to be special," Tyler declared, taking his hand as they sat next to each other in the helicopter. "Because today is our anniversary."

Which one? Alex wondered. *The anniversary of the day you enslaved me? Or the day you killed my friend? The anniversary of the day you sent me to Belvedere? The day I returned?* There were so many ugly milestones in their tortured relationship.

"A year ago today, you begged me to make love to you, and I thought we should celebrate by returning to a place that's special to us both," Tyler explained, clearing up that mystery at least.

A year. Alex was stunned. Had it really been a whole year since that day in the AV when this madness had started?

"I can't believe it," he murmured, smiling at Tyler. "It seems like only yesterday."

"I thought we should mark the day. I have a gift for you." Tyler grinned at him wolfishly, and Alex felt an old instinct stirring inside; he suspected that he wasn't going to like this.

That instinct proved correct when the helicopter landed on a neat green lawn, next to a place he remembered all too well.

Lytton AV

The sign on the door looked old and tired and the building had a rundown appearance, as if limping along on its last legs. He felt much the same. Was he to be paraded in front of his father again? Surely even Tyler wouldn't be so cruel? He didn't even know if Noah was still alive, but if he was, Alex didn't want to cause him more suffering.

Still, it was out of his hands. Tyler jumped briskly from the helicopter and strode into the lobby as if he owned it. Alex followed, his stomach doing somersaults. Was this where his deception finally ended? Gideon had given him the tools to fool Tyler into thinking he was the perfect IS, but he was only human. If Tyler threatened his family, Alex knew he couldn't stand by and watch.

There was a flurry of activity as they arrived, and Alex braced himself for his father's people to turf them out. But instead, one of the senior board members, a man Alex vaguely recognised, walked over and shook Tyler's hand.

"Mr Tyler! Welcome. Simeon Wainright at your service." His gaze passed over Alex blankly, as if he was nothing.

"Ah, Wainright, good to meet you at long last." Tyler grinned, pumping the man's hand.

"Quite so. This deal has been quite the marathon to get over the line, hasn't it?" Wainright grinned back at him delightedly. "But we're there now."

"Absolutely. I believe my terms were more than generous."

"They were, considering the mess we're in. I'm just glad that Lytton AV will survive, in some form at least. It broke my heart to think of all those IS contracts being sold on. The people here are a family, a community."

"I understand," Tyler said crisply.

"Your promise to keep things running as they did before – initially at least – was very welcome. I know the balance sheet didn't justify that commitment, so we're all very grateful."

"Not at all. Anything to help my old friend Noah," Tyler murmured. "Alexander, let me introduce you. You are looking at the new owner of Lytton AV!" Tyler's eyes were sparkling with glee.

"You bought my father's company?" Alex was shocked, but his mask stayed firmly in place, his eyes vacant.

"Yup, down to the last debt, of which there were many." Tyler shot him a triumphant look. When would he stop expecting the blows to land? Alex was giving him nothing, but still he tried.

Countless people lined up to shake Tyler's hand, and then there were some interminable speeches which Alex tuned out. He could barely hear anything anyway; the words of his song were filling his mind, drowning out everything as he stood beside Tyler, his face devoid of emotion. Tyler was the new lord and master of Lytton AV. He didn't just own Alex, he owned everything that should have been his – *his* birthright, *his* inheritance. It was all Tyler's now. The Lyttons were finished – Tyler had completely obliterated them.

Finally, all the niceties were over. Dismissing his staff, Tyler took Alex's hand and led him up the stairs. It was a journey he knew all too well. Last time he'd been here, Tyler had forced him to wear that humiliating outfit. This time, he was dressed like Alex Lytton, the son of the owner, only that wasn't who he was anymore. Now, he was Alexander *Tyler*, the property of the owner.

"Your father couldn't keep it afloat," Tyler said gleefully as he led him down hallways full of ghosts. He'd played on those stairs as a child, sat under that desk with his crayons drawing pictures. He'd worked here and sold his soul here. This place was in his DNA, etched into him.

"Of course, it should have been yours," Tyler said, smiling. "All this should have been yours, Alexander." He stopped outside Noah's office, gazing at Alex keenly, always searching for the chink in his armour.

"No," Alex said.

"No?" Tyler's eyes were bright with the scent of victory. Alex could see that he thought he'd finally cracked his façade and landed a blow.

"I don't deserve it, and *it* deserves better. It deserves someone who'll make a success of it. It deserves *you*," Alex told him firmly.

Tyler sighed. "You could have made it successful," he murmured. "You had it in you."

"No. I'm a dreamer, an artist. All I wanted was to design ducks. You're a businessman. You understand the reality of making money.

Lytton AV has a future with you that it never would have had with me."

Tyler's eyes were dark and intense. He'd wanted his victory acknowledged so much and now he looked overcome.

"Your father ran this company into the ground. He was always a hopeless businessman. I'll restore it to its rightful place. You might think, given our history, that I don't care about Lytton AV, but you'd be wrong," Tyler said fiercely. "My father gave his life to this place, and I respect its role in the history of the Rising. It was Lytton ducks that got everyone moving again in the years immediately after. I want you to know that I'll never subsume it into the Tyler brand. It will always remain its own entity, with its own name. *That* is my anniversary present to you, my love." He wrapped his arm around Alex's shoulder, opened the office door, and pushed him inside.

As Alex glanced around his father's office, he was surprised to find that he felt nothing. It was just an office. He remembered the self-involved boy he'd once been, full of pride and the need to prove himself to his father, to heal the wound of his mother's death. That boy could never have taken over here and made a success of it. He could see now how much sense it had made for his father to insist he learn the business first from the bottom up. He'd been too impatient, too blinded by his own guilt and grief, to see that at the time. It had been hard, and he'd learned some bitter lessons along the way, but he'd finally grown up.

He gazed dispassionately around the room, taking in the imposing black leather chair behind the desk where his father used to sit, and the framed photo of Theo Lytton and Will Tyler shaking hands in front of the first Lytton Classic. There were other pictures on the wall: a nanoprint of a cartoon that Noah had found funny, a holopic of Charles winning his gold medal with Isobel beside him, both of them beaming with happiness, and various other photos, holopics, and paintings that held meaning for him.

"Is my father still alive?" Alex asked quietly as he walked around the room, looking at all the pictures. He dreaded the answer and was angry at himself for wanting to know.

"Yes, but his health has declined, and your idiot brother was never going to be able to run the place."

"No, Charles would be useless at it." Alex smiled at the thought of his good-natured, easy-going brother trying to run a company this complicated.

He stopped in front of an ancient Pre-R print his father had loved. Noah was a Sherlock Holmes fan, and it depicted Holmes and Moriarty fighting on the edge of the Reichenbach Falls. The image had been on this wall for years, and it felt so old and familiar, so normal, when nothing about this was normal.

"It was too much for Noah. The company was on the verge of bankruptcy when I stepped in with a generous offer. I was their only hope. Nobody else wanted it," Tyler continued.

"Thank you," Alex said sincerely. He ran over to Tyler and wrapped his arms around him. "Thank you so much for saving it, sir. Thank you for buying it and helping all these people. Thank you, thank you, thank you."

Tyler put his hands on his shoulders, pushed him back, and looked him in the eyes. "I didn't do it for them. I did it for you, my love." He tipped Alex's chin back and kissed him sweetly on the lips.

Maybe he had, although whether to break him apart or whether to please him was another matter. It didn't matter. At least all the indies at Lytton AV wouldn't have to suffer for the sins of the Lytton family. Tyler would, no doubt, make some sweeping and unpleasant changes, but Lytton AV would survive – and probably thrive – with Tyler at the helm.

Tyler walked jauntily over to Noah's desk and paused dramatically, then took his seat behind it, clearly savouring every second of his victory. He looked happier than Alex had ever seen him. Finally, he had the one thing he'd always wanted.

Alex could see the angry child inside him, the son of an IS, watching the Lyttons exploit his father's gentle nature and make a fortune from his hard work. That had always been Tyler's narrative, and now, finally, he'd slain the Lytton dragon and seized what was rightfully his. It should have hurt to see him there, but Alex found he didn't care.

"So how does it feel to be back?" Tyler asked.

"As if all is right with the world," he replied, smiling. He wondered if Gideon would think it indulgent of him to use this opportunity to find out more about his family, but decided to do it anyway. "My father, does he have enough to live on?" he ventured.

Tyler shrugged. "He's not wealthy anymore. The company was a mess. I was generous, but it had a great many debts. He'll get by, no doubt, but the good times are over. Still, I'd never let him starve, Alexander. You know that."

Oh yes. Alex was quite sure Tyler would step in and buy his father's soul, if he could.

"But... The Orchard... that wasn't part of the deal?" he asked, trying to keep the worry out of his voice.

"No, The Orchard is still his, although I believe it's mortgaged up to the hilt. Your father is impoverished, Alex, but please believe me, that's more of his making than mine. I didn't go after him. He came to me." Alex looked up sharply. "You're surprised? Don't be. Your father is a true Lytton. He'd do anything to keep this place alive, even sell it to his oldest enemy. Now, if he'd had a bright and astute son who could have taken over and helped him after his stroke, then it might have been a different story, but it wasn't to be."

"No. I wasn't a good son. It's better this way," Alex said softly.

Tyler gazed at him for a long time, but if he was hoping he'd break down, show him the raw emotion he craved and reveal the self that Belvedere had taught him to hide, then he was to be disappointed; Alex was too well practised in his deception for that. He just smiled vacantly, and the light faded from Tyler's eyes.

"Come over here and suck me off," he ordered curtly.

Alex was almost relieved by the order, glad of the chance to hide. He slid under the desk to bury himself in the task and was not in the least embarrassed when Wainright popped his head around the door and caught them in the act. He was Tyler's whore and he only had himself to blame. He'd long since made peace with it. It could have been him sitting behind this desk, but he'd thrown his life away. It didn't matter. He wasn't important anymore and hadn't been since the moment Solange died. She was the only one who mattered now.

. . .

His song filled his head for the next few hours as they toured the factory. He concentrated on reciting it as he walked around with Tyler, listening to his plans for the place, nodding and enthusing wherever it seemed appropriate. The factory workers had turned out in force to look at their new owner, and he could see the astonishment on their faces as they watched him go past, Tyler's hand resting proudly on his arse. He was beyond caring. Let them look. He was what he was.

On their return to Ghost Eye, Tyler made love to him repeatedly, still on a high from his moment of glory. When he finally fell asleep, Alex slipped away to the gym, needing his yoga more than ever. He'd kept his mask in place all day in the face of the most impossible provocation. It had been an act of superhuman will and had taken everything he had, and now he desperately needed to recharge and find that place in his head where he could lose himself. Alex Lytton was too present, full of too many feelings. He had to be erased.

"Play *Make Me a Channel of Your Peace*," he ordered the gym smart speaker.

"That song is not available," came the unexpected reply.

Alex whirled around in confusion. "What? Why?"

"That song is not available on the orders of Mr Tyler."

Alex took a deep breath, then another, trying to find a way to process this. He needed that song to survive. He relied on it. Had Tyler somehow figured that out? He could at least do the yoga without it. It wasn't as if he didn't know the song off by heart; he could hum it to himself as he put himself through his poses, but it wasn't the same. The song calmed him. It was his anchor. How was he supposed to survive without it to ground him? Yet, what could he do? Ask Tyler to restore it? For what reason? And how could he do that without giving away all that it meant to him?

He performed his yoga, but the questions continued buzzing around in his head, and it didn't help as much as it usually did. Finally, he gave up and returned to Tyler's bed. He was exhausted but couldn't sleep. Beside him, Tyler snored happily, lost to the world, but Alex just lay there, trying to process the day's events.

At least his father was okay, if penniless. He hoped Tyler hadn't rubbed Noah's nose in his loss too much, but that was unlikely; if George Tyler was going to bail out Lytton AV, he'd want his pound of flesh. First, he'd taken Noah's wife, then his son, and now his company. Alex shivered; it didn't do to forget what a powerful and committed enemy Tyler was.

The next few days were a struggle as he tried to manage without his song. Tyler was upbeat and cheerful, still riding the wave of joy from his acquisition of Lytton AV. Alex tried to suppress his thoughts, but he was restless, full of anxiety for his father and brother, and full of remorse for his part in their downfall.

The sleepless nights began to add up and he thought he was going mad. Every night, Tyler fucked him, revelling in the Lytton in his bed, just as he revelled in being the new owner of Lytton AV. His victory was complete. Every night, he turned over and fell asleep, leaving Alex lying there, burning up inside with too many feelings.

He gazed at Tyler lying next to him. Should he do the world a favour and smother the man with his pillow while he slept? He had this thought on a nightly basis and wrestled with it endlessly. Was it what Joe would do? No. Joe would challenge the man to a fight, give him a fair chance. Alex was an artist, not a soldier; he knew he couldn't do it, and he was by no means sure he could take on Tyler in a fight. He was young and strong, but Tyler was fit and also strong. Besides, Tyler's security team was right outside the door.

The thoughts were taking over his mind and he needed a coping mechanism to stop himself from going completely insane. So he slipped out of bed and walked down the hallway to the gym... only to find it locked.

"Problem, Alexander?" a voice asked silkily behind him.

"No... I just... couldn't sleep." Alex turned to face his houder. "I thought I'd work out, but the gym seems to be locked."

"On my orders. I don't want you doing yoga anymore." Tyler's eyes gleamed as he spoke. "You have a personal trainer to put you through your paces, and you're looking a little sharp around the edges." He traced a finger over Alex's cheekbones. "No more yoga. Not in the gym or anywhere else." He leaned against the wall, gazing at Alex searchingly, still looking for the chink in his armour.

"Of course. Whatever you wish, sir," Alex replied softly, but inside he was screaming. How long could he keep up this veneer of being the perfect IS without his coping mechanisms? Gideon hadn't given him any guidelines for *this*.

Tyler put an arm around his shoulder. "You're cold – let's go back to bed. You know, I've often wondered about the significance of that song you keep playing," he murmured, pushing Alex back along the hallway.

Alex swallowed hard. "It's about service. It reminds me to be humble, so I can be the devoted IS you deserve," he replied softly. "It reminds me that my own needs aren't important. I must dedicate myself only to you and your happiness."

"Ah." Tyler gave a little laugh. "Well, that does sound noble, but I'm sure you don't need a song to help you do that if you are, indeed, the changed person you keep insisting you are."

"No, of course not. It's just a reminder."

"And the yoga?" They reached the bedroom, and Tyler slipped into bed, pulling Alex in beside him.

"It's a discipline. It keeps me in shape."

"Yet there's a ritualistic element to how you perform all those poses. Watch." Tyler brought up footage from his yoga sessions on the smartwall.

Alex gazed at the wall glumly. It seemed that Tyler had finally found his Achilles heel. He watched himself going through his poses, his song playing over and over again, his mouth soundlessly repeating the words. He watched as he gazed at himself in the mirror, saw himself visibly blanking out all aspects of his true personality until there was nothing left.

"You know, it's an interesting trick," Tyler murmured. "It seems to me that when you arrive at the gym, you're agitated. There's this sense of pent-up energy." He rewound the footage and showed it again, pointing. "Then the yoga and the music soothe you. They calm you, and by the end, you're entirely blank. That's what I'm seeing, at least." Tyler turned to face him. "Care to explain?"

Alex felt like he was in a field of snakes and didn't know where to place his feet. He was acutely aware of how very dangerous everything had become.

"At Belvedere, they taught us to put our houders first. I'll admit that didn't come easily to me. This was a way of learning that lesson," he replied eventually.

"Well, I expect my best IS to be able to do that without props." Tyler turned off the footage. "No more yoga, Alexander, no more song. Let's see how well you get on without them, shall we?"

Alex was reminded of that picture in his father's study, of Holmes and Moriarty teetering on the edge of the Reichenbach Falls together, locked in a deadly embrace. That was how it felt being with Tyler. They were going over the Falls together, and they'd both die in the process. It was surely the only possible outcome.

Alex was no Sherlock Holmes. He had no clever plan to escape. His one plan relied on him remaining mentally strong enough to carry it out, and now he'd been deprived of the tools he relied upon to keep him sane, he wasn't sure that was possible.

Chapter Five
MARCH 2096
Josiah

Elsie encouraged Alex to start painting again when his arm healed, and he did so with gusto. Josiah would often come home to find him still in his night clothes, so lost in his work that he'd forgotten to wash, shave, or dress. Josiah never tired of watching him at work, his face lost in concentration. It reminded him of what his father had said about how he could see the beauty in the world and convey it through his art. There was nothing bland about his work, though; it was quirky and creative.

Tyler's trial date had been set for October, and the Inquisitus lawyers insisted that Alex stay in Josiah's custody until then, which was a relief to them both. Josiah hoped it would give him some breathing space to recover, at least a little.

When he wasn't painting, Alex had a rota of visitors – Elsie, Noah, Charles, Ted, Sofie. They all dropped by regularly to spend time with him. Slowly, surrounded by love and friendship, he began to heal. He ate more and lost that sharp, angular, shadow-eyed look he'd had.

Josiah didn't spy on him, so he didn't know what private conversations he had with his father and brother. He had been put under a microscope enough. Josiah wanted him to feel free, even if it was only an illusion.

One day, over breakfast, Josiah casually threw him a biokey.

"What's this?" Alex frowned, looking up.

"For you. It's in the garage." Josiah winked at him.

"What?" Alex jumped to his feet and ran into the garage, with Josiah following behind at a more leisurely pace.

The duck was second-hand but she was sound. Josiah had had Big Jen look her over, just to be sure. Alex stared at the vehicle as if she was made of cheese.

"She's a Lytton Classic," Josiah said softly. "I didn't think you'd want a duck with the Tyler name on it. She's not flashy, but she'll get you around. Now you're feeling a little better, I thought you'd appreciate more independence. You can go and visit your family at The Orchard, if you want. Or go anywhere you like. I'm not keeping tabs on you. Tyler is, unfortunately, but he won't risk messing with you with the trial hanging over him."

"You bought her for me?" Alex asked, wide-eyed.

"Yes. She's second hand, nothing special, but—*Oomph*."

Josiah reeled backwards as Alex threw himself at him. For a moment, their faces were almost touching and Alex's lips were on his, his body pressed up close.

Josiah wanted him with every fibre of his being, and he knew that, right here, right now, he could have him, but that wasn't why he'd bought him the duck. He was enjoying the warmth of Alex's kiss, and it took all his strength to push him away.

"No," he said regretfully, putting a finger over Alex's lips. "You don't have to pay for anything with sex, Alex. Not with me. Never with me."

"I know, but supposing I just really, *really* want you right now?" Alex grinned at him stupidly. "AVs always turn me on."

"Weirdo." Josiah grinned back. "But no. I'm not a commodity, to be picked up and put down on a whim. I'm worth more than that, and so are you."

Alex blinked. "Nobody's ever talked to me like that."

"I know, and that's the problem." Josiah deposited a gentle kiss on his cheek. "The duck's for you, no strings attached. Go and enjoy it," he said firmly. "And if that means you use it to go clubbing, to hook up with some guy – or girl – or even bring them back here for the night, then that's fine. You don't have to ask or explain anything to me."

Alex stood with his hands planted on his hips, looking at Josiah curiously, as if he was some strange new type of person he'd never encountered before. Then, as was the way with him these days, his mood changed abruptly and he wiped his hand over his eyes. Josiah turned away to give him the space to process his emotions. When he glanced back, Alex was sitting in the duck, caressing the steering wheel and looking joyously happy.

Josiah smiled and walked away. Why did he always fall for men who loved vehicles so much? It wasn't a passion he shared.

Alex made the most of his new freedom, flitting around in his new duck, enjoying life for perhaps the first time since his mother died. Josiah loved seeing him so happy. His moods were still a rollercoaster but less volatile than before. He didn't bring anyone home, much to Josiah's relief, although he schooled himself to be okay with it if he did.

Meanwhile, he slowly ticked every area of Alex's life off his list, except one. Finally, he decided it was time to head for Belvedere. He wasn't sure what he was hoping to find, or how it might help, but he couldn't leave any stone unturned. If he didn't find out absolutely everything there was to know, then Tyler might, and that could derail the trial. He didn't want any surprises.

It was a nice day for a drive, the sun bright in a crystal-clear sky. As he drove, he listened to Alex's first trial, following Isobel's death, although it left him none the wiser. He felt like he was pulling threads from a tapestry; they all led somewhere, but the more he pulled, the less clear the big picture became.

Belvedere was an old Georgian manor house that had once been a spa, later converted into an army supply station and then used to train indentured servants. It was a pleasant if unremarkable white building, standing on a clifftop with beautiful sea views.

He was ushered into a hall with a huge log fire burning merrily in a grate.

"Investigator Raine," he said to the homely-looking woman on reception, showing her his ID. "Madeleine Selcourt is expecting me."

"Yes, of course, Investigator Raine. This way."

She led him down many interminable white corridors until finally he ended up in a more modern wing of the house. He was shown into a beautiful room with a sea view, and there, behind a desk, was an equally beautiful woman. She really was stunning – slim and stylish, her sleek dark hair pulled into an elegant chignon. Her clothes were chic – a little cream-coloured suit teamed with a silver silk blouse. Josiah had an eye for sartorial dressing, but even he couldn't find a hair out of place on her. She had large, intelligent, almost soulful dark eyes, her skin was a smooth olive brown, and her nails were perfectly manicured. She had to be in her late fifties, but she could have passed for twenty years younger. She was flawless.

"Investigator Raine, please be seated." Her voice was mellow, cultured, and refined. Josiah adjusted his tie slightly, making sure it was perfect. This was a woman to be reckoned with; there was something about her that made him want to pull himself up by his bootstraps and impress her. She certainly wasn't a woman whose time he could waste.

"I was surprised to receive your call, but I'm happy to help in any way I can," she said, offering him a cup of tea. "I presume you're here to ask about Alexander Tyler, given all the interest in him in the news recently."

"Alexander Ty...?" Josiah frowned. "Oh. I see."

"I've gathered every piece of information we have on him and have prepared it for you." She zapped the document over to his nym, then looked up with a detached smile. "Will that be all?"

"No." He smiled back pleasantly. "Can you advise me what kind of a place Belvedere was when Alexander was here, Ms Selcourt?"

"It was a training facility for indentured servants."

"A very *specialised* training facility, I think it'd be fair to say?"

"We dealt only with high-value servants. There's little point to training someone to do construction or factory work, after all."

"Quite. I gather that some houders paid a high price for your services?"

"Think of it like The New Dorchester, or Rolls Royce." She pursed her lips together. "We offered bespoke training, dealing with only the most exclusive servants for wealthy clients. Mostly, that meant personal servants – those who would have been butlers, ladies' maids, valets, housekeepers, and so on in wealthy establishments."

"What about training servants to offer sexual services?" Josiah felt almost dirty throwing that suggestion at this cultured, elegant woman, but he was interested in her response. Much to his disappointment, she merely gazed at him coolly, as if he were a foul-mouthed schoolboy.

"We certainly didn't deal in anything vulgar, or illegal," she said firmly. "I have no idea how you would even provide training in something so distasteful, but I can assure you it's not something we offered here."

"So, when George Tyler called and asked you to train a difficult servant, you felt you understood the brief?"

"Of course." She inclined her head gracefully. "Over the years, we've been approached to turn all kinds of people into perfect servants. We developed various training schemes and protocols for such eventualities. These arose out of the other work we do here, the more regular courses we offer."

"I see. So you weren't asked to 'break' Alexander?"

"If we had been, it's not a request we'd have agreed to." Her nostrils flared, ever so slightly. "However, we did understand that some people are very attached to their servants and required a personalised approach. We were always happy to tailor our training in those circumstances, for a fee."

"Hmm. How much were you aware of what went on here? I know you own Belvedere, but you own many businesses. You left the day-to-day running to your own indentured servant, I believe? A man called Gideon Bart?"

"That's right. Poor, dear Gideon." She smiled sadly.

"He passed away recently, I understand?"

"Some time ago now. It was in June last year."

"When did he last work here?"

"Oh goodness. Well, he told me about his cancer last February and advised me that he only had a few months to live. He was unlucky. While many cancers are curable these days, his was not. It was caught too late, in any case. He'd never had a day off sick in his life and rather overlooked all his symptoms, only going to the doctor when it was far too late."

"You must have been upset."

She waved her hand dismissively. "Of course. He was a huge asset to Belvedere."

"But on a personal level, too. You'd worked with him for many years."

"Well, quite." She gave a tight, dispassionate smile. "When he told me about the cancer, I immediately released him from his contract and paid it out, in full, so he could live the last few months of his life in comfort."

"I'm sure you were very generous."

"I was." She inclined her head gracefully. "He always worked very hard for me, and I was happy to reward him for that, although saddened that he wouldn't be able to enjoy the fruits of his hard work for very long."

"Then what happened to him?"

"What do you mean?" She raised an eyebrow.

"Where did he go? What did he do?"

"Once he left my service, that was really none of my concern," she murmured. "However, we do have an address for him on file. I can let you have it. I assume it was a rental property, given his situation."

"Do you know what happened to his personal effects?"

"No." She clearly wasn't the kind of person who felt the need to qualify her answers, even in the face of long silences – which was a tactic Josiah often employed to prompt people to speak. She merely sat there, gazing at him expressionlessly.

In the end, he broke first. "I gather there was a memorial service?"

"Yes."

"Did you go?"

"Goodness, no. Gideon was a very good servant, you understand, but he *was* just a servant. We weren't close."

"I see. That's strange. George Tyler went."

"Well, he was so impressed by how well Alexander turned out that he sent several more of his servants to Belvedere after that. I suppose he must have become fond of Gideon in the process, or grateful, perhaps, for his services. Gideon was a clever man. Very particular, very fastidious, which I liked."

"But not enough to attend his memorial service?"

"I'm a very busy woman." She didn't look remotely guilty about this. She clearly saw no reason why she should have been there. "However, as you're so interested in the service, I can send you a link to the live stream."

"Yes, please, if you would." He inclined his head, and she made a note on her holopad. "Did you watch it?"

"No. As I said, I'm a very busy woman. I'm sure it was a tasteful affair, though. Gideon always had excellent taste."

"Was there a funeral?" Josiah asked. "Or just a memorial service?"

"Just the memorial service. Gideon wanted a private ceremony for the funeral. He hated fuss."

"I see. Since Gideon left, who runs Belvedere?" Josiah asked.

"I moved in to assess it and decided to close down the training facility soon after Gideon died. It really was his baby. I had no interest in it."

"So it's not a training facility anymore?"

"No. Gideon made it hugely successful and it brought in a steady income stream, but I wasn't interested in continuing his work. I'm in the process of turning Belvedere back into a high-end spa. I've spent some time here to oversee its closing down and drawing up plans for the refurbishment. Normally, I work from an office in New London, but it's been an enjoyable break." She glanced out of the window, at the sea view. Every movement she made was deliberate and contained, as if anything else would have been unspeakably vulgar.

"It's a lovely location for a spa," he observed.

"It is." She inclined her head, as if granting him a wish. "When I first bought it, most people wouldn't have been able to afford to come to a spa, but there's a growing demand for such luxuries now." She turned back to give him a barely curious glance. "Did Alexander complain about any aspect of his treatment while he was here?"

"No. On the contrary. He viewed it as a respite from his life as an IS. He feels he learned a great deal here that was helpful."

She gave a distant smile, but she looked gratified. "I'm sure he did. Gideon was very good at spotting what people need to know in order to adjust to a life of servitude. I'm sure that was because he was such a natural servant himself. I found him at The New Dorchester, and he quickly impressed me with his attention to detail and eagerness to be of use. Some people are born to serve."

"But he didn't," Josiah pointed out. She arched a questioning eyebrow. "He didn't serve you, did he? He worked here, running this business. If he was such a good servant, I'm surprised you didn't want to keep him close by, to actually serve you."

"We all serve in different ways," she said in a cold tone. "Take yourself. You serve your country, your government. I'm sure you take as much pride in that as Gideon took in serving not only me but also his fellow indentured servants by running a training academy for them. I have absolutely no doubt that Gideon viewed his work here as service."

"He sounds like a remarkable man," Josiah murmured. "I wish I'd met him."

"He's a great loss to us all." She inclined her head. "Now, is there anything else you wish to ask me, Investigator Raine? If there is, I'm happy to help, but I don't have time for idle chit-chat."

"Of course. Just one more thing. I understand that you and George Tyler are friends?"

"I wouldn't go that far." She looked as if she didn't approve of friendship. Josiah wondered if she ever let anyone get close enough to make such a claim. "I know Mr Tyler from various business interests. When he was searching for an establishment that could deal with his difficult IS, I suggested he send the young man to Belvedere. I knew that Gideon would be able to help."

"I see. Well, thank you for your time – and efficiency."

He found a local café and went through the information Madeleine Selcourt had sent, but it was all curiously bland, giving little information apart from the dates Alex had been at Belvedere and the courses he'd attended. Gideon had signed off his stay with what read like an end-of-term school report, asserting that he'd learned all he needed to an adequate standard and had come to appreciate the value of being a committed and eager servant. There was nothing about breaking him, no mention of any special requests Tyler might have made, and absolutely nothing about how to create a mask to obscure all your thoughts and feelings – unless Gideon considered that came under "learned all he needed".

Josiah mused on this over a chocolate brownie. He wasn't sure what he'd expected to find, but he was disappointed. As with everything related to Alex, it seemed the more he learned, the less he knew.

Beginning his long drive home, he felt a little out of sorts and irritable at what had seemed to be a wasted day. His mood was brightened by finding two chocolates in his little silver case. Alex had started slipping them in there again, and it always made him smile.

It was late when he returned home. Alex was already in bed, and Josiah headed straight for his. He wondered if he should tell Alex where he'd been. It felt strange to be digging around in his life while sharing a house with him. But he hadn't told him about Brian's testimony, or about meeting Bax, or any of the other people he'd interviewed. It felt too intrusive. Besides, Alex knew what he was working on and never asked, so Josiah took his cue from that.

The next day was a Saturday, and as Alex was spending it with his family, Josiah decided to work from home. He made some toast for breakfast and decided to work while he ate. He was torn between watching the footage of Alex's two trials again and sitting through the tedium of Gideon's memorial service. He decided on the latter, mainly to get it out of the way.

The stirring sounds of *Amazing Grace* played as the holovid began and people solemnly took their seats in a little stone church. It wasn't widely attended, so it was easy to spot George Tyler as he entered. Why was he there? Josiah knew that some people attended these types of events to network, but that seemed unlikely in Tyler's case. Tyler took his place next to a man with owlish spectacles, who seemed genuinely upset.

A vicar led the ceremony and the man in the spectacles – a Dr Adams – read a moving eulogy, paying tribute to Gideon's sharp mind and superb professional skills. They'd worked together for some years, and it appeared that he'd been an excellent boss and a good friend. Josiah found himself drifting off. So far, so unremarkable. He made himself another cup of tea and treated himself to a couple of chocolates, then returned to watch the last part.

The service came to an end and the vicar said a final few words. Josiah glanced at his to-do list to see what to tackle next, his attention waning. He'd learned nothing, but then he hadn't expected to. He was barely paying attention as the final song played and people began filing out. It took a moment to sink in... and then he looked back at the holovid in surprise. He paused, rewound it, and watched the whole thing again from the start. Then he went through the documents Madeleine Selcourt had given him, looking for a specific image. He stared at the image, then at the paused holovid, sitting back to run a hand through his hair in shock.

He knew who'd killed Elliot Dacre and – he was fairly sure he knew why.

Chapter Six
MAY 2091
Alex

He was in uncharted waters now. Without the anchors of his song and his yoga, he'd been cast adrift, and he wasn't sure how long he could keep afloat.

It didn't help that Tyler's controlling behaviour continued to escalate. He demanded to know every thought going through Alex's head, and on several occasions, Alex woke to find him sitting up in bed watching him, brooding. It was claustrophobic and intense.

Over the Falls we go, Alex thought repeatedly. If only they could get it over and done with. But the falling was taking such a very long time, with neither of them prepared to give an inch.

Tyler was like a spider, watching the prey caught in his web, and Alex was the doomed fly, playing dead in the hope the spider would lose interest and he might escape.

Yet, Tyler prodded him constantly for evidence that the *real* Alex was still in there behind the platitudes and devoted service. Alex's nerves were shredded to pieces and he wasn't sure how he was still alive by this point. For Solange, he reminded himself, but he was starting to think that the task was simply too much. Nobody could endure this amount of scrutiny and keep their true feelings hidden – it wasn't possible.

Forbidden to hear his song, he repeated it over and over in his head. Forbidden to practise his yoga, he used his workout sessions to try and create the same effect. Neither was as good.

There was another problem, too, one that only became apparent a few months after Tyler's triumphant march into Lytton AV; he'd overstretched himself financially.

"You should break it up," one of his advisers told him in a meeting. The man was Dutch, and he'd impressed Alex with his business savvy. His name was Anders Visser, and he also wore a Tyler ID tag, which made his forthright way of talking to Tyler all the more impressive. "You won't get what you paid for it, but it'd mitigate your losses."

"I'm not bloody well selling Lytton AV," Tyler said tightly.

"Well, you have to sell something. You're stretched too thin. All that investment in floating city tech, and then you go and buy a failing AV company with no future."

Alex listened intently, feeling a tiny flare of hope.

"You do have some expensive assets you could sell." Visser glanced at Alex.

"No." Tyler stood up, buttoning his jacket. "Alexander is non-negotiable. Lytton AV is non-negotiable. I've been in worse scrapes than this. I'll survive."

Alex didn't doubt it. What followed was weeks of frantic holochats, wheeler-dealing, and the calling in of favours, to say nothing of the threat of blackmail. Tyler had decades of footage of people in compromising positions and he dug it all out, unafraid to use it. He had a frenetic, nervous energy and clearly thrived on flying by the seat of his pants, but his body was leaner than ever, his dark eyes sunken in his perma-tanned face.

The sex had changed too. Where once it had been raw and passionate, now it had morphed, slowly, into something uglier, the need for control more intense. Tyler took to pinning Alex down every time, holding his wrists so tightly they were covered in bruises.

"Look at me when I'm fucking you," Tyler ordered, slapping his face one night when they were in bed.

"Sorry, sir."

"Where do you go when your eyes are blank like that?" Tyler took his face in his hands and gazed at him searchingly. "Where are you? What are you hiding from me?"

"Nothing. You have me. I'm yours." Alex caressed his cheek gently, feeling like a broken record – they had a variation of this conversation every few days.

"No. I *own* you, but I don't possess you. I need to possess you, Alexander. I need to know you want only me, that you crave only me, that I'm all you think about, day and night." His eyes were dark and savage. He looked deranged.

Alex hummed his song in his head so loudly he was surprised Tyler couldn't hear him. Tyler slapped him again.

"Stop that!"

"What, sir?"

"Whatever the thing is that you're doing. Your eyes go blank and you disappear. Don't do it. I want *you*, the real you. Don't do it. *Don't.*" Tyler took hold of his head and slammed it into the pillow repeatedly. "*Don't disappear!*" he screamed like a madman.

The next morning he was contrite, as he often was after these outbursts.

"I'm sorry. I don't mean to hurt you." He took hold of Alex's bruised wrist and kissed it gently. "Let me make it up to you. How about a little holiday, somewhere warm and beautiful."

A few days later, Tyler took him to a small airport, where a team of people immediately swarmed around them, bringing them champagne, taking care of their luggage, and seeing to their every need. Alex noticed the envious looks they cast at him. If only they knew he'd rather live on the streets and eat trash than stew in the lap of Tyler's luxury.

They boarded Tyler's private jet and took off. Alex stared out of the window, sipping on his glass of champagne, gazing down on the flooded world below. He didn't ask where they were going – he didn't care.

Tyler was in a good mood now, but he was so mercurial that Alex never knew if it was going to last. It was tiring being the perfect courtesan, always ready and willing for sex, always attentive to his houder's every whim, and all without the help of his anchors, his grasp on sanity slipping away daily. All he wanted was respite – a day away from Tyler, a chance to regroup. He needed space.

"So, any guesses where we're going?" Tyler sat down opposite him, clicking his fingers for a glass of champagne.

"I can't think." Alex smiled emptily. Tyler clearly wanted to delight him, but his fingerprints were etched in dark bruises all over his body.

"Well, I think you'll like it. We both need a holiday. I've been a little short-tempered lately. It's been a stressful time, calling in those favours and clawing back some funds, and I've taken it out on you."

Alex supposed that was the closest he'd get to an apology.

"It's just that you make me so angry. I know you're holding back, hiding from me, when all I want is to make you happy."

That wasn't all he wanted. He wanted control. Alex's happiness was irrelevant, yet he'd convinced himself of his own benevolence, like tyrants everywhere.

"This will be a chance for us to unwind together, to take in some sun. You're looking far too pale." Tyler reached across the table for Alex's hand and gently stroked his fingers.

"That sounds perfect," he murmured vacantly.

Tyler's eyes darkened. "Well, try to sound as if you bloody well mean it."

"Oh, I do. I've been so worried about you. You work too hard and you've been run ragged of late." He remembered that endless flattery was a requirement of a good courtesan. "You need a break."

"I do." Tyler pulled his hand to his lips and kissed it, gazing at him meaningfully as he did so.

God, that was corny. "I'm sorry if I haven't helped. I've felt so guilty. You bought Lytton AV for me, after all, and that's what caused you all these financial issues." He knew he was layering it on with a trowel, but Tyler seemed to buy it.

"Well, I always wanted to own Lytton AV. It was rightfully mine, given it was built off my father's hard work."

"Of course. I'm so glad it's back where it belongs."

Tyler seemed mollified by this conversation. "So, any guesses where we're going?"

"I can't even imagine."

Tyler seemed pleased by how mysterious he was being, so Alex pretended to be surprised by every delightful thing on the flight.

They walked off the plane into a beautiful, sunny day a few hours later and were immediately hustled onto a helicopter. Alex still had no idea where they were, and Tyler seemed intent on prolonging the guessing game for as long as possible. They finally landed on top of a cliff with gorgeous views over a beautiful bay. Tyler took his hand and led him through a pretty olive grove to a modern house made, in typical Tyler style, of glass and steel.

"Recognise it?" he asked, smiling as he watched Alex's face.

"Oh!" Alex was genuinely surprised to find he *did* recognise it. "It's your Spanish house. I saw the designs. Is it finished, then?"

"Yes. And look." Tyler led him through a courtyard and then into a beautiful room with views over the bay. "I took your advice. I joined the terrace to the courtyard, and now you can see these beautiful views." He gestured expansively. "I also listened to your thoughts on the décor, and *voila*." He waved at the Spanish-themed rugs and curtains, the *objets d'art*, sofas, shelves, and cushions.

There was still a disconnect between this most modern building and the rustic style inside, but Alex found himself approving all the same. Left to his own devices, Tyler would have decorated it in red, white, and black, stark and aggressive colours, making it feel as cold and sterile as his other houses. By adopting Alex's ideas, he'd made it softer. The smartwalls had been programmed to appear to be of a traditional stucco, and the floor tiles were a warm, faded orange.

"It's beautiful," he said honestly, gazing around.

Outside, there was a crystal-clear infinity pool, a firepit, and a cane sofa hanging on a swing. Gladioli, agapanthus, hibiscus, bougainvillea, and roses flowered in sprays of bright colours along a wall, surrounded by lavender, rosemary, and irises.

"I'm so glad you love it." Tyler took his hand and showed him around, pulling him into every room and closet, all of them beautifully decorated. "We can relax here, just the two of us. Soak up the sun."

How had he afforded it? The man had just fought tooth and nail to keep his business empire together and yet he'd clearly spent a small fortune on this place. How did he do it?

The hacienda was fully staffed, too, with a cook, housekeeper, and gardeners. There was the ever-present security as well, lest Alex think he could somehow escape Tyler's clutches here. Spain didn't recognise the British IS scheme, but they had no wish to interfere, either; this country had its own problems.

"Mr Tyler, sir." A tall man with a completely bald head appeared, his skin dark and smooth. He was dressed in a long black robe, clearly bearing the Tyler livery, although he wasn't an IS. "How lovely to finally welcome you to your hacienda." He had a rich, deep voice and a Spanish accent.

"Alex, this is Jabir. He's the major-domo here." Tyler introduced them. "If you want anything, ask Jabir. He's a local."

Jabir shook Alex's hand, an expression of profound pity in his eyes. His gaze lingered, momentarily, on the ID tag hanging from Alex's necklace, and Alex caught his little moue of distaste.

"You are very welcome here, sir," Jabir said, bowing slightly. "I hope everything here will be to your comfort. Now, I'm sure you are both hungry after your journey. I have laid you a meal out by the pool."

Jabir led them back to the infinity pool, overlooking a glorious blue bay. The food was delicious, and as the sun went down, they swam together in the warm pool, looking out at the lights of the boats in the harbour below.

Later, Tyler made love to him in front of the fire pit, both of them wet and gleaming in the light of the lanterns Jabir had lit. It was the single most romantic moment of Alex's life, but he felt nothing. If all this kept Tyler from hurting him, needling him, and trying to see inside his soul, then that was the best he could hope for.

It wasn't much of a holiday. He was confined to the house, and beautiful though it was, there wasn't much to do. Tyler took trips out, but not with Alex, presumably because if he managed to slip away, then Tyler couldn't compel the Spanish authorities to give him back. The security around the house was impregnable, though, and as it was situated on a remote clifftop, there was no way out. Tyler's ubiquitous smartwalls watched his every move and armed guards patrolled outside. Alex was as much of a prisoner here as he'd ever been in the UK.

Tyler was still a workaholic. He encouraged Alex to swim and relax, but he spent hours holed up in his study working.

"Go and enjoy yourself," he'd order, and Alex would slip away, grateful for the respite. He didn't dare do any yoga – that had been forbidden, and the smartwalls would pick it up – but he lost himself in repetitive lengths of the pool, repeating his song in his head as he swam.

He fell in love with that pool. It was surrounded by flowering shrubs that scented the air and the views were stunning. As he swam towards the edge, it felt as if he'd fall into the harbour far below, an optical illusion that never failed to enchant.

Spain didn't feel real. Left to his own devices for large chunks of time, he felt himself drifting further and further away. He'd wanted space and respite, but it didn't seem to be helping. He recognised that he was depressed, his nerves shot to pieces, and could only watch, almost as an observer, detached from himself, as he sank further and further into a foggy lethargy. He knew that Gideon would chide him, but somehow, he couldn't help it.

Lying in the pool, floating, he gazed at the sky and blanked out. He spent whole days this way, his flesh mottled and prune-like when he finally hauled himself out. He resented every second Tyler spent with him because it meant he had to concentrate when he longed to drift away into nothingness. It was harder and harder to stay in the moment, to live life constantly on the edge in the way that being with Tyler required. He was no longer afraid that he'd snap and give himself away. He was more worried that he'd simply disappear, shrivel into himself and cease to exist.

At first, Spain worked its magic on Tyler. He relaxed in the sun when he wasn't working, and ate a healthier diet. He lost that cadaverous look and the shadows beneath his eyes disappeared. Alex noticed all these things without caring.

The sex, which had once been so passionate, was now almost always violent, and Alex had the bruises to prove it. Mostly on his wrists but also on his thighs and arse, where Tyler grasped him too tightly when fucking him, as if he was terrified Alex was going to escape. *How? Where would I go?* He'd tried that once before, and whenever he thought of it, he saw Peter lying by the side of the road, heard Joe's raw howl of grief, and looked down into Solange's dead eyes. Escape wasn't an option. *Look what happened last time...* No, it was best to just swim and float and swim... and fuck.

Fuck. His cock, which had once been so revitalised by his lust-filled hatred of Tyler, was now experiencing the same lethargy as the rest of him. Yet, Tyler demanded an erection from him every time as some kind of twisted evidence of his power over him. He had no access to the blue pills anymore, so he had to force himself to give Tyler the proof he required. It became more and more difficult, until the day finally came when nothing happened... his cock remained resolutely flaccid.

Panicked, he fell back on an old fantasy and imagined being here with Joe, being himself again – snarky, sometimes bad-tempered and petulant, sometimes charming and fun, but above all real. Not this strange, watered-down version of himself that he'd become. In his fantasies, Joe was a passionate and forceful lover, but also tender and caring. When he was being bratty, Joe picked him up and threw him in the pool. Then he jumped in beside him and kissed him as the water caressed them both. *Forgive me for using you this way, Joe...* But it was the only thing that made him hard now. He tuned out Tyler, gazing at him emptily, and thought only of Joe. He was spent. He had nothing left to give. Maybe Tyler had won after all. He felt as insubstantial as the wind.

When the sex was over, he took to creeping out and jumping into the pool. Only there was he free, swimming naked, cocooned in the warm, gentle kiss of the water.

As he disengaged from Tyler, so Tyler became increasingly frustrated by him. Where was the sassy Alex he'd enjoyed tormenting? The perfect IS, the chatty dinner companion he'd once been, interested in floating cities and all aspects of Tyler's business, delighted and turned on by a trip in a flying duck? Now, it took all Alex's strength to listen and ask questions, and he had no energy for more. His conversational abilities declined and their dinners were more often than not silent.

One night, as he forced himself out of the pool and back into the bedroom just before dawn, he saw lights flashing in Tyler's study. He tiptoed towards them and saw Tyler, sprawled in his office chair, gazing repeatedly at Elliot's two holopics as they swirled and moved around him. One was his mother, looking up, smiling, and walking. The other was himself, caught in that quiet moment, turning and looking straight at the holocam, his eyes visibly draining of personality. Tyler stopped the hologram, placing it on pause just before the mask went on, and Alex knew what he was looking for, because he could see it himself. Alex Lytton was still *in* there, and Tyler wanted him.

Tyler clicked the hologram and it began to move again, its light passing through the illumination from his mother's, the two of them performing a strange, twisted dance. Alex backed away. The expression on Tyler's face was sad, angry, and frustrated… These Lyttons were a mystery he wanted to unravel, to control and possess absolutely, but he never could. When he came back to bed half an hour later, he reached for Alex and entered him so hard that he had to chew on his pillow to stop himself from screaming.

Alex ached all the time now, throughout his body but also in the very depths of his being. It was an ache that exhausted him, leeching out every last ounce of energy until there was nothing left. Tyler shouted at him frequently, but he could barely hear him over the white noise that seemed to play permanently in his ears. If only he had his song, maybe then he could tether himself better to reality. As it was, he struggled to care. He ate like a bird, uninterested in food. He barely slept. He just floated in that pool, gazing at the edge and at the bay far below. If only he could float over it and be dashed on the rocks, but the pool cradled him within, and Tyler's security men watched his every move, so that was never a possibility.

Then it happened. His erection failed to materialise, despite his best efforts to think about Joe. Tyler was angry as Alex's body gave him the evidence he'd been looking for all along, that he was being played, that Alex didn't care about him. Alex was aware of the sharp sting of slaps on his skin, but didn't feel them, aware of Tyler's rage without caring. He knew he *should* care, for Solange's sake, but it was all too much effort. Tyler shook him like a rag doll, then left the room, retreating to the holopics in his office that gave him what he wanted.

Alex lay on the bed, his chest heaving but his mind curiously empty. When, finally, he got his breath back, he hauled himself off the bed and out to the pool. He fell into it rather than jumped. It felt wonderful, like falling into bed. Maybe he could drown, if Tyler's men didn't insist on pulling him out of the water and making him live.

He floated to the surface and lay there, gazing up at the stars, feeling the water wash him clean, gentling the pain in his flesh. He was free here. Nobody could touch him. This was a good place to die.

A splash beside him caught his attention but he couldn't be bothered to look at it. Then his face was grasped between two hard hands.

"Look at me, damn you," Tyler screamed. "You're still in there. I *know* you are. Look at me."

He was aware of a sharp slap across his face, and he managed to force himself to gaze at Tyler. "Oh, hello, sir. Isn't it a beautiful night?" he murmured, as if by rote. It was the kind of thing people said, wasn't it?

"Fuck the night," Tyler raged. "Where are you, Alexander? Where have you gone?"

"I'm not sure. You took away my song, you see," he whispered. "And my yoga. I don't have my anchors anymore, so I'm drifting."

"Don't go nuts on me. It's not who you are," Tyler snapped.

"I was thinking, these are the Falls." Alex gestured to the edge of the infinity pool. "The Reichenbach Falls. We could go over together? Like in the picture." He swam towards the edge, then tried to lever himself up, but lack of food had robbed him of his strength. Tyler threw himself after him, pulling him back.

"Here we go." Alex smiled distantly. "Over we go. We can be each other's fall, sir. We already are, I think."

"Stop it." Tyler slapped his jaw.

Alex wished he could feel it.

"Stop this now, Alexander!"

"Just let ourselves go." Alex thought what a relief the fall would be, after all these years of fighting. To finally let go and just fall – how glorious. Solange wouldn't mind, not if he took Tyler with him, and he could. If he could just grab him and hold on, they could fall together. "Come on! Let's go."

He wrapped his arms around Tyler and tried to pull him to the edge. Tyler yelled and struck out, sending him backwards into the pool. He went under and then felt himself being dragged back up to the surface, winded. When he came to, he found Tyler's hands around his neck, Tyler's dark eyes boring into him, as brooding and obsessive as when they'd been gazing at those holograms.

"You should do it," Alex whispered. "Please, kill me, sir."

Tyler's hands tightened around his throat and he pushed Alex's head under the water. Alex couldn't breathe but he didn't care. He didn't struggle. He would go to his death like a baby, docile and serene. Tyler pulled him up, his hands still wrapped around Alex's throat.

"You're mine," Tyler rasped. "I can kill you if I want."

"Yes, I'm yours," Alex whispered. "I'm happy to die, if that's what you want." He spread his arms, offering himself up. *Let me fall, let me go, please...*

A look of absolute horror crept into Tyler's eyes as sanity slowly returned, and he released Alex abruptly.

"Oh, God." He ran a hand over his smooth scalp. "What have you done to me? Oh, God, Alexander." He took Alex in his arms and held him close, kissing his wet hair. "I'm sorry, I'm so sorry."

Alex felt nothing, only a vague sense of sadness that he was not, after all, to die out here tonight in this beautiful pool.

"We're destroying each other," Tyler hissed, his shoulders hunched. "I love you, but I hate you. You obsess me. It has to stop."

He tilted Alex's chin towards him and kissed his unresponsive lips. Then he stepped back.

"I'm leaving. You'll stay here. I can't let you go. You know I can't let you go, don't you?" His voice was full of despair. "I would, you know, if it weren't for *her*, but I can't because I don't trust you." He released Alex, waded back across the pool, and heaved himself out. "I need a break from you. Jabir will look after you. You can have the song back and the yoga, if they mean so much to you. Just...return to yourself, and to me, Alexander. Please." He wrapped a towel around his waist and strode away.

Alex watched him go, then turned onto his back and floated, gazing up at the stars as they moved overhead. Only when the first light of dawn began to glow on the horizon did he finally force himself out of the water. He walked unsteadily along the hallway to the room he shared with Tyler, only to find it empty. Hearing the whirring of helicopter blades, he glanced out of the window to see Tyler step onboard. The chopper took off into the morning sky, taking his tormentor with it.

He sat on the bed, feeling empty and listless. Then he lay down, gazing out at the morning sky blankly. He'd won a victory of sorts, a respite, if nothing else, and that was a good thing, if only he could feel it. He should be pleased, but he wasn't.

He felt absolutely nothing.

Chapter Seven
JULY 2096
Josiah

Josiah sat staring at the paused holovid, his mind racing. Then he glanced at his watch. 10.15. Alex was out all day, and nobody was expecting him in the office. He considered putting in a call to Esther but decided against it. He wanted to be very sure about this before he stuck his neck out. She'd think he'd gone mad if he went to her with this before he'd investigated.

He flicked through his holopad files to find Gideon's last known address then set off. He arrived at a park home site a couple of hours later – hundreds of AV homes laid out in neat rows, very close together. After the Rising, there had been an explosion in this kind of accommodation: easy, cheap, and movable if the waters rose again.

He found Gideon's among the multitude and knocked on the door. A woman answered, middle-aged, grey-haired, frazzled. He flashed his badge at her and smiled his most charming smile. She peered at him suspiciously.

"I'm looking for Gideon Bart," he said.

"He died ages ago. Last year sometime." She tried to close the door, but he'd taken the precaution of wedging his foot in it.

"Did he leave anything behind?"

"No." She glared at his foot.

"What happened to his stuff? His furniture, personal effects, and so on?"

"No idea. Place was empty when we moved in."

"I see. Well, thank you so much for your help." He removed his foot, and she slammed the door in his face. This seemed to be a dead end, but he wasn't prepared to give up so easily. He walked over to the site office.

"Gideon Bart?" The manager, who had a helpful nanobadge with *Mr Nugent* glowing on it, glanced up. "Yeah. He rented a van home here for a few months before he died. I remember him because he was always so elegant and had such posh manners. You never saw him in a rumpled suit, even though they hung off him. He was skin and bone. Cancer, he said. Liver, I think. He had this yellow tinge." Nugent gestured to his face. "Poor bastard."

"What happened to him?"

"He went into hospital and never came out again. Then we had notification from his next of kin saying he'd died."

"His next of kin?" Josiah frowned. "Who was that?"

"A nephew. I've still got the notification." Nugent found the document and pinged it into the air. It was short and matter-of-fact, simply informing the manager that his uncle had died, and he would arrange for his accommodation to be cleared out as soon as possible.

"Was it?" Josiah asked.

"Yeah, within a few days. All very efficient."

"Did you meet the nephew?"

"Nope. Don't think he came. He sent someone with an AV. They took the stuff and that was that. It was all paid up. Nothing out of the ordinary."

"Did he leave anything behind?" This seemed to be another dead end.

"Don't think so. Let me check." Nugent looked through some more documents on his holopad, then shook his head.

"I see." Josiah was disappointed, although he wasn't sure what he'd expected.

"Oh, hang on! There *was* something else. I forgot about it. He left me a note before he went into hospital that final time. Not often anyone writes anything by hand these days, that's why I remember."

He went out to the back, then returned and handed Josiah a piece of white paper. The writing on it was tiny and a little wavery, the writer clearly not in the best of health, but there was a neatness to it that tallied with what Joe knew about Gideon.

Dear Mr Nugent, I enclose my next month's rent. Thank you so much for your kindness and assistance. It's been a glorious summer, but the raine will come soon, and by then, I'll have gone home.

"What does he mean by that?" Josiah frowned. "This was his home, wasn't it?"

"Dunno. I assumed he meant... you know..." Nugent pointed up at the sky. "Or maybe he meant he'd moved in with his nephew? To be honest, I thought he might have gone a bit nuts."

Josiah read the letter again. Gideon's handwriting was very small but very precise – all except that one word: *rain*. Was that a tiny *e* on the end? Raine? He felt a sudden chill creep up his spine.

"Can I keep this?" He held up the note.

Nugent shrugged. "Be my guest."

Josiah strode back to his duck, his heart beating fast. He read the note again. Was he clutching at straws, or was this a coded message for him? Gideon was such a meticulous person, and the rest of his note written so correctly. How likely was it that he'd make a mistake and add an extra "e" to the end of the word "rain"? What did the message tell him, though? It seemed to be instructing him to search for Gideon at "home", but this *was* his home. His only other home had been Belvedere, and he definitely wasn't there.

Josiah found a café, ordered a hot chocolate and a choc-chip cookie because, right now, he needed as much chocolate as possible, then took out his holopad and searched for everything he could find about Gideon Bart. There wasn't much. He'd worked at Belvedere for years, and prior to that, at The New Dorchester hotel. Then Josiah saw something on the IS database that caught his attention. Gideon had first sold himself into servitude when he was eighteen years old, and the address given for his childhood home was in the Quarterlands.

Josiah left the café in a hurry and directed his duck to take him there. He knew he should tell Esther, who had been very clear he wasn't to go near any area of the Quarterlands again without backup, but he was in no mood to cool his heels waiting for that to arrive.

When he drew up outside the old tower block that had been Gideon's home, he realised this was a very different kind of Quarter. There were no packs of feral children lurking around the entrance; the place was clean, the bricks well scrubbed and the windows all intact. A couple of raftsmen tethered his duck and then ferried him to the entrance, where a welcoming committee of three older women, dressed in plain but clean clothes, greeted him. There would be no need for guns or fist-fights here, and as he entered the building, he could see why. Above the door was a familiar sight: a cross on an ark, a bird circling above it with an olive leaf in its beak – the universal symbol of the Floodites.

The women also wore the symbol on cheap wooden beads around their necks.

"Welcome, sir. How may we help?"

He showed them his badge, and they frowned and discussed it for a moment in a huddle, then returned.

"We want no quarrel with the Thorities," the oldest of the trio said. "We run a very orderly Quarter here. You may enter, but you must leave any weapons with us." She pointed at the desk.

Josiah pondered this for a moment. He wasn't keen to go into any Quarter without at least a stun gun, but their request wasn't unreasonable, and Floodites were known for their strict religious adherence, so he handed it over. He had no intention of telling them about the knife in his sock.

He was taken down a well-lit corridor to a large room with a massive ark symbol painted on the wall. As Quarters went, this one was the cleanest and most orderly he'd ever been in. People walked around freely, and there were no signs of the violence, poverty, or drug use he'd seen in so many other Quarters. Nobody here took the Quarterlands splash, he was sure of that. The people were plainly poor, their clothes bearing the mismatched, threadbare evidence of being third-hand at best, but they were all clean. There was a pervading smell of damp, but it wasn't anywhere near as bad as in some Quarters.

He was taken into a small office and introduced to a woman called Sister Marion.

"This is a religious Quarter?" Josiah asked, taking a seat on a rickety wooden chair.

"That's right. We belong to the Fellowship of the Ark." In other words, Floodites, although he wouldn't call them that to their face as he knew they hated the term.

Sister Marion was a homely-looking woman in her late sixties, a good age for anyone living in the Quarterlands. Most died before they reached fifty.

"Has this always been an Arkian Quarter?" he asked.

"For as long as I've lived here, which is all my life. Now, Investigator Raine, how may I help you?"

"I'm looking for information about a man who lived here as a child: Gideon Bart."

"Ah, Gideon." Marion smiled.

"You know him?"

"Oh, yes. We were close when he was a child. His mother was abandoned by her husband and moved here soon after he was born. She was a religious lady. Very proper. Gideon adored her, and she did her best to school him in Arkian doctrine, but she died when he was seven."

"That must have been hard on Gideon."

"It was. I was a few years older than him and also an orphan. I was tasked with taking care of the little ones who had nobody."

"That's a lot of responsibility for a young girl," Josiah observed.

"Not at all," she said sharply. "Everyone in this Quarter pulls their weight. There's only just enough to go around, but if we share and pull together, nobody goes hungry."

"How do you fund this utopia?" Josiah asked bluntly.

She gave him a cold look. "We bring up our children to be obedient and hard-working. When they reach the age of eighteen, they're encouraged to accept servitude outside the Quarter. We take half the price of each contract, and the rest the employer keeps to give the child on completion. All contracts last for ten years. The child is only twenty-eight when it's finished and hopefully has learned a good trade or has a useful service history behind them. Then, their lives are their own. The Quarter has been paid for bringing them up, and they are equipped to lead a useful life. We also accept donations, of course. The Church of the Fellowship of the Ark is always generous, and our work is well known in the wider community. Those more fortunate than ourselves will happily sponsor a child or elderly person living in our Quarter. We pride ourselves on looking after the most vulnerable in the community."

"That's very laudable," Josiah murmured. "So, do any of your grown-up children ever return?"

"They are welcome to, if we have space, but they must work. There are usually jobs to be had here, caring for the sick, elderly, and the children. There are also maintenance, cooking, cleaning, and other jobs to be done around the Quarter. That's how we are able to keep it in such good condition."

"Has Gideon returned here recently?" Josiah asked.

She looked genuinely startled. "No. Why would he?"

"If he was dying? If he wanted to return to his childhood home for the last few weeks of his life, would he be welcome?"

She hesitated, then gave a tight smile. "If he renounced his sinful ways, then yes. We'd never turn away a member of the Fellowship if truly penitent."

Josiah leaned back in his chair and gazed at her coolly. "And what sinful ways would those be?"

"Gideon was a good child, bright and hard-working. He was never wilful, mean-spirited, rude, or aggressive."

"But?" Josiah had already guessed where this was headed.

She sighed. "As a teenager, he developed sinful lusts. We had many conversations with him about it and how his nature was not compatible with Fellowship teachings. He swore he'd try to defeat his demons, but I don't believe he was successful."

"Are you saying that Gideon was homosexual?"

She gave a regretful smile. "Yes."

Josiah wasn't surprised. Society as a whole couldn't care less who anyone slept with these days, but the whole ethos of the Floodites was that God had sent another flood because of humanity's wickedness and corruption. They believed that only absolute purity would save them from another Rising. Homosexuality was only one of the many things they disapproved of.

"When did you last see Gideon?" he asked.

"He visited us about ten years ago, when his spiritual adviser here, Brother Ezekiel, died. It was good to see him again. He said he still struggled with his sinful inclinations but he found his servitude useful in avoiding temptation."

"And you haven't seen him since?"

"No. Forgive me. Is he in trouble? I'm wondering why an agent from Inquisitus is asking after him."

"I'm afraid I can't answer that." He smiled at her. "One more question, although I think I know the answer: did Gideon have a sibling or... a nephew?"

"No. He had no relatives. He was completely alone in the world. That's why the Fellowship agreed to care for him."

"I see. Well, you've been most helpful. Thank you for your time."

He left the Arkian Quarter feeling unsettled. This Quarter was a sanctuary of sorts. Gideon had been fed, clothed, and educated here. He'd been cared for. Yet he hadn't been accepted. Josiah's own childhood in a different Quarter had been far rougher and more precarious, but also more accepting and less rigid. Nobody had cared that he was gay, and there had been no pressure to become an IS. In fact, his father had always made it quite clear that he was never, under any circumstances, to sell himself.

At least he'd established that there was no nephew. He had no doubt that the person who'd arranged for Gideon's belongings to be cleared out was Gideon himself. He climbed back into his duck and read Gideon's note again.

It's been a glorious summer, but the raine will come soon, and by then, I'll have gone home.

Where might Gideon call home? And why was he leaving a note for Josiah, because that was definitely an "e" on the end of "rain". It was deliberately cryptic, designed to be misunderstood, yet Gideon clearly expected Josiah to be able to decipher it.

Home.

Josiah stared out the window. Why would a man he'd never met leave him such a bizarre note? Alex had said Gideon found him "dead sexy". Had he harboured a strange crush on him?

Home.

Oh, shit.

Josiah put the duck into gear and high-tailed it away from the Arkian Quarter, leaving a small tsunami in his wake.

It was just a hunch… unlikely, improbable, and yet, somehow also the only thing that made sense. He had no other clues, so it was worth a try. He drove for two hours across several lost zones, and as he drew close, he felt a sense of impending dread. He'd avoided this place for years, on purpose, and he'd never had any intention of returning.

Home.

Not Gideon's childhood home – his.

Ahead of him, five tower blocks loomed from out of the sludge-brown water. Greenfields – he could only assume the name was ironic, but maybe it had once been true – was a 1970s-era housing estate, full of high-rises, column upon column of reinforced concrete towers, brutalist monoliths that squatted on the skyline like a row of crumbling tombstones.

He parked his duck next to the middle tower block and climbed out. A pack of kids was on him immediately. They weren't as feral as the kids of the Canary Quarter, but they were wild and rough all the same. He threw them cash cards, waved his badge around, and made it clear that if there was so much as a scratch on his duck when he returned, he'd arrest them all. He could tell by their wide eyes that they believed him: these kids had a healthy fear of Thorities.

He'd left here as a teenager to join the army, but he still remembered every mouldering concrete walkway. Greenfields was rough, but it wasn't as brutal a Quarter as Canary or Shard; it still appealed to families with kids, and the gangs that'd run it when Josiah was a boy still kept it under control. It wasn't a refuge for drug addicts and violent crime, although there was always a criminal element.

It still stank of sewage and damp – that smell never went away – but the place was lit, if dimly, and it wasn't too overcrowded. In fact, there were fewer people here now than when Josiah was a kid. Perhaps because the ceaseless government campaigns to encourage families out of the Quarterlands and into service or work camps had been effective. The world was returning to what it had once been, and the detritus left over from the Rising was slowly being cleaned up. The new floating cities offering cheap accommodation and much better living conditions were also making inroads into old Quarters like this.

There was no welcoming committee at Greenfields like there had been at the Arkian Quarter – this place wasn't anywhere near as well managed – but Josiah knew his presence had been noticed from the moment he'd arrived.

Still, he wasn't challenged as he made his way to the central office hub from where gang business had always been conducted. He walked confidently, remembering the way as if it were yesterday. People moved aside to let him pass. Was that because they could see he was Thorities? Or was it because they recognised him as one of their own? Just a man returning home, nothing to see here.

Very little had changed. The office was still there: a small room with a couple of chairs and a battered old desk with a few old magazines and an old-fashioned walkie-talkie on it. There had always been one gang member on duty at any one time, and that hadn't changed. An obese, middle-aged man sitting behind the desk looked up at him, then burst out laughing.

"What's so funny?" Josiah asked, resting his hand on his stun gun, just in case.

"You are! Heard you were on your way. What's it been, twenty-odd years? And you just saunter back in like it was yesterday, you old fucker. How's life treating ya, Joe? Last time I saw you, you swore you'd never come back, but here you are."

Josiah peered at the man in the poorly lit room and then he burst out laughing, too. "Seamus? Is that you?"

"Yeah. A few years older and a couple of hundred pounds heavier."

Seamus heaved himself to his feet and ambled over to envelop him in a clumsy bear hug.

"And nearly bald." Josiah rubbed the few bristles on Seamus's head affectionately.

"Look at you, striding in here with your fancy clothes, posh accent, and full head of hair." Seamus grinned. "I always said you'd get yourself killed in the army, but nah. No such luck, eh?" He took a step back to admire Josiah's well-cut jeans, maroon polo shirt, and smart linen jacket; even when he was technically off duty, he never let his standards slip.

"How are you doing, Seamus?" he asked softly, taking a seat on a rickety plastic chair and watching as Seamus poured him a typical Quarterlands brew: black tea with a generous dash of whisky, no milk.

"I'm okay, thanks, Joe." Seamus beamed at him. "Took a few years, but I finally managed to take charge of this place. Of course, most of the old guard are dead, as is this shit-heap nowadays. Its glory days are long gone, Joe, but still, I run Greenfields now, and I bet nobody would have put money on *that* when we were kids." He sat back in his chair, looking pleased with himself. "If you'd hung around here, you could have taken over. You had the brains and the muscle for it."

"I didn't want it. I had to get out, Seamus." Josiah took a gulp of the tea, and then another. He didn't usually drink, but this tasted of home. "Dad never wanted me to stay here. He dreamed of bigger things for me, a better life than he'd had. He didn't want me to become an IS."

"Yeah. He always said that to me an' all." Seamus smiled at the memory. "Your dad was good people, Joe. I fucking loved him, and your mum, too. She taught me how to read."

"Me too." Josiah felt a rush of warmth. Maybe it was the whisky in the tea, or maybe it was talking about his parents with people who'd known them. "She was a drybaby before she came here. She went to a proper school on dry land. Then her parents died when she was sixteen and she was turfed out of her home. She had nowhere else to go, so she ended up here. Dad was born here. He knew his way around and he always looked out for her. She said she fell for him because he had kind eyes."

"He did. Mind you, he used to scare the bejeezus out of us kids. I always remember him giving me a clip round the ear for taking apart a fancy duck some idiot had left outside. Now I do the same to the kids here."

"I hope mine's safe, then." Josiah grinned.

"It is. I'm hot on that kind of stuff. We don't want the Thorities making a move on us. We've done well to keep 'em out of our business all this time. No offence." He grinned. "Given that you're Thorities now."

"None taken, I am." Josiah sighed. "But not the kind who clears out the Quarterlands."

"Nah. I know. We've seen ya on the news." Seamus nodded at a battered screen in the corner of the room, next to an ancient two-bar electric fire, which was giving out a faint heat. "Tracking down bad'uns and escaped indies and the like."

"Don't believe everything you see." Josiah shifted uncomfortably. His reputation was a useful smokescreen to hide his role in the Kathleen Line, but he didn't want his old childhood friend thinking the worst of him.

"Oh, I don't. I don't reckon you've changed much, really. Inside, you're still a Greenfields kid. If they cut you, you still bleed Quarterlands sludge." Seamus sat back in his chair and gazed at him thoughtfully. "Reckon I know why you're here, Joe."

"You do?" he asked, surprised.

"Yeah. He said you'd come looking for him. I wasn't so sure, but here you are."

"He's here?" Josiah felt his belly flip. This had been such an unlikely hunch, and yet...

"Yeah. Moved in last year. Nice fella, flashed us some cash, so we gave him what he wanted. He bleeds Quarterlands sludge, too, so he knew the drill. Dunno what he's doing here, and he won't say. All he tells us is he's waiting for something. If you ask me, the only thing he's waiting for is death. He doesn't look far off it. Weird yellow colour. Stick thin."

"He has cancer."

"Yup, I know. He's getting treatment, goes to the hospital every few weeks. Has the money to pay for it. Gets one of the kids to take him. He must be able to afford a proper place on the dry, so I've no idea what he's doin' here, but I ain't complaining. He brings in some dosh for central funds." Seamus leaned back and laced his hands behind his head. "So, what's it all about, Joe?"

"Honestly, I'm not sure, but he's doing well for a dead man; he organised his own memorial service awhile back. He went to great lengths to make people think he'd passed away."

Seamus didn't look surprised. "Yeah, he's an odd one, for sure. Speaks posh though he's a Quarterlands brat just like you and me. But you speak posh, too, these days."

"That's Peter's fault, and my time at Inquisitus too," Josiah admitted.

"You sound like your mum now. She always spoke nice, your mum." Seamus grinned.

"My boss, Esther, talks like Mum. Being around her has rubbed off on me. I didn't do it on purpose, but I suppose I wanted to sound a bit more like a polished investigator and less like…"

"Quarrie scum?" Seamus asked, with a raised eyebrow.

"I was going to say army sergeant. I'm not ashamed of where I come from," Josiah said sharply.

"Nah, but you want to be this person now, I reckon. The one who wears fancy suits and speaks posh. You're that rare thing - a Quarrie kid who made it out in the big wide world without selling himself. It's okay, Joe. I don't blame you. You always had a lot of your mum in you."

His mother had been intelligent and fierce. All the kids had respected her, and she'd taught most of them to read and write. She'd taken Seamus and half a dozen other kids under her wing when their parents had either died or succumbed to their various addictions.

Greenfields had been a different place back then. His mother had passed away when he was thirteen, and his father a couple of years later. They were part of an old guard that had been slowly dying off, even then, and rival gangs had moved in soon after, making Greenfields a more dangerous place.

Josiah had decided to get out, but Seamus had stayed to fight for the soul of the place and had clearly won. Josiah didn't regret his decision. Being back here reminded him how much he'd wanted to leave.

Yet now he'd been forced to return and face the ghosts of the past, and all because of a man he'd never met.

"I need to see him," he said, standing up. He took a final gulp of his tea, draining it to the dregs, glad of the fire in his belly going into this next meeting. "Where is he?"

"Well... here's the spooky part. See, he insisted on us giving him this one particular room. He paid well and said there'd be more every month until he died, so..." Seamus shrugged. "He's a harmless old bugger, no reason to turn him down. Means we can keep the lights on for longer and the central areas heated. Keeps the little kids and old folks warm."

He hauled up his massive frame, grabbed a torch, and escorted Josiah out onto the concrete walkways. As they walked up a familiar stone staircase, Josiah had a sense of foreboding.

"Seamus, are you taking me where I think you are?"

"Yeah." Seamus chuckled. "Sorry, Joe, but it's what he wanted. Reckon he's a bit of a drama queen, but he wants things just so, y'know?" The lights flickered, so Seamus turned on his torch, and they trudged through the gloom until they reached one of the highest floors in the half-submerged building. He paused outside a door and knocked.

"Gideon? I've got a guest for ya. Someone you've been waiting for." He opened the door, then stood aside for Josiah to enter. "I reckon I'll leave you to it," he said, and then backed away, shutting the door behind him.

Josiah stood in the room he'd once shared with his parents and two other families, all squeezed into the small space, huddling together for warmth and a share of the heat from the little electric fire they jointly owned. His parents had both died in this room, lying on an old mattress behind a raggedy curtain.

His mother had gone fast, there one day and gone the next, her poor heart worn out far too young. His father had taken longer to die, slowly losing his battle against pneumonia over several weeks. Josiah had sat next to him on the mattress and held his hand as he'd struggled to breathe. The memories came rushing back and he took a moment to steady himself. Then, slowly, the room came into focus as it was now.

It had been painted white and was in a much better condition than when he was a child. There were a few pictures on the wall, a navy-blue, rather formal-looking sofa, a big mustard yellow armchair, and a comfortable-looking bed behind a painted screen with pictures of birds of paradise on it. All furniture, no doubt, brought from the park home.

On the armchair in the centre of the room, next to a mahogany coffee table, sat Gideon Bart. Seamus was right: he didn't look long for the world. His skin was paper thin, with a sickly yellow sheen, and his clothes hung off him, two sizes too big. He was formally dressed in a grey suit with a purple silk shirt beneath it, a cravat tied around his neck, but his head was cancer-therapy bald and his dark eyes were rheumy and yellow, although still sharp as they studied him.

"Josiah Raine, we meet at last. I can't tell you how much I've been looking forward to this day. I knew you'd come." His voice *was* cultured. "Forgive me for not standing up. I have to conserve my strength these days. Come closer, my dear fellow, let's take a good look at you." He beckoned Josiah forward into the light from the lamp flickering on the coffee table. "Oh, Alex wasn't lying; you are *very* handsome," he declared, with a delighted laugh. "In a brutish kind of way, but that's rather my thing." He gave Josiah a coquettish wink. "Come now, sit down on the sofa. You must have many questions for me."

"You could say that." Josiah took a seat as instructed. "Starting with why you're alive."

"A necessary deception, and not for much longer, I fear, as you can see." He waved a bony hand at his ravaged yellow face. "Still, the wonders of modern medicine are keeping me going far longer than I had any right to expect, and Seamus has made me very welcome here. I gather it's a much nicer place than when you lived here."

"Fewer people, more money. The world is recovering – slowly." Josiah shrugged. "This wasn't the first place I came to after reading your note, though."

"Oh. You went *there*, didn't you?" Gideon looked both delighted and horrified at the same time. "My beloved childhood home." He gave a bitter snort. "I thought you probably would, at first, but they'd never have let me back, and I needed a place where nobody else but you would look. It had to be here."

"Why go to such lengths to lure me here, Gideon? What's all this about?"

"Oh, I think you know why. In fact, I think you've worked most of it out already. I'd expect nothing less of the great Investigator Raine. Now, can I offer you any refreshments? I already have a cup of tea, but I can make you one."

"No thanks, Seamus already obliged."

"Very well. I'm all yours." Gideon sat back in his chair with an exhausted sigh. "Did you bring your e-cuffs with you?" He gave a knowing little wink.

"Do I need them?" Josiah raised an eyebrow.

"Actually, no, if you accept my proposition, but we'll come to that later."

"You've clearly put a great deal of thought into this. Supposing I hadn't figured it out? Supposing I hadn't come in time?"

"I had made other arrangements." Gideon waved his hand. "I'm glad you did, though. I wanted to meet you in person after all this time. It's quite thrilling, like seeing a celebrity in the flesh, which I suppose in a way you are."

"Thrilling enough to kill for?" Josiah asked. Gideon's eyes flashed. "You did kill him, didn't you? You shot Elliot Dacre."

"I wouldn't insult you with a denial." Gideon's expression was crafty, but he also looked more than a little bit pleased with himself. "Of course I did, but you knew that when you came here. Tell me, when did you work it out?"

"Not until this morning, when I watched your memorial service."

"Ah. I thought that might be a clue, but I couldn't be sure you'd see it. I hoped you would. What tipped you off?"

"You played Alex's song at the end – *Make me a Channel of Your Peace*. It felt like a message, so I rewound it and saw you sitting at the back, right at the beginning, before you left. You were wearing a hooded coat, but I knew it was you."

"Oh, yes. It was so delicious to be present at one's own memorial service." Gideon smiled. "I couldn't stay and risk being recognised, but I wanted to drop in briefly."

"That wasn't why you were there," Josiah said, watching him closely.

"Really?" Gideon's face became closed and guarded.

"No. You came to see if *she'd* be there."

"She?"

"Madeleine Selcourt. Your houder."

Gideon took a sip of his tea, but Josiah noticed his hand was shaking. "Well, well, you really are very good at this, which I suppose I knew. Yes, I wanted Miss Madeleine to be there. I adored her."

"But she didn't come, did she? She told me she was a very busy woman, and you were, in the end, *just* a servant." He watched Gideon's eyes darken. "She didn't feel obliged to attend, despite the millions you made for her running Belvedere."

"She told you? You went to see her?" Gideon leaned forward eagerly. "At Belvedere?"

"Yes, I went there yesterday."

"And today you're here. That's really very impressive."

"Is that why you killed Elliot Dacre?" Josiah asked. "In a fit of pique towards houders because Madeleine didn't come to your memorial service?"

"Good lord, no." Gideon took another sip of his tea.

Josiah raised an eyebrow. "It was the catalyst, though, wasn't it? You were devastated. You've been rejected your entire life – by your father, the Arkians, and now by the one person to whom you'd offered your devotion, your life's service. She turned out to be no different to all the others who let you down. It was enough to make you contemplate murder, wasn't it?"

"A very interesting piece of cod psychology, but no," Gideon said waspishly. "I'd already planned Dacre's murder. Why else hold a fake memorial service? I wanted people to believe I was dead, so that I'd be left alone to observe you and Alex from afar. Not that I care about going to jail, given I won't be there for very long, but I didn't want you solving it too soon."

"Too soon for what?"

"I'm a very precise person. A completist. I like things to be just so, as you can see." Gideon waved his hand around the tidy room. "I hate loose ends, Investigator Raine, and I'm dying."

"And before you die, you want resolution to the one big, unresolved story of your life?" Josiah said slowly.

"Quite." Gideon inclined his head. "How is poor dear Alex?"

"Surviving. Just."

"I'm glad. He really hasn't had an easy time of it, but then few of us do, do we?" Gideon sighed. "I'm very fond of that boy. In all my years working at Belvedere, I never came across anyone with such a remarkable story."

"He said he told you everything."

"Well, *almost* everything." Gideon gave a secretive smile. "He told me all about his dear friend Solange, and how George Tyler killed her."

"Yeah, that pissed me off. You could have helped him, you could have reported Tyler."

"I could have done no such thing," Gideon exclaimed. "Nobody would have believed Alexander Lytton. They barely believe him now and he has you on his side. I would have ruined my houder's business and reputation for confidentiality, and all for what? For nothing."

"You could have spared Alex what he's been through these past few years."

"If I'd reported George Tyler to the Thorities, Alex wouldn't be alive right now," Gideon told him crossly. "Come now, Josiah, you know that."

Josiah had to concede there was some truth to that.

"So, you taught him how to hide his true self in order to lull Tyler into a false sense of security, hoping that one day he would find a way to obtain justice for Solange."

"Precisely. He needed to learn how to be a servant. That's what Tyler wanted, and it's precisely what I taught him."

"What you taught Alex almost killed him."

"No, it kept him alive," Gideon declared passionately. "Don't you see, it was the only thing I *could* teach him, Josiah. The only thing in my power to bestow upon him – the ability to pretend to be the perfect servant. He was a wonderful student, in the end, when he realised it was his only hope."

"Were you pretending, too?" Josiah asked. "To be the perfect servant?"

"No. I believe I was. Some of us like living in captivity, Josiah. I wouldn't expect you to understand – you've made such a virtue out of your independence – but not all indies feel the same way. I loved service, I still do, and I loved her. I worshipped her." Gideon looked away wistfully.

"And when you told her you had cancer, what did you expect? That she'd move you into her house and nurse you herself?" Josiah asked cruelly.

Gideon's face seemed to collapse in on itself, as if he'd been punched. "No, but I didn't expect her to cast me off like a shabby old coat, throw some money at me, and leave me to die alone. She broke my heart."

"What was the nature of the attraction?" Josiah asked, leaning forward. "Why were you so besotted with her, Gideon?"

"She was perfect," he breathed, his eyes shining. "She was everything I'd have wanted in a woman, if I'd been... otherwise inclined. Beautiful, cultured, intelligent. She was never boorish or uncouth."

"And you never had to tarnish this perfect goddess with thoughts of sex," Josiah murmured.

Gideon looked horrified. "Sex is for men and dogs. She was untouchable, unsullied, the perfect woman. She never bothered herself with men. She was cool, aloof, alone. I loved that about her."

Josiah could see that Gideon's strict religious upbringing had made him compartmentalise women and sex in this strange way. Of course Madeleine was the perfect woman to him. Forever unattainable, always sitting on the perfect pedestal he'd placed her upon.

"You dedicated your entire life to this goddess and she couldn't even be bothered to come to your memorial service. Did you hope that she'd at least shed a tear for you?"

"Nothing so mawkish," Gideon snapped. "I merely wanted her to attend. I hoped that she would prove, in the end, that I had been of value to her, that she held me in some regard, some affection. I hoped..." His voice faltered.

"But she didn't," Josiah said bluntly. "And you realised it was all a lie. A lifetime of impeccable service, wasted on a woman who couldn't even be bothered to pay her respects at the end. No wonder you were so angry."

"It wasn't wasted," Gideon retorted. "Service never is. It was, perhaps, misguided."

"Were you surprised to see Tyler at the memorial service?"

"Not really. George Tyler is a man of great curiosity and energy. He almost certainly only attended to make sure I was actually dead."

Josiah was taken aback. "Why?"

"I trained several of his servants after Alex. He was a paranoid man, with good cause, and I don't just mean Solange. He had much to hide, and he suspected that I'd learned at least some of his secrets. He was always fascinated by what I'd done with Alex, and by extension, had a certain fascination with me. I suspect all those elements explain his attendance that day."

"It's quite something to fake your own death and arrange your own memorial service."

"It was necessary for two reasons: one, to provide me with an indisputable alibi for Dacre's murder, should you look in my direction; and secondly, to see whether she would attend."

"If she'd been there, shedding a tear for you, might you have decided not to kill Dacre?"

"Unlikely." Gideon shrugged. "I rather fear that Dacre's days were numbered from the minute I found out that mine were. Please don't misunderstand me, Josiah. My mind didn't immediately go to murder. I *did* seek other ways to bring about the resolution I craved. When I first left Miss Madeleine's employ, I looked for Alex. I'd heard very little about him in the intervening years. There had been no news story about Tyler being arrested, so I knew Alex hadn't been successful in his mission. I did see his beautiful face on some holopics, but that's a tedious art form and not one I'm interested in. So, I wondered what had become of him. I must admit I was a tad disappointed that he hadn't fulfilled the only thing in his life that held any meaning for him."

"You wanted Tyler to go down for Solange's murder. Tyler was a bad houder, and you disapprove of bad houders," Josiah guessed.

"Oh, I have no sympathy for Mr Tyler. He's a thoroughly bad man." Gideon shrugged. "We who live to serve must believe that those we dedicate our lives to are worthy of our service. Mr Tyler was decidedly not. I thought maybe that Alex had lost his nerve, so I found a way to return his picture of Solange, to motivate him. It wasn't enough, though. I knew I didn't have all the time in the world, so I decided to take more drastic action."

"So, Elliot was collateral damage in your quest to bring Tyler down?"

"Elliot Dacre was a bad houder, too," Gideon said dismissively. "I gave him a sporting chance, though. I went to him and offered him all my money. I thought I could buy Alex and help him fulfil his vow to poor, tragic Solange. If Elliot had accepted, then he wouldn't have had to die."

"So *you're* the second bidder," Josiah said, that final piece of the puzzle clicking into place. "We knew there were two people bidding on Alex. You were the one we couldn't figure out."

"Well, I made sure not to put anything in writing – I got talking to Dacre in a local café one morning while Alex was at the gym, seemingly by chance. I said I'd noticed him with his stunning IS, and would he be amenable to selling him. We built up a little rapport. He was a very easy man to charm – flattery worked wonders with him. I met him a few times after that, pretending to bump into him and always offering to buy Alex. He loved that I so desperately wanted something that he owned, but sadly – for him – he always refused."

"You almost certainly don't know this, but Elliot wasn't in a position to sell Alex. His contract still belonged to Tyler. Elliot was basically just renting him."

"Is that so? Hmm." Gideon pursed his lips together.

"But I'm puzzled. You'd been a servant all your life. How the hell could you have enough money to buy Alex?"

"Well, I didn't know how much precisely Alex was worth, or what

Elliot or indeed George paid for him in the first place. That information is, of course, confidential to the IS agency, and I wasn't privy to it. But I do have considerable wealth. You see..." He gave a pained smile. "Miss Madeleine believed in incentives. When we started Belvedere, she could see that I was making a go of the place, and she wanted me to think big in terms of what it could achieve. So, every year, she put aside a small percentage of the profits for me. This went into a special account that could only be touched when my contract came to an end, as is the way with most IS contracts. I always told her, 'Miss Madeleine, I will never ask you to terminate my contract, so the money will stay there forever.' It was quite the joke between us." He gave a happy little smile, and Josiah could see how much he'd relished every moment of emotional intimacy with his houder.

"Every year, Belvedere made another healthy profit, and every year, that bank account grew, untouched. It went on for decades, and accruing interest, too." Gideon looked very pleased with himself. "Of course, Belvedere was a huge success, not because I was motivated by the money, but by service to Miss Madeleine."

"But then you fell ill," Josiah pointed out.

"Yes. At first, I dismissed the symptoms as I was too busy running Belvedere to indulge in illness. When, finally, I did seek medical advice, it was too late, the cancer was too advanced."

"What did she say when you told her?"

Gideon's face darkened. "She said that she'd terminate my contract with immediate effect."

"But that wasn't what you wanted, was it?"

"No. I would have died in her service – *that* was what I wanted. But she wouldn't hear of it."

"She didn't want the entanglement of it, the emotion, the sense of obligation to you. She was happy to pay to terminate your contract and say goodbye," Josiah guessed.

"Indeed." Gideon inclined his head. "Those very qualities I admired in her – her precision, aloofness, and sense of business – well, I hadn't quite expected her to turn them so easily on me."

"She could have kept you as her IS, and kept the money when you died," Josiah suggested.

"No, she's a wealthy woman, and shrewd but not greedy. The money was safe for my heirs under the standard terms of my contract, even though I have none. She'd have had to pay it to someone on my death, even if it was simply to the charity of my choice."

"So, she paid you off and turfed you out."

"Quite." Gideon took a long sip of his tea. "All those years of service meant nothing to her, in the end, but they'd meant everything to me. I had hoped to die at my beloved Belvedere, but she said that was out of the question. She wanted me to take my money and go, and not do anything so messy as to die in her service."

"That must have hurt."

Gideon gazed into his tea. "You have no idea," he murmured. He was silent for a long moment, and then he looked up, his eyes bright. "But there I was, not quite dead yet, but with a not inconsiderable fortune in my hands. So, I decided to enjoy myself with it, to use it to bring closure to Alex's story before I died. I was physically fitter back then and devoted myself to the cause. I rather relished it, truth be told. I never got so far as discussing terms with Elliot – money and the like – because he always turned me down point blank before it got to that point."

"So you decided to kill him?"

"Not at first. I studied them from afar for a while."

"You always did like watching people, figuring them out. Alex told me that's how you ran Belvedere."

"Well, quite. I was intrigued as to why Alex hadn't completed his mission, now that he'd escaped Tyler's clutches. I soon realised that he wasn't actually free of that wretched man, that Tyler still watched over him, just as I was doing. Then I understood why Alex hadn't succeeded. Tyler still had control of him and had broken his will somewhat. Something had clearly occurred after he left Belvedere that I wasn't privy to. I was disappointed but undaunted. I considered killing Elliot at that point, but I'm not a natural killer, unlike some people." He shot Josiah a sharp glance. "I thought about it a great deal. I did genuinely try to find another way. Then I saw Elliot taking Alex to those awful shows and prostituting him to other houders, and that made up my mind for me."

"You knew about that?" Josiah asked, surprised.

"Of course. I observed his every move. I knew then that Elliot Dacre deserved to die and steeled myself to do the deed. Please understand that my motives were pure. I reasoned that with Elliot dead, Alex would very likely fall into your hands, and then he would have his chance."

Josiah was startled. "You wanted *me* to arrest Alex?"

"Of course. You're a very famous investigator, and your agency holds the government's homicide contract. Obviously, Alex would be a suspect. We indies always are, aren't we?" Gideon gave a bitter smile. "I wanted him to fall into your hands, but I didn't want him to be blamed for a murder he didn't commit, so I sent you the gun afterwards to show it couldn't possibly have been him."

"*You* posted the gun?"

"No, I paid one of Seamus's delightful friends to do it. I did stress that he should be careful about being seen with the parcel. He reported back that he'd given it to a random woman to post for him, which was very wise."

"So, it was all planned?"

"As much as it could be. I'm rather a meticulous fellow, you know." He looked pleased with himself. "I knew that if I threw Alex on your mercy, he'd be able to tell you his story, and it worked, didn't it? That's why George Tyler has finally been charged with poor Solange's murder."

"So, you bought a gun, walked into Elliot Dacre's house, and shot him, at point-blank range?"

"Yes," Gideon said nonchalantly, without a trace of guilt. "I even chose the date on purpose. Another clue, but maybe you didn't realise?"

"You deliberately killed Elliot on the anniversary of Peter's death... So that wasn't a coincidence...?" Josiah felt the hairs on the back of his neck stand on end.

"*Au contraire*, it was the result of careful planning. You first met Alex on the night your husband was killed. I wanted to reunite you on the anniversary of that date. It was a delicious symmetry, far too perfect to pass up." Gideon grinned.

Josiah stared at him in horror. He'd long ago worked out that Elliot's murder was about Alex, but he'd never guessed it was also about him. It made his stomach churn to think that while he'd been polishing Peter's car and dealing with all the memories the anniversary of his death threw up, Gideon had been using his grief for the "delicious symmetry" of the timing.

"Tell me about the murder," he said at last, covering up his distress.

"Well, Elliot let me in. In fact, he was quite happy to see me. I'd never been to his house before, but he didn't seem bothered by the intrusion. He already knew and trusted me by this point. Besides, he was the kind of man who enjoyed flaunting what he owned. I dare say he was looking forward to me repeating my desire to buy Alex so that he could shoot me down again, but instead, *I* was the one doing the shooting." Gideon clapped his hands together sharply, making Josiah jump. "I'm not a practised marksman, but really it was impossible to miss at such close range. He wasn't expecting it – the expression on his face was most surprised. I stayed only long enough to wipe the smartwall data and check that he was dead, and then I left. I must say, it was all rather more thrilling than I'd expected." He gave a shivery little laugh.

"Thou shalt not kill," Josiah quoted. "What would the Arkians say?"

Gideon's face darkened. "I'm *dying*, I have nothing to lose. I don't believe in God, or hell, and I despise Elliot Dacre and all his ilk. I don't care what the Arkians would say. They did nothing but lecture me, then threw me out as soon as they could and told me not to come back until I was cured of my wickedness. They had half my contract fee for raising me, so they didn't exactly do it out of love or compassion. I owe them nothing. Any debt I owed them has been long since paid off, and any affection I had for them died with poor Brother Zeke. He was the only one I'd have returned there for. He was a good man."

"That's a shame. Sister Marion is clearly still fond of you."

"She was good to me once, but she's a Floodite to her core. She can't look at me without disgust. I refuse to feel the shame they want me to feel. You must understand that, Josiah," he said impatiently.

"I've never felt any shame about who I am."

"How fortunate for you. You think I went too far? I'd have thought that you, of all people, would understand. I wanted Alex to have his victory, and I also wanted for him to have *you*. If I can't, at least one of us should." He gave another of those coquettish winks.

"Alex and I aren't a couple, Gideon," Josiah told him quietly. "You can't possibly believe that throwing us together in this way would mean we'd automatically fall in love."

"He was already half in love with you, that was evident. As for you, I'd studied you for a long time and could see how lonely you were since your husband died."

"You studied *me*, too?" Josiah asked, taken aback.

"Of course. From the moment Alex showed me your photograph and told me your tragic story, I admit I had something of a fixation on you. A crush, if you like." He gave a flirtatious smile. "I felt sure if you were forced together by circumstance that you'd fall in love. I know you're still grieving for your husband, but why wouldn't you fall in love with such a beautiful, tragic young man?"

"I'm not saying there isn't an attraction there, but Alex didn't really know me. How could he? If he *was* in love with me, it was a fantasy. The real me is less interesting, I'm afraid, and far less attractive than he thought."

"Having met you in person now, I can assure you that is absolutely not the case," Gideon said stubbornly.

Josiah sighed and sat back, shaking his head. "So, you did all this – faked your own death, killed an innocent man – to give Alex his happy ending?"

"Doesn't he deserve it?" Gideon raised an eyebrow. "I won't get mine, but at least he can have his – and you can, too."

Josiah stared at him, completely and utterly lost for words.

Gideon made a face like he'd sucked on a lemon. "Oh, don't look at me like that. It's true that the cancer has spread to my brain, but I can assure you that I'm of sound mind. None of what I've told you has been illogical or without sense."

"No, it all makes perfect sense," Josiah said slowly. "But even you have to admit it's diabolical, in both planning and execution."

"Diabolical? Or justified? Alex told me how he helped you fight that vagrant who attacked your husband. It was so desperately sad. I felt your grief and read everything I could find about you, trying to understand you. You could say I was a tad obsessed." His eyes twinkled. "Alex didn't tell me everything, of course, but I'm no fool. I guessed your secret. I know what you and Peter were doing that night."

Josiah took a sharp intake of breath. He hadn't expected this.

"You intended to rescue Alex but it all went wrong. Who could blame me for wanting to bring the pair of you together and move this whole sorry story to a satisfactory conclusion? Oh, don't worry, I won't tell anyone." Gideon leaned forward and patted his knee reassuringly.

"In exchange for what?" Josiah asked. This was worrying. With Tyler's trial imminent, he couldn't afford for Gideon to reveal the existence of the Kathleen Line to the media.

"So cynical."

"You won't tell my secret in exchange for not arresting you? Is that it? Is that the proposition you mentioned when I first arrived?"

Gideon looked outraged. "No. I don't care if you arrest me or not. I won't live to see my own trial, so it'd be a waste of your time. It's not important to me. However, I would like to see *another* trial – one that is shortly about to start."

"George Tyler," Josiah said softly.

"Quite."

"Why not just kill him, if you wanted revenge on houders?"

"That's a misrepresentation of my motives, Josiah, and not worthy of you," Gideon chided. "I didn't kill Tyler for two reasons: one, he's very hard to get close to, given all the security he has, and two, I wanted him to face justice, and I wanted you and Alex to bring that about. I want to see his fall from grace and the loss of the power and control that he loves so much."

"So, what is it that you want from me?"

"I want to see Tyler's trial. I know it's going to be livestreamed. I want to watch it every day and see you and him do battle, and I want to know the outcome of that battle. It's really all I'm hanging on for now." A shadow of pain passed over Gideon's face, and he leaned forward, holding his stomach and grimacing. "I don't have long, but

I'm determined to see him go down. I do hope you've created a watertight case against him, Josiah. Have you?"

"Honestly? I'm not sure. It hangs in the balance. We know he'll play dirty."

"Of course he will."

"So, you're asking me to hold off from arresting you, so you can follow the trial? The law doesn't work like that, Gideon."

"Come now, we both know you aren't averse to breaking the law when it suits you."

Josiah shifted uncomfortably, but he couldn't deny it. "This doesn't suit me."

"It might. You see, I still have most of the money Miss Madeleine gave me. It's my intention to leave it all to you."

Josiah was aghast. "What would I do with it? I already have more money than I need."

"Don't be so slow, Josiah. That's not why I'm leaving it to you," Gideon chided.

"Oh." Josiah stared at him, the realisation dawning.

"Precisely. If Tyler's ill treatment of his servant is revealed in court, then it's likely they'll order Alex's contract be sold, whether Tyler is convicted of Solange's murder or not."

"You want me to buy his contract," Josiah said slowly.

"Yes. Then set him free, obviously."

"Obviously." Josiah nodded. "All this, in return for not arresting you?"

"I'd rather see out my days here where I can feel close to you than in a dingy cell somewhere, away from all the news."

"You really have thought all this through, haven't you?" Josiah couldn't help admiring the man's attention to detail, especially given his frailty.

"Yes." Gideon gave a smug smile. "It's my talent, Josiah. So, what do you say?"

"I say that Elliot Dacre didn't deserve to die, and when Alex finds out why he was killed, he'll be incredibly upset."

"I'm sure, but it wasn't his choice, it was mine." Gideon waved his hand in the air. "He has no reason to feel guilty."

"He will, anyway. He already does about Peter, and Solange, and his mother... This will be one more burden for him to carry."

"Then you must persuade him otherwise." Gideon gazed at him curiously. "Tell me, did you ever discover his secret?"

Josiah almost jumped out of his skin in surprise. "What secret?"

"Oh, please. You know there is one, even if you don't know what it is. I knew of its existence, of course, but I could never get him to reveal it. He shared so much else but not that one thing. I knew it was about his family, but I couldn't quite work out what it was."

"Do you have any idea?" Josiah leaned in close. "I wondered if it was about his brother."

"My bet was the mother. Has he ever told you about his first sexual experience?"

"No." Josiah frowned. "Do you think he was abused as a child?"

"I'm not sure, but I don't think that's it, although it's something just as damaging in its own way. Something he's ashamed about, and I should know. I know all about early sexual experiences and shame." He gave a sharp bark of laughter. "You should find out what it is, Josiah, because I think it's important."

"Easier said than done. He says there are no more secrets."

"He would. This is one of those secrets a man takes to his grave, unless he's forced to give it up." Gideon shrugged. "I studied him in great depth. Poor dear Alex – beautiful, wealthy, and utterly doomed. Those good looks were quite his undoing. People expected him to be arrogant, but in my view, he has quite low self-esteem. He's quirky and artistic, but his looks and his family's wealth fooled people into thinking he was something else. Then there's the awful brother..." He made a sour face.

"Charles – you dislike him too?" Josiah couldn't help being pleased that someone else shared his antipathy towards the smiling, affable, utterly vacuous Charles.

"Oh, completely. Charles was the golden boy who ate up all that family's attention. Alex was groomed from birth to be second best. The place of the good child was taken; the position of bad child was all that was left for him to fill. Charles was the gold medallist child, the only important one in the family. Everything was always about him."

"Alex loves his brother. He won't hear a word against him," Josiah sighed. "He says Charles was always good to him."

"I'm sure he was. I'm not suggesting he's evil or malicious, but he sucked up all the resources that family had and left Alex with very little. He loves it, doesn't he? The praise, the limelight, the national treasure status. He doesn't care that Alex was the... What was the phrase you used? Collateral damage? That was irrelevant, as long as Charles got what Charles wanted: the undivided attention of his mother and that bloody gold medal he was so obsessed with. Alex was brought up to believe that Charles and that medal were the only important things in the world. Certainly much more important than him."

"I agree. Alex was badly damaged by the whole family, but they *are* still his family, and he loves them."

"Oh, I understand. It takes a great deal for us to walk away from the ones who raised us." Gideon gave another of those bitter little laughs. "But we've rather strayed from the subject, haven't we? On purpose, I suspect, as you've been playing for time. So, tell me, dear Investigator Raine, do we have a deal?" He held out his hand expectantly.

Josiah gazed at it, mulling it over. He preferred to do things by the book, but his life with Peter and his years working for the Kathleen Line had forced him to take a more pragmatic view. The world wasn't fair, the rules not always right, and every person had to find their own way through the moral maze that was existence in this complex, post-apocalyptic world.

Did Gideon really have enough money to buy Alex? He doubted it, but it might be enough to mount a good legal challenge to persuade the courts to free him, although that was a long shot. Still, he'd do almost anything to be able to set Alex free, and the money would at least give them options. It wasn't as if Gideon was going anywhere, or posed a threat to anyone. He clearly didn't have long left.

He reached out, taking Gideon's bony hand and squeezing it.

"Deal," he said.

Chapter Eight
AUGUST 2091
Alex

Sunlight crept around the side of the blinds, and then darkness. Sunlight. Darkness. Sunlight... and then a persistent knocking that finally permeated his consciousness.

"Mr Alexander? Please, are you well?"

Alex moved his head slowly, with great effort. His body ached, his tongue felt swollen, and his head was on fire.

"Who...?" The word came out more like a gasp, his thick tongue getting in the way.

The door opened and a man entered the room.

"Forgive me, Mr Alexander, but I'm worried about you." The man was carrying a jug of water and a glass. He set them down on the nightstand, then leaned over him with a concerned frown, placing a cool hand on his head. "You are not well." The frown deepened. "But you have no fever."

"I'm fine." How to explain that the malady was within the mind, not the body?

"You have not left this room in many days. You haven't eaten or drunk anything. You are most certainly not fine."

Alex gazed at the man, wondering who he was. He was tall and thin, and his skin was as dark as polished ebony. He seemed vaguely familiar. Had they met? Was Alex supposed to entertain him?

"I don't have my blue pills," Alex mumbled.

"You require medication?" the man asked. "Tell me where I can find it, and I will assist you."

Alex blinked. "Who are you? Do you want to fuck me?" he asked blankly.

The man recoiled, as if struck. "Mr Alexander, my name is Jabir. We have been introduced, remember? I take care of Mr Tyler's hacienda. I am instructed to also take care of you in his absence. Now, sit up, my friend, and drink some water." He helped Alex up and held a cup of cool water to his parched lips. Alex drank, and slowly the aching in his head subsided a fraction.

"You are dehydrated, Mr Alexander," Jabir chided mildly. "I have brought you a tray of food also." He opened the blinds, which made Alex's eyes hurt, then left the room briefly, returning with a bowl of fresh fruit, cut into bite-sized pieces, and some bread and cheese, also in little chunks. "You will feel better if you eat," Jabir said, setting the tray on the bed. He propped some pillows behind Alex and then stood beside him, gazing at him with what appeared to be genuine concern.

"Am I supposed to be doing something?" Alex slurred, squinting up at him. "Does Mr Tyler require anything of me?" A panicked thought gripped him. "Has he returned?"

"No, Mr Tyler has no plans to return. I spoke to him this morning. He told me I must rouse you and see that you eat, drink, and take care of yourself. He's worried about you."

"I'll be okay. I was just..." What? How could he possibly explain that he'd been lying here simply ceasing to exist for however many days had passed since Tyler left? Most of the time he'd slept, but when he was awake, he'd gazed blankly at the ceiling, unable to move.

"You are very tired, I think," Jabir said gently. "You need to rest."

"Yes. Very tired," he whispered. There were smartwalls here, just as there were in all Tyler's properties. He was still being watched. He still needed his mask... but where was it? "I think I left it over there," he murmured, pointing vaguely in the direction of the pool.

"We will fetch it later," Jabir said with a kind smile. "For now, you will eat. Here, I will help." He sat on the bed beside Alex and gently placed a piece of melon in his mouth. "This is how I feed my children when they are sick," he murmured.

"You have children?" The melon felt like nectar in his mouth, a sweet explosion of juicy coolness.

"I have many children," Jabir laughed. "We've been called selfish, given the situation in the world, but my wife and I both come from big families and we always wanted to have one of our own."

He continued to feed Alex from the tray, while telling him the names and ages of his children. Alex couldn't follow any of it, but he recognised kindness even in his current weakened state and relaxed. Jabir meant him no harm. He doubted the tall, gentle man was capable of harming anyone.

He managed to eat a little of the food, and when he'd had enough, Jabir stood.

"You must wash and dress, Mr Alexander. Take a few steps outside into the fresh air. Then you will feel better."

Alex wasn't sure he could stand, let alone take any steps, but Jabir helped him. He was wearing the loose cotton robe he always pulled on after swimming, and as he stood, it fell open. He heard Jabir stifle a gasp, and when he caught sight of himself in the mirror opposite, he understood why. His body was covered in bruises, particularly his throat and wrists, but also his ribs and thighs. They were of various colours – purple, yellow, red, green – some more recent than others.

"I will help you to wash," Jabir said softly, holding his arm as he walked him across the room to the bathroom.

It felt good to stand beneath the warm spray, even if he did need Jabir to support him as if he were an infant. His new friend washed him, then gently dried him and guided him back to the bedroom. He dressed Alex in a pair of soft linen trousers and a tee-shirt, both of which hung off him, then slid his feet into a pair of sandals.

"Come. I've prepared the courtyard. You can sit, and we will talk," Jabir said, helping him to stand again.

It took all Alex's strength to walk the short distance along the hallway to the beautiful courtyard. It was a hot day, but one side of the courtyard was shady and cool. Jabir assisted him to a sun lounger and helped him onto it. Then he sat in front of him, placed a towel on his knees, and took his feet into his lap.

"Allow me, Mr Alexander. My wife says I give the best foot rubs in all of Spain." Jabir's teeth were bright white against his dark face as he grinned.

Alex had no strength to protest. He lay back and allowed Jabir to rub his feet gently with an oil that smelled of rose blossom. He closed his eyes and felt tears running down his face. How strange it felt to cry without the accompanying mellow high of croc. Why was he crying anyway? He hadn't wept for a very long time, so why now? They weren't sobs, though. His eyes simply seemed to be excreting tears under their own volition. He was barely inhabiting his body now; it seemed to be doing its own thing. Jabir was polite enough to pretend not to notice as the tears fell copiously down his cheeks, on and on and on. Why was it always so much worse when people were kind than when they were mean?

"I think you have been through some very trying times," Jabir murmured, which Alex thought was an understatement. "And now, you must rest, sit in the sun, swim in the pool, and eat all the lovely fresh food I will bring for you. Soon you will feel well again, Mr Alexander."

"Please call me Alex," he whispered.

But Jabir shook his head. "I cannot do that, sir."

Alex couldn't be bothered to protest. He sat back and allowed the other man's strong hands to gently but firmly massage his feet back into existence.

The next few days passed in much the same way. Jabir would help him to wash and dress, feed him like a child, then assist him to the courtyard to sit while he massaged his feet – and then his hands, and finally his head and shoulders, his strong fingers working magic on the tight knots in Alex's muscles. Each day he relaxed a little more, and became a little stronger.

Jabir wore a little gold cross around his neck, and sometimes, when he took a break from his duties to drink a cup of the strong coffee he favoured, he read his bible. Alex wondered what comfort he drew from it. His own experience of religion had been the fire and brimstone kind, but Jabir seemed to worship a different god.

"Do you pray, Mr Alexander?" Jabir asked him one day.

"No. My father was religious, and we were brought up in the church, but now... I have no faith." Alex shrugged. "My father is a Floodite," he added, gazing at the glorious blue sky, completely devoid of clouds. "An Arkian?" he clarified, seeing Jabir's look of blank incomprehension.

"I have heard of them." Jabir's mouth settled into a disapproving line. "I do not care for their views. I worship a loving, forgiving deity. I do not believe he punishes innocent children by sending floods to drown them and cast them from their homes."

"I don't think my father really believed that, either, but his father loved all that thunderbolt-and-lightning stuff – my grandfather enjoyed the idea of a vengeful god. My dad was kinder than that, at heart."

Jabir was a peaceful presence to have around. Under his gentle ministrations Alex soon started feeling better, physically at least. Mentally, he knew he was spent. He had no energy or drive. He knew he should be plotting how to stay one step ahead of Tyler, figuring out his next move, and planning for Tyler's return. He should be scoping out his new home, observing the security, maybe even contemplating escape, but he couldn't. It was all he could do to dress himself each day and sit by the pool. There was a continuous fuzzy sound in his head and the smallest activity exhausted him. He was burned out.

One day, a short round woman walked through the courtyard, holding the hand of a young boy. She smiled at Alex and made a little bow.

"Mr Alexander, sir, I am Jabir's wife, Maura. Mr Tyler has kindly allowed us to bring our little ones to teach them how to swim. I thought to start with Razin." She gestured at the small boy. Alex smiled at the child, who immediately stepped shyly behind his mother.

He lay back on the lounger and watched as Maura helped Razin into the pool. The kid seemed thrilled to be splashing around in the water with his mother.

Alex closed his eyes. Blue skies, water, bright sunshine, a mother and a son... he was back in Minneapolis at the 2082 Olympic games.

———

It had been forty-eight hours since Charles had won his medal, and the furore still hadn't died down. Charles was being invited to parties everywhere, and he dragged Alex along with him. This was wonderful for a seventeen-year-old boy, high on the excitement of it all.

Alex groaned, his head aching. He glanced at the clock on the hotel nightstand – nearly noon. What time had they rolled back in last night? He and Charles were sharing a room in an expensive hotel near Long Lake, with their parents next door. His mother hadn't approved of Charles staying in the Olympic village and had insisted on having him close by.

"Hey, sleepyheads! Rise and shine." Isobel entered through the connecting door and pulled the curtains open, causing bright sunshine to flood the room. Alex groaned again.

"Mum!"

She laughed and pulled the sheets off his bed.

"Up," she said, bestowing a kiss on his tousled hair. She performed the same routine with Charles, who grumbled, then sat up. Even just waking up after a night partying, he looked perfect. His blond hair was always flat and tidy, his tanned skin never sallow from drinking too much.

"C'mon, Alex! Let's go and have more fun." He grinned, throwing his pillow at him and rolling out of bed.

It took Alex longer to come to. He emerged from the shower half an hour later to find a fully dressed Charles talking quietly to his mother, their heads pressed together. They drew back and smiled as he entered the bedroom, but he had the sense, as he so often did, that he wasn't welcome in their little world.

He opened the fridge, yawning, a towel wrapped around his waist. Finding a can of fizzy water, he opened it, then downed the contents in a few gulps. The fridge was full of potions – Charles's supplements and protein powders, and the vials of blood that Alex was used to seeing from The Orchard.

"It's like living with a vampire," he'd once grumbled. "Does he have any blood left?"

"We have to test, test, test, darling, to make sure he's always in tip-top shape," Isobel had told him.

Alex threw the empty can in the trash. "What's the plan today?"

"I was just telling Charles that he has a few interviews later, and there's a reception this evening, followed by yet another party. I suggested to your father that maybe Charles should have his own room..." Isobel shot Charles a little wink. "I know it's expensive, but with all the companies lining up with sponsorship deals, he can afford it, and, well, I thought you both might like some privacy to really, ahem, take advantage of all that's going on."

"Mum," Alex said again in an agonised voice. Charles burst out laughing.

"I was young once, I know what it's like." Isobel laughed as well. "Charles has worked hard – he's entitled to play hard, too."

"And me?" Alex asked, grinning. "Can I play hard as well?"

"Well, you're only seventeen, darling, but why not?" She grinned. "I can't believe that a year ago you were a scrawny, dark, glowering little thing. You seem to have shot up overnight and blossomed into such a handsome young man. Any young lady would be lucky to land you. Just make sure she's not using you to get to your brother."

Alex fought down a wave of irritation. He turned away sullenly, grabbed his clothes, and returned to the bathroom to get dressed, emerging a few minutes later still feeling annoyed.

"I'm going out for a walk," he snapped, and then left, slamming the door behind him.

He pulled his baseball cap over his eyes, ran down the back stairs, managing to avoid the ever-present gaggle of reporters and news crews in the hotel lobby, and slipped outside. It was hot and sticky, and he found he missed the A/C almost immediately.

He walked to a quiet spot near the water and sat with his feet dangling in the lake, cooling his hot skin. He wished he'd eaten something. His head still hurt, and he was ashamed of himself for snapping like that. Why did he always have to antagonise everyone with his moods?

He mulled over what his mother had said. He'd seen people looking at him lately, checking him out. Nobody had ever noticed him before, but suddenly he felt visible, and he wasn't sure he liked it. He'd never been a pretty child, unlike Charles. He'd always been the weird-looking, difficult one, and he was struggling to adjust to this new reality. On the one hand, people were nicer to him now, but on the other, it felt as if they'd stopped seeing *him* and were only interested in his newly acquired good looks, which made him feel invisible in a different way.

He was jolted out of these thoughts when someone sat down beside him. He caught a whiff of his mother's perfume before he saw her – he'd know her scent anywhere. She rolled up her trousers and slipped her long, elegant legs into the cool water.

"Sorry, darling. It's all been about Charles lately, hasn't it?"

"It's not that." He stared into the dark water. Was now the right time to tell her? When *would* be the right time? He didn't like keeping secrets from her.

"Still, I didn't mean that girls wouldn't find you attractive, too, because you're quite the looker these days. I just meant that Charles is famous now, and I don't want you being used to get to him. I don't want you getting hurt."

"I knew what you meant." Alex watched as a gaggle of ducks fought over a morsel of food floating in the lake.

"You're still very young, darling." She pressed a little kiss to the side of his head. "I don't wish to pry, but you've never mentioned a special girl. I know, I know. These are things a young man doesn't like to discuss with his mother, but you know you can, if you want to, don't you?"

She smiled at him, and that made it worse. The sense of shame and guilt twisted inside him. He had to tell her.

"There's no special girl," he muttered.

"Ah. Well, I'm sure there will be, one day."

"What if there isn't?" He turned to look at her, holding his breath.

"A beautiful boy like you? You'll be fighting them off." She gave him a sympathetic hug. "Look, it's difficult at your age, and I know you've struggled to make friends. You've never found it easy to talk to people, but that comes with maturity, it really does."

"That's not what I meant," he said quietly, although she was right.

She looked at him for a long moment, and then realisation flooded in.

"Oh," she said. Then, again, more emphatically. "*Oh!*" And then she burst out laughing.

He stared at her. "Why are you laughing?"

"Because I remember thinking when you were a little boy that you'd probably grow up to be gay, but your father became cranky whenever I mentioned it, so I shut up, and I haven't thought about it since."

His father. Alex stared glumly into the water. It had been hard enough telling his mother. He and Noah were finally getting along a little better; he didn't want to mess that up.

"And, of course, it's so very obvious, now you say it," Isobel continued.

"Is it? In what way?" He hunched his shoulders miserably. Did everyone know, just by looking at him?

"Well, you were always such an artistic little boy."

"Mum! That's the worst kind of stereotyping," he admonished. "You can be artistic and not gay, and anyway, I'm not sure I'm completely gay. I mean… I don't know. I like boys… but sometimes I really fancy girls, too."

"Well, that's what your teens are for, experimenting," she declared. "I rather hope you *are* gay. Think of all the fun we could have together."

She nudged him, and he brightened. Her relationship with Charles had always seemed so impenetrable and exclusive. This might be something special that only he could share with her.

"Really?"

"Oh yes! Shopping, flirting with hot men and gossiping about them afterwards." She laughed.

"What about Dad?" He turned to face her anxiously.

"Oh, don't worry about him." She waved her hand dismissively in the air.

"He believes God sent a flood to wipe out half of humanity because we're so full of sin, so I do kind of worry about what he'll say," he muttered anxiously.

"Well, don't. You take some time to figure out who you are and then we'll deal with it. In the meantime, it'll be our little secret." She nudged her shoulder against his, smiling. "Yes?"

"Yes," he said happily, smiling back. "Will it cause trouble between you and Dad?" He couldn't help worrying. He'd heard them arguing more often lately, usually about money, but also about her flirting. Noah was so busy running Lytton AV, and she moved in very different circles. Were they growing apart?

"Not at all. I'll talk him round when the time comes. Your father can be an old fuddy-duddy, but he's a good man at heart. I wouldn't have married him if he wasn't."

"Why *did* you marry him?" Alex asked. It was something he'd often wondered. His mother was so bright and vivacious and his father so strait-laced and, well, dull by comparison.

Isobel stared straight ahead. "I've not been entirely honest with you about my childhood, darling. Your father knows, but I kept it from you and Charles because it was a world away from the life I wanted to give you. You know I was born in a government work camp, but my father didn't die young, like I told you. The truth is, I never knew him. I'm not sure Mum knew which man my biological father was, to be honest. She had to do some desperate things to survive in the camp." She gave a sad smile. "Secrets, darling. I'm trusting mine to you, so that you know you can trust yours to me."

"God, that's awful, Mum. I had no idea." His grandmother had always struck him as a very proper kind of person, but she'd died when he was eight, so he hadn't known her very well.

"Growing up in the work camp was bloody horrible. That's why she fought so hard for me to get out. She wanted a better life for me. When I won that scholarship to Oxford, the first thing she said was, 'You must find a rich man there.'" Isobel gave a sad little smile. "When Noah came along, she was ecstatic."

"That's not why you married him, though, is it?"

"Oh, God, no." Isobel laughed. "I love your father. He's a good man, like I said. I know it looks like we have nothing in common, but he grounds me. Also…" She lowered her voice, as if confessing some dark secret. "The truth is that he loves me more than anything or anyone else in the world, and I need that. There's nothing I can do that will make him stop loving me, and I need someone who'll always be there for me, no matter how many mistakes I make." There was a wistful expression in her eyes as she turned to him. "I hope you find someone like that, too, one day. We need it, I think. You and I are alike in that. Find him, Alex, find that one person who sees beneath your looks and loves you for you, who grounds you and keeps you safe, no matter what silly mistakes you make. Someone steadfast, who never wavers. I know stoicism and stability are old-fashioned values, but there's a lot to be said for them. Find someone who looks at you like your father looks at me, Alex – he'll be worth it."

Alex coloured at the "he", and his mother laughed again. "You should get used to it, darling, if that's how it's to be for you."

"Sorry, I didn't mean to make it all about me. It's Charles's time," Alex mumbled.

"It's been Charles's time for years. Now he's won his medal, I rather think it's Alex's time, don't you?" She put her arm around his shoulders and squeezed. "When we get home, we'll talk about next steps. It was terribly naughty of you to be expelled again, but I must admit I'm glad you're not going back to boarding school. We'll spend some time together and have tons of fun." She leaned back on her hands and gazed out over the water, her blonde hair rustling in the light breeze. "You know, darling, this has all been quite an endeavour and I'm rather glad it's done."

"You aren't going to stop coaching Charles, are you?"

"Oh, I didn't mean that. I just mean that your brother is older now and he's achieved what we set out to do. Anything else he accomplishes is a bonus. He may wish to retire, or forge a new path. He's certainly set for life with all these sponsorship deals, and maybe he'd like to try broadcasting – he has the looks for it. It's been glorious, but I'd like a new challenge now." She smiled at him. "I always used to resent my mother for living through her child, and then I did the same. I need to forge my own path, now your brother's had his success. I need to find new challenges."

He'd felt so grown up with her talking to him in that way. It was one of his most treasured memories. He wished she'd had a chance to find those challenges she sought.

Maura and Razin giggled and splashed happily in the pool, making him smile. He watched until Razin grew tired and Maura insisted it was time for his supper. The little boy threw a minor tantrum, but she was having none of it, and soon they'd said their goodbyes and left him there, all alone.

It was quiet without them. They'd injected a sense of normality into his very abnormal existence. He couldn't say he missed them because he wasn't aware of feeling anything, but it was so very quiet now.

The pool looked inviting. He removed his robe and sank, naked, into the water. Was that when it had started, this long, slow descent into hell? On the shore of Long Lake, all those years ago, with one little secret? He thought maybe it was. One secret that had led, inexorably, to so many others.

He turned onto his back, gazing up at the stars, slivers of memories slipping into his mind, jumbled up and disjointed. A moment from his childhood, a brief scene from his university days, a few words, a vivid sunset, little fragments of time long since gone. Often, they made him smile, but then, without warning, flashes of other memories slipped in like unwelcome guests: his mother, her neck twisted at an unnatural angle, her lipstick still perfect on her dead lips; Peter, blood flooding out from his neck, while Joe clamped his hand over the wound in a hopeless attempt to hold back the inevitable; Solange, lying on the floor in a cloud of her own hair, a jagged red mark on her head. These were memories that haunted him, and he wished he could forget, yet still they came when he least expected them. Only the gentle motion of the swimming soothed him when they invaded his mind.

He floated for hours, watching the stars scurrying overhead. How fast they moved. He'd always thought of them as constant, but they were ever-moving, racing across the firmament. Sometimes, he let his head fall beneath the water, hoping somehow to disappear, but he always came up for air, gasping.

Soon, far too soon, he could see the faint rosy glow of the sun on the horizon. He pulled himself out of the pool and wandered, slowly, back into the hacienda. Had he been in the water all night? His skin was wrinkled like a prune. He went to Tyler's study, some impulse drawing him there. He didn't even know if it'd still be there, but he had to find out. The room wasn't locked. Maybe that was surprising, but he couldn't be sure. It was neat inside, just a desk and a chair. All very Tyler. No paperwork, no work in progress, no mess. All utterly stark and sterile.

Alex knew his every move was being videoed, but he didn't care. He didn't even have to look in the desk drawers. He found the two light boxes lying on the desk, side by side. He clicked on the one nearest to him and the holographic image of his mother sprang to life in the room, vivid and real.

As she smiled and walked towards him, he wondered if he'd ever really known her. Maybe you only came to know your parents later, as an adult, and she hadn't lived long enough for that. He sat in Tyler's chair and watched her, over and over again, never growing tired of that beaming smile.

Oxford gave out one scholarship a year to a student from the work camps, and she'd been a recipient. Had he ever really understood the kind of misery she'd come from, or what his grandmother had endured in the camp? His mum had been bright, and while the level of schooling wasn't great in the camps, the smart kids tended to work hard because they wanted to escape so much. They could envisage the kind of future they'd have if they didn't. He could see now how well she and Tyler had been suited to each other. She was always hustling, always wanting something better, always trying to escape the camp, long after she'd left it.

She'd said that she loved his father, and he thought maybe, paradoxically, that was true, too. Noah had offered her the one thing she'd never had – stability. Tyler was the son of an indentured servant, with no real prospects beyond servitude himself. She could have thrown in her lot with him, but Noah was the sure thing, a way to escape the grinding poverty of the camps and be forever free. He didn't blame her for choosing his father over Tyler. He was sure that her mother had pressured her to make the best choice for them both.

However, the repercussions of that choice still echoed down the generations. Alex doubted now whether any of them had seen more than a glimpse of the real her. She'd hidden herself too well. He wished he'd had more time to get to know her better, to be a friend to her. She'd told Tyler she'd leave Noah when he turned eighteen, but she'd also told him she'd spend more time with him to make up for all the years she'd invested in Charles. Had she been lying to one of them? Both? Or had she somehow thought she could make it all come right in the end? Leave Noah and take Alex with her? Stay and end things with Tyler? It was impossible to know what she had planned.

He watched the hologram look at him, smile, and come towards him, over and over again for a very long time, just as Tyler had. Unlike Tyler, he grasped, in the end, that she would remain unknowable.

Instead of frustrating him, he found it comforting. It was as if she'd been playing a game with them all and had never fully shown her hand, right to the end. He liked that. Admired it. She'd checked out far too early, but on some level, he rather thought she'd won.

Chapter Nine
JULY 2096
Josiah

As Josiah made his way home, he pondered whether he should tell Alex what he'd learned. On the one hand, he thought Alex deserved to know, but on the other, his mental state was still fragile, and with the trial looming, was it wise to let him know that Gideon was alive and had killed Elliot Dacre?

Gideon had told him in no uncertain terms that he didn't want to see Alex before he died, and Josiah was pretty sure he knew why. Gideon had a list of excuses and justifications for his actions, but he had to be worried they wouldn't withstand Alex's reactions to them. Alex hadn't been in love with Elliot, but he'd been fond of him; he'd be devastated to learn why he'd been killed.

On balance, he decided it was best not to tell Alex before the trial. He needed him alert and focused on Tyler, not upset about Gideon.

It was just after 7 p.m. when he returned home, and his heart sank to see Charles's duck in the driveway. Charles and Alex had been spending a lot of time together lately, which was fine, but Josiah didn't enjoy Charles's company.

"Hey," he called when he entered.

"Hey." Alex ran to greet him, looking excited, and pressed a kiss to his cheek. "Charles is going to stay over. He's taking me out to some fancy restaurant on Ghost Eye tonight. It'll be late after and easier for him to stay here. If that's okay?" he added anxiously.

"Of course it's okay," Josiah said firmly. "I told you to treat my house as your home for as long as you're here, and that includes inviting guests to stay over."

"Cool. I said he can sleep on the sofa. I'm not sure he'd manage the stairs anyway. He struggles with his legs, but did you know that his upper body strength is still excellent? He's talking about training again, maybe even competing."

Josiah gazed at him steadily. "And how do you feel about that?"

"I suppose it's fine if it makes him happy. I mean, it's nothing to do with me." Alex shrugged. "The spotlight will be on me for the next few months anyway. Nothing Charles does will make that any worse."

That was certainly true. Josiah stepped into the living room to be greeted by Charles's familiar, affable smile and good-natured, boyish charm. He wasn't sure why, but it always rubbed him up the wrong way, and tonight he was tired after a gruelling day and not in the mood to deal with it. It was hard to actively *hate* Charles – he was far too bumbling and ineffectual for that – but Josiah found him irritating.

Charles was jabbering on excitedly about the fancy new restaurant on Ghost Eye. Josiah had vaguely heard of it. He was excited about showing it off to Alex and had arranged to meet a bunch of his friends there.

"My treat." Charles beamed.

"I hope it's not too expensive," Alex said anxiously.

"I can give you the money if it is," Josiah said. He already gave Alex a monthly allowance because he wanted him to have as much freedom as possible to enjoy life. Alex usually spent it on art supplies; the house was full of his sketches, to the point where it was difficult to find anywhere to sit at times. Josiah liked it. He'd always complained about Peter leaving engine parts around the place, and this was a damn sight easier to live with, as hobbies went.

"No, I won't hear of it. I want to pay," Charles insisted.

Josiah remembered those bank statements Charles had shown him. He wasn't exactly rolling in money, but he'd been splashing the cash around on Alex a lot lately. Perhaps it wasn't surprising. He'd been reunited with his brother, who'd been through a hard time. It was natural for Charles to want to treat him. Yet, the investigator in him couldn't help wondering if he was compensating for something – maybe for not saving the money to buy Alex's contract, the way he'd promised, or... perhaps for something else?

"I'm going upstairs to get changed. I'll be ready soon," Alex said, disappearing into the hallway.

Josiah stared glumly at Charles. He hated making small talk and had nothing to say to this man. Charles flashed him that bright, sweet smile that had charmed the nation, and Josiah wasn't sure why, but something inside him snapped.

"There's something I've been meaning to ask you," he said.

"Oh, hello!" Charles laughed. "That sounds serious."

"When I last visited The Orchard, you said something that stuck with me. I almost missed it, but it came back into my head again recently, and I thought I'd ask you about it. It might be nothing, but..." He shrugged.

"Fire away." Charles beamed at him.

"When I told you what had happened to Alex, you were understandably upset, and you said something that struck me as strange."

"Did I? What on earth was it?"

"You said, 'All this because he told one mistake.' That seemed to me an odd choice of language."

Charles gave an easy laugh. "Oh, lord! I was in such a state I knocked over a glass of water as well. I'm sorry. I don't think I really knew what I was saying."

"So, it didn't mean anything?" Josiah gazed at him keenly. "Just... one *tells* a lie, one *makes* a mistake."

Charles stared at him blankly. "I suppose so. I wasn't thinking clearly. I have no idea what I said, but I'm surprised it was coherent at all, given the circumstances."

Josiah gave a tight smile. "Understandable."

"Honestly, Josiah, I was babbling. I can be an utter klutz at times. Ask Alex." He gave a roar of laughter.

"Ask me what?" Alex appeared in the doorway, wearing a pair of black jeans and a vivid green shirt, with a dark purple jacket over the ensemble. He'd let his hair grow, so it hung in dark curls around his neck.

Josiah's heart skipped a beat; he looked stunning, and, more importantly, he looked happy. "Nothing," he said quickly. "Now, you two go and have a good night out. Any plans for tomorrow?"

"We're going shopping," Charles announced cheerfully. "Alex has something very particular he wants to buy." He winked at Alex, who put a finger over his mouth and whispered a theatrical "shh!"

"It's a surprise," Alex informed Josiah, pressing a kiss to his cheek, and then they both left, still laughing and whispering.

The house seemed oddly lonely and empty without them. For the first time since Hattie's death, Josiah wished he had someone to share it with. Living with Alex, loving Alex and not being able to have him... it was hard.

He sat on the sofa and gazed around the room. Alex had turned a sad, shabby house into a home. His eye for design meant that the place was now full of delightful cushions, lamps, throws, and other little touches that brightened it up without changing its character. He found he liked it much better with Alex in it than he had before.

He thought for a moment that he could feel Hattie's cold, wet nose snuffling in his hand, but when he looked down, there was nothing there. Leaning back with a sigh, he allowed his mind to wander over the events of the day. How he wished Peter was here to help him through the complexity of it all.

Gideon's motive for killing Dacre – dragging not only Alex but also himself into his warped reasoning – still disturbed him. Then there was that conversation with Charles. He'd given no indication that he was lying. In fact, his explanation was entirely reasonable. So, why couldn't he let it go? Was it because he didn't like Charles? Did he even envy Charles the time he was spending with Alex, while he worked his arse off on the case Alex had thrust upon him, upending his life in the process? Yet, he'd been the one encouraging Alex to live his life; he'd wanted to give Alex that.

He sighed. This was doing him no good. Taking off his shoes, he padded into the kitchen. He didn't usually drink, but that Quarterlands brew earlier had reawakened his taste for it. He made himself a black tea with a dash of whisky, rummaged around in the pantry for a box of his favourite chocolates, and returned to the sofa with both.

He gazed vacantly at the screen, finding it impossible to switch off. If he closed his eyes, he could see Gideon's yellow skin, remember his cultured voice speaking such appalling truths, hear his coquettish laugh. He knew he should tell Esther, but he also knew he wouldn't. He'd made a deal with Gideon, and he couldn't risk screwing it up. Alex's future depended on it.

He turned to his holopad and made a private entry, visible to nobody unless he died. Then Reed would no doubt be tasked with looking through all his files. He wanted to make sure there was some record of Gideon's crime somewhere, just in case. As it stood, Neil would likely be blamed for Dacre's murder, and as unpleasant as he'd been, it didn't sit easy with Josiah that an innocent man should take the rap for such a crime. He finished the entry and put the holopad to one side. He'd done enough work for one day.

"Have you discovered Alex's secret?" He remembered the exact cadence of Gideon's voice as he spoke. *"You should – it's important..."*

Poor Alex. Befriended by Solange as part of an elaborate trap, filmed having sex for use as blackmail material, watched by Gideon to uncover his secrets at Belvedere. Josiah had prided himself on giving Alex back his freedom, and now he found he couldn't leave him be either. Digging into his life, allowing no stone to remain unturned, leaving him with no secrets. Not even this one. The one he'd clearly spent years hiding, so that nobody – not Solange, not Tyler, not even Gideon – came close.

Josiah reached for his holopad again, despising himself. He was just as bad as all the rest, because he couldn't stop digging. He had to find out what Alex's secret was. He could fool himself it was for the case, to ensure there were no surprises going into court against Tyler, but he knew that was only a small part of it. The truth was, he was an investigator, and this was what he did.

He pulled up the court transcripts from Alex's trial for dangerous driving, then looked at the official report on the accident. There hadn't been much of an investigation because Alex had pleaded guilty and it was clearly an open and shut case. He studied the mortuary report on Isobel Lytton, gazing at photos of her wide, open eyes as she lay dead on the slab. Then he read the statements of the landlady and various witnesses from the pub where Isobel and her sons had eaten lunch. Isobel had drunk two large glasses of wine, but her sons hadn't touched any alcohol. Had she been driving at the time of the accident? Was it possible that Alex had covered for her? If so, why?

He flicked through the statement. Witnesses reported that when they left the pub, Alex had definitely been driving, and the accident had happened barely ten minutes later. It made no sense that Alex and his mother had swapped places. Alex had also been adamant that he was to blame for the accident and clearly felt it deeply. Why would he feel that way if he hadn't been at the wheel?

Burrowing deeper, he found that Isobel Lytton didn't have a driving licence. He supposed that made sense. She'd grown up in a work camp and wouldn't have had the opportunity to learn there, and after she'd married Noah, she'd have had servants to drive her anywhere she wanted to go. Why would she suddenly take the wheel of a duck if she didn't know how to drive, especially after drinking two glasses of wine?

Could Charles have been driving? But the whole point of the duck trip that afternoon had been for him to sit in the back showing off his medal to the local people. There were several reports of him doing just that. Besides, he hadn't been drinking at lunch, so why would Alex have needed to lie to cover for him?

Maybe the secret wasn't about the accident. Then what else? How did any of this fit with what Gideon had said about Alex's first sexual experience, or had that just been the dying man's prurience talking? He doubted Isobel had abused either of her sons, although it was possible. What about Noah? Alex was always desperate to please his father and seemed to love him very much, although they'd clearly had their differences. Josiah hoped it wasn't that. He liked Noah.

He read every single thing he could find but came up with blanks. Finally, he took himself off to bed. It was cold and empty, as it was every night. For the first time since Peter had died, he seriously considered going to a club, picking up a man, and fucking him into the mattress, but he didn't move. He didn't want sex. He wanted answers.

No, he wanted Alex, and he couldn't have him, any more than he could have Peter. Finally, exhausted, he fell asleep.

He woke early the next day, feeling refreshed. He knew himself well enough to know that he wasn't going to let this drop. Even if it ruined his friendship with Alex, he was going to find out what his secret was. He was Investigator Raine of Inquisitus; it was in his bones. He couldn't stop now.

He showered, shaved, and dressed, then tiptoed down the stairs. Peering into the living room, he saw that Charles was fast asleep on the sofa, a huddled mound under a blanket. Josiah grabbed his holopad and a handful of chocolates and climbed into his duck.

He drove, first of all, to the scene of the accident. It was a quiet country lane, with very little traffic. Nobody had witnessed the accident; no other ducks had been on the road when it took place, and no pedestrians. In fact, no more witnesses had come forward between the Lyttons leaving the pub and the accident taking place. Now he was here, Josiah could see why. It was off the beaten track, a winding byway in the middle of nowhere.

He stopped his duck and climbed out, examining the road at the precise place where the accident had taken place. Alex had lost control on a bend, and the AV had rolled over several times, throwing out Charles and Isobel through the open roof, before slamming into a tree. Josiah glanced at the report again. Alex had said in his statement that he'd come to inside the wreckage of the duck and had climbed out to find his mother's body further up the road. Josiah studied the photos of the wreckage. The front section was entirely smashed in. It was a wonder that Alex had escaped with only cuts and bruises.

He returned to his duck and drove back along the lane, retracing the route they'd have taken, and reached The Dark Horse pub. Above the door hung a sign depicting a beautiful black stallion standing in a storm, with a lost zone framed behind him. There was something oddly haunting about it.

Josiah entered the pub, and the woman behind the bar looked up. Josiah recognised her from the photo on his holopad: Kim Moore, the landlady. She was a few years older but had the same distinctive dyed red hair and large looped earrings.

"We're not open yet, and if you're here for Sunday lunch, we're booked up if you don't have a reservation," she told him.

"I'm not here for lunch." Josiah showed her his ID, and her whole demeanour changed. She finished up behind the bar and joined him at one of the tables.

"I've read your report on the accident that killed Isobel Lytton. I just wanted to ask you a few more questions," he informed her.

She looked taken aback. "It was years ago."

"I know. Do you still remember it?"

"Like it was yesterday. Charles Lytton, the national hero, in my pub? Of course I remember it. Those poor kids, they were so happy."

"I just want to check. Was Alex Lytton driving the duck when they left?"

"Absolutely. My wife took a photo – she was so excited." She pointed at the wall behind him. Josiah turned and saw the nanopic on display. It showed Alex behind the wheel, with Isobel sitting next to him, laughing and waving. She was wearing a jaunty red silk scarf, her lips painted cherry red to match. The roof of the AV was pulled back, and Charles was sitting directly behind Alex, beaming and waving. He was wearing his gold medal, and a happy, excited crowd had gathered around to see them off.

"Did you hear the accident?" Josiah asked, hooking the picture off the wall and gazing at it.

"No. It was too far away for that. First I knew about it was the sirens in the distance. The younger Lytton boy called for an ambulance."

Josiah held the photo up to the light, examining it closely. The photographer clearly hadn't been interested in Alex. Charles was the photo's main subject, a bright, shining, golden-haired young man, so strong and handsome, full of joy at his recent victory. He was framed in the centre, and only half of Alex's face was visible. Josiah frowned as he caught a gleam of wetness on Alex's cheek. Tears. No, not just tears, crocodile tears. But he knew Alex had been off his head on croc at the time of the accident. It had been in the toxicology report. How had Isobel not noticed? Or maybe she had and hadn't cared. He put the photograph back on the wall.

"Was there anything that struck you as strange about them before they left?" he asked.

"No. They had a good lunch. They were happy. It was awful what happened. That was the last picture taken before the accident." She nodded at it.

Josiah glanced at it again. There was always something so poignant about scenes like this. He could see why she'd hung it on the wall. It evoked so many reactions: sadness, but also a certain kind of mawkish curiosity. People loved revelling in these emotions – they could feel how awful it had been without it directly affecting them. There was something vampiric about it, feeding off the tragedy of that day.

He asked Kim Moore a few more questions, but she had nothing of interest to say. Josiah left, wondering if he was wasting his time. But if it wasn't the accident, what was it?

Next, he drove to the training facility where Charles and Isobel had spent so many long years building his path to the gold medal. It was a bright, sunny day, and there were plenty of boats out on the water already. He entered the clubhouse and ordered a cup of tea to get a feel for the place. There was a holographic shrine to Charles, dominating one wall. Here he was training, his face creased with effort, then standing in the clubhouse holding up a drink, laughing, and finally, a familiar image from his Olympic win: sitting in his boat, his arms held aloft, an expression of pure joy on his exhausted face.

Rowing. It was hard to get excited by it, but then Josiah found ducks equally dull, while other people loved them. He wasn't into sports generally, and would have been just as nonplussed by a famous footballer or track athlete. The people in this clubhouse were clearly passionate about their sport, though, and the rest of the country had been so ecstatic that one of their athletes had finally won an Olympic gold medal again after thirty years that they'd become experts in rowing overnight. The entire nation had suddenly formed an opinion on the direction of the wind, the pulling of the oars, and the timing of the famous late burst.

Josiah got talking to the young woman behind the bar.

"I was wondering if anyone here trained with Charles Lytton?" he asked.

"Oh, loads! Jim Lacey will be in shortly. I'll send him over to you."

Lacey was a tall, muscular man in his thirties.

"I hear you've been asking after Charles?" he said, taking a seat opposite Josiah a few minutes later. They had a good view of the water and watched as a team of young men whizzed past in a boat.

"Looks like hard work," Josiah observed.

"It is. Not as hard as the single sculls, though."

Josiah raised an eyebrow.

"That's the event Charles won, and it's the hardest. That's why it's sometimes called the king's class. It's tough – physically, mentally, and emotionally. It's just you out there with an oar in each hand. It's the hardest rowing event of them all."

"Right."

"You could do it. You've got the physique for it," Lacey said, glancing at Josiah's muscular chest and shoulders. "Hey, you're not from the media, are you? Only, a few journalists have been sniffing around lately because of this Tyler trial. Looks like the Lyttons will be in the limelight again." He rolled his eyes.

"Charles will be pleased," Josiah commented slyly, sensing an undercurrent.

Lacey snorted. "Oh, yeah. Charles loves all the attention."

"Was he always that way?"

"Yup."

"Were you close?" Josiah took a sip of his tea.

"Nah. Well, we trained together sometimes, but I wouldn't say we were close. Charles was popular. Everyone liked him. But to be honest, I wouldn't say he was that close to anyone. Too focused on his training."

"What about Isobel Lytton? Did you see much of her?"

"Well, yeah. She and Charles were joined at the hip. She pushed him."

"Did he need much pushing?"

"No, he was up for it, but..." Lacey paused and glanced out of the window.

"But?" Josiah prompted.

"He wasn't the brightest button in the box. She was the brains behind his whole regime. She ran his training schedule. He just did as he was told."

"Did you see George Tyler hanging around here?" Josiah asked.

"Yeah, a few times." Lacey looked uncomfortable. "Hey, you never answered my question. Are you media?"

"No." Josiah shook his head firmly. "I'm from an IA." He showed Lacey his badge.

Lacey looked at it, then at him. "You're that indiehunter. I don't follow the news much, but I've seen your face a few times. Hey, do I need to be worried? Is this official business?"

"None of this is on the record. I'm not taking your statement. It's more by way of background checks on the Lyttons, so I can understand them," Josiah said.

"Okay, cool. I'm not sure I'm the best person to ask, but fire away."

"What's your opinion of Charles as a rower?" Josiah asked.

Lacey looked surprised. "Well, he was good enough to win a gold medal."

"Was he?" Josiah sat back and stared at the man. He didn't have a particular line of questioning, but he had a technique of randomly challenging people's statements during informal interviews like this, to see what happened. "I know nothing about rowing, that's why I ask." He followed that with a disarming smile.

"Well…" Lacey gave an uncomfortable shrug. "I guess he had a lot of help. His dad was loaded, and his mum was forever pushing him. Most of us don't have that kind of support."

"So, it was a team effort, rather than his natural talent and hard work?"

"Sure. It always is, really, but yeah, in his case, more than most, I think." He chewed on his lower lip.

"Do you think he deserved the medal?" Josiah took another sip of his tea. Something was bothering Lacey. What was it?

Lacey shrugged. "I guess. He trained hard, so, yeah. I suppose…" He hunched his shoulders and leaned forward. "It was surprising. I mean, he's a nice chap, hard-working, decent and all that, but he seemed to lack the killer instinct, you know what I mean? Nobody here thought he'd do it. He was good, but was he good enough? He surprised us all."

Josiah remembered some media reports that had questioned much the same thing prior to Charles's win. Maybe they'd been managing the country's expectations. "One of the reporters asked if he was just too nice to win," he said.

"Yeah. There was that famous quote his brother gave: nice guys *do* come first." Lacey sat back.

"What was your view of Isobel's relationship with Tyler?" Josiah asked.

"Well, we all assumed they were shagging." Lacey grinned. "Isobel Lytton was hot – I mean, sizzling. Plenty of us had a crush on her. Then Tyler showed up and he was all over her. I saw them holding hands a few times. I did wonder about her husband, but really it was none of my business."

Josiah thought of Tyler with all his smartwall footage and his known blackmail operation. Then there was Isobel and all the accounts she'd had to submit to Noah, who went through them with a fine-tooth comb. Noah had said he'd give her any money she needed, so why was she going to Tyler for cash? What was it for? Was it possible that Tyler was bribing officials to make sure Charles won?

"Did you ever meet Noah Lytton?" he asked Lacey.

"No. He was always busy working. I saw him from afar during a few of Charles's races, but didn't speak to him. He never came to training. That was just Isobel and Charles, and sometimes Tyler."

"What's bothering you, Lacey?" Josiah asked, throwing caution to the wind and slinging it out there. "Something is."

"Nah. I mean... no. It's nothing."

"Tell me," Josiah urged. "I promise it won't go any further."

"No. Honestly." Lacey shook his head firmly. "That poor bastard broke his spine, and his mum is dead. Best let things rest there."

"It's off the record. Your name will never be attached to any information you give me," Josiah said softly.

"I can't." Lacey turned to look around the clubhouse. "It's not fair. I don't know anything. It's just..." He hunched his shoulders.

"A feeling? An inkling?"

"Something like that." Lacey made a face.

"Do you think bribery was involved?" Josiah asked, showing his hand. He didn't want to lead his witness, but Lacey was clamming up.

"What? No. I don't think so." Lacey looked so bewildered that Josiah knew he was barking up the wrong tree.

"So, what was it? Do you think Charles cheated in some way to win the gold medal? Did Tyler somehow swing that win for him?"

"No." Lacey glanced around the clubhouse again to make sure they weren't being overheard, then leaned forward. "I know I'm not the only one to suspect it, but nobody said anything. Why would we? He was never caught."

"Who wasn't? Tyler? Charles? Caught doing what?"

"Flex." Lacey spoke the word in such a low voice that Josiah struggled to catch it.

"What's that? Some kind of training programme?"

Lacey suddenly turned bright red and got to his feet. "Forget I said anything. It's just gossip. I shouldn't have mentioned it," he muttered. Then he left.

Josiah turned to his holopad and searched for Flex. He read for over an hour, considering all the possibilities, and then put his holopad to one side and rubbed his face wearily.

He gazed out of the window for a long time. He could leave this, drop it and walk away. He'd be serving no great public interest by pursuing it. If his suspicions turned out to be correct, then everyone would be much happier if he left it, including Alex.

He considered it, weighing up all the pros and cons, then reached for his holopad again and made some calls. He was an investigator – this was what he did. Maybe he was wrong. He hoped he was, he really did, but he couldn't bring himself to drop it. He had to know the truth.

A couple of hours later, he knocked on the door of an unprepossessing house on the edge of a lost zone. A thick-set, middle-aged man who at best could be described as plain and at worst as downright ugly opened the door. He had thinning dark hair and ferociously bushy eyebrows, and was wearing a bright yellow polo shirt which stretched a little too tightly over his big belly.

"Thank you for agreeing to see me at such short notice, Mr Buzzard, and on a Sunday, too," Josiah said politely.

"Well, it sounded important. I take my work extremely seriously, and when WADO told me that Investigator Raine of Inquisitus had asked for me personally, I felt duty-bound to see you."

He ushered Josiah into a small, sunny conservatory and offered him a seat on a comfortable wicker armchair, then sat down opposite.

"So, how can I help you?" He looked cautiously intrigued, but calm.

"You work for WADO – the World Anti-Doping Organisation?"

"Yes."

"Am I right in saying you took a blood sample from Charles Lytton at The Orchard a few weeks after his gold medal win?"

Buzzard's jaw tightened almost imperceptibly. "That's correct."

"You're aware that was the day he was involved in a terrible duck accident?"

"Yes. It was tragic for all concerned." Buzzard nodded brusquely.

"Can you explain the testing regime for world-class athletes such as Charles Lytton?"

"Of course. Charles gave a urine sample immediately after he won his Olympic gold medal. He would have been accompanied at all times by a chaperone."

"Was his urine sample clear?"

"Yes."

"What other testing is there?"

"Charles, like all other athletes competing at the highest level, was subject to routine blood and urine tests."

"Were these conducted at hospitals?"

Buzzard shook his head. "A trained phlebotomist, such as myself, attends the athlete at their own home or training facility with a medibot."

"Are they given any warning?"

"No. They must submit a list of the places where they will be within certain dates. Doping can be quite sophisticated. The aim is to catch cheats, so the regime must be stringent."

"I see. What was the result of Charles's blood test on that morning?"

"It was clear. We detected no evidence of any banned substances."

"Did that surprise you?"

Buzzard gave him a hard stare.

"I only ask because you were vocal at that time in finding Charles's improvement hard to credit without pharmaceutical aid."

"I did wonder, yes, but I was proved wrong," Buzzard said stiffly. "His sample was clear."

At that moment, an elderly woman wandered in. She was a large lady with an ample bust, wearing a homely apron over a floral dress.

"Oh! Hello." She stopped in surprise when she saw Josiah. "Adrian didn't tell me he was entertaining. Has he offered you tea and biscuits? Adrian! You haven't made your guest feel at home," she chided.

"Please, Mother, this is official business. It's not a social call," Buzzard said hurriedly.

"It's fine, Mrs Buzzard, I don't need any tea, thank you." Josiah smiled at her.

"Very well. I'll be in the kitchen. Just call if you or your guest want anything," she said, and then she left.

Josiah took a moment to glance at his notes before looking up and hitting Buzzard with the question he really wanted the answer to.

"Can you tell me, did you test Charles for a banned substance known colloquially as Flex?"

"Yes," Buzzard replied, looking completely unsurprised by the question. "We found no trace of Flex in his blood sample."

"Is it true that Flex doesn't show up in a urine sample?"

"Yes, it is. Some banned substances don't, which is why we take random blood samples."

"Can you tell me what kind of advantage Flex would give an athlete?"

Buzzard relaxed a little, clearly keen to impart his professional knowledge of banned substances. "It gives sudden, explosive bursts of energy, but it can also cause lack of inhibition and reckless risk-taking."

"Explosive bursts of energy of the kind Charles showed at the end of his gold medal-winning race?"

"Charles's test results were clear," Buzzard repeated firmly. "There's absolutely no suggestion that he was using Flex. It's quite common for athletes to find extra reserves of energy towards the end of a race. Some are very strong finishers while others are not."

"But he wasn't known for being a particularly strong finisher, was he? He was more of a steady-as-you-go type of rower."

"Agreed, but that's not to say that under race conditions he couldn't find extra reserves. That's what happens to some athletes. They dig deep when they need to."

"I'm sure. Why were you suspicious of Charles before the race, Mr Buzzard?"

Buzzard looked irritated by the question. "I didn't like Isobel Lytton," he blurted. "In my opinion, she flirted her way around the race circuit, and I was concerned in case any previous blood tests were unsafe. That was why I insisted on going myself that day. I wanted to be assured that the tests were done properly."

"And were they?"

"Absolutely."

"You'd have been very unpopular if that blood test had come back positive." Josiah gave a disarming smile.

"I don't care about being popular," Buzzard said bullishly, and Josiah believed him. "If Charles Lytton had won that medal under false pretences, I'd have been the first to denounce him. The integrity of the race is more important than anything else. The standards of the sport can't be maintained if the athletes are using drugs to unfair advantage. It's also not fair if wealthy nations do better because their athletes can afford expensive drugs, whereas countries still struggling after the Rising can barely muster a decent team." He sounded quite passionate on the topic; it was clearly something he felt deeply.

"Is Flex expensive?"

"Yes, very. Few of our athletes would have been able to afford it."

"Surely not a problem for the Lyttons, though, given their wealth at that time?"

"That was my concern. Some of my colleagues seemed to worship Isobel Lytton, but I was highly suspicious of her."

"Not of Noah?"

"No." Buzzard shook his head vehemently. "I barely ever saw the man. He was always working. But Isobel ran Charles's Olympic bid, everyone knew that. She was the brains behind it."

"Well, it certainly wasn't Charles." Josiah gave a sly grin.

"Quite." Buzzard relaxed enough to smile back.

"So, on the morning he was selected for the random blood test, you went to The Orchard to take the sample?"

"Yes." Buzzard nodded.

"Was there anything unusual about that visit?"

"Such as what?" Buzzard demanded stiffly.

"I don't know. I just wondered if anything struck you as strange that day."

"Not really. Isobel seemed annoyed to see me, but then she and I didn't get on."

"You'd met?"

"Many times. The world of elite athletes is really quite small. We'd rubbed shoulders at various functions and events."

"Did she try to flirt with you?"

"Isobel Lytton flirted with everyone, but it didn't work with me." Buzzard seemed pleased with himself.

"Because you're gay?" Josiah raised an eyebrow. He'd clocked that from the minute Buzzard had opened the door. Josiah was an imposing, muscular man, and gay men always reacted to meeting him. There were just little tells that couldn't be faked – the dilating of pupils, the quick look up and down lingering a fraction too long in places. It would have been imperceptible to most men, but not to him.

"Absolutely not." Buzzard bristled. "Plenty of gay men were charmed by Isobel. She had a way about her. You know the kind of woman that certain kinds of gay men adore. Isobel was certainly that."

"I see. So, you knew the Lyttons. Had you ever taken blood from Charles before?"

"Not until that day, no."

"And what happened when you arrived? You said that Isobel was annoyed? Any idea why?"

"Yes. She said they were getting ready to go out for lunch and a little victory tour around their local neighbourhood as it was such a beautiful day, and that my visit was inconvenient. I reminded her of Charles's obligations as an athlete and she let me in. She had little choice."

"Did you see anyone else apart from Isobel and Charles during your visit to The Orchard? Noah Lytton, maybe?"

"Not Noah, but the younger son was there... Alexander." Buzzard threw out the name casually but his jaw was tight. "The one who caused all that trouble later."

"Did you meet him?"

"Only briefly. Isobel left me with Charles in the living room. I oversaw the medibot taking the sample, and then it was stored in a specially refrigerated section of the medibot, as required by WADO. After we were done, Alexander wandered in to see what was happening. I asked to use the toilet and he showed me where it was. I relieved myself, then said goodbye to the Lyttons and left."

"Did you take the medibot with you when you went to the toilet?"

"Of course," Buzzard exclaimed. "Charles's sample never left my sight. Those are the regulations."

"I see." Josiah sat back in his chair, gazing at Buzzard thoughtfully. "Could the results have been tampered with when the sample was returned to the lab?"

"Absolutely not."

"Could an official have been bribed to turn in an incorrect result?"

"No. Look, I'm not saying it's impossible, but we have very strict procedures. Everyone is vetted and the samples are anonymised – nobody in the lab would have known it was his. Also, as I had concerns about Charles's win, I was extra vigilant during the whole process. I'd have known if a false result was generated, I'm sure of that."

"So, you are absolutely, one hundred per cent sure that Charles was not on Flex when he won that gold medal?"

"Absolutely. Flex stays in the blood for around six weeks after ingestion. I visited The Orchard four weeks after his gold medal race. If Charles had been on Flex, it would have showed up in his blood, and it simply didn't. I can assure you that Charles Lytton wasn't taking Flex."

"I see." Josiah got to his feet. "Well, thank you for your time."

"What's this all about? Why are you asking these questions?"

Buzzard asked, looking relieved that the interview was over. "Is it anything to do with the upcoming Tyler trial? I heard Alexander is involved in that in some way."

"No, it has nothing to do with that. It's a quite separate matter," Josiah said smoothly. He paused to glance out at the view of a small, tidy garden. "This is a lovely place. Your mother lives here, too?"

"Yes. She's elderly now and enjoys the company."

"Just you and her? You don't have a partner, then?" Josiah raised an eyebrow, aiming to be intrusive and clearly hitting a nerve.

"Not right now," Buzzard said sharply. "I'm not exactly catnip to gay men, but I doubt you know what that's like." He had every justification for being annoyed by his impertinence, so Josiah let that pass.

"Nah, I do alright." He gave a big grin. "See, I've got Alex living with me now, and he's quite the sexy young thing." He gave a lascivious wink and saw Buzzard's eyes widen, the pupils dilating, and watched as his neck turned a peculiar shade of purple above the collar of his polo shirt.

"Well, yes, obviously, he's very attractive," he spluttered.

"Is he your type?"

"I'd imagine he's most people's type."

"Yeah." Josiah gave a little chuckle. "He's hot. I bet you'd like to get down and dirty with him."

Buzzard flushed bright red. "I doubt he'd look twice at someone like me."

"True. A stunning young man like him... why would he?" Josiah pressed remorselessly.

Buzzard's eyes widened as if he'd suddenly realised something, and he looked completely stunned. Josiah knew that he'd seen all he needed.

"Well, thanks for your time." Josiah shook his hand and then returned to his duck.

He sat there for a long time, his hands resting on the steering wheel, staring at nothing. He was pretty sure he'd figured out Alex's secret, and now he wished he hadn't. Finally, he put the duck into gear and began the long drive home.

Chapter Ten
OCTOBER 2091
Alex

Slowly, Alex's body healed. His mind was another matter. After several weeks of sunshine, rest, and good food, he knew for certain now that his sense of malaise was more mental than physical. It was as if his body was in control, and his mind was simply coming along for the ride. He didn't choose to eat or wash or swim, he just did it. Tyler might have given him back his song and his yoga, but he couldn't see the point of them anymore. He'd given up. He knew he should apologise to Solange for failing her, and to Ted for not being as strong as he'd believed him to be, but he didn't have the strength to even feel bad about it. He'd failed. He'd never bring Tyler to justice now, and he didn't care. He didn't care about anything.

He watched as Maura brought her children to swim, watched Jabir working around the hacienda, instructing gardeners, seeing to a blocked drain, and checking in with the security detail. The security presence was heavy: smartwalls, CCTV, and men with dogs continuously parading the boundary. There was a room inside the hacienda that was manned 24/7, filled with real-time footage showing his every movement. They were here to protect the hacienda, yes, but their primary purpose was to ensure that he didn't escape. Not that he had plans to even try. He was too tired, too mentally ill.

He had no screen, no holopad, and no access to the internet, so he was cut off from the outside world in every way. However, there were hundreds of books in the library. Normally, he'd have relished reading them, but now, he couldn't concentrate for more than a few sentences before his brain asked to rest. His mind was filled constantly with a fuzzy sound, perpetual white noise that was worse when he was tired.

One day, Jabir brought in a padded table and set it up in the courtyard. He had Alex lie on it, and his strong hands made short work of the knots and aches in Alex's shoulders and legs.

"Mr Alexander, this is a lonely life for you, so I was wondering if you would like to come to dinner at our house?" he asked as he worked. "Maura is a great cook, and the children are always asking about you. Razin has a kitten. He has named him Alexander after you. He's a shy boy, but he's curious about you. He sees you sitting watching him swim but never speaking. I thought maybe you would enjoy our company?"

Alex was glad he was face down, so that Jabir couldn't see the tears in his eyes. His heart longed for the company of decent, honest people. He wanted to caress his namesake kitten and answer all Razin's innocent questions about the stranger who sat so silently, watching while he swam. He wanted to eat Maura's delicious food, to make conversation and feel normal again... but he couldn't do any of those things.

"I would love to," he said softly. "But I don't think Mr Tyler would like it."

Jabir's fingers dug deeper into his shoulders, finding a sore spot and gently teasing it out. "He instructed me to take care of you. I am sure an invitation to dinner falls into that category."

"You would think so." He heard Gideon lecturing him. *"You can't have friends, Alex. You must never let anyone get close."*

Of course not. He heard the loud crack of Tyler's hand on Solange's jaw, saw her falling backwards. He couldn't bear the thought of anything happening to this kind man and his lovely family. He couldn't drag them into the insane psycho-drama between himself and Tyler. It wasn't worth the risk.

"It's best not to. Thank you all the same, and thank Maura, too. It's most kind of you both to offer."

Jabir asked again, many times, but Alex's answer was always the same.

Razin had a little brother, Zayd, and Maura often brought the two of them together to the pool. Zayd was bolder than his brother, less solemn, and often caused mayhem, but Razin was always kind and patient with him. Alex loved watching them playing by the pool, their dark heads pressed together as they dug little holes in the flower beds with sticks, or ran around the courtyard chasing each other. One time, Zayd fell over, and Razin was the first to comfort him, throwing his skinny arms around his brother and holding him gently as he sobbed.

It reminded Alex of his own brother. How was Charles? Did he ever think about him? Was he saving up his money as he'd promised to buy Alex's contract the second he was allowed? Not that Tyler would ever let him go, so it was pointless, but he liked to dream of a world in which it could happen.

Family legend had it that Charles had been so excited when their mother brought Alex home from the hospital that he'd brought all his toys and placed them in Alex's cradle, covering him completely. Isobel had gently explained that he wouldn't be old enough to play for a while, but Charles had continued to do it, right up until the time when Alex did finally play with him. Charles had always had time for him, always given him anything he asked for, even if it was his most treasured possession.

He'd been so excited when his parents had told him he was going to the same boarding school as his beloved big brother.

―

"Oh, it's fantastic. You'll love it," Charles told him, enchanting him with stories about midnight feasts and a seemingly endless amount of pranks.

Charles had been right. There were plenty of midnight feasts, but Alex was never invited, and he was usually the butt of all the pranks. He wondered what he was doing wrong and studied his brother for clues. Charles was always smiling, always happy, and so good-natured that he attracted friends wherever he went. What was his secret? Where did that effortless charm come from? Alex felt difficult and complicated in comparison. For Charles, every day was a sunny one, even when it was pouring with rain. He was also physically strong and so good-looking. Alex was scrawny and dark, pale and uninteresting by comparison. The ugly Lytton.

As the months passed, Alex sank into a depression. He'd made no friends except the art teacher, a flamboyant woman who reminded him a little of his mother. He missed Isobel. Whenever he called home, she regaled him with stories of trips to the theatre and lunches with her friends in expensive restaurants. She sounded happier now he was gone, even if she didn't mean to. Later, it occurred to him that she might have been filling up her life because she missed him, but at the time, he simply thought she'd moved on.

One day, Charles found him up to his knees in mud, wading through a little trench out in the woods filled with sludge.

"Alex? Brown says you took all his clothes and threw them into the pool. Why would you do that?" Charles asked. "And, also, what on earth are you doing?" He planted his hands on his hips and gazed at his little brother, a perplexed frown creasing his forehead.

"I made a drawing for Mum's birthday. I was going to send it to her, but Brown took it and threw it in this ditch. That's why I threw his clothes in the pool." Alex searched through the muddy water for the drawing, found it, and pulled it out. It was wet through, smeared with mud, and completely unsalvageable.

"Oh, dear." Charles grimaced.

"I hate it here," Alex seethed, tearing up the painting and scattering the remains back into the sludge.

"You are having a bad time of it, aren't you? I can't think why." Charles looked completely bemused by Alex's lack of popularity.

"I'm not you! Nobody likes me here."

"I do," Charles said stoutly. "Come on, let's get you out of there." He offered Alex his hand and made short work of plucking him out of the mud. Then he wrapped an arm around his shoulder as they walked back to the school.

As they drew near, Brown came charging out with his little posse of friends, looking ready to do battle.

"Hey, fellas," Charles called in a cheery voice. The gang of boys paused. Charles was well liked, and a few years older. Nobody wanted to include him in their fights with Alex. Charles flashed them his most genial smile. "I'm rowing in a regatta next weekend and have six free tickets," he announced. "Five are up for grabs. Alex gets first dibs. There'll be girls there." He gave a knowing wink. "Alex gets to choose who comes along."

That took the wind out of their sails and ensured that, for the next few days at least, Alex wasn't short of friends. Charles used his charm instead of his fists, and generally preferred to avoid confrontation, but he was a steadfast ally.

Alex was devastated when his parents removed Charles from the school a few months later to concentrate on his rowing. He missed his brother badly and, without his friend and protector, went completely off the rails. Before long, he'd been expelled, which he was glad about as it meant he got to go home... only home was different now. Charles and his mother were always off training, and his father was upset with him for being expelled, and before long he was packed off to a new boarding school and was soon expelled from that, too.

When he returned home after that, he felt even more alienated. His father was working all hours, and his mother and Charles were only interested in Charles's blossoming rowing career. He took to stealing Charles's motorbike and roaming around the local area with his sketchpad, stopping wherever the fancy took him and drawing what he saw there. It was a lonely life, but he preferred it to being tormented at school.

Inevitably, he was sent away to another school, and that was where he discovered croc. It soothed him, made him feel mellow, and helped him get by. He even made a couple of friends, until his croc habit was exposed and he was expelled from that school, too.

Croc. He hadn't thought about it in years, and yet there was something about his current state of mind that reminded him of it. There was a haziness to his life in Spain, a lack of clarity and focus that resembled a croc-induced high. He liked it. It was easier than having to feel anything.

More weeks passed, and he was now able to read for twenty minutes at a time before the fuzzy sound recurred, forcing him to put the book aside. He tried not to think about the future as he was reconciled to not having one.

Every day was the same: he wandered listlessly around the hacienda, watched the hologram of his mother, read a little, and swam a lot. He didn't feel bored. He didn't feel real. He was the ghost who inhabited this place, not a flesh-and-blood person. He was sure he was see-through, transparent and insubstantial. A wraith. Sometimes, he was surprised when he caught glimpses of himself in the mirror, or the gardener wished him good morning. Surely he was invisible? How could anyone see him?

He was so used to this routine that he was confused when he heard the sound of a helicopter landing just beyond the olive grove, and then, a few minutes later, George Tyler strode into the courtyard.

"Alexander!" He looked jovial and relaxed as he took Alex by the arms and gazed at him. "You're looking so much better. Your tan is darker than mine now."

He swept Alex into a hug, holding him tight, then pushed him back to look at him again. "God, I've missed you," he whispered, holding Alex's face between his hands and kissing him gently on the lips. Alex stood there, unmoving, quiescent. He felt nothing. Not hatred, or lust, or any of the feelings he'd once had towards this man. He was completely numb.

"I realised I only left you with summer clothes. I wasn't anticipating you still being here when the seasons changed, so... I've made up for that." Tyler clicked his fingers and a couple of security guards staggered forward, carrying two huge suitcases. "I have a present for you, too."

He took a beautifully wrapped gift box from his jacket pocket and handed it to him. Alex gazed at it, befuddled. What on earth was he supposed to do with it?

"Come on, open it," Tyler chided, and that, at least, was a clue.

Alex opened it slowly, smoothing the paper as he went, and all the while Tyler hovered over him, waiting to see his reaction. Inside was a plain black leather box.

"Come on, come on!" Tyler chivvied again. Finally, he took the box from Alex's nerveless fingers and opened it himself, to reveal a stunning watch inside.

"How beautiful," Alex murmured, wondering why Tyler would think he cared about watches, of all things.

"It should be. It cost a fortune." Tyler took it out of its box and strapped it to Alex's wrist. Then he took his hand and led him to their bedroom, where he commanded Alex to unpack the suitcases.

The new clothes were beautiful, too: all the latest designer gear, perfect for the climate, elegant and well tailored. Alex managed to stumble out a few words of appreciation. He'd been perfectly happy in his old clothes. Most days, he wore the same thing – comfortable, soft sweatpants and a tee-shirt, with a sweater when the weather was colder.

Now, at Tyler's insistence, he dressed himself in a pair of navy-blue chinos and a soft silk tee-shirt, with a thin cashmere sweater over the top in a gorgeous shade of deep purple. Tyler had even bought him some beach jewellery: a seashell bracelet and a leather amulet with a piece of perfectly polished blue-green sea-glass in it. Alex put them on and slipped on a pair of new trainers. He detected Andrew's hand in the meticulously chosen clothes and well-packed suitcase. The new outfit was comfortable and suited him. Suddenly, he looked like a person again as he gazed at himself in the mirror.

Tyler stood behind him, with a little whistle of appreciation. "That's my beautiful lover. Much better than loafing around every day, barely getting dressed."

Ah, so that was why Tyler had bought all this stuff; he was irritated by his lethargy. Alex could understand why a man as driven as Tyler would find it both mystifying and annoying that he'd become such a lump.

"Come on, let's eat." Tyler led him back to the courtyard, where Jabir was scurrying around, laying out a delicious lunch. It was colder than in the summer, but still warm enough to sit out and eat on a sunny day, and there were patio heaters for when there was a chill in the air.

Tyler was in a good mood, full of anecdotes and happy smiles, as he sat opposite Alex, regaling him at length. Alex did his best to concentrate, but he wasn't used to conversations that lasted this long, and his mind wandered. He managed to make noises in the right places, though, and that seemed to satisfy Tyler.

After they'd finished eating, Tyler sat back and gazed at him, clearing his throat.

"I hope you're feeling better now," he said earnestly, and Alex knew that he meant it. "I was worried about you when I left."

"I *am* feeling better." Alex managed to drag a smile from far away.

"I'm glad. I've been watching you, and you seem happier. You're reading again." He picked up the book Alex had left on the low wall beside the table, earlier in the day. "What's it like? Any good?"

"It passes the time." Alex gazed at him vacantly. He could hear Gideon in his head, chiding him for not being better prepared. *"You've had weeks. He gave you back your yoga and your song. You must have known he'd return. You could have armoured up. You're lazy and complacent."*

Tyler leaned forward across the table. "Listen, I want you back," he said.

"Back?" Alex asked blankly. He hadn't gone anywhere.

"Back as you were before, when we used to talk. Remember that first time in the Destiny duck? Remember how hot we were for each other? I want that again. I want that night in front of the fire at La Papillon. I want those conversations about floating cities. I want all that back, Alexander."

"Of course. How lovely," Alex murmured.

"I know I didn't behave well towards the end of our last time together. I was frustrated. I want to make it up to you. I'm going to show you a good time. The best."

Tyler was true to his word. Over the next few days, he took Alex out on several boat trips around the bays and caves nearby. They were always surrounded by security, and Alex never had a chance to interact with any ordinary Spaniards, but no opulence was spared.

On warm days, they had fine lunches on Tyler's private yacht and lazy afternoons sleeping it off in hammocks on the deck. Tyler kissed him every so often, but he never made any other kind of move on him. He was the perfect gentleman, entertaining, funny, and solicitous. If Alex hadn't known better, he would have thought he was attempting to woo him. It reminded him of how important his enthusiastic consent had been to Tyler in the early days.

Tyler brought out plans for his new floating cities, laid them on the table in the hacienda, and talked Alex through them. He was excited, full of passion for his pet project. Alex remembered he'd once felt the same, but now he could barely summon an interest. He expressed polite curiosity about the plans, managed to ask pertinent if uninteresting questions, and then lapsed back into silence.

"I want you again," Tyler told him on his yacht one day, after he'd been back for a week. He reached for Alex's hand.

"You can have me whenever you like," Alex murmured. "I'm yours."

"I want you to want me," Tyler told him.

"Ah." Alex gave a distant smile.

"I want that heat, that passion that was always between us. I liked the fire, even though it burned us. It was always so hot between us, wasn't it?"

Alex turned his head to gaze into Tyler's brown eyes. "Yes. Hot." He smiled emptily.

Tyler gave an irritable sigh. "It seems that no matter how hard I try, you don't respond."

Alex had no reply.

Tyler raised his hand to his mouth and kissed it. "Come on, let's go to bed. We always did our best talking in the bedroom."

He led Alex to the large red bed in the black-and-white bedroom on the yacht and kissed him gently.

Alex had to hand it to him, he really did try. He spent ages kissing, licking, and caressing him, but Alex's cock remained resolutely soft, despite his best efforts. Alex kissed him back, caressed him where directed, and generally went through the motions without any of the heat that Tyler so desperately craved. He wished he could oblige, but he was so disconnected from himself that it was impossible. He didn't want to anger his houder, but he simply had nothing to give. If that meant arousing Tyler's anger, then so be it. It didn't matter. Nothing did. However, on this occasion, Tyler was gentle and solicitous, pretending not to notice that Alex failed to achieve an erection.

As the days passed, though, his frustration returned. He stopped wooing Alex, taking him roughly whenever he was in the mood, his lovemaking becoming more and more brutal as he substituted violence for the passion he was seeking.

Alex took it without complaint. He felt as if they were acting out some great opera and this was the final act. He wasn't consciously goading Tyler into killing him, but he hoped he would. He couldn't see any other way for this to end.

One night, as Tyler was pounding into his body in their bedroom in the hacienda, he gazed up at the ceiling and wondered if there was a mirror there because he seemed to be looking down on himself. He could no longer feel his body, or what Tyler was doing to it. He watched dispassionately from afar as Tyler finished inside him then rolled over, wrapped an arm around him, and fell asleep.

He didn't remember anything about the next few hours. He didn't think he slept, but he wasn't sure he was awake, either. He wasn't aware of anything until he heard someone shouting in his ear and he came to, to find himself standing by the pool with someone shaking him, their fingers digging roughly into his shoulders.

"Oh my fucking God! You've got to be kidding me. What have you done?"

Tyler's voice. Alex shook himself awake, wondering what the hell was going on. It took him a few moments to understand, and then he gazed at the pool in shock. All his clothes were in the water, a rich mixture of pale linens and vivid silks, cashmere and cotton, swirling around in a tangle of arms and legs, as if they'd taken themselves off for a swim.

"Why the hell did you do that?" Tyler demanded.

Alex stared at him blankly. "I don't remember doing it," he whispered. He really didn't. What had happened? Had he been sleepwalking? Or had he somehow been re-enacting that memory of throwing Brown's clothes into the school pool?

"You little shit. I bought these for you and this is how you repay me? And where's your new watch?" Tyler grabbed his wrist to find it empty. "I suppose that's in there, too?"

"I don't know. I don't remember."

"We'll see about that, shall we?" Tyler growled.

He dragged Alex along to the security room and had them replay the courtyard's CCTV footage. Alex raised his hand to his mouth in shock as he watched himself carrying armfuls of clothes to the pool and dropping them in without emotion, then returning for more. Then, finally, looking completely blank, he'd removed the watch and simply allowed it to fall from his fingers into the water. There was no anger in any of his actions, and while his eyes were open, there was no expression on his face.

"Hmm, maybe you really *were* sleepwalking," Tyler said grudgingly, giving him the benefit of the doubt. "You'd better shape up, though," he warned. "I'll give you more time, but when I next visit, I expect things to be different."

Then he left, and peace returned to the hacienda once more.

Chapter Eleven

JULY 2096

Josiah

Alex called as Josiah was on his way home. "Hey. How are you doing?" He sounded bright and happy.

"I'm fine. A bit tired. Been a long day," he replied, every word feeling like a betrayal, but he couldn't face telling Alex he'd spent the day investigating him. "How was your day?"

"Fantastic. Charles and I spent the entire day shopping. Are you on your way home? I thought we could eat together, have a catch-up."

Josiah hesitated. He could be home in an hour, but he couldn't handle a cosy dinner with a happy Alex right now.

"Go ahead and eat without me," he said. "I'm going to be late back."

"You okay?" Alex asked. "I haven't seen you for a few days. Has anything happened? Is it Tyler?" His voice was suddenly anxious.

"I'm fine," Josiah snapped. "Not everything is about George *fucking* Tyler." There was a shocked silence and he felt ashamed of himself. Alex didn't know what he'd been doing, so it wasn't fair to snap at him. He knew a showdown was looming but he didn't want it to be tonight. He was too tired and his mind was too full. "Sorry. Like I said, I'm tired. Look... why don't we spend the day together tomorrow?"

"What about work?"

"I've been working all weekend. You're right, we haven't seen each other lately. My fault. Work is taking up all my time. I'm glad you're having fun, though. Look, let's catch up properly tomorrow, okay? If you're free?" He felt like he was walking on eggshells.

"Yes, I'm free. I'd like that. I'll make us a late breakfast, so you can sleep in."

Josiah chewed on his lip in silence, dreading it.

"Are you sure you're okay? Has something happened?" Alex asked tentatively.

"I'm fine. I just need to do some more work."

That was a lie. He wasn't going to work any more this evening. He was going to do something else entirely, something he hadn't done in a long time, but it was what he needed, tonight more than ever.

An hour later, he pulled up outside the rundown gym next to the lost zone near his house, grabbed the bag of workout clothes he kept in the back of his duck, and strode inside.

"Well, well, well... look who's crawled outta the water." Winston glanced up from reading a crumpled magazine, his cigar perma-clamped between what was left of his teeth. "Been a long time, Sergeant."

"Been busy." Josiah shrugged.

"Yeah, I bin watchin' the news. You still livin' with that model?"

"Model...? Alex?" Josiah rolled his eyes. "He's not a model."

"Well, he's too pretty to be a regular bloke. He why you haven't been around lately? Too busy shagging him to need to fight?"

"I'm not—" Josiah began, then he stopped and sighed. "Something like that."

"Hah! Thought so. So, what's up tonight? You lookin' for a fight?"

"Yeah. You got anything for me?"

"Yup. Crowd of new regulars will take you on, I reckon. Just what you're looking for. Do 'em good, too. They're too used to having things their own way around here. Session with you should sort that out." He gave a dark grin.

Josiah changed and warmed up, then stepped into the ring. Winston had rounded up five men, all young, toned, and fit.

"Reckon you can beat 'em?" Winston winked at him. "Or has all that soft living with your pretty boy made you lose your edge, Sergeant?"

"I can take 'em," Josiah said grimly.

He wasn't wrong. The young men were good, but he was in the zone, so he was better. He took a few blows but landed more than he received. Soon, his blood was buzzing with adrenaline, his head had cleared, and he was starting to feel better. He lost himself in the sheer, exhilarating joy of fists connecting with flesh, with breathing coming in ragged gasps, and with that sense of being truly alive that he rarely felt outside of fighting or fucking. As he fought, he was able to forget what he'd learned over the past couple of days and be only in the moment, which was a blessed relief.

An hour later, he looked up to see that he'd worked his way through all of Winston's promising young fighters, one after the other. His fists ached, his forehead was bleeding, and he'd taken a few bruises to the ribs, but he felt fantastic.

"Reckon you've been cheating on me with some other gym," Winston grumbled. "Thought you'd be slack, but you're fitter than ever."

"Just because I haven't been here for a while doesn't mean I haven't thrown a punch – or several – since last time." Josiah grinned. "I do a dangerous job, Winston."

"Well, I'm glad to see you ain't lost your edge." Winston leaned in close, treating Josiah to a whiff of his tobacco-scented breath. "Hate admittin' it, but I always love watchin' ya in action, Sergeant. Nobody else comes close. It's a thing of beauty. If you ever wanted to turn pro, even at your age, there are proper fights I could get you in on."

"Nah, I already have a day job." Josiah climbed out of the ring, feeling much better than when he'd climbed in.

Winston laughed. "That you do, Sergeant. That you do."

. . .

It was midnight by the time he returned home, and the place was in darkness. He was relieved not to have to face Alex tonight, and not looking forward to tomorrow.

The fighting had worn him out, so he slept well, emerging the next morning washed, shaved, and dressed to find Alex singing as he brewed a pot of tea.

"Morning!" Alex's good mood from the previous day was still in evidence, and Josiah hated the thought of puncturing it. "I heard you in the shower, so I've made you a cuppa. Then I'll cook us both breakfast... Oh shit." He looked at Josiah for the first time and took in his bruised cheekbone and the cut above his eye. "What the hell happened?" He put down the teapot and came over to examine Josiah's wounds. "Chasing bad guys again?" He reached out a gentle hand to touch Josiah's cheek, but he brushed it away.

"Something like that," he muttered.

Alex stood with his hands on his hips gazing at him searchingly, but Josiah wouldn't meet his eye. Eventually, Alex gave an exasperated sigh, then went to the cupboard under the sink and took out the first aid box.

"Sit down. Let me see to this."

Josiah sat cautiously, his ribs aching.

"Okay, where else hurts?" Alex asked.

Josiah lifted his polo shirt to reveal the huge bruise on his ribs.

"Oh, for fuck's sake." Alex crouched down in front of him and began gently administering arnica to the bruise. He was good at it, and Josiah felt soothed by his ministrations but also vaguely guilty as his injuries were all his own fault. Alex tended to his cut face and then packed the first aid kit away.

"You weren't in a fight," he accused. "You went to the boxing gym."

"Yup," Josiah grunted.

"You wanted release? You could have asked me." Alex wrapped an arm around his shoulder and pressed a kiss to his hair. "You know I'd have helped."

"No." Josiah pushed him away. "We agreed not to go there. You aren't responsible for me, Alex, and you don't have to put out for me."

"Sure, but it's not exactly a chore." Alex ruffled his hair affectionately. "I mean, I enjoy it."

"Let's not complicate things. With Tyler's trial hanging over us, we have enough to handle without sex and emotions getting in the way."

"Are you worried about getting hurt?" Alex asked quietly. "I mean, after the trial, whatever the result, I have to leave."

"I know." Josiah gazed at him glumly, unwilling to contemplate that reality. He was by no means convinced that Gideon's offer of money would amount to anything, and it certainly wasn't something he was going to share with Alex in case it gave him false hope. Besides, Gideon's money was only of use if they won. If they didn't, then Alex's life didn't bear thinking about because Josiah had no doubt Tyler would make it a complete misery.

"We could share a bed again. Make the most of what time we have left," Alex suggested.

"I think that'd be a mistake. You're doing so much better now. I don't want it to be too much for either of us when this is all over and you have to go. Let's make it easier on ourselves."

"Okay, but no more going into the boxing ring. Please," Alex begged, squeezing Josiah's shoulder gently.

"Fine." Josiah caught his hand and dropped a little kiss on it. "Thank you, Alex."

"I was going to give you this last night over dinner." Alex disappeared into the dining room and returned a few seconds later holding a large, wrapped present. "But this seems like a good time." He handed the gift to Josiah.

"You didn't need to buy me anything." Josiah felt another wave of guilt. How could he tell Alex he knew his secret when he was being this sweet? He couldn't bear to shatter his joyful mood.

"Well, technically speaking, *you* bought it as it's your money, but, well, it's *from* me, as you'll see when you open it." Alex sat down at the kitchen table, gazing at him expectantly. "I've been working on it for a few weeks. Charles helped me find the perfect thing to put it in yesterday."

Josiah tensed at Charles's name. Giving a brusque grunt, he slipped his fingers savagely through the wrapping paper. Then he sat gazing wordlessly at the picture beneath, taken completely by surprise. Alex had painted a beautiful landscape in bright acrylic paints, showing a pathway between two rolling green hills, without a lost zone in sight. The sky was blue, the sun shining, and two men were walking hand in hand along the path, with a black dog trotting along beside them. Josiah felt his breath catch in his throat as he recognised himself and Peter. They were smiling at each other, while Hattie looked up at them both, tongue lolling, eyes bright, tail held high. The painting exuded a sense of joy and quiet serenity.

"Do you like it?" Alex asked anxiously. "I hope you do. I spent ages on it, trying to get it right. In the end, Elsie told me to stop bloody well tinkering with it and just give it to you."

"Like it? Alex, it's beautiful."

There were none of the usual flourishes that he was familiar with in Alex's work: no flying cars or the quirky visual jokes that made him laugh. This picture was full of love, both in tone and execution, and completely unironic. Alex wasn't trying to be clever, only sincere. A lump rose in his throat.

"I did think about giving Hattie wings but decided against it." Alex grinned. "Charles helped me choose the frame yesterday when we were out shopping. He hasn't got a bad eye – for a rower." He laughed.

Josiah stroked the brushed-silver frame lightly with his fingers. It was perfect, even if Charles *had* been involved in choosing it.

"I hope you don't think it's too sappy, but I wanted it to reflect how I saw your relationship with Peter. I know I didn't see you together for long, but you were so relaxed and happy, and I loved the banter you had." He gazed at Josiah anxiously. "I hope you don't mind that I put Peter and Hattie in it."

"Why would I mind?" Josiah held it up, unable to take his eyes off it.

"It wasn't my intention for it to be a sad painting," Alex explained. "I wanted it to make you smile whenever you look at it because it brings back happy memories. Peter and Hattie are always a part of you, Joe. That won't ever change, whatever new things happen in your life, or new people come into it."

"I love it," Josiah whispered.

"Good, because it's more than just a painting. It's a message, too, and an important one."

"A message?"

Alex rested his hand on Josiah's arm. "The message is, 'Don't be lonely,' Joe. When I'm gone, and you're here all by yourself, I want you to know that you aren't ever really alone. We're all here with you, the people you rescued. You touched our lives and made them better. Without you..." Alex broke off and looked down, blinking hard. "When I'm gone, I want you to look at this and remember that. I made you promise this once before, but I wanted to remind you because it's important. Don't be lonely, Joe. It doesn't have to be a man, but it could at least be a dog, or you could let your friends into your life more. Just promise me you won't be lonely." He looked up again, his eyes gleaming.

"Thank you. I'll try," Josiah said softly.

Alex squeezed his arm. "No, promise me, Joe."

Josiah remembered the countless evenings he'd returned home late to a cold house and eaten a lukewarm takeaway hachée on the sofa before he'd sleepwalked his way up to bed. He dreaded being that person again, frozen inside, locked up in all that grief and misery. He was taken aback by how well Alex knew him, and that he'd been so concerned about him that he'd thought to make this touching gift, with its important message lovingly rendered in every brush stroke.

"I promise," he said, his voice breaking a little. He didn't want to be that lost, lonely man again. He wanted more from life than that. The future was in his hands. It was his choice, and this picture would always remind him of that.

"Alex, this really is the most beautiful gift," he said softly, leaning forward to press a kiss to his cheek. "I'll treasure it forever. Now, instead of breakfast here, why don't we go out for brunch? It's a beautiful day, let's make the most of it."

Inspired by Alex's painting, they drove out into the country. Alex directed him to a restaurant not far from The Orchard where they could sit outside and enjoy a beautiful view over rolling hills.

"I know we don't have much longer together," Alex said. "And I want to thank you – for everything. Whichever way the trial goes, I know you've done all you can to bring Tyler to justice."

"I wish I could give you some assurances about the future, about the trial and your life after it." Josiah sighed. "I wish that was in my power."

"But it isn't. What you've done is give me the time and space to recover, at least a little. I'm not in the bad place I was in a few months ago, and that's because of you. I know it hasn't always been easy, but please know that I will always be grateful."

They decided to take a walk. It was a glorious summer day, the sky a vivid blue above them and the countryside as green and perfect as in Alex's painting. As they walked, Alex slipped his hand into his, and Josiah let him because somehow, on this precious, beautiful day, it belonged there. Alex wasn't his. Alex might never be his, but right here, right now, they had each other.

He knew he should speak up about what he suspected, but he couldn't find the words. How could he admit that he'd gone delving into Alex's life, not to win the case against Tyler but out of sheer curiosity, because being an investigator was who he was and he couldn't resist a mystery?

Alex had endured years of misery without revealing his secret. Was Josiah going to expose it to daylight after all this time? Throw it at Alex and watch his face fall and his heart break?

Yet with Tyler's trial looming, he couldn't in all conscience remain silent, either. It was unlikely Alex's secret would come up during the trial, but Josiah couldn't run the risk of going into it with such a massive potential bombshell hanging over them.

Josiah knew himself to be many things, but he wasn't a coward, either physically or emotionally. He'd put off the moment for as long as he could; it couldn't wait any longer.

A thought occurred to him on the way home, and he deliberately drove in the direction he'd taken the day before. Beside him, Alex suddenly fell silent as he realised where they were.

"Why are we driving this way?" he asked, gripping the door handle tightly, as if afraid they'd crash.

"Why not? It's a pretty route."

They passed The Dark Horse pub, where a crowd of people were sitting outside, enjoying the sunshine.

"This isn't the way home," Alex said, a note of panic in his voice.

"I know."

Josiah drove on implacably. Had Alex been back here since the crash? He doubted it. It was such a beautiful day that he opened the duck's roof hatch, and the sun flooded them with warmth. The accident had happened on a day like this, in a duck like this, with the hatch open and happy people inside.

"What are we doing here?" Alex asked urgently. "You know where we are, don't you?"

"Yes. I know."

Josiah turned into the lane where the accident had taken place, drove a little way along, and pulled over onto the grass verge. Then he turned to face Alex.

"I know," he said again. "Alex – I know."

Alex's face drained of blood. He sat quite still, staring ahead.

"What do you know?" he whispered.

"I know you weren't driving the duck when the accident happened," Josiah said softly.

Alex turned to look at him, and Josiah could see him visibly struggling to suppress a rising tide of alarm.

"Of course I was driving," he snapped. "There were witnesses. People saw me."

"They saw you driving away from the pub, but my guess is that around about this precise spot, right here, your mother looked at you, saw the tears streaming down your face, and realised you'd taken croc. She knew it was too dangerous for you to continue driving and she couldn't drive because she'd never learned how, so she told you to swap places with Charles."

"No. That's not what happened," Alex said firmly.

"Yes, it is."

Josiah took out his holopad and brought up the photos of the wreckage. They hung in the air, visceral and shocking. Alex looked away.

"I had an instinct about it when I first started investigating this case back in October. When we saw that media report about the crash, I knew there was something wrong, but I couldn't place it at the time. I finally revisited that instinct, and when I looked at the investigative reports about the accident, I knew something was off; I just wasn't sure what. Then I figured it out. You said that when you came to after the crash, you were still in the duck. You said you pulled yourself out of the wreckage and found your mother and brother on the road. The thing is..." Josiah paused and glanced at Alex, to find him staring straight ahead, his arms folded across his chest.

"That's just not possible." Josiah gestured at one of the holopics showing the wreckage of the duck. "The front of the duck was all but obliterated by the force of the impact with the trees. Anyone sitting there wouldn't have been able to climb out afterwards and walk away with just a few cuts and bruises as you did – they'd have been crushed to death. Charles and your mother were both thrown out through the open roof when the duck tumbled over. It's possible the duck landed on top of Charles at least once as it tumbled, although I suspect your mother was thrown clear and killed instantly on impact with the road." Josiah continued on relentlessly. "You sustained the fewest injuries because you weren't driving. You were sitting in the back."

Alex started shaking. He wrapped his arms around his body and rocked back and forth. "Why would I lie?" he asked, his jaw jutting out defiantly. "Why would I lie, Joe?"

Josiah sighed. "You lied because Charles was taking a banned drug called Flex. I'm not sure how long you'd known about that, but you did know. Maybe, somehow, the pair of them had drawn you into their inner circle and made you feel part of their world. The price for that was protecting their secret at all costs."

"No." Alex shook his head vehemently, still refusing to look at the holopics.

Josiah put the holopad away and drove further along the road, stopping at the bend where the accident had happened. Alex started humming loudly, a song that Josiah was all too familiar with.

"What's going on, Alex?" he asked gently. "Why do you need your song right now?"

"Because you brought me here to this place where my mum died. I didn't think you could be so cruel, Joe."

Josiah glanced around. "After you swapped places, Charles drove – too fast – around that bend back there. He lost control and the duck tumbled over and over and then smashed into this little group of trees. He was thrown out along the way and the paramedics found him here." Josiah climbed out of the duck, leaving the door open, and pointed at the spot. "You crawled out of the duck when you came to and called for an ambulance. It took twenty-three minutes to arrive, plenty of time for you and Charles to have a conversation."

He walked back to the duck and leaned through the open door. "I don't know if he asked you to lie, or if you volunteered, but you had to know that whoever was driving would have their blood tested for banned substances. A lot of duck accidents were – and still are – caused by croc, or sable, or good old-fashioned ketamine or cocaine. However, Flex is also tested for, because it can cause risk-taking behaviour and adrenaline surges. Charles relied on those surges to win races."

"None of this is true," Alex said tightly. His humming was repetitive and high-pitched now. "*I* was driving. The accident was my fault."

"I think you believe the second statement, if not the first," Josiah said gently. He walked around the duck and opened the passenger door, crouching down next to Alex. "Is that why you've consistently taken the blame all these years?" he asked, gazing at him intently. "Partly to protect your brother, but also because you blame yourself? You promised your father you'd give up croc. You'd been expelled from school for taking it only a few months previously. But something triggered you to renege on that promise. Something happened at that pub to make you take it again. What was it, Alex? What was the trigger?"

"Nothing. This didn't happen!"

"You blame yourself because if you hadn't taken the croc you'd have been driving, not Charles. Now, Charles is, by nature, a mild-tempered kind of man. Flex didn't have a noticeable effect on him except in that one respect – he became more of a risk-taker, souped up on the drug in his system."

"He drove all the time," Alex protested. "Why would Mum allow him to take over the driving if she thought he was high on Flex?"

"She didn't have much choice. You were clearly even higher on croc, and she'd never learned how to drive. I'm guessing that was because she grew up in a work camp and after she married she had servants to drive her everywhere. Besides, Flex was normal to them; neither of them thought it made Charles a dangerous driver, and for the most part it didn't. Flex magnifies the adrenaline in your system. It gave him a surge when he needed it most, when he was racing and already in a heightened state because of that."

"No." Alex gazed straight ahead, refusing to look at him.

Josiah ploughed on regardless. "On the day of the accident, you were doing a victory lap around the area where you grew up, and Charles was showing off his medal to everyone you saw along the way. He was wearing it, for fuck's sake. He was hyped up on the adoration he was getting, and Flex took that adrenaline surge and tripled it. He was on a massive high at the time of the accident."

"You don't know any of this. You're reaching," Alex accused. He began humming his song again, still rocking in his seat.

Josiah put a gentle hand on his arm. "I'm a good investigator, Alex. I know that is what happened. Charles was taking Flex when he won that gold medal. If he was tested and found positive, they'd have taken his medal away. You already knew your mother was dead, and Charles was badly injured. You couldn't bear the thought that he'd lose the one thing that had given his life meaning. Besides, you'd been brought up to believe that Charles and his rowing career must be protected at all costs. You and your life weren't anywhere near as important."

"That's not true. Mum and Dad loved us both," Alex whispered.

"I know, and I'm sure they didn't mean to make you feel second best, but look at you – taking drugs, being expelled... You felt unworthy and neglected, and that was how it manifested. You were the problem child, and you never felt good enough next to the bright, shining golden boy, Charles."

"That's all bollocks. Cod psychology. You're better than that, Joe," Alex spat viciously.

"I don't believe your father knew that Charles was taking a banned substance," Josiah continued, getting up and pacing around the outside of the duck again. "Your mother started her affair with Tyler because she needed the money to buy Flex. It's not cheap, and she had to account for every penny to Noah. You know what that's like. He made you do the same thing when you went to university."

Alex shook his head mutely, humming loudly again.

"But you weren't aware of her affair with Tyler at this point. You hadn't been to Charles's training sessions and seen them together. Only Charles knew about their affair."

"Charles knew?" Alex's head snapped around to look at him.

"Yes, they were in on it together. He knew she needed money to afford the drug. I suspect, also, that she spent some of Tyler's money on bribes. She was an adept flirt, who made it her business to become close to the WADO officials, but there would have been some money changing hands, too."

"No, that's not true," Alex protested. "Charles was tested on the morning of the crash. His blood test was clean."

"Oh, Alex. Don't make me spell it out." Josiah crouched down beside the duck again, leaning against the open door. Alex turned slowly to look at him. His face was white, his skin clammy, and he was shaking uncontrollably now.

"I went to visit Adrian Buzzard yesterday – the doping official who took Charles's blood on the morning of the accident. He didn't like your mother, and the feeling was mutual, so he was immune to her flirting, unlike some of the other officials who tested Charles over the years. He also wasn't the kind of man to take a bribe. However, he does have one weakness – beautiful young men – and given how unattractive he is, they never looked twice at him. Did your mother ask you to distract him that day, or did you offer?"

Alex shook his head mutely, but his humming went up a notch in volume.

"Isobel kept clean blood samples in the fridge, didn't she? All you had to do was distract Buzzard for long enough for her to make the swap. Buzzard said he used the toilet when visiting The Orchard, and that you showed him the way. I'm guessing you went in with him. Did you suck him off in there, Alex? Or maybe it was a hand job. But you certainly had sex with him in there."

Alex was now humming so loudly that Josiah had to shout to make himself heard.

"Was that how you distracted him while your mother or Charles made the swap? He says he took the medibot containing the sample into the toilet with him, and he probably did, but he'd hardly admit he didn't have eyes on it the whole time because you distracted him with sex, would he? I don't think he realised until yesterday that the Lytton family had played him. He was convinced that blood test was clean, but then the realisation hit him like a ton of bricks when I questioned him."

Alex suddenly flung himself out of his seat and shoved past him, causing Josiah to fall onto his side, and then he ran towards the bushes and threw up. Josiah got to his feet and went after him, stroking his back as he heaved up into the bushes.

"You were only seventeen," he said softly. "Was it your first real sexual experience? I suspect it was. You were quite a late developer and always struggled to form relationships, and you didn't have any friends. I don't think you'd found a sexual partner before then. Did your mother know that? You'd come out to her, hadn't you? I suspect she was pleased. Isobel strikes me as someone who'd have enjoyed having a gay or at least bisexual son. Your father, though, was a Floodite. You both knew it wasn't a good idea to tell him, not while he was still so angry with you for being expelled."

Alex finished throwing up and stood there, his chest heaving. Josiah returned to the duck and retrieved a bottle of water for him. Alex took it wordlessly and gulped it down. Then he slumped on the grassy verge by the side of the road, looking as if all the life had been forcibly sucked out of him. He lay there, doubled over, for a long time. When he finally looked up, the sense of betrayal in his eyes hit Josiah like a fist in the gut.

"You've been investigating me."

"You know I've been investigating you."

"No. This wasn't for Tyler or Elliot, this was for *you*. You were investigating me because you can't help yourself. Any more than you can stop yourself beating the crap out of people at that gym you go to." Alex grabbed Josiah's bruised fist and held it up. "You didn't need to do this – any of it – but you just couldn't let it go. You had to know, didn't you?"

"Yes," Josiah said bluntly. "I *asked* you, Alex. I asked you if there were any more secrets, and you said no. You lied to me, and I knew it was a lie."

"You asked me if there were any more secrets that would have a bearing on Tyler's trial!" Alex rounded on him angrily. "This has nothing to do with him. It's irrelevant to Solange's murder."

"You lied under oath," Josiah pointed out. "You stood up in court and said you were driving at the time of the accident. That *is* pertinent to Tyler's case. If you've lied under oath once, what's to stop you doing it again at Tyler's trial?"

"I'm not lying about Tyler. Everything I've told you about him and what happened to Solange is the truth."

"And I believe you." Josiah gazed at him steadily. "But I had to know what you were hiding in case it came up during the trial. I had to be prepared for that eventuality."

"No, you had to know, period," Alex spat. "You had to know all of me, didn't you? You couldn't leave it. You're allowed your secrets, Joe, you're allowed your precious bloody Kathleen Line, but I'm not allowed the one thing that's mine. Not one secret."

"It's a pretty big secret, Alex." Josiah sat back. "When did you find out that Charles was doping?"

"You still have to know, don't you?" Alex gave a twisted smile. "Of course you do. If you must know, it was at the Olympics, after he won the medal. I saw him and Mum make the swap when a WADO guy came to take his blood. I was devastated because Charles was my hero, so I ran off, but Mum came after me. She convinced me that it was all okay, and persuaded me to be okay with it, too."

"She convinced you to keep it quiet and not to tell your father?"

"What else was I going to do?" Alex asked in a despairing tone. "Maybe, in time, I'd have grown a pair and said something to him, but I was so shocked, and everything she said was so reasonable. I hated what they'd done, but I still loved them." He looked at Josiah beseechingly. "If I'd said something, maybe she'd still be alive today."

"Maybe, but you'd have caused a huge rift in your family."

"I believed in Charles. I'd bought the same lie as the rest of the country. I felt angry and betrayed." Alex's face crumpled again. "But then they told me that I could be part of it – part of *them* – and I was seduced by that. I wanted that so much."

"Of course you did." Josiah sighed. "It was all you ever wanted. Were you never tempted to tell Tyler the truth? The only reason he persecuted you was because he believed you killed your mother."

"All the time!" Alex flared. "All the damn time, Joe. Do you have any idea how much it took for me to keep that promise to Charles? The promise I made to him on this road, when he was lying over there, crushed and paralysed." He pointed. "I didn't know if he'd survive. If he did, I didn't want them taking his medal away from him. He begged me to take the blame, and I did."

"Ah." Josiah nodded. "I wondered if he'd asked or if you'd offered."

"He asked. He knew they'd take his medal from him if he was found to have been doping, and he knew he'd be disgraced in front of the whole country. Then it'd all have been for nothing. All those years of training, all that sacrifice. He *needed* that medal. We'd lost Mum – I could see that she was dead. Who knew what condition Charles would be in, if he survived? The least I could do was take the blame."

"You have to know that it wasn't your fault, Alex. You weren't driving, and you weren't the one cheating by taking Flex."

"You have no idea how many sleepless nights I've had wishing I could turn back time, wishing I hadn't taken croc that day in the pub," Alex growled. "I *do* blame myself. It *was* my fault. I didn't have to be driving for it to be my fault."

"Why did you take the croc?" Josiah asked quietly.

Alex stared into the distance. "Mum was having a cigarette, but Dad hated her smoking. When I caught her, she laughed. 'It's our little secret,' she said." His face crumpled. "I don't know why but it made me want the croc. I had a stash in my wallet that I'd almost forgotten about, but then I remembered, and I wanted it so badly."

"'Our little secret'? Like earlier, when you had sex with Buzzard in the toilet at The Orchard? Like when you found out about Charles taking Flex, and your mother persuaded you not to tell Noah? 'Our little secret'...?" Josiah raised an eyebrow. "No wonder that was a trigger for you. You loved your father, and you weren't comfortable with all this lying. It came easier to Isobel and Charles than it did to you. For all your moodiness, you're a straightforward kind of man, Alex. You don't like lying to the people you love."

Alex took another gulp of the water. "I don't know."

Josiah put his hand on Alex's back and rubbed gently. "I'm so sorry."

"Don't be. I made those decisions. Me. I was stupid and venal and weak. I did all those things, and I stole that money from Dad. You always make excuses for me, Joe, but I'm a pretty awful person."

"You were a neglected kid who wanted his mum's attention. Yes, you made some bad decisions, but you were only young and you've more than paid for them. You always tell me all the ways you're a bad person, but you forget all the good, noble, and brave things you've done, too," Josiah told him firmly.

"Bullshit," Alex growled.

"No, it isn't. Let me tell you some of the things I've found out about you in these past few months. Number one: you're loyal. Fiercely, stubbornly loyal. You stick by your friends. Solange and Gideon weren't always good to you – they lied to you and deceived you – but you've always been loyal to them. Number two: you could never harm anyone. I've killed people, Alex, many people, but you never could. If that had been even remotely possible, then you'd have found a way to kill Tyler, and you never did. Number three: you're a sensitive soul, an artist and a dreamer – you never wanted to be dragged into any of this. Number four: you're brave; you were fighting Lars Driessen when I ran back to the car that night. You tried to stop him attacking Peter again, and he was twice your size. You could have run away, but you stayed and fought to help me save Peter's life. Number five: you're *kind*, Alex. Kinder than me, or your mother, or your brother. You painted that beautiful picture for me because you were so worried about me being alone. I think all you ever really wanted was to pursue your art, but your looks and notoriety got in the way."

Alex was gazing at his feet, his cheeks flushed bright red. "I don't know about any of that," he muttered.

"Stop it," Josiah told him fiercely. "You made me promise to let my friends in, to not be alone, and I needed to hear that. Now, I'm telling you something *you* need to hear. You're not the villain in any of this – you never were. See yourself in the round, Alex, not just as the sum of your mistakes. See yourself as I see you."

Alex managed a tentative smile. "I dunno. Mostly I think I'm an idiot."

"No. You're a lost soul who made some bad choices, but they don't have to define your life forever," Josiah insisted. "Believe me, I should know."

"You'd have said something," Alex murmured. "*You* wouldn't have gone along with Mum and Charles for a second."

"I don't know." Josiah shrugged. "I did some pretty stupid things as a teenager too. I was even a prize-fighter for a bit, and that was both illegal and stupid. You loved your family, and we sometimes do the wrong things for the people we love."

"Have you?" Alex asked.

"Yes." Josiah sighed. He sat down on the ground opposite Alex and leaned his head back on the open duck door. "I loved Peter, like you loved your mother and brother, but…" He hesitated. It felt like such a betrayal, but he'd forced Alex to tell the truth, so shouldn't he face some truths, too?

"Peter often didn't listen to me – to anyone. We always did what Peter wanted. He was very persuasive, and often what he said was reasonable, but sometimes I wasn't comfortable with it, and he'd talk me round, convince me to do things I didn't think were right. I did them because I loved him, but… I wish he'd listened to me more."

"I always thought Peter was perfect."

"So did I." Josiah sighed. "But he wasn't. None of us are. Peter always got his way, even about the stuff that I thought maybe didn't matter. I kept on giving up pieces of myself because I loved him so much, and maybe he took advantage of that." Josiah rested his head on the duck door and gazed at Alex sadly. "That's not something I've ever admitted to myself before, but it's true."

"We love who we love," Alex murmured. "I know you don't much care for Charles, but he's my brother and I love him. I know he lied and cheated, and I hate that he's not who I thought he was, but he's still my brother."

"I know," Josiah said softly. "I think in this that you and I are quite alike. We give ourselves away for the people we love, when really, we should draw some lines in the sand."

"Peter was always the captain, wasn't he? And you were always the sergeant?" Alex suggested. "He was always the one calling the shots. The one in command."

"Yes. And Charles was always your shining, golden big brother, and Isobel, your beautiful, glamorous mother."

"Maybe neither of us wanted to see the ways they used us."

Josiah felt himself bristling, wanting to refute that Peter had ever used him, but Alex was right. It wasn't as egregious as what Charles and Isobel had done, but Peter had often overridden his wishes and somehow always got his own way. He'd been so charming, so charismatic, and Josiah had been so much in love that he'd been blind to the ways in which their relationship wasn't perfect. It hurt to realise it now, to think ill of Peter now he was dead, but he'd been far too dazzled by him when he was alive to have such thoughts.

He could see now that he'd been desperate for love, much like Alex. He was the poor Quarterlands orphan, coming out of Rosengarten with so much damage. He'd been gauche, much younger and far less educated than Peter, who'd picked him up, dusted him down, and made him feel loved and whole again. He knew Peter had loved him, and he didn't doubt that Charles and Isobel had loved Alex, but the relationships had been unequal all the same.

"Yes," he agreed softly, and it hurt, but it was the truth.

"I won't ever betray Charles, so please don't ask me to," Alex told him fiercely. "I won't do that, Joe."

"I knew you'd say that." Josiah sighed. "I don't think he's worth all you've endured to save his sorry hide, but I understand that *you* do."

"I made him a promise out here on this road. I'm not breaking it," Alex said.

"God, I know that. You always keep your promises, even when you really *should* break them." He nudged Alex gently with his elbow. "I can't believe you never told Tyler the truth, despite all you endured."

"Do you really think he'd have believed me if I had?" Alex snorted.

"No. No, I don't."

"So, there was nothing to be gained by telling him."

"All the same, that must have been hard, keeping that secret for all those years, when maybe it could have made a difference. If he'd believed you, he might have set you free."

"And have him go after Charles? Do you think I could have lived with myself if I'd done that?"

"No. Like I said, you're loyal to a fault. You're a good person, Alex. I wish I could make you believe that."

"Well, I don't." Alex hunched his shoulders miserably. "Mum didn't ask me to seduce Buzzard," he said suddenly. "It wasn't like that. She'd never have asked me to do that. It just seemed like something I could do to help, so I offered."

"You've always viewed sex as transactional. I guess that's where it all started."

"Not with you," Alex refuted. "I didn't view it that way with you."

"Sometimes you did," Josiah told him quietly. "Sometimes, Alex." He looked at him for a long time, until he could no longer hold his gaze and looked away.

"Yes. Sometimes," he whispered.

"That's why it had to stop. Your mask is too good, and it was too hard for me to tell whether you really wanted me or not. The only reason you should ever have sex is desire, Alex. *Your* desire. It's not a means to an end. It's not a bribe. It's not to keep someone from hurting you, or to please them. You're worth more than that."

"I'm not sure I am." Alex gazed into space.

"Believe me, you are."

They were silent for a long time, wrung out and exhausted.

Then, finally, Alex spoke. "What now?" He turned to look at him. "What will you do with my secret, Joe?"

"I don't know."

"Please, don't tell anyone," Alex begged. "It will make it all so pointless, all those years of suffering and enduring Tyler's hatred – and not just Tyler, either. The entire fucking country hates me because of what happened to Charles. It will all have been for nothing if you speak out."

"I won't lie under oath to protect Charles."

"There's no reason it'll come up at the trial."

"No," Josiah agreed. "But it might."

"Please, Joe, please promise me you won't reveal it to anyone. *Promise* me."

"I don't know..."

"That's not fair, Joe. *You've* broken the law. You've helped countless indies to get out of the country. Why do you get to keep your secret and not me? You even lied to Esther about Peter. You lied during a murder investigation! That's worse than what I did. Why should you get away with it and not me?"

Josiah gazed at him glumly. He had a point.

"Please, Joe. Promise me you won't tell anyone. I want Charles to be happy. I want him to keep his medal, and I want Mum to have what she always wanted for him, and for us as a family."

"Your mother is dead."

"It's what she wanted," Alex cried brokenly.

"I know, but it's a lie, Alex. Charles didn't win that medal fair and square. He wouldn't have won it at all without Flex."

"Please," Alex whispered. "My whole life, everything I endured at Tyler's hands, it's all for nothing if people know. Please, Joe. Promise."

"Okay." Josiah couldn't help himself. Alex needed this, and was it really so much to ask? Who really benefitted from knowing? It surely had no bearing on the trial.

"Say it," Alex demanded. "Say it, Joe."

"I promise," Josiah told him. "I promise I won't tell anyone, Alex."

It was the second promise he'd made to Alex today. He'd do his best, he really would, but he didn't know if he'd be able to keep either of them.

Chapter Twelve
OCTOBER 2091
Alex

Alex was shaken by the incident with the clothes and the watch. With Tyler's words of warning reverberating in his head, he knew he should try and pull himself together. What was stopping him? Was it all these memories that kept replaying as he swam? Were they trying to tell him something? If so, what? Or was he simply trying to make sense of it all, finally, after all these years?

He tried not swimming, but he yearned for it; it was the only thing that soothed him now. A few days after Tyler left, he couldn't hold out anymore. He slipped into the pool, and immediately, he was back at Long Lake, sitting next to his mother on the day he'd told her about his sexuality.

Isobel reached out and tidied a lock of hair away from his face.

"My beautiful boy. You've been so brave to tell me all this. I love you very much." She kissed his cheek, and he wrapped his arms around her and held on tight, inhaling the scent of her perfume.

Her nanopad chimed, and she drew back and answered it, her expression changing instantly.

"Now? Where are you? I'll be right there." She jumped to her feet.

"Where are you going?" Alex asked, startled.

"Back to the hotel. WADO are there."

"The doping people?" He knew his mother found them a pain in the arse as they could turn up at any time; Charles had to submit weekly diaries of his movements, which she found a drag.

Isobel didn't reply – she was already running back to the hotel.

He caught up with her only as she entered Charles's room, breezing inside with a flurry of her famous charm.

"Ezra! Long time no see, darling." She took the hands of a bespectacled, middle-aged man and kissed his cheeks. "Would you like a drink? It's so hot, isn't it?"

The doping control officer happily accepted, and they went out onto the balcony, where they chatted and sipped cocktails, while Alex sat on his bed, reading his nanopad. He'd never met Ezra, but Isobel and Charles clearly knew him well. They were all laughing and joking, discussing the games and the famous winning medal.

"It was a fantastic race. This is just a formality, you understand." Ezra beamed as he activated the medibot.

"Of course." Charles put his arm on the table while Isobel drifted back into the room and opened the fridge to top up her drink. She had her back to the balcony, but Alex could see her clearly as she took a vial of blood from the fridge and slipped it into her bra, all while continuing to laugh and joke. There was an odd incongruity between her easy banter and her sly movements that startled him. Then she wafted back to the balcony, chatting away, more vivacious than he'd ever seen her. She ruffled Charles's hair playfully at one point, and he looked up, laughing.

"I'm trying to decide on an outfit for this party tonight," she announced. "Perhaps Ezra can help me choose." Disappearing into her own room, she returned with a couple of dresses, holding them up. "What do you think, Ezra darling? The gold or the black?"

"Both are lovely," Ezra assured her. He oversaw the taking of Charles's blood, then placed the full vial in the medibot's refrigerated storage unit.

"Will I show too much cleavage in the black? Here, tell me what you think." She slipped into the bathroom and emerged moments later, looking stunning in the black dress. It was low cut, but that never normally bothered her, so Alex had no idea why she was worried about it.

"Too much?" She waved her hand at her cleavage. Ezra leaned forward, enjoying the invitation to ogle her beautiful breasts. Alex rolled his eyes; she was such a flirt.

Then he saw it out of the corner of his eye. Charles, opening the medibot while Ezra's attention was elsewhere. Alex watched, stunned, as Charles removed the vial of blood he'd just been given and replaced it with the one Isobel had hidden in her bra. When had she passed that to him? Alex hadn't seen the sleight of hand taking place.

It was so silently done, so easy. Ezra didn't notice; Isobel was busy commanding his full attention. She didn't hurry him out of the room once the swap had taken place, though. She carried on joking and flirting with him for several more minutes before, regretfully, he took his leave.

When he'd gone, she fell into Charles's arms.

"Gawd, that was a hard one," she exclaimed dramatically, looking exhilarated.

"You were magnificent, Mum." Charles laughed, twirling her around.

"As were you." She kissed his cheek. "Oh!" She drew back as she saw Alex, staring at them both from shocked eyes. Unable to speak, he ran for the door.

"Darling! Alex. Come back."

Ignoring her, he ran downstairs – straight into a huddle of paparazzi lurking in the lobby.

"Alex! How's Charles today? Hear it was a late night."

He shielded his face as he was temporarily blinded by camera flashes. Why were they still taking pictures of him? Charles's victory was two days old. Surely there was nothing new to see or say about this whole ridiculous hoopla now?

He shoved his way through the throng and out of the door, then he ran and didn't stop until what felt like hours later. Only then did he realise that he'd returned to where he'd been earlier, to the shores of

Long Lake. His heart was thudding in his chest as he tried to calm down. What had he just seen? What did it mean?

The hot weather broke with a sudden cloudburst of rain that was more than welcome. It poured down, the storm almost tropical in intensity. Alex kept on walking, head down, so he didn't see her coming until she was upon him.

"Alex, darling, please, let's talk about this." Isobel put her arm around him, but he pushed her away. "Alex, please, it's not what you think."

Did she think he was an idiot? It was exactly what he thought.

"Does Dad know?" he growled. Were they all in on it? Was he the only one who didn't know? Always the outsider, the family fool?

"No, of course he doesn't. Please, darling, let's sit over here." She waved at a sodden picnic table nearby, and he allowed her to lead him there and push him onto the bench. She sat down opposite him.

"You must have so many questions," she said, smoothing her wet hair away from her face. She was still wearing the evening dress and it looked ridiculous, soaking wet, clinging to her curves. How Ezra would love to see her like this, Alex thought bitterly.

"Why?"

"Because Charles was never going to win without it," she told him, her voice harsh and flat.

"And winning is that important?"

"Yes." Spoken like a girl born in a work camp. For all the advantages she'd won by marrying his father, he could see how her childhood had scarred her. Born into the worst of circumstances, she'd become hardened, desperate to escape. But she *had* escaped.

"Why risk everything for the stupid gold medal?" he demanded.

"We had to have it," she exclaimed, her eyes burning with an almost religious fervour. "I'm ambitious, darling, always have been, and that ambition needed somewhere to go. Your father has Lytton AV. He didn't want me to work, but I wanted success too. Charles was my way of getting it."

"Charles agreed to this?"

"He wanted it as much as me." Her face was cold and closed off. She'd made her decision years ago, and she clearly didn't regret it.

"It's cheating, Mum," he told her desperately.

"Oh, grow up, Alex. Everyone cheats," she snapped. "In sport, in life. Do you think I won that scholarship to Oxford by being a good little girl in the work camp? Bullshit! Mum and I had to hustle our way out of there. If we hadn't, we'd still be there." He didn't know precisely what that meant, but he didn't want to. He could guess.

She leaned across the picnic table, grasping both his hands.

"Listen to me, Alex. Charles wanted that gold medal more than anything, and I wanted him to have it. So, we did what we had to do."

All those years of listening to their tedious stories about training schedules, diets, and muscle strains... they'd all been a deceit. They were cheats, lying not only to his father and to him but to the entire country – to the world. Had they been laughing at him all this time? Amused by his naivety, his excited joy at Charles's win? At his stupid, misguided quote – "nice guys do come first"? Only, it seemed, Charles wasn't so nice after all.

He stared at her in disgust. Even though her honey-blonde hair was sticking to her head, she still looked beautiful. Feeling a sudden wave of nausea, he leaned over to retch. He hadn't eaten anything, so there wasn't much to come up. When the sickness eventually subsided, he realised she was stroking his hair.

"I know this has been a shock," she murmured soothingly.

"A shock? For fuck's sake! This isn't about me, it's about what you're doing. It's so fucking risky," he yelled, sitting up. "What if you're found out? How many times have you done that routine of switching the blood samples?"

"Not as often as you might think. I sometimes use bribes, but I know most of the Doping Control Officers. I've made it my business to get to know them, and I knew Ezra wouldn't pass up an opportunity to stare. Sometimes, I let them have a good feel, too."

"Stop it," he growled, hating to think of his beautiful mother whoring herself out in this way.

"It's exciting." Her face lit up. "Darling, the truth is, I'm so bloody bored I could shoot myself some days."

He was more shocked by this than anything else she'd said.

"You're still a child. You just see me as your mum, and I am that and proud to be so, but I'm a person, too. I know children never think that about their parents, and sons certainly never think it about their mothers, but it's true."

"Of course I know you're a person."

"Oh, darling, you have no idea." Her face changed in front of him, and he felt as if he was seeing her – really seeing her – for the first time. "Life is tedious, monotonous, and watching your brother row a boat up and down for hours on end is boring beyond belief. Yes, I know it's risky, yes, I know it's bad and wrong and all that. But darling... it makes me feel so alive."

She looked luminous, sitting there in her wet evening gown, her blue eyes positively sparkling. He saw then that she was a gambler, prepared to risk everything on one throw of the dice.

She placed one perfectly manicured hand on his arm. "The world is fucked up, Alex, and I am, too. I'm sorry I'm not the perfect mother all boys want their mums to be, but trust me when I say I think you'll find I'm much more fun."

"Fun? You think any of this is fun?"

"Don't be boring like your father. You have too much of me in you for that." She smiled. "Live a little, darling. Be daring. Yes, we might lose everything, but that's what makes life exciting. Now look, I need you to promise that you won't say anything to your father about this."

"What?" He stared at her.

"You have your little secret, darling, and now I'm trusting you with mine."

"Are you saying you'll tell Dad about my sexuality if I tell him about this?"

"Oh, God, no. I'm not blackmailing you, Alex." She squeezed his arm gently. "I'm just saying, a little secret doesn't do any harm, does it? Look, the reason I don't want you to tell your father is the same reason you don't want him to know you're into boys. We don't want to break his heart, do we? He's lovely, but he's so... him." She gave a regretful sigh. "He's not one of life's natural law-breakers, is he? He was brought up never having to fight for anything. He wouldn't understand."

"How have you even managed to keep it a secret from him? Doesn't he go through your accounts?"

Everyone knew that Noah was obsessed with spreadsheets. Alex often joked that they were his idea of a fun bedtime read.

"Accounts can always be fudged." She waved a hand as if that was a tedious detail, not worthy of her time. "Shave a bit off here, add a bit on there, put some money aside for bribes and to pay for the drugs." She shrugged. "I learned to be resourceful as a little girl, Alex. You're lucky, you never had to. So, please don't stand there on your high horse looking down on me, when you've had every privilege a young man could possibly be given in this fucked-up world."

How could he refuse her? How could he tell his father anyway? He couldn't even tell him about his sexuality.

"Okay," he whispered wretchedly. "I won't tell him. Or anyone."

"Good." She leaned across the table and wrapped her arms around him, hugging him tightly. "I'm actually relieved this has happened because now you're one of us and we don't have to keep this secret from you anymore. You and me and Charles, we're all in this together. Me and my two beautiful boys." She pressed a kiss to his cheek. "Yes? We'll do lots of things together, go on trips. I know you've felt left out, but not anymore. Everything will change now, you'll see."

He hated himself for brightening so much at her words. To be part of their little gang, to be included... it was all he'd ever wanted. *How easily bought you are*, he thought as she stood up and dragged him to his feet.

"Come on, now, we must get ready for this party. Who knows what hot young men might be there ready to whisk you off your feet." She prodded him slyly in the ribs, and he couldn't help smiling. Somehow, she always knew the best way to cajole and charm him, just as she did with everyone else.

Alex sank under the water and waited until his lungs felt ready to explode. If only he didn't have to surface. He was a weak man, he could see that now. He deserved all the bruises Tyler had punched into his flesh. Hopefully, one day soon, Tyler would return to finish him off.

He'd made one terrible decision after another and he didn't deserve to keep living. He could only hope that the end would be swift.

Tyler returned a few weeks later, bringing more gifts. This time, it was drawing materials, the most beautiful Alex had ever seen: exquisite canvasses, superb charcoals, and the finest paints.

"The very best money can buy and all for you," he proclaimed.

"How thoughtful of you," Alex replied, gazing at them blankly. He hadn't felt the urge to draw in a very long time.

"I bet you don't throw these into the pool." Tyler laughed.

Alex took them with murmured words of thanks and did his best to appear grateful.

This visit went much the same way as the last. It started well and then, inevitably, degenerated, as Alex failed to give Tyler what he wanted.

One night, as they ate in the scented air of the courtyard, the crickets chirping all around them, Tyler leaned across the table, an ugly look on his face.

"What do you want from me, Alexander?"

"Nothing." Alex shrugged. "Nothing at all, sir."

"You don't care if I'm kind, and you don't care if I hurt you."

Alex frowned. "But you wanted me broken," he said softly. "Didn't you?"

"Not like this." Realisation flooded into Tyler's eyes. "Is that what this is? You play-act being a broken doll and you think I'll set you free? Is that it?"

"Oh no. I don't want to be free, sir. I don't deserve freedom."

"What then? What *do* you want?"

"I told you last time: I'm hoping you'll kill me."

Tyler stared at him in disbelief. "No." He threw his napkin onto the table and stood up. "If you want to be dead so much, why not kill yourself?"

"How? I'm always watched." Alex gave a helpless shrug, although, to be honest, he didn't have the energy to even contemplate taking his own life.

"No." Tyler gripped hold of his shoulders. "I *own* you, Alexander. There's no escape from me – ever."

"As you wish, sir." Alex smiled at him serenely, unable to care even about that.

"Oh, you're loving this, aren't you?"

"What?" he asked blankly.

"This. Trying to control me."

Control. There it was again – Tyler's fatal flaw. Alex heard the crack of his hand on his jaw, but the next few minutes were like a strangely choreographed performance, with the moon covered in wispy clouds far above the only audience. Tyler hit him repeatedly, but he felt no pain. He fell down, but only as required by the pantomime they were enacting. None of it felt real. He was an actor on stage, each movement carefully rehearsed, everything familiar, as if he'd done it a hundred times before.

He heard the sound of footsteps striding away, making little staccato taps on the flagstones, and then there was silence. He was alone in the darkness, lying on the ground beside the upturned table. He rolled his tongue, tasting blood, and his body ached all over, which thrilled him because he so rarely felt anything these days.

The stone tiles of the courtyard were hard and cool under his cheek, and he found himself travelling back in time once more.

He was standing in the corner, watching the party whirling on around him. Everyone was young and attractive, albeit a few years older than him. Surely he could lose his virginity here? Plenty of his contemporaries at school had been shagging like bunnies for years – but how? Talking to people was so hard. He should learn how to flirt but it seemed so fake. His recent transformation from ugly duckling meant people looked at him more now, but he wasn't sure what to do with that attention, or how to turn it into sex.

Charles was at the centre of the room, laughing and drinking. He looked like a Greek god, tanned, fit, and strong. It had been a month since his life-changing race and people gravitated towards him, eager to bask in that gold medal glow.

Charles didn't have any trouble talking to people; it came effortlessly to him. Pretty girls threw themselves at him all the time. Alex watched him turn down various invitations to disappear into a back room, seeing the disappointed expressions on the girls' faces as Charles made it clear he wanted to stay here, where everyone was crowded around him, admiring and adoring him. He knew Charles had had plenty of sex with any number of pretty women, but it didn't seem to motivate him. He'd rather stand in the centre of the room being worshipped by everyone than slope off somewhere for a shag.

A cute boy walked past, handing out tabs of croc. God, how he wanted some right now. Croc would make it easier to simply go with the flow and enjoy the party. Why *did* people enjoy parties? They were so boring.

A girl sidled up to him wearing a very short skirt and a very tight top. He tried to talk to her, wondering what it'd be like to kiss her, but then she asked if he'd introduce her to Charles. This often happened. His mother had warned him, but it stung all the same.

He turned around, looking for the cute boy handing out the croc, but no. He'd promised his dad. Yet, croc made him feel so mellow. If he took it, he wouldn't mind that pretty girls only talked to him because they wanted to meet Charles.

What about the pretty boys? It still felt transgressive to even think about kissing a boy. He'd sat through so many of those thunder-and-lightning sermons at the church his father dragged him to. Fancying boys was sinful. Yet, he knew that he did. Maybe if he actually slept with boys and girls, he'd find out which he liked best, or maybe he'd find out he liked both equally. He felt a wave of angry impatience. When would his life bloody well start? How could he hurry it along? He sipped on his drink, only Coke, nothing stronger, because he was desperately trying not to disappoint his father right now after the last expulsion.

One of Charles's rowing friends, Simon something, shot a few glances his way, but Alex felt awkward and stupid, so he looked away. How was he ever going to have sex if he was going to stand in a corner all the time, looking miserable?

He wondered if the trick was to pretend to be someone else. Alex Lytton was rubbish at talking to attractive people, but supposing he was a more confident boy, the kind who was good at sport, loved working out, could talk to people easily, and had tons of friends. Someone like... Charles? He plucked up the courage to walk up to Simon.

"Hey."

Simon smiled at him. "Hey, Alex. How are you doing?"

"I'm great. I've been working out," he lied. Simon was wearing a tight tee-shirt that showed off his impressive muscles. Surely this was something Simon would find interesting?

"Really?" Simon glanced at Alex's slender frame.

"Well, I just started, but I'm loving it. I'm going to take up rowing, too."

"Right." Simon gave him a pitying look, and Alex felt crestfallen. He was getting this all wrong. "I heard you were an artist," Simon said. "I think that's much cooler than rowing; I'm studying history of art at university."

"Oh." Alex felt a wave of relief. This was something he could talk about. Simon was sweet and kind, and later, he drew Alex into the cloakroom and kissed him. Any doubts he might have had about finding men attractive vanished with that kiss. Alex melted against him. He'd have let him do anything in that moment, but Simon drew back with a sigh.

"Sorry, Alex," he said regretfully. "I'm not sure Charles would like me messing around with his kid brother."

Alex was sure Charles wouldn't care, but Simon wouldn't be persuaded.

He woke up the next morning still buzzing. He'd had his first kiss, and it had been awesome. It was already mid-morning by the time he emerged and the sun was shining outside. He floated downstairs on a post-kiss high, feeling invincible, and found his mother pacing around the hallway in a panic.

"What's the matter?" he asked. "Is something wrong?"

"That fat slug Adrian Buzzard from WADO just turned up to take Charles's blood," she fumed.

"Well, can't you just, you know, do your thing." He gestured at her cleavage, flushing slightly.

"Not with Buzzard. He's gay, and he hates me. He's also not open to bribes, more's the pity. Fuck it." She paced around. "I'll have to distract him somehow. Maybe a medical emergency?"

"He's gay?" Alex grinned. "Well, why don't *I* distract him, then?" As soon as he said it, he regretted it. He'd had one kiss. That in no way equipped him to flirt with a fully grown man, and he was rubbish at flirting anyway.

"Oh, darling, no. I'd never ask you to do that." She shot him a grateful smile. "This is our mess, mine and Charles's. We'll handle it together, the way we always do. I'd never drag you into it."

Oh, but how he longed to be dragged into their orbit, to be part of what they had together. This was something he could do, a way of being useful to them.

"I'll do it," he said firmly. All he had to do was to pretend to be someone else. It had worked last night, hadn't it? Kind of...

Without waiting for her reply, he waltzed into the dining room. Charles was seated at the huge mahogany table in the centre of the room, opposite an ugly, pot-bellied, dark-haired man with a cold, closed-off face. Buzzard, his mother had called him. Weird name.

"Sorry, I didn't know anyone was in here," he exclaimed. "Oh... and who is this?" he purred, remembering how his mother had played Ezra. Instead of being Charles, he'd be her. How hard could it be?

"I'm Adrian Buzzard." The man looked him up and down for just a fraction too long. Aha. His newly acquired good looks were working. He could see the man was attracted to him. He could do this.

"Hey, Adrian. I had no idea Charles was entertaining." He grinned.

"I'm from WADO. I'm here to take a blood test."

"Cool. I've always wondered how the whole dope testing thing works." He sat down, gazing at the man adoringly as he asked a few questions. Buzzard was all too eager to show off his knowledge and clearly flattered by the attention of a beautiful young man.

The inspector oversaw the medibot taking the samples, then stored them in the refrigerated storage unit, just as Ezra had done.

"I'd like to use the facilities, please, and then I'm done here," he said stiffly.

"I'll show you the way," Alex offered. His throat was dry as he reached out and touched Buzzard's hand, letting his fingers linger a little too long, and then led him down the hallway.

Buzzard was holding on to the medibot. Alex knew he had to separate him from it, but how? Was he really going to do this? *You're not gawky, awkward Alex Lytton*, he reminded himself. *You're confident and attractive, and this man clearly wants you.*

"Here it is." He opened the toilet door, then slipped his hand into Buzzard's. "Shh." Heart pounding, he put a finger over his lips. "We don't want Charles to hear us. He always thinks he's the big 'I am' around here, but why shouldn't the rest of us have some fun?" Giggling, he pulled the inspector into the toilet and pushed him up against the wall.

Buzzard's eyes widened, but Alex saw immediately that he wasn't going to refuse, and a heady wave of power flooded through him. This was easy. Buzzard dropped the medibot onto the floor, grabbing Alex hungrily. Alex pulled him further into the toilet, keeping the man's back to the medibot. Buzzard's mouth was suddenly on his, hot and hungry, far more forceful than Simon's had been the night before.

He grabbed the man's buttocks and squeezed, loving the little panting sounds Buzzard made. He didn't find him attractive, but he did, oddly, find his desire a turn-on. There was a feeling of such satisfaction about giving someone pleasure. It was entirely new to him, and he loved it.

"Here... here... suck me..." Buzzard pushed him down towards his groin. "God, you're beautiful... I've never had anyone as beautiful before... I want to feel your lips on me..."

Alex knelt in front of him and opened the man's trousers. He was almost shocked by how erect he was. He'd watched porn and he'd fantasised about doing this, but now the moment was here...

Out of the corner of his eye, he saw his brother open the toilet door silently and lean forward to grab the medibot. To cover any possible sound, Alex took the plunge and wrapped his lips around Buzzard's erection.

He'd never imagined his first time would be this furtive, this weird... but it didn't matter. His first blow job was clumsy and noisy, but he gave it his best shot, and Buzzard didn't seem to notice or care.

He stroked Alex's hair, moaning and panting the whole time. It was easy enough for Charles to return the medibot a few seconds later – job done.

Afterwards, Alex emerged from the toilet wiping his lips, feeling triumphant. Buzzard left without so much as a smile in his direction, which stung a little. He felt used, which was ridiculous as he'd been the one who'd initiated the whole thing. Surely if anyone had been used, it was Buzzard, wasn't it?

As soon as Charles closed the front door, the three of them burst out laughing. Alex ran around the hallway, needing to burn off some weird excess energy. Charles chased after him, picked him up bodily, and danced around with him for a few minutes, shrieking his head off. The sense of relief and excitement was palpable. Alex suddenly understood what his mother loved about all the deception, the gambling, the dicing with disgrace… it was thrilling.

"Alex! You wonderful, fabulous boy," Charles exclaimed, still carrying him around the hallway.

"He is! Oh, darling, you saved our bacon." Isobel wrapped her arms around him and kissed him all over his face.

When all the emotion had subsided, Alex felt an odd emptiness settle inside. Was that it? Was that sex? Once the adrenaline surge abated, he felt crushingly low. How did his mother handle all these extreme emotions? He wasn't sure he was cut out for this kind of risk-taking.

She noticed his low mood. "Darling, Charles and I thought we'd go to The Dark Horse for lunch. It's a glorious day, and your father is working as usual." She rolled her eyes. "Charles is going to take his medal to show everyone. The local people have always been so supportive, and we thought a little victory circuit might be a nice way of repaying them. I was going to ask Henry to drive us, so that Charles could sit in the back and wave at everyone. But you could drive instead, if you'd like to come? Would you?"

Of course he would. His mood lifted immediately, and he was happy to jump into the duck a little while later and drive Charles on his victory round. His older brother was in his element, wearing his gold medal around his neck and waving at everyone they passed.

Alex stirred. Where was he? It was still nighttime; stars were twinkling overhead and the sky was an inky black. Such a beautiful night. If only he had his paints, he'd love to try and capture the different tones and accents of that darkness.

He raised his hand and imagined trailing a brush across his canvas. Should he get up and find his art stuff? But he was so comfortable here. The stone was cool beneath his aching flesh and the sky so very pretty. Maybe he'd stay here and imagine painting it instead. He tried very hard to do that, but he was so tired. He closed his eyes and drifted back in time again.

The Dark Horse was always packed for Sunday lunch but a table was immediately found for Charles Lytton. Lunch took ages because people kept coming over and congratulating him. Charles barely touched his meal. Food, like sex, held little interest for him when his drug of choice was on offer.

After lunch, his mother disappeared. Alex found her outside, puffing away on a cigarette.

"Mum! They're illegal," he scolded.

"Oh, darling, don't be such a killjoy. Everyone still smokes, including you. Don't think I don't know." She offered him one, and he took it, grinning. "Please don't tell your father," she begged, although he sensed she didn't really care if he did or not. She just liked inventing these little dramas to spice up her life.

"I won't." He opened his wallet, found a strip of matches, and lit both their cigarettes.

"Thank you. It'll be our little secret." She pressed a kiss to his cheek, leaving a bright red mark from her lipstick. As he put the matches back in his wallet, he saw the tab of croc he'd stashed there months ago, that he'd never quite been able to bring himself to throw away.

Charles was still making his way through a throng of admirers. So he went to the toilet, feeling low again for some reason. Today had been such a weird rollercoaster of emotions.

Our little secret.

He felt suddenly impatient. His mother was smoking, drinking, cheating, and deceiving their father – why shouldn't he? He wanted that croc so badly. Fishing it out, he tapped the contents onto the back of his hand and inhaled, then threw his head back, breathing deeply. Oh, yes… there it was… that beautiful, mellow high. God, how he'd missed it.

He was feeling much happier when he returned to their duck. Charles was already sitting in the back, his gold medal glinting in the sun. Isobel was in the front seat, gazing at herself in the mirror as she reapplied her lipstick.

"Are you ready, Alex?" she called.

"Yes – coming." Wiping away a sprinkling of crocodile tears, he climbed into the duck beside her. They waved cheerfully to the crowd of people who'd come outside to see them go, and then they set off.

He'd only been driving a few minutes when the flow of tears down his cheeks became a flood. That was when he realised he'd taken too much. He felt fantastic, but he could barely see the road. He slowed down, blinking furiously.

Isobel turned in surprise. "What's the matter… Oh." She saw the tears running down his cheeks. "Alex!" she chided. "You said you weren't going to use croc again."

"Oh, please. You're lecturing me about drugs, given what you feed to Charles?"

"That's different. Pull over!"

He'd virtually stopped anyway, his vision completely blurry. He nudged the duck onto a grassy verge, bringing it to a halt.

"Charles, you'll have to drive," Isobel ordered, turning to him. "Your brother clearly can't."

"Do I have to?" Charles was so obviously enjoying sitting in the back, waving when they passed through villages as if they were on a royal tour.

"Well, I can't drive," she said. "So it'll have to be you."

"Fine." Charles climbed out of the duck and hauled Alex out of the driving seat. "Come on, you silly old croc-head." He gave an easy, cheerful laugh.

Alex jumped into the back, and Charles turned to grin at him.

"Ready?" He gave a manic laugh. "Then let's *go!*"

Isobel screamed with laughter as he slammed his foot down hard and the duck sped off.

The croc high soon returned, and Alex joined in their happy chatter. Finally – finally! – he was on the team.

Charles's shirtsleeves were folded back to the elbows and he was careening around the bends of the twisty little lane like a motor racing pro, chortling when their mother screamed and held on to the door, berating him for going too fast. Then suddenly, in the blink of an eye, he changed, as if taken over by some demon.

"Charles, stop! It's too fast."

"Calm down, Mum. I know what I'm doing."

Another bend loomed ahead and, still laughing, he sped up even more, approaching it at high speed...

Alex felt a sudden lurch, then a wrenching, churning, and tumbling that jarred every bone in his body. Over and over he went, and all he could hear was the screeching and tearing of metal that continued for an eternity before it ended abruptly with a loud bang.

Everything was suddenly, shockingly, quiet. He lay there dazed, his body aching. Blood was streaming down his face and his thigh felt wet. At first, he thought he couldn't move, and when he tried it hurt so much that he screamed. His cries filled the air, but nobody answered. Nobody came. Where was his mother? Where was Charles? He forced his eyes open and sunlight flooded in. He was lying on his side in the wreckage of the duck. It was still a beautiful, sunny day, and overhead, trees were swaying gently in the breeze. His arm was caught but he managed to pull it free. His shoulder ached, and his back, but his thigh... his thigh hurt the most. He looked down and saw blood pouring through his torn clothing.

"Mum? Charles?" he cried, but there was no reply. Looking around, he took in the enormity of what had happened. The back of the duck was still largely intact, but the front was completely caved in from where it'd smashed into a huge tree.

Where were they? They'd all been wearing seatbelts, but given how the duck had tumbled over and over, it was entirely possible that Charles and his mother had been thrown out of the open roof. At least, he hoped so, because nobody could still be alive in the mangled wreckage in front.

He forced himself to sit up, his head pounding, his leg aching. Kicking his way out, he fell onto the grassy verge. Crocodile tears were still flowing freely from his eyes, but now his vision was stained a blurry red as they mingled with the blood trickling from the cut on his head. He wiped his sleeve across his eyes to clear his vision... and that's when he saw her. She was lying in the road, her body twisted at an unnatural angle, her lips still perfectly red from when she'd reapplied her lipstick in the pub earlier. Her eyes were wide open, gazing at him sightlessly. She was so obviously dead, but his brain struggled to process it all the same.

"Mum?" he whispered.

There was a sound behind him, little more than a whimper.

"Charles?" He forced himself to stand and turned around, dreading what he'd find. Charles was lying a few feet away by the side of the road. For a big, strong man, he looked somehow small and diminished, his body crumpled into a heap. He wasn't moving, but he was groaning. Alex limped towards him.

"Charles, it's okay. I'm here." He crouched down, ignoring his aching hip, found Charles's hand, and held it tight.

Charles's eyes fluttered open. "Alex... what happened?"

"There was an accident. The duck came off the road. It's okay. You'll be okay." There was blood on Charles's arm, and his face was scratched. "Let me help you sit up."

"I can't," Charles whispered. "I can't feel my legs."

Alex froze. "What?" He looked at his brother's legs, but they appeared uninjured. He touched one, gently. "Can you feel that?"

"No."

He prodded harder, but Charles shook his head. "Okay, just concentrate on breathing. I'm going to call for help." He found his nanopad, miraculously still in his pocket. The case was cracked but it was still working. Shakily, he called for the emergency services.

"How many are injured?" the call handler asked.

"Two," he whispered. "Please... hurry." He was able to give a precise location, but it was fairly remote, so he doubted the ambulance would be here soon.

There was a tug on his arm as he finished the call.

"Two? What about Mum? Is she hurt?" Charles asked.

He tried to move his head to look, but Alex blocked his view. He didn't want him to see their mother like that, with her neck twisted at that terrible angle. He stroked Charles's hair gently; he was panting, his skin clammy and deathly pale.

"Mum...?" he asked again. "Please, Alex... where's Mum?"

Alex screwed up his face, not wanting to say it because that would make it true.

"Alex?" Charles asked urgently.

"She's gone, Charles. Don't look. Please, don't look."

Charles began sobbing uncontrollably, and Alex held on to him, stroking his hair gently, trying to be strong for him.

Suddenly, he was aware that Charles had gone limp in his arms and his eyes were closed.

"Please don't let me lose them both," he whispered, pressing his fingers to Charles's wrist. He couldn't bear to be alone on this road with the bodies of his mother and brother. Then he felt the thrumming of Charles's pulse beneath his fingers, thready but strong, and sighed with relief.

Charles's eyelids fluttered open. "Hurts," he whispered. "Why can't I move?"

"I don't know."

He was still in that same crumpled position, but Alex didn't want to move him in case it caused more damage.

"Alex..." Charles reached out and tugged on his ripped shirt. "They'll test me."

"What?" Alex frowned. What on earth did he mean?

"For drugs. They'll test me because I was driving. If they find out..."

"You can't worry about that. You must only think about pulling through this and getting better."

"If they find out, they'll take my medal away. Please, don't let them take my medal."

For years now, his mother and brother had been obsessed with winning that bloody gold medal, so he wasn't surprised that, even now, lying here seriously injured, it was foremost in Charles's mind.

"What do you want me to do?" he asked.

Charles's face twisted in pain and his body spasmed.

Alex held on to his hand helplessly, desperately afraid that he was losing him. "Charles? What do you want me to do?" he repeated. He could hardly tell the doctors not to test Charles for banned substances.

"Tell them I wasn't driving," Charles said hoarsely. "Say it was you. Please, Alex."

He wasn't in any frame of mind to consider the consequences of such a lie, or understand what he was agreeing to. He just wanted to give his brother comfort in his hour of need.

"Of course. I promise. Now, don't worry about it. Please, Charles, just stay with us. Don't leave me."

In the distance, he heard sirens. Thank God. He levered himself to his feet, slowly, scanning the horizon and feeling a wave of relief when he saw the ambulance. A jolly-looking giant of a man stepped out, accompanied by a medibot.

"Our duck crashed," Alex told him hoarsely. "My brother was thrown out, and my mother, too, but there's nothing you can do for her."

That's when it sank in and his legs gave way. The giant reached out and caught him just in time, calling to his companion to bring a stretcher.

"Alright, mate. Just sit down here for a mo. Do you have a name, son? I'm Graham." He knelt down in front of Alex, instructing the medibot to begin examining him.

"I'm Alex. We'd been for lunch at the pub. I don't know what happened. The duck just tumbled over and over, then hit that tree. Mum..." He gestured up the road. "She's gone. Charles can't feel his legs. Please help him. Leave me. I'm fine."

"Alright, Alex. You just sit here for a second, okay?" Graham glanced at his companion, who was already kneeling beside Charles.

"Shit..." Graham took a good look at Charles and then turned back to Alex. "Is that Charles Lytton?"

"Yes, he's my brother. Please help him."

"Don't worry, he's in good hands. We'll get you both to the hospital. Now, what about you, Alex?" The giant touched the gaping hole in Alex's ripped jeans where blood was still streaming down his leg.

"I'm fine. Please, help Charles."

"We will, don't worry, I just want to be sure you're not seriously injured, too." Graham gave him a reassuring smile.

"I was driving," Alex told him urgently, needing to make good on his promise to Charles. "It was all my fault." It was in a way. He *should* have been driving. If only he hadn't taken all that croc.

Oh, shit, what had he done?

He drifted out of the memory to find the moon had travelled halfway across the sky. What would happen if he told Tyler the truth? He'd always shut down that thought before, his greatest fear being that Tyler would turn the full force of his wrath upon his beloved brother instead. There was no point in them both suffering at the man's hands, and Charles had surely suffered enough. Besides, he'd promised Charles, and that was a promise he'd never break. So no, he'd never tell Tyler, or anyone else for that matter. Not now. Not ever. It was a secret he'd take to his grave.

There was no point in telling Tyler now, anyway. Even if the man believed him, too much water had passed under the bridge, and what lay between them had evolved far beyond his obsession with Isobel's death. They were trapped in Tyler's sticky web together, neither of them able to break free.

Alex lay on the cool stone beneath the dark night sky for what could have been days but was probably only a few hours. Somewhere in the distance he heard the whirr of helicopter blades, and then he felt gentle fingers on his face.

"Mr Alexander, sir, Mr Tyler said you'd fallen. Please, let me be of assistance." Jabir went to put down his torch, giving a startled gasp as it flashed on Alex's face. "You are injured, Mr Alexander. Tell me where it hurts."

"It doesn't hurt, Jabir, but thank you for asking."

"Let me help you up."

Alex tried to rise but his legs wouldn't work. In the end, Jabir managed to haul him to his feet and half walk, half carry him back to his room. He set Alex on the bed and gently eased off his shoes.

"Poor Mr Alexander. Poor dear man." He washed the blood off Alex's face, brought him painkillers, helped him out of his stained clothes and put him to bed. Then he stood by the door, his hand hovering over the light switch.

"I will be just outside if you need me. Call me if you do, please," he said, his face desperately sad. "I'm here for you."

Jabir took care of him for the next few days, helping him to wash, bringing him food, and offering massages. It was as if they'd travelled back in time to the first occasion when Tyler had left.

"The olive grove looks very pretty. Would you like to walk there with me?" Jabir offered when Alex was back on his feet again. He threaded Alex's hand through his arm and refused to take no for an answer.

Jabir took him right to the edge of the olive grove, to an old wooden door set in the high stone wall, and then spoke to him in a low, quiet voice.

"I know the movements of the security guards. When you are fully better, I can arrange to leave this door open and a parcel beneath this tree with food and a passport."

Alex glanced around anxiously.

"We cannot be overheard here, and if we are seen, it will simply look as if we are walking, which we are." Jabir moved Alex on slowly, as if he was simply helping him to regain his strength.

"Thank you." Alex smiled and nodded serenely for the benefit of the camera on the wall that was following his every move. "But I wouldn't risk you or your family. If Tyler found out..." He was back in that room, watching as Tyler smacked Solange and she fell. He flinched, hearing the crack her head made as it hit the fireplace.

"It is a small risk."

"No!" He spoke more heatedly than he'd intended. He calmed down, smiling for the camera. "No. I can't risk it. I couldn't bear it if anything happened to you, or Maura and the children."

"Mr Tyler has always been a generous and decent employer, unlike some others," Jabir said darkly. "I do not believe he would harm us." Then he frowned. "Yet I know he harms you." His worried gaze took in the bruises that were slowly fading on Alex's face. "I thought, maybe, this was a personal matter between the two of you. You are lovers, yes?"

"He uses me for sex, if that's what you mean. Lovers..." Alex sighed. If that term had ever been accurate, it certainly wasn't now. "I don't know that you'd call it that."

"Some people are very passionate. It is not my place to interfere with my employer's personal affairs." Jabir's gaze travelled to the ID tag attached to Alex's necklace. "But..." He paused, uncertainly. "I don't understand the system in your country. We don't have it here. You work for him, yes?"

"Yes. Or at least I did. Now... I don't know. He hasn't made me work for a long time."

"No, I think he is still making you work," Jabir said softly, his gaze never leaving Alex's face. "I am uncomfortable with this situation, Mr Alexander. It tests me. I pray for you every night. I discuss it with Maura."

"It's not your responsibility, Jabir. It's nothing to do with you," Alex told him firmly. Leaning heavily on the other man's arm, he directed him back towards the house.

"No man is an island," Jabir murmured unhappily. "The bible says, 'Truly I tell you, whatever you did for one of the least of these brothers and sisters of mine, you did for me.' I cannot in all conscience ignore your suffering, my dear Mr Alexander."

"It's my cross to bear," Alex replied, using language he thought Jabir would understand. "But thank you. My father's church only cared about sin and punishment. I'd forgotten that some people live their faiths differently."

"Then I'm glad to have at least shown you that, as little as it is," Jabir said softly. "You have seen the worst of people, I think, Mr Alexander."

"And the best, too." Alex thought of Joe and Peter, of Solange and Ted, of Barney Bates.

"I hope that is true."

They reached the courtyard, and Alex slid gratefully back onto a sun lounger to rest with a blanket pulled up over him. When he awoke a few hours later, he lay gazing up at the cloud of sweet-scented bougainvillea that hung above him and wondered about the old wooden door in the olive grove. It was a way out other than the death he'd been anticipating – should he take it? He'd given up on the idea of obtaining justice for Solange, so why not just leave?

He was paralysed by his own indecision. On the one hand, it was a way out; on the other, it felt exhausting to even consider it. How far could he reasonably expect to get in an unfamiliar country where he didn't speak the language? He'd utterly failed to escape in the UK, where the odds had been much more in his favour. He didn't even know where in Spain they were. He knew nothing except the inside of this compound where Tyler kept him a closely guarded prisoner.

Jabir was as naïve as Solange had once been when she'd helped him escape, whereas he'd seen first-hand what Tyler was capable of. No, if he ever made an escape attempt, it wouldn't involve help from anyone else. He couldn't risk it. He wouldn't have any more dead bodies and ruined lives on his conscience.

"Explain to me the significance of the tag you wear," Jabir said to him the next day as he massaged his hands. "I've heard there is a system in your country which prevented you all from killing each other after the Rising. We envied you that in the beginning. How does it work?"

Alex explained, and Jabir listened as he massaged.

"I cannot say it sounds appealing," Jabir said uncertainly when Alex had finished. "And yet... my country tore itself apart after the Rising, and wars seem to end only to begin again. Who am I to say whether the peace you created with this system is a bad thing?"

"If the IS system ever played a useful part in preventing war, then that time is long gone," Alex replied. "We've grown fat and complacent and far too reliant on it. It's time we ended it."

"Maybe this could be your task one day?" Jabir suggested.

Alex shrugged. He doubted he'd live long enough, and he wouldn't know where to start.

Jabir took him for little walks around the olive grove every day after that, until he was strong enough to walk there himself. Each time, Jabir would linger by the door and say, "You know you only have to say the word, Mr Alexander."

Alex just smiled and assured him that he never would.

Tyler returned, eventually, several weeks later, his eyes haunted and desperate, as if searching for another fix of a drug he couldn't quite kick. Alex recognised that look – he'd once felt a similar yearning for croc. Everything proceeded in much the same way as last time, and ended the same, too. Jabir took care of him once more, but he could see that the man was growing increasingly uncomfortable with the situation.

"I've spoken to Maura about the possibility of leaving Mr Tyler's employment," Jabir said on one of their now familiar walks around the olive grove.

Alex felt hollow at this news. Much as he'd tried not to view Jabir as a friend, he was only human, and he yearned for the kindness and compassion that Jabir provided. Still, he wouldn't beg him to stay. He wouldn't be responsible for anything that happened to him.

"You must do as you wish," he said softly.

"The only reason I stay is out of concern for what would happen to you if I left."

"That is kind, but you mustn't factor me into your decisions."

"If only I understood what lies between you and Mr Tyler. Why does he come here to make love to you, to shower you with gifts, only to then end up beating you?" Jabir asked fiercely.

"I could not tell you, even if I wanted to," Alex said wearily. How was it possible to explain to anyone, least of all this kind, decent man, all that lay between him and Tyler, their complicated web of desire and hatred, and all of their terrible history?

"I will stay," Jabir said softly. "I cannot leave you. Maura agrees. If I left, I would only fret about what was happening to you."

After that, Alex took care to distance himself from Jabir as much as possible. He'd never so much as spoken to the man's children, for fear of what Tyler might do to them if he thought Alex was fond of them. Now he withdrew from Jabir, too. Jabir still tried to engage him in conversation and looked puzzled when Alex rebuffed him. It hurt to be cool to this man who had been so kind to him, but Alex knew the rules. Gideon had been very clear, and he'd been right. He couldn't have friends; he'd only put them at risk.

When Tyler next returned, he brought the usual suitcases full of gifts: more clothes and some new books for him to read. They'd been carefully chosen, precisely the kind of reading material Tyler knew Alex loved. He barely glanced at them.

Tyler looked upset that his grand gesture had elicited so muted a response.

"I'm trying, Alexander. At least give me that," he exclaimed.

"You are very kind," Alex agreed. Sometimes, he heard himself and thought it sounded like that game kids played, where they agreed with the other person until it drove them mad. He could see why Tyler was so irritated, but he couldn't stop.

Days passed, and Tyler didn't sleep with him, but he did watch him constantly, clearly searching for some sign that he was still in there. Alex didn't mind. He had no need of his mask anymore, or possibly it was so ingrained that he'd succeeded in erasing all trace of himself, just as Gideon had wanted. Either way, there was nothing for Tyler to see.

At the end of the week, Tyler took him for a trip on his yacht. He was solicitous, kind even.

"I want to make love to you tonight," he said. "Dress for dinner. Let's enjoy ourselves."

Alex dutifully dressed in one of the new outfits Tyler had brought for him, and joined him on deck for a delicious dinner, managing to smile and nod in all the right places.

When Tyler made love to him later, he was as acquiescent and dutiful as ever, but something had changed. Alex waited for the hands to fasten around his throat, for Tyler's rage to consume him, but it didn't happen. Tyler made love to him sweetly and tenderly, treating him as a cherished lover, not a punchbag. There were soft kisses, gentle caresses, and kind words. It made no difference to Alex, who couldn't have cared less either way.

Afterwards, Tyler held him in his arms, trailing his fingers lovingly over Alex's skin and pressing little kisses to his hair until he fell asleep.

When he awoke sometime later, Tyler was sitting on the balcony, gazing out over the moonlit waves as he sipped a glass of whisky. Alex watched him. He didn't think Tyler was aware he was awake, but he must have made a sound, because Tyler suddenly spoke.

"I did wonder whether to come." He gazed at Alex broodingly through the open balcony doors. "I don't like the hold you have over me. I thought that by leaving you here, far away, out of sight, out of mind, I'd be free, but I still think about you all the damn time." He looked weary, full of despair.

Alex actually felt a twinge of pity for him. "How can I help?" He slid off the bed, pulled on a light cotton robe and padded silently over to him.

"I don't know," Tyler said wearily. "I look at you and I see Izzy. I never used to. I know she'd be horrified by what I've done to you, but you're in my veins – I'm addicted to you. I can't live with you, but I can't live without you."

"You should have killed me that time in the pool," Alex murmured.

"I can't kill you. Despite what you think, I'm not a killer. Besides, I can't because..." He looked away. "She'd haunt me if I did."

"Solange?"

"Isobel!" Tyler looked furious that he'd mentioned Solange. "I can't kill you, Alex. I could never do that."

"Then how does this end?" Alex asked helplessly.

"All I want is for you to—" Tyler broke off abruptly.

Alex waited.

"I need... I want..." Tyler's face twisted in pain.

"Tell me." Alex took hold of his hands and gazed at him.

"I love you," Tyler whispered, and Alex was sure he believed it. "I love you, and I want you to love me back. If you could do that, I'd give you the world. I'd lay all my wealth at your feet. It's all I want."

Alex released his hands and sat back in his chair, staring at the moonlight shining on the gentle waves below.

"You have me. My every hour is yours to command," he murmured. "You can send me anywhere you like and do anything you wish to me. I'm yours completely. I will give you everything you could ever ask of me as my houder." He glanced at Tyler. "But my feelings? You cannot dictate those, George. They are mine and mine alone. You know this, and it's what drives you mad. I would give you what you ask for if it was in my power, but it isn't. I'm lost to myself. I feel nothing. It's all the same to me whether you lay all your wealth at my feet or close your hands around my throat and strangle the life from me. I am yours and that is not enough. You want more. You will always want more. I'm sorry for that." Alex gave him a pitying smile. "I truly am. If I could give you what you want, I would, but I can't, and I never will."

It was, he thought, the most honest conversation they'd ever had. Here they were, finally, after all these years, exhausted by each other. There was nothing left, no fresh ground to explore, no new hand to play. Surely Tyler saw that?

Tyler took a sip of whisky, his eyes dark with unshed tears. Alex almost felt sorry for him.

"Thank you. I needed to hear that. You're right, of course." Tyler looked straight at him. "You still want me to kill you, don't you?"

"I don't see any other outcome." Alex shrugged. "I make you angry. It's not my intention, but I do. Why not finish it? I'm sure you could make it look like an accident. Throw me overboard, and let my body wash up in some lost zone somewhere. Then you'll be free."

"I could never do it in cold blood. I don't want to do it at all." Tyler gazed dourly into his drink. "You fill me with such rage. I never mean to hurt you, but..." He finished the whisky in one gulp. "You're right. One of these days, I *will* kill you. I won't mean to, but I will all the same, and I don't want that. I don't want you on my conscience. It's bad enough having *her* there." He stared out at sea for a long time, and Alex wondered what was going on in his head.

"I see your mother," he said finally. "In my dreams. How she'd hate me for what I've done to you. I hate myself for it, too. I miss you, Alexander. I know you might find it hard to believe, but I do. I didn't mean to fall in love with you, but you're so bright and smart and so fucking enigmatic, and you're all I have left of her, and somehow – and I don't know how – I fell for you. You *get* me. In a different time and place, we could have been perfect for each other."

Really? Alex thought. *Could we?*

Tyler turned to look at him again. "You're sure you could never love me?"

"I've never been in love with anyone. I don't think I'm capable of it," Alex told him honestly.

"I've only ever loved your mother. I thought I'd never love anyone else as long as I lived, until... you." Tyler sighed. "What a fucking mess. You're wise to never fall in love. It makes you vulnerable, makes you weak. That's how I feel around you – weak."

"Yes." That was why he had to lash out. George Tyler wasn't a man who could bear to feel weak.

"I don't like feeling weak, but I don't want to kill you." Tyler's face twisted into a mask of sadness. "I'll figure something out." He stood up. "Goodbye, my love." Leaning down, he pressed a kiss to Alex's lips. "Sorry," he whispered, and then he left.

He took a dinghy back to shore. Alex watched him from the yacht, not even remotely curious as to where he was going or what he would 'figure out'. It didn't matter.

A few weeks later, a helicopter arrived at the hacienda, and Alex's security detail appeared in the doorway.

"You're leaving. Now. No need to pack."

There was no time to say goodbye to Jabir or Maura. He was bundled out of the door and taken to the waiting helicopter. Where to? It was out of his hands. He didn't care enough to even wonder.

They landed in a cold, wet New London a few hours later. Alex shivered in his thin linen trousers and tee-shirt, completely unprepared for the English weather. Tyler wasn't there to meet him, but a familiar figure *was* waiting at the airport.

"Alex!" He was wrapped in a warm bear hug. "You're freezing. You poor old thing. The tan suits you, though."

"Elliot?" Alex blinked in surprise.

"Yes, it's me. Do you have any luggage? Well, never mind, I can buy you anything you need."

"Am I to be your muse again?" Alex asked as Elliot drew him towards a waiting duck. "Like last time?"

"Not exactly like last time, but yes, I very much hope you'll be my muse again. I'm counting on it, in fact." They reached the duck, and he tugged Alex in close, trying to kiss him.

Alex pulled back. "My houder wouldn't like it," he demurred. "You know what his instructions were last time. He doesn't want anyone touching me but him."

"Ah, but you have a new houder now," Elliot told him, with a delighted smile.

"What?" Alex gazed at him blankly.

"You're mine, Alex. George sold your contract to me. All the paperwork went through this morning."

Alex's head was spinning as he climbed into the duck beside Elliot. Could this be true? Would Tyler really sell him, given what he knew?

"Oh, wait, I'm forgetting something." Elliot was grinning from ear to ear as he took out a little black box and opened it. Inside was a beautiful gold necklace with a designer ID tag attached. It must have cost a fortune.

"Put it on," Elliot urged, clapping his hands. "Let's make this official."

He batted Alex's hands away impatiently, removed Tyler's necklace and ID tag from around his neck, and then fastened his own there instead.

"Oh, yes. Look." Elliot pointed at Alex's reflection in the mirror. "Don't you look gorgeous?"

"It's very pretty," Alex murmured.

"Aren't you excited, sweetie?" Elliot asked, beaming from ear to ear. "I am. This is the start of a wonderful new chapter – for us both."

As they drove away from the airport, Alex glanced in the wing mirror to see a black SUAV trailing them. He wasn't surprised. Of course he wasn't free of George Tyler. He would never be free of George Tyler. Not now. Not ever.

Chapter Thirteen
OCTOBER 2096
Josiah

The first day of Tyler's trial dawned bright and sunny. Josiah came downstairs to find Alex sitting in the kitchen wearing a smart burgundy suit, a grey shirt, and a pair of highly polished shoes. Josiah's shoes were on the kitchen mat, also polished to a high shine.

"Couldn't sleep?" Josiah sat at the table and pulled on his shoes.

"Nope. Spent the night polishing. Did some ironing, too, and some cooking." Alex nodded at a pile of freezer containers. "Batch-cooked some food to last us through the trial. Thought we might not be in the mood to cook during... and frankly dreading how much takeaway hachée you'll make me eat." Alex shot him a grin that didn't quite reach his eyes.

Josiah reached across the table and squeezed his arm. "Hachée is delicious," he said solemnly. "Food of the gods."

Alex managed a little laugh. "I can't believe the day has finally arrived."

"Because of you. You hung on in there and made this happen, Alex."

"And you – you took it on. Most investigators wouldn't have believed me."

"There's a chance the jury won't, either," Josiah warned him. "I'm trying to manage your expectations. Our case isn't as strong as I'd like, and Tyler has engaged some very expensive lawyers."

"You gave it your best shot." Alex smiled at him. "If we lose, we go down fighting. You hungry? I cooked you breakfast." He gestured at the frying pan on the hob.

"Not in the mood," Josiah said with a sigh.

"Me neither. Couldn't eat right now if you paid me." Alex stood up. "Shall we go, then?"

"Yup." Josiah finished tying his shoelaces and got to his feet. He was wearing one of his finest suits – a charcoal-grey three-piece, with a burgundy silk tie and matching pocket square. Without trying, he and Alex matched, their outfits complementing each other.

"Wait." Alex put a hand on his chest. "You're missing something." He produced the little silver chocolate box and tucked it into Josiah's pocket. "In case you get peckish in court."

Josiah smiled and pressed a kiss to Alex's cheek. The little shared rituals were what he'd loved so much about being married to Peter. As much as he wanted this trial over and done with, he also dreaded it because then, regardless of the outcome, Alex would leave, and his life would return to what it had been before. No more chocolate box rituals, nobody to sit next to on the sofa in the evenings. He and Alex might not be a couple, but they'd shared this house for almost a year and become accustomed to each other's ways. Josiah would love him to remain forever, but it wasn't in their hands. It was true he still had Gideon's offer of money to help him buy Alex's contract, but he didn't think it was wise to count on that. He took a deep breath, adjusted his tie, and then held out his hand.

"Let's go."

The High Court was based in a plain, functional building on Ghost Eye. Long gone were the days of the Old Bailey and barristers in wigs and gowns scurrying through the Inns of Court. Justice in post-Rising Britain took place in more mundane settings and the lawyers wore suits. The cash-strapped state had outsourced the process and paraphernalia of upholding the law to private companies, just as they had with investigation.

Many aspects of the legal process had changed, too. Not necessarily for the better, but it was the best they could do right now. Josiah had to hope it would be enough to see George Tyler brought to justice.

He knew the presiding judge to be a fair woman, but she was also brusque and impatient with grandstanding lawyers. Maybe that would work in their favour. He'd worked closely with the prosecution for months, and they'd put together the best case they could. The years of footage from all the smartwalls at Tyler's houses had never been found. He was sure the servers they resided on were located in some foreign jurisdiction, far out of the reach of British law enforcement. He'd searched everywhere but had uncovered nothing that even spoke to the existence of those compromising files.

Tyler had insisted any footage taken inside his home was for security, and that it was usually deleted after a month. He'd even supplied detailed logs showing the process in action, and it was exactly as he said. Of course it was. Josiah knew he was dealing with a very slick operator in George Tyler. Nothing would have been left to chance.

The one place he'd been unable to search was Tyler's Spanish property. The authorities there, locked in an arcane battle with their British counterparts that went back to the Rising and was so complicated that nobody fully understood it, refused to allow any investigation on Spanish soil. Tyler would have known that, of course. Josiah had no doubt that was why he'd bought the property in Spain in the first place. He was certain that either hard copies of the blackmail footage were being stored there or even that the hacienda housed the servers containing the original material proving the extent of Tyler's blackmail operations. Without the kompromat, they were reliant on eye-witness testimony of Tyler's treatment of Alex and his occasional wild rages.

Tyler's lawyer, Henry Marshall-Shaw, was the most expensive money could buy, almost as much of a celebrity as Tyler himself. He was so well known that he was referred to by his initials – HMS – on all the popular media sites.

"Sounds like a bloody ship," Josiah observed. HMS looked like one, too; he was a man of large buttressing, much given to dramatically sallying forth across the courtroom to play to the jury. Josiah loathed him.

The prosecution team was led by Mona Byrne, a short, stocky, foul-mouthed Irishwoman, who was always ferociously well prepared in their meetings and like a dog with a bone when she sensed weakness. Josiah often hadn't enjoyed their encounters, and he hoped that Tyler would feel the same way.

The news crews were out in force outside the court building. It had been dubbed "The Trial of the Century", and was all that anybody was talking about.

The Indiehunter Versus the Tycoon! was the headline on the large screen outside the court, together with unflattering photos of both himself and Tyler. Josiah knew his reputation was on the line. Tyler might walk all over his carefully prepared case, and then the famous indiehunter would be crucified by a media that already thought he'd been seduced by the pretty face of a notorious liar.

All major trials were broadcast on livestream. In an age of smartwalls, holovids, contact lens cams, and other sophisticated tech, the state had given up trying to control what the juries or witnesses were privy to during the process. It was imperfect, but then so many of their systems were.

Josiah shielded Alex from the media scrum as best he could and they scrambled breathlessly into the court building.

The Inquisitus team was already there – Esther, Sofie, Reed, and Mel – together with all the prosecution lawyers. Only Esther would stay for the proceedings. The others were simply there to offer support at the start of the trial.

Ted was in court, too, with his wife beside him, a plump woman with bleached-blond hair and a fearless expression. Mick was next to them, squeezed into a suit two sizes too small that barely stretched over his belly. Charles and Noah were standing in a little huddle with Elsie. All were there to support Alex.

Josiah found it hard to look at Charles without wanting to punch him, but he managed a coolly polite greeting. He saved a warmer welcome for Noah, who he'd come to rather like, and pulled Elsie into his usual bear hug. Then they moved into the courtroom and took their seats.

Tyler and his team were already inside. Their adversary looked more cadaverous than ever, without a scrap of spare flesh on him, his body tautly muscled. Alex had told him that Tyler coped with stress by eating less and working out more. Judging by his appearance, he was extremely stressed right now, which gave Josiah a smidgen of comfort; at least Tyler wasn't entirely confident the case would go his way.

Tyler was dressed from head to foot in his trademark black. As they entered, he glanced across the court and shot Alex a dark and sinister smile. Josiah drew Alex's attention away, not wanting him to be spooked.

The court was called to order. There were some tedious formalities. The jury selection process had already taken place and both sides were comfortable with it. Josiah watched as the twelve men and women took their seats, looking solemn but with an undercurrent of excitement at being present at *this* famous a trial.

The judge entered, the courtroom fell silent… and then it began.

Byrne gave the opening statement for the prosecution. "George Tyler is charged with the manslaughter of an indentured servant in his care and employ, one Solange Alajika." She outlined the basics of the prosecution case and described what had happened on the night Solange was killed. "Mr Tyler might not have meant to kill Ms Alajika, but he certainly intended to punish her for her part in Mr Lytton's escape. The situation got out of hand, resulting in her death: a death that Mr Tyler subsequently hushed up by disposing of the body in a lost zone under cover of darkness. The defence will argue that the DNA evidence does not match that of Ms Alajika in the IS agency database. We would move that the evidence has been tampered with at the behest of Mr Tyler by an agency official who was being blackmailed."

A low rumble went around the room. It was all shaping up to be extremely spicy.

Then it was the defence's turn. HMS stood up and addressed the jury.

"You are aware that you are sitting on a unique trial. George Tyler is a well-known businessman, philanthropist, and media personality. He's particularly famous for his investment in the floating cities that currently house thousands of people, liberating them from the Quarterlands and the work camps. The idea that he prostituted his indentured servants in order to blackmail business partners and IS agency officials is inconceivable. The truth is that the body Inquisitus dredged up is not that of Solange Alajika. We refute, utterly and completely, the idea that anyone from the IS agency has been bribed to alter the database."

HMS called Martin Bagshaw to the witness stand. He was all smiles and effusive unction, directed mainly at the judge, but also to the jury and the world in general. A more affable man would be hard to find.

"Mr Bagshaw, you are in charge of the government's indentured servant agency, I believe?" HMS asked.

"I am, sir," Bagshaw said proudly.

"For how long?"

"Five years."

"And before that?"

"I worked at the IS agency, handling the accounts of high-profile clients such as Mr Tyler."

"So, you were Mr Tyler's account handler when Ms Alajika was first registered on the IS database?"

"Yes, sir, I was."

"In all the time you've worked at the IS agency, have there been any instances of the database being tampered with?"

"There have been incorrect registrations," Bagshaw replied uncertainly.

"I'm talking about instances where the security of the database itself was undermined," HMS explained. "Where it was hacked, or the information in it altered without the knowledge of the authorities."

"No, sir, that couldn't happen." Bagshaw launched into a detailed explanation as to why. Several members of the jury immediately entered notes on their court-issued nanopads, looking impressed.

"Could the database be altered by an employee of the ISA?"

"Of course, but we have robust alteration policies in place. The system notes any changes, so there's always a data trail."

Solange's IS records were brought up for the jury to examine. Josiah heard Alex take a sharp intake of breath as her registration photo flashed up on the court smartwall. He realised that Alex had only ever seen one photo of Solange in years – the one he'd kept with him for so long – and that was seared into his brain. He was transfixed by the new image, his eyes shining wetly. Ted glanced at him, his eyes also glassy, and Alex met his gaze. She was the reason they were here, the reason why they'd risked so much. Gone, but never forgotten, these two men had carried her memory in their hearts for years, waiting for this moment. Whatever happened, Josiah was moved by their bravery.

Byrne took over and was a lot less impressed by Bagshaw's attempts to ingratiate himself.

"Have you ever been asked to take a bribe in order to falsify IS records?" she asked.

"Good lord, no. Investigator Raine requisitioned all my bank statements as part of his investigation and he found nothing amiss, no large incoming amounts of money."

"What about a different kind of bribe – a sexual bribe," she pressed. "Mr Tyler owns the contracts of many different indentured servants. Did he ever offer you their sexual services in exchange for your professional cooperation?"

Bagshaw was clearly waiting for the question. "Absolutely not," he said firmly.

Josiah was aware of Alex staring at the man, his eyes boring holes into him, but Bagshaw didn't once look in his direction.

"Running the IS agency isn't a glamorous job," Bagshaw explained. "It's mainly record-keeping and policy. We're also tasked with ensuring the welfare and proper treatment of the country's indentured servants. That's a mission I feel passionately about. I would hardly jeopardise my career and all I believe in for the sake of an assignation. Prostitution of an IS is illegal, and rightly so. That is one of the primary rules our agency exists to protect. Indentured servants are not our slaves. The nature of their contracts means we have a special duty of care towards them, and my agency takes great pride in upholding that, as you can see by our record. Under my directorship, we've successfully prosecuted hundreds of houders who have not conformed to the rigorous standards we set."

"Yes, your record is most commendable." Byrne gave a tight smile. "Are you married, Mr Bagshaw?"

"Yes."

"Happily?"

"Very." He looked angry, as well he might at the personal nature of the questioning.

"And you have two sons?"

"Yes." He relaxed a little at that, his mouth curving into a gentle smile. Josiah had no doubt he loved his children.

"Did George Tyler ever offer you sex with Alexander Lytton, either with or without strings attached?"

"No!" Bagshaw looked appalled.

Alex's hand landed on Josiah's arm and his nails dug in hard. Josiah didn't blame him.

"Did you receive a call to the ISA helpline from Alexander Lytton on Tuesday, September twenty-first, 2088?"

"Yes, we did. It's documented in his records."

"What did he say?"

"He was distressed. We do see this sometimes with those who are sentenced to servitude instead of prison time. They haven't chosen the life and it can be an adjustment."

"What did you do when you received the call from Mr Lytton?"

"I called George – uh, Mr Tyler – and advised him, and then I went straight to his residence."

"What time was this?"

"Evening. I don't recall a precise time."

"Was it usual to perform agency business in the evening?"

Bagshaw puffed out his chest. "I made it my business to be available to my account holders twenty-four-seven."

"*Your* account holders?" Byrne raised an eyebrow. "The ISA is a government agency. *They* pay your salary. You may well have handled several big accounts, but those people had no call on your time outside hours, and they were not *your* account holders."

"It's just a figure of speech. The people whose accounts I looked after on behalf of the agency," Bagshaw said quickly.

"What did you do when you went to Mr Tyler's residence?"

"I asked to speak to Mr Lytton."

"In private?"

"Yes, absolutely. We had a nice little chat, and I was able to reassure him that his treatment had been exemplary, and he was merely experiencing distress at his loss of independence and status – no different to being in prison."

"Was he satisfied with that?"

"Oh, yes. He had a little weep on my shoulder and that was that." Bagshaw gave a saintly smile.

Alex's nails dug deeper into Josiah's arm.

"I see. Mr Bagshaw, have you ever had sexual intercourse with Alexander Lytton? Either before or after this encounter?"

"Absolutely not," Bagshaw exclaimed, his face flushing an indignant shade of red.

"Thank you. That's all." Byrne gave a curt nod.

Josiah sighed. He'd done considerable digging on Bagshaw but found nothing – no suspicious payments into his bank accounts, no evidence that he'd had affairs outside his marriage, or an interest in young – the younger, the better – men. He was sure such evidence existed. He doubted a man like Bagshaw would be satisfied with the handful of young men Tyler threw his way. But Tyler had performed a very efficient job of sweeping away the evidence. It had been clear to Josiah from the lack of evidence everywhere that Tyler had been preparing for this trial, not simply from the moment of his arrest but since the night he'd killed Solange.

There was a break for lunch, and when they returned, HMS stepped forward, his entire body quivering in anticipatory glee.

"Oh, shit," Josiah whispered.

Alex glanced at him, startled. "What?"

"Brace yourself," Josiah warned.

Mona Byrne had not shared all the details of the prosecution's case with him. In fact, she'd thrown him out of her office weeks ago, telling him to "feck off, you big, interfering goon. This is my fecking case, and I'll conduct it my fecking way." So he knew there would be some surprises, the first of which, he suspected, was about to appear.

HMS surveyed the court for a few minutes, waiting until everyone's attention was fixed completely on him. Then he dropped his bombshell.

"I call Solange Alajika to the stand."

"What?" Alex craned his head as the side door opened and a beautiful woman walked in. She had the most stunning hair, which settled around her slender shoulders like a cloud. She was wearing a navy-blue suit over a cream blouse and smart knee-length boots.

Alex grabbed Josiah's arm. "No," he said in a strangled whisper.

"Solange" took her place on the stand, right next to the picture on the smartwall from her registration ID. The two women looked almost identical – one, it seemed, an older version of the other. Alex looked at Ted, who looked back at Alex in disbelief. Josiah suspected the photograph on the IS database that had affected them so much was of this woman, not of Solange, and he fought down a surge of anger at Tyler's manipulations. They'd been so touched by that photo, but it wasn't even real.

"Solange?" Ted whispered, reaching out his hand. The woman on the stand didn't look at him.

"Please give your name," HMS invited.

"I'm Solange Alajika," she said, looking serious but serene. "And I'm George Tyler's goddaughter."

Pandemonium broke out. The jury looked mystified. Was this huge, important trial all a mistake? It all seemed unbelievable. Josiah sat beside Alex, unmoving, his arm now covered in indentations from his fingernails.

"Ms Alajika. In his witness statement, Mr Marlon Baxter stated that he met you at Oxford, and you told him you were Mr Tyler's goddaughter. Is that correct?"

"Yes." She shot a fond smile at Tyler. "My father was a designer at

Tyler Tech. He and Uncle George were good friends, so he was delighted to be asked to be my godfather." IS database records were produced, showing photos of Solange's supposed "father".

"What happened to your parents, Ms Alajika?"

"They were killed in a duck accident when I was seventeen," she said in a low voice. She took a moment to close her eyes and compose herself. Josiah had to admire her acting ability.

"Leaving you in the care of your godfather?"

"That's right." She smiled. "He was always very good to me. Dad had wanted me to go to Oxford to study art, if I was good enough. I went off the rails a bit after my parents died, but Uncle George encouraged me in that dream."

"Mr Baxter says you weren't wearing an identification tag when you were at Oxford. Are we to understand, then, that you weren't Mr Tyler's indentured servant when you went to university?"

"That's right. Uncle George paid for my tuition and expenses at uni. That was his gift to me. Besides," she added in a very serious tone, "it's illegal for an IS not to be registered and microchipped. As you can see from the database, I wasn't registered as his IS until after I left university."

"Why was that?" HMS asked. "I mean, why make you his IS if you're his goddaughter – his best friend's daughter?"

"I believe in paying my way," she replied earnestly. "Uncle George had already been so generous to me, and I wanted to give something back, so I asked if I could join Tyler Tech as an IS. Besides, there's no shame in being a servant – it was good enough for my dad. I didn't ask for any special treatment. I wanted to start out in the TT IS programme, if he'd accept me, which he did." She shot Tyler a grateful smile.

"Did you do well at Tyler Tech?"

"I think so. I remained for a few years until my contract completed, and then I decided to leave. I'm an artist at heart, you see, and Uncle George understood that."

"Did you stay in touch with him?"

"Of course. He's like family to me. I visit him occasionally, but I'm a busy married mum now – an artist, too, when I have time. So I don't, perhaps, see as much of him as we'd both like. Sorry, Uncle George." She gave him a little wave.

Josiah was taken aback by how convincing she was. She seemed so sure of the lies she was telling. If he was on the jury, he'd be convinced.

"So, you're saying that far from being killed in an argument in 2088, you're actually alive and well and living your best life?" HMS smiled at the jury smugly.

"As you can see!" She gave a light laugh.

Her evidence was perfect. She'd clearly been well rehearsed. She made it clear that she took the proceedings seriously, but at the same time, found it a little amusing that people thought she was dead.

Tyler glanced over with a triumphant expression in his eyes. Josiah shrugged; there was still a long way to go.

Byrne stood up. She interrogated the fake Solange at length but found no weaknesses in her story. Fake Solange's DNA matched that registered in the IS agency database. Byrne called Ted to the stand.

"I don't know who that woman is," he said stoutly, "but she's not Solange. I know that because I saw her being thrown out of a duck seven years ago with a bloody great crack on the side of her head."

Byrne spent some time drawing out the best in Ted. He spoke movingly of his romance with Solange. "She wasn't a designer at Tyler Tech," he spat. "Tyler used her to blackmail people he wanted to keep in his pocket. He used to whore her out, and Alex, too."

This sparked another furore, requiring the judge to intervene. It took several minutes to settle the courtroom down again.

"That lady can't be Solange, because me and Solange was in love," Ted insisted. "We were making plans together. Solange grew up in the Quarterlands – she never even knew her dad. We spent hours talking and I knew all about her. I used to love her hair, so she pulled a few strands out one day and gave them to me. I kept them in this locket for all these years." He pointed to the locket he was wearing. "My girl's DNA was in that skeleton they dragged from the water. It matches what's in my locket."

The court adjourned for the day halfway through Ted's evidence. Tyler had produced records that backed up everything Fake Solange said. It looked perfect, and it would be very easy to believe it. That was the line of least resistance. The prosecution's version required a suspension of disbelief that would stretch the jury's credulity far more. Tyler had provided them with an easier, more prosaic explanation.

Glancing over at his adversary, Josiah found him looking supremely confident, as well he might. There was no doubt who'd won the first day in court.

Josiah waylaid Byrne on his way out of the courtroom, beckoning her into a nearby meeting room and shutting the door behind them.

"You could have warned me about fake Solange," he remonstrated when they were alone.

She shrugged. "I told you weeks ago to get the feck out of this case. You're too involved, Raine. It's too personal for you. You were driving me nuts with all your nitpicky queries and interventions."

"Seeing her was a shock for Alex," he snapped. "A heads-up would have been nice, as a professional courtesy if nothing else."

Byrne gazed at him coolly. "I understand that you're the lead investigator on this case, but when I was appointed to prosecute, it became *my* case, and I don't play well with others."

"That's obvious!" he snorted. "You must have known for weeks that Tyler would produce that woman, but you never said anything."

"I didn't owe you that information. Yes, Tyler tried to have the case thrown out long before it reached trial on the grounds that Solange Alajika was still alive. There were some pretty heated pre-trial exchanges, I can tell you. The judge was this close..." She held up her thumb and forefinger, "to declaring there was no case to answer. I worked my arse off to get it before a jury, and I did it because I'm like a dog with a fecking bone when I get going, and because I believe that bastard killed that poor woman, and I won't let him get away with it. You're not the only one who bloody well cares about justice, Raine! Rich tossers like George Tyler get off scot-free far too often, but not on Mona Byrne's watch." She planted her hands firmly on her ample hips and glared at him.

"Fine, I believe you." He glared back at her. "But would it have hurt you to have shared this with me?"

She rolled her eyes. "Oh, for feck's sake! I'm up to my eyeballs in this, and I don't have time to deliver constant updates to you. I'll involve you when I need you and no further. That's how I work."

They continued glaring at each other for a long moment, and then she sighed. "This is not the strongest case you've ever delivered for prosecution, Raine."

"I know," he said tightly.

"It could go either way."

"I know that too."

"Then back off and let me do my damn job. I'm the best chance we have of nailing that bastard, and you know it."

"Fine," he sighed, knowing she was right. "But are there any other surprises I should be aware of?"

"I have no idea, but if there are, you'll find out the same as everyone else, in the fecking courtroom. Now, bugger off and let me get on with this. Believe it or not, I know what I'm doing."

With one last glare, she swept from the room.

Neither he nor Alex spoke on the way home. They were both too dispirited.

"It's not looking good, is it?" Alex said as they heated up some of the food he'd made the previous night. He pushed his meal around his plate listlessly.

"No, but you knew this wouldn't be easy."

"She looked so like her. It was like having her back again. When I saw that photo, I was sure it was Solange. Where did he find someone so perfect? How did he manage that so quickly?"

"Oh, Alex." Josiah put his knife and fork down, shaking his head. "He's had her in place for years. He probably started looking for her the day after he killed Solange. He figured out exactly the evidence he'd need in place should the truth ever come out, and he made sure the paper trail was all there. The fake father he was so close to that he honoured his wish to send his beloved daughter to Oxford, the story as to why she became an IS at all, given she was supposedly his goddaughter. All thoroughly thought through with plausible explanations for everything."

"Solange once told me he advertised for her, then spent weeks polishing her up and rehearsing her, so she could convince me of her story. I suppose this was no different."

"No. It was the inevitable outcome of him altering the DNA on the IS database. I'm sure he found a Quarterlands girl who looked like Solange, set her up in a nice flat somewhere, gave her lots of money, and polished her to be precisely what he needed. I wouldn't be surprised if he paid for her to have plastic surgery to look even more like Solange."

"He did a good job. I almost wanted to believe it was her, if it meant having her back," Alex said softly. "Seeing her there, older... made me think of all he stole from her. All the living she was never able to experience."

"I'm sorry. She *was* very convincing, but this is just the first day – we're not giving up yet."

As they drove to the courtroom the next day, Josiah's favourite talk radio station was full of trial news.

"This is Alan Brady for *News-Spec*, where the only news anyone is talking about today is, of course, the trial of tech entrepreneur George Tyler. Amanda, what's the word on the street?"

His co-host gave a breathless chuckle. "Well, I think we're all asking, has Josiah Raine bitten off more than he can chew? I mean, we're all aware of his record in court. Inquisitus has never lost a case where he was the lead investigator. But taking on George Tyler?" She gave a long whistle. "Could that be a career-ending mistake?"

Alex slammed his hand on the mute button. "That's quite enough of that."

Josiah turned it back on. "Nah, let's hear what they have to say. It'll clue us in to how the jury is likely thinking."

Amanda was in full flow. "Tyler's team seems to be running rings around the prosecution right now. You have to wonder whether the judge will move to abandon the trial altogether, given that the lady in question seems to be alive and well and living her best life."

"Why would Raine bring a case this risky unless he was sure of his evidence?" Alan mused.

"Why indeed? We're all used to Josiah Raine being the steely-eyed indiehunter, but is it possible that on this occasion he's less the hunter and more the prey?" Amanda mused. "You have to hand it to Alexander Lytton. If anyone could melt our indiehunter's stone-cold heart and make him believe a pack of lies, it's clearly him. Alexander Lytton: face of an angel, soul of a demon."

Alex laughed out loud. "Remember to put that on my gravestone," he told Josiah. "I like that one."

"Hah! And I'm steely-eyed with a stone-cold heart."

"They know you too well," Alex joked, and they both burst out laughing, grateful of some relief from all the tension.

"I must say, I find the presence of his brother, Charles, in court very poignant," Alan continued in a more reverential tone. "To still be there, supporting his no-good brother, after all he's been through."

Josiah's fists tightened on the steering wheel.

"He's a true national treasure," Amanda added, sounding ever so slightly choked with emotion. "Now, let's go to Sandra from Essex. Sandra, what do you make of proceedings so far?"

"Morning, Amanda and Alan. I just wanted to say I'm very cross with Investigator Raine. I thought he was on our side, but he seems to have been taken in by this Lytton boy."

"*Our* side?" Amanda queried.

"You know, against indies stealing our jobs, murdering us in our beds and running off with all our money."

"I suppose we don't know what Josiah Raine thinks about anything. He never gives interviews," Alan hedged.

"But he's the indiehunter," Sandra snapped.

"Not a title he's ever claimed for himself," Alan warned, sounding a rare note of sanity in a show not well known for it.

"But an indie murdered his husband," she protested. "We all know he hates them. Why is he letting this one run rings around him?"

"Why indeed? Let's ask Hameed from Carshalton that same question."

"Maybe the Lytton lad has something on him," Hameed offered.

"This is a trial all about blackmail, after all, and I doubt Lytton would have any problem stooping to it. Poor Charles. Sitting in that courtroom supporting his low-life brother, still wanting to believe the best of him, no matter what."

Josiah felt the beginnings of a headache brewing. The problem was always that the public perception of Alex was so negative, it would be all but impossible to turn it around. Everyone wanted to believe the world was black and white, that Josiah Raine hated indentured servants, and Alexander Lytton was a villain. Nobody wanted a more nuanced version. This trial was entertainment, and people wanted everyone to play the part they occupied in the public imagination. The scale of the task facing them seemed almost insurmountable. Alex was the baddie and nobody was going to believe a word he said, and that was that.

There was no question of the judge abandoning the trial. "You've been given two conflicting versions of Ms Alajika's story," she told the jury. "It will be for you to decide which one is true."

Yet, Josiah knew the burden of proof lay with the prosecution. They had to convince the jury that Alex, Ted, and Mick were telling the truth about what happened that night, that Bagshaw had been blackmailed into altering the IS database, and that Tyler was a far bigger villain than Alex. None of which would be easy. Tyler was a famous, successful entrepreneur. The idea that he'd prostituted his indentured servants in order to blackmail business partners seemed inconceivable, and that was the mountain they had to climb. This trial was shaping up to be as much about public perception as reality, and Josiah didn't have a huge amount of faith in the public.

Ted returned to the stand. Josiah could see how nervous he was, how out of his depth and scared of Tyler. He drew strength from his wife, Trudy, often looking to her for support. He was no match for HMS, although Tyler's smug barrister wasn't as tough with him as he could have been. Ted was too sympathetic a witness for that, and Josiah had a suspicion HMS was saving his roughest mauling for Alex.

"Was Mr Tyler a good houder to you?" he asked.

"He was a bully. He had Solange beaten by his major-domo once."

"Was he a good houder to *you*?" HMS emphasised. "Were you fed and housed, were your conditions as specified in your contract?"

"Yeah." Ted shrugged.

"And after you left Mr Tyler's employ, were you automatically enrolled in his IS Leavers' Scheme, and given aid and support in establishing yourself in a new job?"

Alex glanced at Josiah. "IS Leavers' Scheme?" he mouthed.

"I dunno about no leavers' scheme," Ted replied. "He helped me set up in an army shop, but that was hush money for staying quiet about Solange."

"On the contrary, Mr Tyler runs a generous programme for IS leavers. All his indentured servants are enrolled in it when they complete their contracts. You were given support like countless others." HMS took a moment to read out some sworn testimonials from happy leavers.

Ted stared at him miserably. "Like I said, I dunno about no leavers' scheme," he said when HMS was finished.

"I've been told something rather different. I put it to you that you developed a crush on Ms Alajika, and when she rebuffed your advances, you became obsessed with her. In the end, she reported you to Mr Tyler and he removed you from his security roster. You were let go early for that reason, although he paid out your contract in full, which speaks to his generosity. However, you were angry with him for intervening as you had deluded yourself that you had a chance of romance with Ms Alajika. That is why you colluded with Alexander Lytton in this concoction of lies against Mr Tyler."

It was breath-taking in its chutzpah. Josiah had wondered how they'd blacken Ted's motives, but it hurt to see a good man traduced in this way.

"That's not true," Ted cried, looking towards Trudy in distress. She crossed her arms over her chest and nodded to him, bolstering him up.

"Solange and I were in love," he said forlornly. He' cut a pathetic figure standing up there, stooped, lanky, and emotional, with his drooping moustache and scarred face.

"Solange Alajika – this woman – was in love with you?" HMS spoke in a tone of sneering disbelief as he brought up Solange's picture on the smartwall again. She was stunning, and his insinuation was clear. Would a woman this beautiful have looked twice at a man like Ted? The Solange they'd seen in court was beautiful, cultured, and elegant. She was in a completely different league to this shambling, scarred, uneducated man. It was laughable to think that *she* had ever been interested in him.

"Poor Ted," Alex whispered. "Fuck Tyler."

Byrne gave Ted an easier time.

"Tell us about the Solange you knew, Mr Burgis," she instructed.

Ted smiled. "Well, she was like me. We both came from the Quarterlands, and we were both indies. Sure, she was dead pretty, but she was like all the girls I knew growing up, all desperate to get outta the Quarterlands, to start living. She knew she had to put in the time doing Tyler's dirty work for a few years, but then she'd be free to pursue her dreams. It was the same for me. Sell yourself for a few years, and then hopefully be able to rent a little place on the dry and start making something of yourself. She wasn't artistic like they made out. She wasn't a reader or a thinker, really. She was warm-hearted and kind. She wanted kids above everything else. She was a traditional girl at heart, my Solange. She didn't dream that big. She just wanted a bloke who wouldn't let her down, and I wanted to be that for her."

"She sounds lovely," Byrne said softly. Josiah exhaled. She'd brought out Ted's sincere love for Solange and showed that they were just two Quarterlands kids who'd found each other in servitude. *This* Solange had much more in common with Ted than the fake version, but he doubted it would be enough to convince the jury.

"Tell us about the events of the night of November third, 2088," Byrne requested.

Ted took a deep breath before launching into a detailed account of the night Solange had died.

"Tyler was hopping mad that Alex had got away. Of course, he knew that Solange had helped Alex. He made her watch Alex being punished because he knew she'd be upset. She and Alex were close, really good friends. Not at the beginning because of how he felt she'd betrayed him. But they became real close over time. I can still see her face. She was crying, horrified by what Tyler was doing to Alex. He was beating him so hard. I was worried because I thought he was gonna kill Alex. I'd never seen Tyler like that – he lost control. Solange ran forward and yanked at Tyler's arm, and he kept trying to shake her off. Then he grabbed hold of her hair and hit her several times. I ran forward to stop him, but I was too late. He hit her across the face so hard that she fell against the fireplace and her head cracked back... and then she was gone. It all happened so fast."

Josiah glanced at the jury. They looked touched by his story, perhaps on their way to being won over. They'd clawed back a little of the ground they'd lost.

Byrne finished questioning Ted, and HMS stood up.

"I have a few more questions. So, Mr Burgis, your houder is beating the woman you proclaim to love, and you just stand there and do nothing until it's too late?" he asked in a sceptical tone.

Ted looked as if someone had punched him. "You gotta understand, we were all scared of Tyler," he said. "All of us were beaten at some point. We expected it."

"It's illegal to beat an indentured servant," HMS said.

Ted laughed. "Well, that must mean it never happens then, like all illegal stuff."

The jury gave a little laugh at that.

"So, if this beating was as bad as you say, then it stands to reason that Mr Lytton would still have scarring?"

"Yeah, I guess." Ted shrugged.

"Scars like these, perhaps?" HMS clicked, and images of Alex flashed up on the smartwall. They showed his back with the faint, silvery scars that Josiah was familiar with. "These pictures were taken at the time of Mr Lytton's registration as an IS, long before the events of the night in question. I'm sure you're aware that Mr Lytton was involved in a serious duck accident at the age of seventeen. His mother was killed and his brother was seriously injured. Mr Lytton was found guilty of causing that accident by taking the street drug known as crocodile tears before getting behind the wheel. The scars on his back are a result of that accident, not some frenzied assault by one of the country's most respected and successful businessmen."

Alex buried his face in his hands. Josiah rested his hand on his thigh and squeezed gently. How hard it must be to have the facts of your life rewritten in this way. Tyler had obviously falsified those photos, as he had so much else, but the balance of probability was slipping away from them again.

Josiah knew that Alex's medical records would have been transferred to Tyler's keeping for the duration of his servitude. There had been plenty of time and opportunity to have them altered. Byrne could put Charles and Noah on the witness stand, have them testify as to what they knew of Alex's injuries, but Charles had been unconscious for days after the crash, and Noah had been in shock. HMS wouldn't have to do much to paint their recollections as unreliable without traducing their characters as he had Ted's.

Ted stepped down from the stand. Medical experts from both sides were then called to testify as to whether the scars on Alex's back were consistent with a beating from a whip or whether they could have been caused by the road accident. While the truth seemed perfectly obvious to Josiah, Tyler had enough medical experts in his pocket to cast doubt on the issue.

There was a recess for lunch, and Alex ran to give Ted a hug once they were outside the courtroom.

"Bloody hell, mate, I didn't expect it to be that bad," Ted said shakily. Trudy came to stand beside him, and he reached for her hand, holding on tightly.

"At least my Trudes knows me," he said, smiling at her.

"We all do, Ted," Josiah said, shaking his hand firmly. "You did well up there."

"They made out I was a stalker. That I was after that cow pretending to be Solange."

"Solange loved you, and you loved her," Josiah said firmly. "We all know the truth. Don't let them get into your head."

"It's not going well, is it?" Ted asked. "That bastard is gonna get away with it, like I always knew he would. System's rigged, Joe, no offence."

"None taken. I agree, it's not looking great at the moment, but we have a long way to go yet, and I've seen trials turn around out of nowhere before."

"How are you holding up, Alex?" Ted asked kindly. "Must be hard for you to listen to all that bollocks when we were there and know what happened. I *saw* you bleeding all over Tyler's fancy white sofa."

"I'm okay." Alex gave a strained smile.

Josiah was worried about him, they all were. His friends and family knew what he'd been through to get this far, and the mental health struggles he'd battled. He stood to lose far more than the rest of them if Tyler was found not guilty. The pressure had to be almost intolerable, but Alex was fulfilling his vow to Solange, and Josiah knew that was sustaining him right now.

Mick gave evidence next. Even dressed up in his best suit, he still looked shabby. Both he and Ted were such unsophisticated witnesses compared to Martin Bagshaw and Fake Solange.

Byrne took him through the events of that night, which he described in much the same way as Ted had. Then HMS stepped up. Josiah was coming to loathe the way the man sallied forth like a ship in full sail, awash with smug righteousness.

"Mr Reynolds, you worked for Mr Tyler as a security guard for many years."

"Yeah, I did." Despite his size, Mick looked diminished on the witness stand, cutting a forlorn, pathetic figure. He was clearly overawed by the proceedings and utterly out of his depth.

"What were your duties?"

"I guarded his property."

"By which you mean?"

"His houses and stuff but also people. Well, mainly Alex... Mr Lytton. None of the rest of his indies needed it, really."

"Well, Mr Lytton was expensive," HMS said. "He was a well-known public figure owing to the success of his brother and his father's business endeavours. He also attracted a considerable amount of notoriety owing to his role in the AV crash that killed his mother and maimed his brother."

Josiah noticed how often HMS reminded the jury of the crash.

"It's not unreasonable that Mr Tyler might have wanted dedicated security for such a person, for his own safety, is it?"

"Well, no," Mick answered, taken aback. "But that's not really what we was doing. I mean, we weren't protecting him against people trying to hurt him. We was there to stop him escaping."

"Was Mr Tyler a good houder to you?"

"He was okay." Mick shrugged.

"Come now. After you left his service, he entered you into his IS Leavers' Scheme. You were given money and helped to find decent accommodation. In fact, that continued until very recently, didn't it?"

"Yeah, but that was to pay for me staying quiet about what went on that night with Solange."

"There are hundreds of ex-indentured servants in Mr Tyler's leavers' scheme. Were they *all* there that night? It must have been very crowded in that room." HMS bounced up and down on his heels, looking very pleased with his joke. A few members of the jury smiled.

"I dunno about anyone else. I dunno about any leavers' scheme, either."

"Well, it's an officially registered scheme. There is detailed paperwork, which we've submitted to the court, and which the jury can examine later." HMS smiled at the jury, then turned back to Mick. "The truth is, Mr Reynolds, that until recently Mr Tyler was very generous towards you, more than was required by the terms of your contract. In fact, he only stopped payments to you when you were convicted of illegal trading. Under the terms of the scheme, anyone acquiring a criminal record is automatically expelled."

Mick's face went bright red and he glanced furtively around the court. "It was only some fags and booze," he muttered. "Black market stuff. Everyone does it."

"And crocodile tears. You were dealing in drugs too. In addition, you have several criminal convictions for drunk and disorderly behaviour."

Byrne objected, but the judge allowed it, saying Mick's reliability as a witness was pertinent to the case. Josiah sighed. He'd always known it was risky putting Mick on the stand.

"I put it to you that you were angry that Mr Tyler cut off the small stipend he was paying you, and that is why you agreed to testify against him. It was revenge, pure and simple, towards a man who'd been nothing but generous to you."

"Nah," Mick growled. "That's a fucking lie."

The judge intervened to remind him that he was in a court of law, while HMS glanced at the jury with a raised eyebrow as if to say, "See what kind of man this is?" Josiah was confident the jury were going to happily discount Mick's testimony.

Each night, he and Alex drove home in glum silence, ate sparsely from Alex's stash of pre-prepared meals, then sat on the sofa for a couple of hours watching mindless shows before crawling off to bed. They barely spoke. Did Alex blame him for not putting together a better case? He blamed himself; if only he'd found the blackmail footage, or convinced Rebecca Lang to speak out.

The press made lurid headlines out of their misery every single day, and now Josiah forced himself to listen to *News-Spec* as a kind of torture, hearing his and Alex's names dragged through the mud by every caller. Nobody believed their version of events. It all seemed so improbable, so far-fetched.

Mel was called to the stand to go through the DNA evidence. She was as professional as always, managing to make the dry nature of the subject easy for the jury to understand.

"In my professional opinion, the victim was killed by a blow to the head," she said.

"Is it hard to extract DNA from a body that's been underwater for a long time?" Byrne asked.

"Hard, yes, but not impossible. This is a field that has gone through rapid advances since the Rising."

"Have you any way of knowing how long that body was in the water?" HMS asked. "Could it be a very old skeleton? Perhaps dating back to the Rising or even before?"

"Unlikely. I mean, it's hard enough extracting DNA from a corpse that's been underwater for seven years, so seventy is even harder. You might get partial mitochondrial DNA suitable for maternal lineage identification, but a full nuclear DNA profile for individual identification would be much less likely. The fact we were able to get a full DNA profile indicates the body hasn't been underwater longer than, probably, a decade, at most."

HMS asked her another question, but Josiah missed it because his holopad vibrated. He glanced at it to find it was Reed. He knew it had to be important for Reed to call him during a trial, so he slipped out into the hallway to answer it.

"You need to come back to the office right now," Reed said urgently. "There's a man here who says he has important information about Tyler, but he'll only speak to you."

When Josiah strode into the SID a little while later, he found Reed talking to a tall, dignified-looking man in his early forties, with a completely bald head and skin like burnished mahogany.

"Who's this?" Josiah asked as he strode up.

"Jabir Aldaba. He's the major-domo of Tyler's hacienda in Spain."

"Oh, really?" Josiah felt his heart skip a beat. He'd had no luck with any of his Spanish investigations, so this was something of a development. He stepped forward and shook the man's hand. "I'm Josiah Raine, the chief investigator on the Tyler case."

"Yes, of course. I recognise you from the news, sir." Jabir bowed his head nervously.

"What can we do for you, Mr Aldaba?"

"I wasn't sure what to do." Aldaba spoke perfect English. "Mr Tyler has been good to me, but I couldn't remain silent any longer. May God forgive me if I do him wrong."

"You have information for us?" Josiah asked, hoping against hope that he did.

"No." Josiah's heart sank. "I have something else." Aldaba lifted a large rucksack and spilled its contents onto Reed's desk. "Many months ago, Mr Tyler came to the hacienda in a hurry and deposited these in his safe under the cover of night, and the next day he left, also in a hurry. I cannot say what is on them, but..."

Reed gave a low whistle. In front of them were hundreds of nanodrives, neatly arranged in little boxes. Reed and Josiah exchanged glances. Was this the blackmail footage?

Aldaba looked troubled. "I know I will lose my job for bringing them here. I have wrestled with my conscience ever since I found out about the charges against my employer. As I said, he has always been good to me. But, despite that, I do not believe he is a good man."

"What makes you say that?" Josiah asked, while Reed grabbed one of the drives and inserted it into his screen.

"The way he treated that poor young man." Aldaba shook his head. "I saw the bruises on him, and I know how he came by them, but he never once complained. He never said a bad word against Mr Tyler. I hope I'm doing the right thing."

"You are," Josiah told him firmly. He turned to Reed. "Cam – anything?"

Reed shook his head. "It's heavily encrypted. It might take weeks to crack, if that's even possible. Given what we believe is on them, Tyler would hardly make it easy, would he?"

Josiah put his hands on Reed's shoulders and gave a firm squeeze. "You're the best, Cameron Reed, and I *know* you'll crack that encryption and get access to whatever's on those drives. That's why we pay you the big bucks."

"Those bucks aren't nearly as big as they could be," Reed grumbled, but he was already engrossed in his work, his fingers flying across the keyboard as he tried to gain access to the encrypted files.

Josiah turned back to Aldaba. "Thank you for doing this."

"It might be nothing, I don't know, but I do know from reading about this trial that we are being asked to choose between Mr Tyler's and Mr Alexander's version of events. It seems that most people believe Mr Tyler, so I had to ask myself, having spent a little time with both men, which one would I believe?"

"And?" Josiah asked.

Aldaba sighed. "Mr Alexander haunted the hacienda then, and he haunts me still. I wish I could have been more of a friend to him." He took Josiah's hand, as if seeking absolution. "I hope that now, by doing this, I am finally righting a terrible wrong."

Chapter Fourteen
APRIL 2092
Alex

"Those clothes won't do at all," Elliot chided as they entered his home in Crystal Palace. "You'll be freezing in them. And we have a lunch reservation at Marmaduke's for 1.30. Oh, I know what! You can wear Christopher's clothes. You're about the same size."

He took Alex's arm and hurried him up the stairs in a frenzy of excited activity. "You'll sleep in here. This is where Chris kept his wardrobe. He was such a vain tart that he needed a whole room for all his stuff." Elliot gave a delighted grin. "Here!" He flung open one of the four closets in the room and plucked out a pair of sparkly maroon LaRay trousers, a slinky green luminet shirt, and a cerise bubble-print scarf. "Oh, yes. This was one of Christopher's favourite ensembles. You'll make all those lecherous old queens at Marmaduke's salivate in this. Hurry up. I'll see you downstairs in five minutes."

The clothes were far too neo-glam in style for Alex's taste, but it hardly mattered. Christopher had clearly been a certain kind of man because the trousers fitted *very* snugly, while the shirt seemed to be missing any buttons at all above the belly button. The scarf was noisy and frankly clashed, but Alex didn't care. He'd worn far worse. He was struggling to get his head around the sudden change in his circumstances, not to mention make sense of it, but there was no time to think because, as he was about to find out, life with Elliot was a constant whirlwind.

"Oh, yes," Elliot breathed as he walked down the stairs. "Oh, darling! Don't you look a picture? I'd get my holocams out right now if it wasn't for lunch. Never mind, we'll get straight down to that tomorrow. Come on now, Chris. You always keep me waiting while you tart yourself up."

Humming to himself, he bounced excitedly as he grabbed Alex's arm and pulled him back outside to the duck. Alex noticed the black SUAV was still there – did Elliot know?

Marmaduke's was one of those snooty eateries where the staff seemed to feel that serving people was beneath them. Elliot made a huge entrance, loudly declaring his name and complaining about the terrible parking situation.

"Crystal Palace is the best place to live but the traffic is hideous these days. My usual table, please." He didn't wait to be shown to the table, waltzing over and plonking himself down by the window. "Come on, Chris, it's not like you to be shy," he called.

Alex wondered if he even knew he was calling him Chris and referring to his personality as if it was the same as that of his dead husband. Elliot talked such a lot that it was entirely possible he didn't know what he was doing. He was a strange person – sweet but capricious, prone to sudden outbursts that quickly blew over. He wasn't tricky like Tyler, though, and Alex started to relax. Whatever was happening, he should appreciate it as the respite it was.

Marmaduke's seemed to be a hub for local gay men as it was packed with them, and Elliot wasted no time in showing off his new acquisition. He held court as if he were a king, waving to friends and acquaintances while fawning over Alex so everyone could see he was with a beautiful young man. It was harmless, and Elliot had an easy-going charm that made him impossible to dislike.

"He's my new muse. I mean, of course he is. Look at him! Such divine beauty. He'll inspire me to produce works the world will swoon over." Hyperbole, it seemed, was Elliot's dish of the day.

After lunch, he whisked Alex off to an exclusive men's boutique and sipped champagne while he selected various outfits for Alex to try on.

"Just the basics for now," he announced. "Things for you to be seen on my arm in. You can wear Christopher's clothes, too, but I want some outfits tailored precisely for you, my darling. Those trousers are a little *too* tight, fetching though they are, and a little too long on the leg as well."

Alex was surprised that he'd noticed.

"Oh, I'm all about the details," Elliot exclaimed. "I have an eye for these things. I'm a creative. When we've sorted out your everyday, we'll come back another time and find you some fabulous fantasy costumes."

Alex tensed, wondering what, precisely, that meant.

Elliot frowned and stroked his arm gently. "For the holocam, my love. We want to create moods and drama and themes, and—Oh! This will be such fun, trust me."

Later, clutching several bags, they arrived back at Elliot's house. Alex noticed the black SUAV had trailed them throughout but had made no move to intervene at any stage.

"Run upstairs and put your new clothes away, darling," Elliot instructed. "No! Wait." He pulled Alex back and wrapped his arms around his waist. "Don't you have something to say to me for buying you all these lovely things?"

"Um… thank you?" Alex offered.

Elliot pouted, and Alex realised something more was required. He leaned forward and pressed a little kiss to the older man's cheek.

"Oh! That's better. Dear, sweet boy." Elliot pulled him in for a more thorough kiss, then released him with a pat to his bottom. "Go on. Run along. And change into the gorgeous green velvet suit with the purple shirt. We're going out tonight."

Out? They'd only just got in. After the peace and quiet of Spain, it was all rather too much for Alex. He walked slowly up the stairs, his head pounding. He could hear Gideon giving him a pep-talk. *"He's your houder and you're his servant. You'll give him exactly what he wants."*

Unbidden, his song entered his head for the first time in months and worked its old magic, calming him. When he reached the privacy of his bedroom, he hurriedly put the clothes away and then spent ten minutes performing a sun salutation. The familiar actions, combined with his song, restored him even more, and he was able to dress himself in the ludicrous green velvet suit and purple shirt combo before returning downstairs, ready for whatever Elliot had planned.

He could have spent longer on his yoga because Elliot didn't emerge for another hour. Alex spent the time wandering around the lounge. Elliot had several beautiful pieces of furniture that he admired: a Japanese lacquered cabinet and a stunning cream-coloured sofa by a modern designer whose work he was familiar with. There were vases of flowers everywhere, dominated by Asiatic lilies that gave off a heady scent.

It was hard to ignore the lightboxes on the walls showcasing Elliot's holopics. He appeared to have updated his collection since his last visit, and Alex noticed that he'd improved. There was no denying that Elliot had an exceptional eye; he was right about his meticulous attention to detail.

He paused, startled, in front of a picture of himself. It was nothing special. In fact, compared to some of Elliot's works, it was positively dull. In it, he was gazing into the holocam, unblinking. It was the first holopic Elliot had made of him, telling him to relax, that it was just a test pic. But clearly he'd liked it enough to keep it. He wondered why, as it was such a relatively uninteresting picture, but as he studied it, he understood. It was the mask. He'd felt self-conscious, so he'd sung his song in his head to make himself feel better, and Elliot had taken the photo just as the mask had fallen into place. Alex gazed at himself, fascinated by his expression. He'd seen it in the mirror, but it was so much more interesting gazing back at him from a hologram.

"Beautiful, isn't it?" a voice behind him murmured; Elliot had appeared. He wrapped his arms around Alex's waist and rested his chin on his shoulder. "The holocam loves you, darling."

"It was the first holopic you took of me. I thought it was just a test."

"It was supposed to be, but then I saw the ineffable mystery that is you, my dear heart, and I knew I had to fully render it and have it in my house. There will be many more such pictures now that you're mine." His lips trailed up the side of Alex's face, kissing him repeatedly.

Alex did his best to hold still as the picture in front of him watched, unblinking. Elliot sighed and pulled away.

"You'll warm up," he said.

"Sorry," Alex whispered. "Just... it's been a long day."

"Yes, of course. You'll soon feel better when I tell you where we're going."

Alex managed to raise a polite eyebrow, although all he wanted was to lie down and rest.

"It's the premiere of Hudson Brink's new movie," Elliot exclaimed delightedly. "And my date is even more beautiful than Hud himself."

It was startling to be whisked out of the quiet, insular sanctuary of the hacienda to attend, of all things, a movie premiere. Alex felt as if he was in a dream as Elliot led him down the red carpet, beaming and waving as if *he* was the star, not Hudson Brink. He fell asleep during the film, which was quite a feat as it was a noisy holomovie with the action swirling all around and constant explosions.

Later, Elliot took him to the after-show party, and Hud greeted his new houder like the old friend he presumably was.

"Ell! How are ya doing?" Hudson Brink had a relaxed American drawl and was so impossibly handsome close up, with sparkling green eyes and blindingly white teeth, that even Alex was dazzled by him. He stood to one side, saying nothing as Elliot and Hud caught up. Hud glanced at him once or twice but didn't speak to him.

"Are you in the UK for long? Can we go clubbing?" Elliot asked.

"No can do. I'm on a worldwide press junket for the next few months for this heap of shit." Hud put two fingers up at the holoposter of the film Alex had just slept through.

"When are you back in the UK? I'll hold one of my parties and you can be guest of honour." Elliot clapped his hands together in excitement.

"Well, if I'm free, sure." Hud gave a slow, non-committal grin, and then, with a last glance at Alex, he moved away.

In the duck on the way home, Elliot chatted away about everything and nothing, but Alex felt himself growing increasingly tense. He knew

Elliot wanted to sleep with him – he'd made that plain from the minute he'd first met him. Alex would go to his bed – he had no choice – but it had been some time since his cock had worked, and he doubted it would tonight. Not without the blue pills, and he hadn't had any of those for a long time.

He was feeling more and more anxious as they neared Elliot's house. What would Elliot do if he couldn't perform? Would he send him back to Tyler? Alex had resigned himself to dying by Tyler's hand, and he couldn't cope with the mental gymnastics of the past twenty-four hours. His head ached, and he dreaded what would happen when they reached the house.

He became quieter and more withdrawn with each passing minute, not that Elliot seemed to notice, as he talked enough for them both. Finally, they reached the house, and Alex walked wearily inside, a couple of steps behind his new houder.

"He wouldn't have a career at all without me, so he bloody well *should* come to my party," Elliot carped, still complaining about Hudson Brink's lack of enthusiasm for his invitation.

Alex came to a stop at the foot of the stairs and gazed up them, longing for the quietness and serenity of a bed of his own, without company.

"Everyone loves my parties. We dress up. And…" Elliot lowered his voice theatrically, although they were quite alone. "I have access to some of the finest party drugs in all of New London."

Alex barely heard him. He just stood there, unable to move.

"You like croc, don't you? Well, I have croc. Lots of it." Elliot moved his arm, and Alex, reacting purely on instinct, flinched. Elliot suddenly stopped talking.

"Oh, my dear boy. You really have been through the mill, haven't you?" Elliot said softly. "I'm sorry. There's me rabbiting on, but I have noticed how out of sorts you are. You slept all through Hud's movie, although it was unbelievably tedious, so I'm not surprised. I was just going to brush that lock of hair away from your face. There." He gently raised his fingers and smoothed Alex's hair out of his eyes. Then he took Alex's face in his hands, gazing at him sadly.

"Our friend George has been unspeakably vile to you, hasn't he, sweetheart? Did he beat you? I think he did, and that's a crime against beauty. To hurt such an angel. To lay one single finger on someone this heartbreakingly beautiful." He pressed a gentle kiss to Alex's lips.

"*I* will never hit you, my darling, rest assured about that. You will be safe here, with me."

"Thank you," Alex whispered. "I'm just very tired."

"Of course you are. Have I been ever so selfish showing you off today the way I did? I just couldn't wait for people to see you. I can see how it might all have been a bit too much, so run along upstairs to bed, my sweet. Tomorrow is a new day."

Alex was relieved that nothing more would be required of him tonight. He walked slowly to his bedroom and lay down on the bed the minute he reached it, unable to even remove his clothes. He needed time and space to process the complete change in his circumstances, and it seemed that Elliot was going to give him that – for now, at least.

For the next few days, Elliot was kind and solicitous. He took out his holocams and set up numerous shots of Alex, but they went nowhere and saw nobody. It was a relief after the whirlwind of that first day, and Alex was grateful for it. He was, therefore, taken by surprise at the end of the week, when he was sitting in the dining room eating breakfast with Elliot, by the sound of the front door opening. He looked up, startled.

"Don't worry, my love. It's just the housekeeper. Chantal. In here, my dear." He turned back to Alex. "She's been with me for years and adores me. I gave her some time off to settle you in, but she usually comes most days at ten-thirty. She's terribly sweet – French, you know. Had a beastly time of it over there. All those awful wars. She's ever so grateful to be here in the land of peace and plenty."

Alex never found out if that was the case because Chantal rarely spoke. She was a tiny bird of a woman but very efficient at her job, which was a good thing because Elliot was a messy man who left piles of detritus in any room he was in.

Elliot introduced them, and Chantal glanced at Alex's ID tag with some curiosity, then back at Elliot sadly. She must have known dead Christopher with the terrible taste in clothes. She never said as much, but Alex had the feeling she disapproved of him. It was as if she thought he was using Elliot, taking advantage of his grief over his dead husband to inveigle himself into his life, even though none of this had been his doing.

When Elliot was working, he was tireless in pursuit of precisely the shots he wanted. He arranged Alex in numerous positions, had him make faces, walk forwards, backwards, sideways, bend over, smile and pout for hours on end. It was so tedious that Alex wondered how professional models could bear it. How was this considered glamorous? Still, it didn't require anything of him except to be Elliot's animated marionette, simply doing whatever Elliot asked, without the need for any input from himself, and it was better – by far – than the alternative.

Then, suddenly, everything changed. Elliot stopped working, and for the next couple of weeks it was one party, club, and social event after another, a merry-go-round of fancy restaurants and non-stop revelling that would have exhausted most men half Elliot's age.

Alex soon came to understand that this was Elliot's lifestyle. He cocooned himself while working, emerged to throw himself into a wild bout of partying, and then returned to his work.

One morning, a few weeks after his arrival, Elliot sat him down and spoke to him in a firm, direct way.

"Darling, I know you've been through hell, but you weren't cheap, and I want my money's worth. Now, listen. You know I sometimes call you Christopher, and you, frankly, could do with a completely fresh start. So, I've been thinking. Why don't I change your name to Christopher Dacre on the IS agency database? You see, my love, it's not enough for you to be as beautiful and obedient as you are, and, lord love you, you really are so good and do everything I ask. But modelling requires a tad more effort than that. I need you to engage with the work, my pretty. So, why don't you become Christopher? You can be my muse and forget you were ever sad old Alex, who beastly George was so mean to. What do you say? It'll be a nice new beginning for us both."

Alex gazed at him, wondering if he should be surprised, but then realised he wasn't. Elliot was a profoundly silly man and all too likely to believe that a name change would be enough to alter someone's entire personality and outlook on life.

Yet, he was curiously drawn to the idea. Christopher was a role he could play, a persona he could draw on, an extension of his mask. He already knew who Christopher had been because Elliot had made that entirely clear. He was a flamboyant airhead of a man, interested in clothes, parties, drugs, and sex. In short, the perfect partner for Elliot Dacre.

"Okay," he found himself saying.

"Oh, good." Elliot clapped his hands. "I'll send off the paperwork today, *Christopher*. Now, as to other, ahem, matters, it's really time for some fun, isn't it? Chris was always up for some fun. You know what I mean, darling. I've been terribly patient, but you're making me wait ever such a long time."

Alex smiled and got down on his knees in front of Elliot. Then he pushed open his houder's legs, opened his trousers, and gave him one of his best blow jobs, with Elliot's hand tangled in his hair the entire time as he squealed, "Oh, yes, *please*," over and over again.

That night, for the first time, Elliot asked Alex to stay over in his bedroom. He acted shy and coy, but the minute Alex undressed, he let out a sigh of almost orgasmic delight.

"Oh, my sweet, look how gorgeous you are. I'd run for my holocam, but we can save that for another time. Come here, my lovely, and let me touch you."

Alex slipped into bed with him and did his best to show him a good time. Later, Elliot sighed and held him close, kissing his cheek every so often.

"Such a lovely boy. So kind and beautiful. My lovely Chris," he whispered. "It's wonderful to have you back, my darling."

Did he really think Alex was his husband, returned to him? Alex suspected not. He was sure Elliot knew it was a fantasy, but he didn't want anything to puncture the illusion he'd created. Well, there were worse things than being a rich old fool's plaything, he supposed.

The following morning, he woke to find Elliot creeping out of bed.

"*No!* Don't look at me," he screeched. "You must close your eyes." Alex did as he was told, mystified.

"Now you can open them," Elliot declared a few seconds later. Alex looked at him, bemused. What had that been about?

"It's just..." Elliot slipped back into bed beside him, patting his hair. "It might shock you to know this, but I wear a little hairpiece, sweetie, and it slipped off in the night. I had to adjust it before you looked at me, in case you found me utterly hideous, like that wretched creature in *Beauty and the Beast*."

Alex couldn't help laughing, mostly because he was amused that Elliot seemed to think his toupee fooled anyone. Elliot joined in his laughter, and they cuddled in bed together for the next hour, chatting and giggling. It was nice, Alex thought. He could get used to this.

He decided to treat being Christopher like he'd treated those dossiers of Tyler's. This was his job, and even if it wasn't what he'd have chosen, he might as well try to perform it to the best of his ability. So, he spent some time in his bedroom dressing in Chris's clothes, trying to get a feel for the man Elliot wanted him to be. In some respects, Elliot hadn't been wrong. It was much more appealing to be Chris than it was to be Alex, with all his history.

He'd been with his new houder a couple of months when Elliot threw his first big party. He hadn't been lying about the costumes. The house looked like a film set, with cowboys, bishops, aliens, and an assortment of historical figures and famous movie characters all jostling side by side.

Alex was barely dressed at all, in a tiny white loincloth and a wig made entirely of blond ringlets, and carrying a little bow and arrow.

"You're my beautiful Cupid," Elliot said, adjusting the costume he'd picked out for Alex excitedly.

Elliot himself was wearing a tight red rubber outfit with horns that stretched over his paunch in a way that was unflattering, and yet somehow he could pull it off. "And I'm the devil!" He laughed, chasing a giggling Alex around the lounge.

"I have a job for you, Chris," Elliot announced as the party took off. "Offer our guests some happiness dust, will you?" He gestured to four bowls neatly arranged on little trays. "Croc, sable, cocaine, and ecstasy," he said, pointing at each in turn. "Which is your poison of choice, my lovely Cupid?"

Croc. Alex hadn't had any in years, but now he found he yearned for it again.

Elliot saw the look in his eyes and laughed. "Here you go, my sweet," he said, handing him the bowl of croc. "You go first. I'm sure you'll look beautiful on your knees with tears falling down your face."

Before too long, that was precisely where Alex was. As Christopher, he danced around the party, handing out the 'happiness dust', feeling himself drift away on a mellow haze of croc. It felt so good to be high again.

Soon, the tears were flowing and he was whirling around the room, making everyone smile at his antics. He wasn't Alex anymore, and it was such a relief. He was Chris the party boy, showing all their guests a great time.

Eventually, he was on his knees, as Elliot had predicted, sucking Elliot off, while all around a bunch of people were engaged in similar acts with each other.

Alex soon came to realise that all Elliot's parties descended into orgies at some point. That was why his guests enjoyed them so much. The drugs and alcohol flowed freely, and Elliot and Chris created the kind of atmosphere in which everyone had a good time.

A few days later, the partying stopped and the holocams came out again. This time, Alex knew what was required of him. Elliot didn't want him to just do as he was told, he wanted him to perform for the holocam.

Alex wasn't much of a performer, but Chris, loosened by partying and drugs, had no problem. He strutted and simpered, laughed and splayed, and soon came to understand that there was an art to modelling.

He started asking Elliot questions about the equipment. He'd always loved that point where art and technology met, and the more he understood holotech, the more he was able to give Elliot precisely what he wanted for his shots.

They developed a shorthand and would often lie snuggled up together in bed, talking about what the next shoot should be. Elliot had a good creative imagination, and Alex was able to riff off him in a way that was satisfying to them both.

Soon, Elliot's work hit new heights. He was being shown at trendy galleries, parading Alex on his arm, and his artworks were all over social media. He was, quite simply, becoming a sensation, and it was in no small part due to Alex.

They went to costume fittings, pored over designs for sets, and scouted out unusual locations together. Alex pitched ideas, and Elliot ran with them. They created all kinds of scenarios, including one involving a friend's tame raven and a ruined castle that was so over the top it always made Alex laugh whenever he looked at it.

It was creative and exciting, and one day, Alex realised that a year had passed since he'd left Spain. He thought maybe he'd needed Elliot to drag him back into the land of the living. He'd been in such a bad place in Spain, so mentally fractured, but Elliot had forced him to engage with the world again… or at least, not him but his avatar, Christopher.

He liked being Chris. He didn't come with Alex's baggage; he wasn't trying to seek justice for his murdered friend, or come to terms with a shattered life. His world revolved around parties, drugs, sex, photoshoots, and nothing else. He was simply too busy to be Alex.

If he was completely in character, he could even bring himself to not notice the black SUAV that was always parked outside, and that followed them whenever they left the house.

That first year passed in a haze. The drugs helped, and somewhere along the way, Alex's libido returned. He didn't exactly fancy Elliot, but he did enjoy the way his houder squealed with pleasure in bed. He wasn't a hard person to please, and Alex had always liked pleasing his sex partners.

Elliot loved showing off his beloved Chris at parties; he wanted other men to desire him, but then he'd move in and make it clear that Alex belonged to him and him alone.

Alex soon came to understand that this was part of the Chris persona. He was to flirt with other men, even kiss them. Elliot would see them and come charging over, and massive drama would ensue that always ended in passionate sex. That pressed all Elliot's buttons, so Alex engineered these scenarios at every party.

Hudson Brink did finally come to one of Elliot's parties. He showed up with an entourage of hangers-on and stood there, like the big "I am", clearly enjoying the way everyone fawned over him.

Alex knew he was the ideal person to fulfil Elliot's jealous-lover fantasy, so he danced over to Hud with the bowls of drugs, dressed as skimpily as ever, as a Roman slave in a teeny-tiny tunic.

Hud grinned as he took a pinch of sable. "You're the kid who came to my premiere, ain't'cha?" He took a sniff of the drug, then leaned back, looking Alex up and down lasciviously.

"Yeah."

"Gawd, you're pretty, and those lips… now, they're what I'd call 'cock-sucking lips'." He grinned.

"Oh, they are." Alex laughed, taking a big sniff of croc and waiting for the high to hit.

Hud reached out a lazy hand and grabbed Alex's wrist. He was a big man, with hard, solid muscles, and Alex was reminded, suddenly and inexplicably, of Joe. He squashed that memory down. He was Chris, and Chris didn't know or care about Josiah fucking Raine.

"Who are you supposed to be, then?" Hud drawled, looking at his costume.

"Spartacus, I think. A Roman slave, anyway."

"Oh, yeah, I see it now. Hmm." Hud licked his lips. He was dressed like a cowboy, in leather chaps and a plaid shirt, and he was hot as hell.

"Well, if you're a slave, you should put out for me, yeah?" Hud pulled him in close, wrapped his arms around him, and kissed him hard.

On cue, Elliot rushed over as Alex wriggled in Hud's arms.

"Oh, Elliot." Alex was actually relieved. Hud's grasp on him was uncomfortably tight and he had a mean look in his eyes.

"This little slut was flirting with me. Would you like to see me fuck him?" Hud asked, grinning at Elliot.

Elliot stood there, frozen to the spot, and Alex realised suddenly that this game had a darker element than he'd appreciated. The lust was evident in Elliot's eyes; oh yes, he *would* like to watch, thank you very much. A handsome stud like Hud, with a beautiful young man like Alex? Who wouldn't? He could see all these thoughts flit across Elliot's face.

"Elliot!" he protested, realising he'd lost control of the situation.

Elliot smiled at him a little sadly, then put his finger over Alex's lips. "I've loved having you all to myself, sweetie-pie, but really, isn't it nice to share?" he murmured.

"I thought you'd say that," Hud chuckled.

It was a warm summer's evening, and they were outside in Elliot's spacious garden, with dozens of people all around.

Hud suddenly tipped Alex over the back of a nearby garden sofa, flipped his little tunic up, and ripped his briefs down. It all happened so fast that it took Alex completely by surprise. Then Hud's big hands spread his arse cheeks and he rammed his cock straight into him.

There was no preparation and no warning. Alex let out a hoarse scream, but Hud just laughed and clamped a big hand over Alex's mouth, holding him in place while he skewered him like a piece of meat.

A little group of men saw what was happening and moved over, silently, like a troupe of ghouls, their mouths open and their eyes hungry. They formed a little circle around Hud and Alex, their hands working furiously in their underwear as they watched.

The croc suddenly kicked in and the tears began to fall down Alex's face as Hud pumped into him over the back of the sofa. It hurt, but what hurt most was seeing Elliot's face, his eyes dark with arousal, his hand wrapped firmly around his cock as he enjoyed the show.

The next day, at breakfast, there was a wrapped gift sitting on Alex's plate.

"What's this?" he asked, sitting down gingerly.

"It's for you. A little present for being so wonderful last night. What a little treasure you are."

Alex picked up the gift, wondering if Elliot felt a tinge of remorse for what had happened. It was wrapped in tasteful navy-blue paper and tied with a big sky-blue bow. Alex slid his finger under the wrapping and opened it to find a picture he was all too familiar with. It was a still version of *Halo of Fire*, featuring Hudson Brink standing in a ring of flames, looking like a burnished Greek god.

"Oh," he whispered, and suddenly he was back in that flat he'd shared with Neil at university.

"I thought you'd like it as a memento of the night you snared the biggest movie star in the world." Elliot sat back, looking smug.

"I'm not sure I snared him so much as he speared me," Alex murmured, gazing at the photo. God, how he hated it. Firstly, because it reminded him of Neil, and now, because it reminded him of Hudson Brink, who was a shitty human being, even if he *was* hot.

"I know you prefer not to have light boxes in your room, so I dug out this old still version that I keep in my study. I thought how perfect it would be for you. After breakfast, I'll help you hang it over your bed."

Alex knew it wasn't meant as an apology. Elliot really *did* think he had enjoyed Hud's attentions, and he was full of himself for providing him with what he was sure was the perfect gift. Maybe Chris would have loved it. Elliot always assumed that Alex felt the same way about everything as his dead husband. Maybe Chris would have been thrilled to be Hud's plaything at a party.

The encounter with Hud changed their dynamic, opening up a floodgate. Now, Elliot wanted to watch Alex being fucked at all his parties, and sometimes just when mingling over dinner and drinks with his coterie of gay friends, and that became their new normal.

For some reason it turned him on to see Alex being bent over and fucked by another man. As a precaution, Alex made sure to carry lube with him at all times, leaving tubes of the stuff in all his pockets.

"I was thinking," Elliot said one day over breakfast, while Alex was between his legs delivering his usual morning blow job, "why don't I take you to an indie show?"

An indie show? Alex looked up at him. What the hell was that? Elliot gave a delighted laugh and directed Alex's head back down to his cock. "Don't stop, Chris."

Alex redoubled his efforts, while Elliot explained, "An indie show is where you can take your beautiful servant and swap him for someone else's beautiful servant." Elliot beamed. "Doesn't that sound exciting?"

Alex was glad his mouth was full, saving him from having to reply, because it didn't sound remotely exciting.

It wasn't. Their first show was in a hotel in St Albans, far away from anyone Elliot knew. He wanted it to feel illicit and forbidden, because that aroused him. He knew he shouldn't be prostituting Alex, but the idea of swapping him for another boy was too thrilling.

Alex gazed out of the window as they drove there, watching the ever-present black SUAV trailing behind them. He never mentioned it to Elliot, but he must have noticed. Did he know why it was there?

"You'll enjoy this," Elliot declared, smiling at Alex as he drove. "I'm aware that I'm much older than you. This will be exciting for a young slut like you. A chance for you to sleep with other men without little old me around, cramping your style. I don't like to think of you missing out."

Alex suppressed a smile. Elliot's self-delusion knew no bounds. He wasn't doing this for Alex but for himself. *He* was the one who wanted an endless stream of beautiful young men to sleep with. He'd had Alex many times and he was bored. He wanted someone new and exciting. Elliot's leg jiggled up and down as he drove, exuding a fractious, nervy sense of anticipation.

"Did you do stuff like this with Chris?" Alex asked, hoping to jolt Elliot out of his edgy, aroused mood.

His cheek suddenly stung and he put up a hand to where Elliot had slapped him.

"You *are* Chris," Elliot snapped.

Alex nursed his cheek, wondering if Elliot even remembered what he'd said the first night he'd arrived. *I will never hit you, my darling.* So much for that.

Elliot glanced sideways at him, looking embarrassed by his outburst. "I'm sorry, my love. Don't be angry with me. I just want you to be Chris, that's all. Is that too much to ask?" He pursed his lips into a huge, exaggerated pout.

Alex wasn't angry with him. It was hard to ever be angry with Elliot because he was such a child, and a grieving one at that. He'd slapped Alex because he was having a tantrum. It was as if he thought that if he called Alex by his dead husband's name, dressed him in his clothes, and did the kinds of activities they'd once done together, Alex would magically become Chris.

The hotel was small, damp, and ugly. The whole event shrieked of a certain kind of sleazy seediness. The bar area, next to a dismal, decaying ballroom left over from a different age, was where the show was being held.

Alex was given a band with the number twenty-three to attach to his arm and sent off to a room where a number of other indies were hanging around, waiting for it to kick off. This was an exclusively gay event, and only men were present.

After about an hour, during which they were served enough drink to encourage a party atmosphere, the door swung open, and they were called to strut out onto the stage at one end of the ballroom. The event was packed with men staring intently as the indies were paraded around. It was all Alex could do not to laugh. This was like one of those old-fashioned beauty pageants but with far more sleaze.

The indies, by and large, were young and attractive, the men watching not so much. They skewed older, which made sense. Alex wondered how many of the young indies were Quarterlands kids, selling themselves like Solange and Ted, desperate to get out of the slums and live a decent life on dry land. If this was what it took, they'd do it. Many would view it as better than working all hours in a factory or in construction, and definitely better than a government work camp, where conditions were notoriously squalid.

"Number three," the compere called. "A lovely young indie whose skills are making his houder dinner and having a very talented mouth. At least, that's what it says here!" The compere laughed, reading off a card in his hand. Number three sashayed happily around the stage, clearly enjoying the catcalls and whistles that came his way.

This was a furtive, underground event, and that seemed to only add to the febrile atmosphere. As the evening wore on and the drinks flowed freely, the mood of the watching houders turned ugly. They were openly leering, assessing and discussing which of the young men they wanted. No money would change hands. This was skirting dangerously close to the edges of the law but just about staying within it. The houder whose indie received the most votes would have his first pick of the boys on display, and then the one with the second most votes, and so it went on. It was a cattle market. Alex was only surprised nobody checked his teeth or shoved a finger up his arse.

Soon, it would be his turn. How would Chris behave? he wondered. It would be easier if he could be someone else as he paraded around that stage. Chris was a tease who liked showing off his pert bum in tight-fitting trousers. He'd play the crowd and enjoy every minute of being admired. That wasn't Alex, but if the only way to get through this was to play-act being someone else, then so be it.

The boy in front of him grinned and waved as he stepped onto the stage, walked a little way across it, pretended to drop something, then bent over, wiggling his arse at the crowd, who roared their approval. He stood up, cheeks flushed, winked, and carried on. Alex knew he couldn't do that. He didn't have it in him.

Finally, it was his turn. He played it cool and aloof, his mask firmly in place. Nobody looking at him would know if he was loving or hating this. His face was a perfect blank as he walked onto that stage, then paused, turned his head, and slowly let his gaze wander over the watching men, checking them out. An uneasy murmur went up from the crowd. This indie was looking at them the way they were looking at him, and they didn't like it. Finally, with a cold, hard stare, he turned and stalked off the stage. He could have kicked himself as he left. He'd got their attention, when he should have scurried on and off and left no impression at all.

There was an interval while the houders considered their decision, and then they wrote down their first, second, and third choices and put them in sealed envelopes, which were collected and counted up.

While all this was going on, there was some "entertainment" in the form of a couple of male strippers. Elliot pushed his way through the crowd and grabbed Alex excitedly.

"Oh, you were good, Chris," he exclaimed. "They couldn't take their eyes off you. Well done." He planted a smacking great kiss on Alex's cheek.

The votes were counted and the compere took to the stage again.

"Well, this is unusual. One indie received the top vote from every houder here. Step forward, number twenty-three."

Alex felt his cheeks burn and heard Elliot squeal, just like he did when they were having sex. He walked onstage with his houder, and Elliot gushed about how delighted he was.

"Which indie do you choose as your prize?" the compere asked, waggling his eyebrows suggestively.

"Number fifteen," Elliot said immediately, choosing a somewhat shy-looking, red-faced boy with a sweet smile.

"Number fifteen's houder – come and claim *your* prize, you lucky bastard."

Fifteen's houder leapt onto the stage, pulling his indie behind him. His hands went immediately around Alex's waist, positively salivating at the sight of him. He shoved his indie in Elliot's direction, then dragged Alex away without another word.

Alex went with the man to the hotel room he'd been allocated for the night. The arrangement was that you stayed overnight and were reunited with your houder in the hotel cafeteria for breakfast the following morning.

Alex's houder for the night was plain and portly, but beyond demanding vigorous sex for half the night, he made no unusual or unpleasant requests. When it was all over, and the man was finally sated, Alex lay looking at the wall. It wasn't, he supposed, as bad as it had been at Tyler's, but often he'd felt he had the upper hand there, by virtue of all Tyler's clients being vetted, the dossiers that had given him an inkling of what lay ahead, and the constant security presence outside his bedroom door. This, by comparison, was sketchy and dangerous, and he felt more used, like a piece of meat.

"How was it?" Elliot asked eagerly on the drive home the next day. "Did you love it? Wasn't it fantastic? That boy... his arse alone was worth the entry fee. Oh, it was so good."

Alex said nothing. He just gazed into the wing mirror at the black SUAV driving along behind them.

Thereafter, Elliot took him to a show every month. Alex learned how to appear boring onstage, but Elliot always dressed him to best effect, and it was impossible to hide his obvious good looks. He always won the contest for Elliot, who therefore always had his pick of the indies on display.

Months passed in a haze of holophotography, wild parties, drugs, and shows. Alex went along with all of it because what else could he do? He hadn't expected to still be alive after Spain, and yet here he was, somehow living a life of sorts.

One morning, they woke up to a thick fall of snow outside. The sky was dark and ominous, and the nearby lost zone was as grey as iron.

"Let's do a shoot," Alex suggested.

"In this? It's freezing." Elliot shivered theatrically, despite the fact they were tucked up warm indoors.

"But look at the colours." Alex pointed at the sky. "Look at how still everything is, waiting for the snow to fall again."

He could always appeal to Elliot's artistic side, and soon they were outside, dressed up against the elements, trying to find the right place to film. Alex spotted it – an area where the grey of the lost zone seemed to meet the fullness of the snow-filled clouds.

Elliot was taking forever to set up, and even though he was dressed in a heavy black winter coat, Alex was freezing. He could hardly complain; this had been his idea, after all. Usually, living Elliot's high-octane life meant he rarely had time to think about anything, but all of a sudden, standing here in the snow waiting, he did.

What the hell was he doing? Solange lay dead in a lost zone just like the one behind him. He'd vowed to bring her killer to justice, but what had he done? Nothing. He hadn't even attempted to report Tyler. It was as if he'd given up on his mission altogether. What would Ted say? He'd trusted Alex to bring Tyler down. Or Gideon, who had given him all the skills he needed to pass as the perfect servant until his moment came to act. He thought about Joe; he'd pursue Tyler as if his life depended on it, if he was in this situation. But Alex? He felt like Hamlet, endlessly procrastinating, frozen like the scene around him, completely unable to take action.

As he stood there lost in thought, the snow began to fall again, dizzying swirls surrounding him like a shroud. He was silent, still, completely motionless. He felt as if he'd been asleep for years, biding his time, waiting for... what? Was this the life he was settling for, or did he intend to make good on his vow to Solange? He stared sightlessly into space, hating himself. If he'd been sleepwalking for so long, then surely it was time for him to wake up?

At that moment he blinked, startled by that realisation.

"Got it," Elliot called, and he came to.

"I didn't realise you'd started," he murmured.

"You were half asleep, and there was a beautiful stillness to the composition. I got all I needed. Now, let's go back. It's freezing."

Later, when Elliot had run it through all his filters, edited and trimmed it and created a beautiful render, Alex thought it was the most beautiful holopic he'd ever made, but every time he looked at it, he couldn't help thinking of Solange and his mission to seek justice for her.

He'd been asleep for long enough. It was time to wake up.

Chapter Fifteen
OCTOBER 2096
Josiah

While Reed was examining the nanodrives, Josiah took Jabir to the interview suite and recorded his testimony.

"Can you tell me why you brought us these nanodrives?" he asked.

"I regretted that I wasn't able to help Mr Alexander when he lived with us in Spain. It has always weighed on my conscience," Jabir replied.

"Why is that?"

"He was such a lost soul. He was scared to be my friend. I worried for his health. He was tired all the time, and he seemed to have given up."

"Do you know why that was?" Josiah asked.

Jabir hesitated.

"You can talk freely," Josiah prompted.

"I cannot say for sure, but he and Mr Tyler seemed to be in a relationship of sorts."

Josiah stiffened. Tyler had already told him this, but he'd struggled to believe it, and Alex hadn't been forthcoming on the subject.

"A romantic relationship?"

"I believe so. I often saw them kissing and they shared a room."

Josiah felt as if he'd been punched in the gut. "Do you believe they were in love?"

Jabir considered this. "I cannot say. Or, at least... I believe Mr Tyler was. I'm unsure whether that was also true of Mr Alexander. I believe, maybe, this was the source of the conflict between them."

"You heard them arguing?"

"Not exactly. Mr Tyler frequently brought Mr Alexander gifts and took him out on his yacht. He seemed very attentive, but Mr Alexander was quiet and distant with him, as he was with everyone. This seemed to frustrate Mr Tyler."

"How did that frustration manifest?" Josiah asked.

Jabir paused again, then sighed. "I never saw Mr Tyler strike Mr Alexander, but I did see the bruises on him many times. One time, I found him in the courtyard lying on the ground, badly hurt."

"Tyler hurt him?"

Jabir paused again. "Well, I cannot say for sure as I saw nothing, but... who else could it be?"

"Is it possible..." Josiah sought for the kinds of arguments Tyler's defence might use when confronted with this testimony. "Could these injuries have been sustained as part of a sex game?"

Jabir looked shocked. "I don't know. I suppose they could, but... Mr Alexander did not seem to be enjoying it, if that was so. I had the sense of an unequal relationship. I offered Mr Alexander a way to leave, a chance to escape the security guards, but he refused."

"Because he didn't want to, or because he was afraid of what might happen if he did?"

"He said that he didn't want to place me or my family in danger, but that didn't seem likely to me."

It did to Josiah, but then he was aware that Jabir didn't know the whole story. He could see, all too clearly, that Alex's actions were influenced by what had happened to Solange; he was terrified that someone else might get hurt.

He took Jabir's testimony, then made sure the man had a safe place to stay.

"You might be called on to give evidence in the trial," he advised.

Jabir looked strained, but he nodded. "I do not wish Mr Tyler ill," he murmured. "He has always been a kind and generous employer to me and good to my family. It pains me to be here, but I cannot forget poor Mr Alexander. I liked him. He has a gentle soul, I think."

Josiah gave a tight smile. If anyone could recognise a gentle soul, it was Jabir, who was clearly precisely that.

***

Josiah arrived home late. Alex had been dropped off hours ago by an Inquisitus agent and had already texted that he was going to bed. Josiah parked his duck in the garage and climbed out wearily. He glanced at the red Jag, parked next to his duck... and that was when it hit him.

"Fuck." He looked at the date on his watch for confirmation, then leaned against the side of the Jag, winded. He stood there for ages, unable to move, hating himself.

"Hey," a voice said softly from the direction of the house. He looked around to see Alex standing in the doorway.

"I thought you'd gone to bed."

"I did, but I couldn't sleep. I heard you pull up, but then you didn't come into the house, so I thought I'd check you were okay."

"Me? I'm fine." Josiah pushed himself away from the car.

"Are you?" Alex walked over to him, his fingertips brushing the side of the Jag. "I wasn't sure if I should say anything, but I know what today is. I've known all day."

"You did better than me, then. I forgot." Josiah's voice was ragged and broken. "For the first time, I forgot, until I saw his car just now."

"Don't beat yourself up." Alex took hold of his face, gazing at him intently. "Peter would prefer you to forget than to be how you were a year ago, locked up in all that pain. I know he would."

"Yeah." Josiah gave a shaky laugh. "Today's the first day I haven't polished the stupid car. I've done it every year on the anniversary of his death. Every damn year. Even last year, until I was interrupted by an urgent call about a case." He gave a wry grin. "And you ran full tilt back into my life."

Alex wrapped his arms around him. "You've had a lot on your plate. It's not surprising you forgot with the trial going on."

"Eight years. It's been eight years." Josiah threw his head back, swallowing down the lump in his throat. "Hard to believe."

"Eight years since he died – and since we first met." Alex rubbed gentle circles on his back.

"It's so bizarre that those anniversaries are on the same date."

"Even more bizarre that Elliot should have been killed on that exact same day, too," Alex said.

Josiah made no reply. There was no mystery there – Gideon had planned it that way – but he wasn't going to tell Alex that. Besides, today was Peter's day. He closed his eyes and was immediately back on the side of that road, holding Peter's bloody body, with the rain pouring down and Alex standing under a street light transfixed with panic.

"I'm glad I was there that night," Alex said softly. "So that you have someone to share that memory with now, and don't have to bear it alone."

Josiah swallowed hard, then opened his eyes and smiled down at him.

"Me too." It was true. He'd been alone with this memory for all these years, but Alex had been there, too, and sharing it made the burden easier somehow. "I still miss him so much," he said, aching.

"Of course you do. He was special." Alex smiled up at him. "I barely knew him, but even I could see how wonderful he was."

Josiah lost it for a moment, then, but Alex's arms were a comforting haven from the storm. They stood there for a long time until he was able to pull himself together, and then, finally, with one last sad look at the Jag, they walked back into the house, hand in hand.

Josiah decided not to tell Alex about Jabir's visit. They had no idea what was on those nanodrives, and no way of knowing whether Reed would ever crack the encryption. He didn't want to give Alex any false hope, especially as he was about to testify soon.

Alex was nervous the night before he was due to take the stand. He paced around the living room for half the evening until Josiah ordered him to bed.

"Just get some rest, even if you can't sleep."

Josiah didn't get much sleep himself. He knew HMS would do his best to tear Alex apart on the witness stand, and it felt almost cruel to send Alex to this fate after all he'd endured. Still, Alex had proved himself to be nothing if not resilient. This was just one more hurdle for him to jump.

Around 3 a.m., he heard a muffled thumping from Alex's room and knew that he was performing his yoga. Unable to sleep, he slipped into the box room and took out his own nervous energy on the punchbag; they each coped in their own way.

Neither of them mentioned it the next day. Alex appeared, smartly dressed as usual, with highly polished shoes, not a hair out of place, the dark shadows around his eyes the only clue to his sleepless night.

"Please promise me you won't leave while I'm on the stand," Alex begged as they climbed into the duck.

"I promise."

"You left the other day," Alex pointed out.

"Unavoidable, but it won't happen today," Josiah told him firmly. "I'll be there for every second of your evidence."

"Thank you." Alex took several deep breaths.

For fun, and because it had become their ritual, they listened to the radio on the drive to the court building. They heard very little that was good about themselves but were beyond caring. Now, they revelled in little in-jokes based on the wildly inaccurate public perception of their characters and motivations. Today was no exception.

"So, Amanda, today's the big day," Alan exclaimed. "When we finally hear what Alexander Lytton has to say for himself. Are we expecting any revelations?"

"Oh, I'm sure there will be many." She sounded as if she was rubbing her hands together in glee. "This is the moment we've all been waiting for."

Melissa from Swanley came hesitantly onto the line. "Is it possible that he's telling the truth?" she asked. "I mean, everyone seems to assume he's lying, but supposing he isn't?"

Shaun from Reigate wasn't having any of it. "Come on! So far, we've heard from an obsessed weirdo who runs an army shop and a low-life croc dealer with a grudge against Tyler. Are we really supposed to believe that the director of the IS agency and the owner of the biggest tech firm in the UK are the ones lying here? It's absurd. I don't even know why the judge is allowing this nonsense to continue."

"Because there's a skeleton, and a lock of hair with DNA that matches that in the locket. You can't discount them," Melissa argued. "Inquisitus investigated this, and I'd trust Josiah Raine with my life. He's not making any of this up. He believes it."

"Ah, Melissa. Our heroine." Alex smiled at Josiah. "She believes us, even if nobody else does."

"Where there's one, there'll be others," Josiah said with more confidence than he felt. For the next half hour, all the callers to the programme disabused him of that notion, and he was thoroughly depressed by the time they arrived at the courthouse.

He sent Alex on ahead and took a moment to call Reed, whose rumpled suit and haggard face made it clear he'd pulled an all-nighter. The charge in his holotie had almost completely run down and was glowing a sinister orange.

"How's it going?" Josiah asked.

"Badly," Reed growled. "Tyler has access to the best IT techs in the world. It's madness to think I can crack their encryption in one night. I could work at it for forty years and still get nowhere."

"I have more faith in you than you do," Josiah told him patiently. "You're a world-class brain, Cam. You *chose* to work for Inquisitus rather than go and work for a shit like Tyler. You could have earned a fortune at a company like Tyler Tech, but you're a decent man, and you wanted to give something back."

"I'm an idiot who could have afforded a dozen Destiny ducks by now if I'd only made different career choices," Reed grumbled. But Josiah could see his eyes were still scanning his screen, his fingers scrabbling at top speed across the keyboard, even as they spoke.

"I'll leave you to it. Remember to eat."

"Yeah, you too," Reed muttered absently. "Wait – what?"

"Never mind." Josiah finished the call and stood there, considering their options. He couldn't ask the judge to delay the trial on the vague hope that new evidence might come to light at some point. Their only course of action was to soldier on and hope that Reed came good, and draw out their testimonies as much as possible in the meantime to buy him time.

Alex was rocking back and forth in his seat by the time Josiah took his beside him. Realising that Alex was reciting his song in his head, Josiah put a firm hand on his knee, which immediately calmed him. The entire court was buzzing as the assembled media and public anticipated Alex's evidence. Finally, the judge entered, the court was called to order, and Byrne called Alex to the stand.

Gone was the scared teenager who'd appeared at his trial for driving under the influence of drugs. Gone, too, was the shell-shocked, ashamed young man who'd embezzled his father's money. This Alexander Lytton wasn't one that the media had seen before. He held his head high and spoke in a clear voice, taking his time to consider each question, speaking earnestly and honestly straight from the heart. Josiah was so proud of him. It couldn't be easy facing a hostile press and George Tyler across the courtroom and holding his ground, but Alex did – and some.

He spoke eloquently of his past, clearly owning his mistakes, making no excuses for himself. There was no sign of the petulance that had marked his brother's paralympic win, or his old antagonistic relationship with the press. He was a compelling witness, raw in his honesty, sparing nobody, least of all himself.

"When you first met Solange, what did you think?" Byrne asked.

"That she was gorgeous, breathtakingly beautiful, and she was, inside and out. She was a lovely person."

"What was the nature of your relationship?"

"We became lovers very quickly. I felt as if she understood me. She said her parents had died in a duck crash, and that bonded us. I didn't realise it was a lie, that she'd been rehearsed on how to get close to me."

An excited gasp went around the court. This, finally, was the meat of the story. Alex went on to explain Solange's past and how Tyler had found her in the Quarterlands with the intent of trapping him.

"Can you tell us why Mr Tyler went to all this bother?" Byrne asked.

"Yes. He was having an affair with my mother. He was devastated when she died, and he blamed me. He wanted his revenge on me."

There was a startled silence, and then the courtroom erupted in a low hum of noise. They had expected revelations, but this was juicy stuff. Alex explained that his mother had met Tyler at university and fallen in love with him before she met his father. Byrne had statements from Noah and Charles corroborating both the university romance and the affair.

Tyler looked murderous, his face tight and pinched, although he had to have known this would be revealed.

Alex continued with his testimony. It was long, detailed, and slow. All the better for their purposes, with Reed bashing away at cracking that encryption back at Inquisitus.

Alex told a story that was truly shocking. Josiah glanced around the court as Alex spoke of being prostituted, with agonising pauses, often looking down, his eyes haunted. Surely, only a trained actor could produce a performance so touching? The press, who had so far viewed this case as an absurd spectator sport, suddenly looked chastened as, for the first time, they entertained the possibility that Alex might be telling the truth. What about the jury, though? They were harder to read, but they listened carefully, and Josiah thought he detected some pity in their expressions as they heard Alex out.

Alex's testimony took several days. He was allowed frequent breaks, and he needed them. Josiah made sure he ate and drank during every recess, however little he felt like it. In the evenings, he flopped onto the sofa, exhausted, the minute they arrived home.

One night, Josiah sat beside him, removed his shoes, drew his legs onto his lap, and massaged his feet.

"S'nice," Alex murmured. "S'like Spain." He rarely mentioned his time in Spain, but Jabir's statement had filled in the blanks. Josiah wasn't surprised that Alex didn't want to talk about it.

"What happened in Spain?" he asked quietly.

"I barely remember it. I was in a bad way mentally." Alex shivered. "I hope I never feel that way again. It took me a long time to decide I wanted to live and to feel halfway normal again."

"You're doing a great job on the stand," Josiah told him encouragingly. "Brilliant, in fact. The jury might be able to discount Ted and Mick, but you're on a different level."

Alex managed a grateful smile but was clearly too exhausted to reply.

Byrne's questioning was measured and, for her, relatively gentle, but at least it eased Alex into being on the witness stand. Josiah knew HMS's questions would be very different in tone, and they were.

"You're asking us to believe that Mr Tyler went to all these lengths to create this elaborate plot, and all to pay you back for what happened to your mother?"

"It's what happened," Alex replied politely. "If you find it unbelievable, you should ask Mr Tyler what's in his character that compelled him to go to such lengths, not me."

"Mr Tyler is busy running one of the world's biggest tech companies, but somehow we're led to believe that he had the time to find a girl in the Quarterlands and tutor her in how to attract you and then to go about ensnaring you?"

"As I said, it's what happened," Alex replied firmly but without anger. "Anyone who knows Mr Tyler is aware that he's an extremely driven man, with huge reserves of energy."

"What was the plan in sending this Quarterlands girl to you?"

"To make me fall in love with her, and then to reveal it was all a lie, so I would experience the same heartbreak he'd felt when he lost my mother," Alex explained.

"That wasn't what happened, though, was it? Why?"

"I didn't fall in love with her." Alex gave a rueful smile. "In fact, I finished with her, so he came up with a different plan to destroy me."

"Why didn't you fall in love with her, if she was designed to be so perfect for you?" HMS had a sneering tone in his voice as he tried to show how absurd this whole scenario was.

"I don't know, but the truth is, I've never been in love. I think my mother's death broke something in me." Alex's voice cracked with the force of his honesty. "I think, maybe, I've never allowed myself to fall in love because of her, because I don't deserve it, or because I'm scared of the pain of losing someone I love, the way I lost her. I've pushed away some wonderful people as a result of that, people I adore and wish I could love in the way they deserve." He looked straight at Josiah as he spoke. "Solange was one of them."

HMS looked momentarily wrong-footed by Alex's candour. He cleared his throat. "Let's move on to the agreement you and Mr Tyler made to create a new kind of duck. You say this was all part of this scheming to get back at you? Are you saying that *he* was behind the theft of millions from your father's business?"

"No," Alex said firmly. "Tyler didn't make me steal that money. I did that myself. I wouldn't lay that on him. He set the trap, but I was the one who walked into it."

The press looked impressed by his honesty and refusal to pass the buck, but whether they actually believed him... Josiah guessed he'd find out when he read what they had to say about it.

"I put it to you that you invented this whole pack of lies because your pride was hurt when the court sentenced you to servitude. Not just any servitude, either. You'd viewed Mr Tyler as a friend and then you were forced to become his servant. It rankled with you. You came from a privileged background, and you envied your brother, Charles, his success. You were angry with everyone that you'd failed to make the duck design work."

"I was mostly angry with myself," Alex said mildly. "I loved those designs, and I desperately wanted them to work."

"Ms Alajika testified that you were a moody and difficult boyfriend."

"I was, but not to her," Alex replied. "I've never met the woman who was in this courtroom claiming to be Solange."

"George Tyler is everything *you* wanted to be. The successful businessman, running a successful tech empire," HMS continued. "You ruined your own life, and then decided to ruin his. In fact, Mr Lytton, I put it to you that ruining lives is what you do best. Your mother, your brother, your father, yourself, and now you're attempting to ruin Mr Tyler's life. It's what you do. It's all you know."

Alex's face had a haunted quality, but he managed to dredge up a rueful smile. "Yes. You're right. I've hurt many people as a result of my failings, but I'm telling the truth about George Tyler."

HMS looked annoyed that his attempts to needle hadn't resulted in the petulant outburst he was expecting. It was obvious that he'd read all about Alex and viewed all the news reports. He'd seen him pissing on journalists from an upstairs window when his brother won a gold medal at the Paralympics. He was so sure he knew what he was dealing with, and he was wrong.

Alex was finally allowed to leave the stand, and Josiah bought them both fish and chips to celebrate on the way home.

"Thanks for what you said, about falling in love," Josiah told him when they'd both finished. He pushed his plate back and patted his full stomach.

"It was all true." Alex reached across the table and stroked his hand. "All of it. I wish it wasn't."

"Me too, but one thing I'm absolutely sure of is that you *do* deserve love, Alex. As for being afraid of losing it, well, I'm not the best person to talk to about that. Losing Peter was the worst thing that ever happened to me, but I survived, and I'm very much open to the idea of falling in love again. It's taken some time, but I got there in the end, thanks to you."

Alex smiled. "I'm glad. You'll make some lucky man very happy one day."

Josiah smiled back. "I could say the same for you."

Reed seemed to be getting by on three hours' sleep every night. He had Inquisitus's entire tech team working on the encryption, but there were no breakthroughs. Josiah wondered if Alex's compelling testimony might have done enough to sway the jury. The tone on *News-Spec* had certainly become more muted since Alex had taken to the stand.

"I mean, I can see why the indiehunter was swayed by him," Becky from Banstead mused. "I liked him more than I thought I would. I just assumed he was lying from the get-go, but the more I heard from him, the more I liked him. It's just... it all sounds so mad, doesn't it?" she said, echoing what most people thought.

The papers also took a more temperate tone, clearly swayed by Alex's humble demeanour on the witness stand.

"This was an Alexander Lytton we've never seen before," the *Daily Times* wrote. "Contrite, reasonable, articulate, and even, dare I say, gentle? Quite the sweetheart. Was it all an act? His story is hardly credible, as he well knows. If it were true, it would overturn everything we believe not only about George Tyler but also about Alexander Lytton himself. I doubt the jury is ready to do that. The presence of both Charles and Noah Lytton in court, both victims of Alexander's behaviour in the past, calls into question anything he has to say. Noah looks frail after suffering two strokes, and who can look at Charles without remembering that glorious day at Long Lake in Minnesota all those years ago, and the devastating events a few weeks later? I doubt the nation – or the jury – is in any mood to forgive Alexander Lytton just yet, or give him the benefit of the doubt."

Josiah had always known it was an uphill battle. As always, Alex's reputation went before him.

George Tyler was called to the stand next. HMS greeted him like an old friend.

"I think we can all agree that this is a preposterous charge against a respectable businessman," he said pompously. "You know Mr Lytton. Do you have any idea why he'd make up such a story?"

Tyler looked pained and solemn. "He's a troubled soul. Isobel often talked about his problems. He was expelled from several schools for being difficult and taking drugs. She despaired of him."

"Can you explain to the court why you bought his contract after he betrayed you so badly over the duck designs?"

"I loved his mother." Tyler sighed. "I wanted to do right by her son."

"What service did you ask him to provide when you made him your IS?"

"I hoped to tutor him in the business. I'd always thought him a promising young man, if prone to moody outbursts. I took him to several business meetings with me and tried to show him the ropes. He has a fine mind. I thought he could be of use in the business."

Testimony from several witnesses to that effect was shown to the court, along with footage of Alex in various different business suits, trailing behind Tyler on many occasions during the following years.

"We usually delete footage from our smartwalls after a few weeks, but I wanted to compile a little video to show to Alexander's family, so they could see that he was being well treated," Tyler said, clearly having an answer for everything.

"Noah Lytton publicly disowned his son after the theft. Did you manage to reconcile them?" HMS asked.

"No. I took Alexander to his father's office on one occasion to attempt a reconciliation, but Noah refused to talk to him."

"Both Alexander and Noah Lytton have testified that you took Alexander there wearing inappropriate clothing in an attempt to humiliate him and embarrass his father."

Tyler looked sad. "The truth is, Noah's business was struggling. I was his old love rival and one of his main competitors in business. There was a lot of bad blood between us. It's a matter of public record that I bought his business from him when it went under, and I think that, and the fact his wife intended to leave him for me, rankled with him. That's why he gave that testimony," Tyler said smoothly.

Tyler was just as impressive as Alex had been, and Josiah could see the jury being swayed back the other way. They were losing them again.

"To understand why, you have to understand the Lyttons," Tyler continued. "They're a rich, privileged family, and I was the son of their IS. My father designed the original Lytton Classic AV." Tyler gave a proud smile, which soon faded. "But we had nothing. I was grateful when Theo Lytton paid for me to accompany his son, Noah, to Oxford, but the family wanted me to take a contract with Lytton AV after I left, to repay them."

"And you didn't want that?"

"No. I was grateful, but I found Noah arrogant and difficult. Sadly, Alexander takes after him. The Lyttons are used to throwing their money around and having everything go their way."

There was a restive noise in the courtroom as this chimed with the press and jury. Nobody liked the rich and arrogant, and the Lyttons were perceived as precisely those things.

"When I refused their contract for indentured servitude, they were angry with me, even more so when I eventually became a competitor, and finally, bested Lytton AV in business. Noah hated me for that, as did Alexander. I'm a self-made man, you see, whereas Noah wasn't a great businessman. He couldn't build on his father's success, and Alexander was even worse. Indulged and entitled, they basically frittered it all away."

Josiah put his hand on Alex's thigh, which was tense with anger.

HMS moved on. "Can you explain why you didn't sell Alexander's contract to Elliot Dacre? Instead, you created a rather unorthodox leasing arrangement with him."

"I wanted to help Alexander because I wanted to do right by his mother, whom I'd loved. However, it wasn't working out for Alex at Tyler Tech, for the same reason it didn't work out for him at Lytton AV. He just wasn't cut out for business. He didn't want to work at it."

"Why not just sell his contract on?"

"I had a soft spot for him, and I wanted to remain invested in his life and what became of him. I didn't think, in good conscience, that I could just sell his contract and forget about him. Elliot was a good friend of mine. He'd made a name for himself in the world of holophotography and I thought that might appeal to Alexander's more creative side. He'd always expressed an interest in art and design, and I thought it could be a good opportunity for him to explore that. However, Elliot couldn't afford an IS as expensive as Alexander, so I came up with the leasing plan. That way I could remain a positive influence in Alexander's life, while also giving him a chance to grow and develop his skills."

"A very kind and generous gesture."

Tyler looked solemn. "His mother meant the world to me. I wanted to do right by her son."

Josiah glanced at the jury; they seemed moved by the evident sincerity in Tyler's voice.

Byrne stepped up. She did her best to rattle Tyler, but he kept his temper in check throughout and answered every charge she put to him. Smooth, commanding, and urbane, he was a man used to giving orders and being listened to. He didn't lose his cool when Byrne gave him a hard time, and he had a plausible answer for everything. In fact, he was the personification of reasonableness. Everything he said seemed to scream, *Look! How can this nonsense be true? I'm a serious businessman, not some two-bit crook from the Quarterlands.*

By the time he left the stand, Josiah knew they'd lost the jury. They'd also lost the press. The good impression Alex had made on them turned suddenly and ferociously in a heartbeat. Now, the press screamed their support for Tyler and hatred of Alex.

Spoilt son of a spoilt family! one headline on a news site spat, seemingly having forgotten that Charles was the bona fide national hero they all adored. *When all this is over, George Tyler deserves our support and sympathy as he tries to rebuild a life destroyed by an arrogant, entitled family who never forgave him for besting them in business.*

"We aren't going to win, are we?" Alex asked quietly as they drove home.

"The trial isn't over yet," Josiah replied grimly, but he knew Alex was right; they weren't going to win.

However, they still had a couple of good cards still to play, as Byrne called first Barney Bates and then Jabir Aldaba as witnesses for the prosecution.

Barney was overawed by the occasion, but he spoke up well, confirming he'd picked up Alex on the road and given him a lift and a warm meal during his escape attempt. Byrne linked the dates with Alex's visit to his father in hospital.

Jabir was up next. He was a late addition to the prosecution case but the judge had approved his presence, even if the defence were angry about it. They'd had a few days to prepare, but Josiah could see that Tyler was furious. His eyes burned angrily as Jabir stepped onto the witness stand, but apart from that, his expression didn't change, although he surely had to be worried, given Jabir's proximity to the blackmail footage.

Alex's reaction was equally interesting. He turned to him in surprise.

"Jabir?" he whispered urgently. Josiah shrugged and turned his attention back to the witness stand. He didn't feel bad about not warning Alex in advance. Alex hadn't exactly lied to him about his relationship with Tyler, but he hadn't told him the full truth, either. He wasn't surprised that Alex looked so uneasy.

Byrne introduced Jabir to the court and had him explain who he was, then got down to business.

"Mr Aldaba, can you describe the nature of Mr Tyler's relationship with Alexander Lytton during the time you witnessed them in Spain?"

"They were lovers," Jabir said. A buzz went around the court at this new revelation.

"Are you sure?"

"Yes. They shared a bedroom, and I often saw them kissing and holding hands."

"Was it a happy relationship?"

"I do not think so," Jabir replied. "Mr Alexander had many bruises on his body."

More shock waves went around the court. This cast doubt on Tyler's version of events.

HMS gave Jabir a harder time. "Did you ever see Mr Tyler hitting Alexander?" he asked sternly.

"No, I never saw that," Jabir replied. "But who else could it be? I heard raised voices, and Alexander was always bruised when Mr Tyler was in residence, and never when he wasn't."

HMS asked him many questions about whether Tyler was a good and decent employer, and Jabir admitted that he was. Josiah could see the jury and press wondering what the hell was going on. It all seemed so contradictory. Jabir's evidence was compelling, but Josiah wasn't sure it was enough to sway the jury.

As they left the courtroom at the end of the day, Alex made a beeline for Jabir's tall, elegant frame.

"Jabir!"

"Mr Alexander." Jabir whirled around to greet him.

Alex ran straight into his arms for a heartfelt hug that Jabir returned with real feeling. Then he put his hands on Alex's shoulders and gazed at him with tears in his eyes. "It's good to see you looking so well. I've been worried about you since you left the hacienda so suddenly."

"I'm fine." Alex waved an impatient arm. "But what about Maura, Razin, Zayd, and all the other kids, and Alexander the kitten?" he asked excitedly. "How are they?"

"They are well, thank you for asking, Mr Alexander, and the little kitten is now a huge, lazy cat."

"I hope you have pictures of them all, and please, will you call me Alex now?"

"I will try." Jabir laughed.

Josiah invited Jabir for coffee so they could catch up properly. There was something so endearing about Alex when he was with Jabir. He was oddly childlike and vulnerable, and Josiah sensed they'd shared a particular time in Alex's life when he'd felt precisely that way.

"Jabir used to give me these amazing foot rubs," Alex told him over coffee. "You were so kind to me, Jabir."

"I didn't do enough. It has always weighed on my conscience. I hope you forgive me, Mr—Alex, for not doing more."

"There's nothing to forgive."

"Maura and I often wondered what had happened to you. I hoped you were well, but in my darkest moments, I worried that you were no longer with us," Jabir admitted. "You were such a lost, fragile soul, Alex. I wanted to help you far more than you would allow."

"I was terrified that Tyler would hurt you or your family," Alex told him. "I couldn't tell you about Solange because Tyler listened to everything I said, and I was afraid that if he thought we were close, he'd hurt you, or Maura, or the children – or even the kitten. So I pushed you away. But I want you to know how much your friendship meant to me. I was in a very dark place during that time, mentally and emotionally. I wouldn't have survived without you."

"I'm glad I was of some use." Jabir gave a gentle smile. "Although it felt to be not enough at the time."

"It was everything," Alex said in a heartfelt tone. "What brought you here to testify, Jabir?"

Jabir exchanged a glance with Josiah. They'd agreed that they wouldn't tell Alex about the nanodrives in case they turned out to be a dead end. Josiah was always anxious about Alex's mental state, and the trial was difficult enough for him to navigate without throwing in that rollercoaster.

"I read about the trial, and I felt I must seek out Mr Raine and tell him what I knew of your relationship with Mr Tyler, hoping it would have some bearing on the outcome."

"Tyler won't be happy about it," Alex warned.

"He has already terminated my employment, but Maura and I knew he would do that." Jabir shrugged. "It doesn't matter. It was the right thing."

"But what will you do for work?" Alex asked anxiously. He looked unhappy about the Aldaba family suffering any hardship on his account, but Jabir waved his concern aside.

"Please don't worry about that. We aren't extravagant people, and Mr Tyler paid well. We've saved. I will find another job."

On the drive home, Josiah was aware that Alex was shooting him little glances, and he knew why. Alex had always been very reticent about what, precisely, had taken place between himself and Tyler. Jabir had testified in no uncertain terms that they were lovers, and Alex was concerned about his reaction.

"Do you have any questions?" Alex asked when they reached the house. "About what Jabir said on the stand today."

Josiah sighed. "I have a thousand questions, if I'm honest, but I won't ask any of them because I'm not sure I'll hear the truth from you on this subject, Alex."

"I haven't lied to you about any of it," Alex said defensively.

"Maybe, but you also haven't told me the whole truth."

"I'm not even sure I know what the truth *is* where this particular relationship was concerned. It's not that simple, Joe."

Josiah shot him a hard glance. "I think you know more than you want me to know." He left it at that. He was in no mood to hear more of Alex's half-truths.

. . .

The next day, HMS called Tyler back to the witness stand.

"Yesterday, you heard Mr Aldaba state that you and Mr Lytton were lovers. Is that true?"

"Briefly, yes." Tyler sighed. "Alexander can be very single-minded in pursuit of what he wants, and he definitely wanted me."

"Why didn't you mention this before?" HMS pressed.

"Why didn't *he*?" Tyler challenged, coming out fighting. "I didn't want to stoop so low as to imply Alexander's vendetta against me is a result of me ending our affair, because I'm sure that's only part of his motivation in pursuing me. He seduced me because he wanted me to end his contract and free him from his indentured servitude. He made me believe he loved me. He broke my heart."

Josiah glanced at Alex, who looked devastated by this new turn of events. It had been a risk putting Jabir on the witness stand. Josiah had anticipated that Tyler would respond like this. But Jabir had spoken of Tyler's mistreatment of Alex, and they needed to keep drumming that home to the jury.

"Did you physically harm him during your relationship?"

"No, although we were very passionate. That is where the bruises came from."

"So, you're saying you were in love with Alexander, but he was just using you?"

"Yes."

"Let's see some smartwall footage of that time, shall we?"

Josiah felt as if he'd been punched in the gut as he watched Alex pressing himself against Tyler in an elevator, hungrily searching for kisses. There could be no denying the heat between them. He turned to Alex, his eyes flashing angrily. So *this* was the truth he hadn't wanted him to know. He'd asked Alex if he'd told him all he needed to know, and he'd never once admitted that he and Tyler had been engaged in a full-blown affair – because this was clearly more than just sex.

There was shot after shot of the two of them together: dining alone in Tyler's apartment; talking, with their heads pressed close together; laughing and kissing as they walked hand in hand. Even cuddled up on the sofa, like a loving, cosy couple. He remembered Tyler's words of warning to him on the day of his arrest. *It took me a long time to get over him*... He hadn't wanted to believe him, but now he did. George Tyler had been well and truly head over heels in love with Alex.

Bile rose in the back of his throat. Did he know Alex at all? He turned slowly and shot him a look of wordless betrayal. Alex's expression said it all; guilt, panic, and abject misery were writ large on his features. Josiah remembered how Alex had tried to seduce him when he'd first taken him home. Had it all been a lie? Had Alex ever really cared for him, or had he been using him the entire time, the way he'd used Tyler?

He felt an overwhelming need to escape. He couldn't stay here in this stifling courtroom a second longer; he needed some air. He clambered past the row of people next to him and then strode towards the door, aware of Tyler's amused gaze as he watched him from the witness stand.

The little rustle of noise from the press and the turned heads of the jury made it clear that his departure hadn't gone unnoticed by them, either. He knew it didn't look good for the case, and he knew the press would report on it, but he didn't care. He just knew he had to get out of there.

Chapter Sixteen
JANUARY 2094
Alex

Alex spent the next few weeks considering how he might report Tyler for Solange's murder. He had more freedom now than when he'd belonged to Tyler. But he was with Elliot nearly every hour of the day, and the black SUAV followed them everywhere outside the house.

He examined Elliot's holopad when his houder was out of the room, but it was biolocked. He left the house to walk to the nearby shops as a test, but the black SUAV followed him immediately. It seemed that Tyler didn't quite trust that Alex wasn't a threat to him – not that Alex would ever expect George Tyler to take anything on trust. He tried giving the SUAV the slip by running down a narrow side street, but within seconds, burly men in the trademark Tyler livery were on his trail. Defeated, he returned to the house.

Another problem occurred to him. How did he even go about reporting it? He'd always had a vague fantasy about fleeing to Inquisitus and finding Joe, who would recognise him immediately and believe every word he said, but now, several years on from Peter's murder, he wondered if Joe *would* recognise him. He'd seen him only briefly during the most traumatic of circumstances. He could explain their connection, but just because he'd been there when Peter was killed didn't mean Joe would believe him. The more Alex mulled it over, the more impossible it all became. Anyway, he stood no chance of reaching Inquisitus, so it was all conjecture.

He was so paralysed by his own inaction that he wondered if he'd lost his nerve somewhere along the way. Spain had been a turning point, and he now recognised that he'd experienced a complete breakdown there.

He wasn't sure he was the same person who'd vowed to seek justice for Solange's death. Did he have any fight left in him? Maybe he should just accept the life he had now. Being Elliot's IS wasn't terrible, and it was certainly far better than belonging to Tyler.

A thought struck him. Had he, somewhere along the way, simply accepted his own servitude? Was he institutionalised? He thought of Gideon, refusing Madeleine's offer to pay out his contract because he *wanted* to be her servant; it had conferred a sense of belonging and proximity to the one person he admired – maybe even loved – above all others. She'd been placed in a position of being forced to care about his welfare in a way that wouldn't have happened if he'd simply been her employee. By remaining her IS, he'd created an illusion of intimacy. It might have been one-sided and utterly without substance, but it was important to *him*.

Had Alex accepted the inevitability of his own servitude to the point where he had no other aims and ambitions in life outside of service? It wasn't as if he'd made a success of his life when he'd been free. Had serving Elliot simply become comfortable and familiar?

He wrestled with these problems for weeks, turning them around in his head. Elliot didn't like it when he disappeared inside himself. Elliot wanted Chris, the fun-loving party boy, to be in evidence at all times, and Alex was starting to find being Chris as difficult to maintain as Gideon's blank-mask persona.

He looked at himself in the mirror, wearing tight jeans and a loud shirt, the kind of clothes he'd never choose for himself, and he saw Alex staring back, a little glimmer of distaste for the outfit simmering in his eyes. He'd tried so hard to make Alex disappear, but it seemed that he kept returning. Maybe it was impossible to *truly* be someone else forever. He was stumped. What should he do next? If only he could receive some kind of sign.

. . .

Within a few weeks, he got his wish. Elliot loved his holotech, and had a state-of-the-art holoscreen. One night, as they were watching the news, a familiar image appeared in front of him, and he was suddenly gazing at a man he hadn't seen in years. Josiah Raine looked superb, dressed in an elegantly cut suit that accentuated his muscular body and great height.

"Well, *hello*, darling," Elliot whistled, ogling the holoimage. "Who is *this* hunk?"

"Emma James was a much-loved media personality," Joe announced solemnly. "I promise that I will find the person who killed her."

"Is it true that one of her indentured servants has gone on the run?" a reporter asked.

"Yes, it is, but I'll track him down." Joe spoke straight to the camera in a hard, determined voice. "Bram Janssen won't be able to hide from me forever. I'll find him."

Alex drank in the sight of him. Elliot's holotech was so good that it was almost as if Joe was right here in the room with them. Had he recovered from losing Peter? Did he have a new man in his life? Did he remember Ben Smith? He wanted to watch that clip over and over again, searching for the smallest clues that might answer these questions. But with Elliot around, he was denied the chance.

Joe's pursuit of the hapless Bram Janssen, however, went on for weeks, and he became a national celebrity in the process. There were articles about him everywhere, although as he didn't give any interviews, they were largely conjecture or downright made up.

It became Alex's guilty pleasure to source every single news report and magazine article mentioning Joe by name. On one memorable occasion, Joe even scored the lead story on *The Daily Lowdown*, the biggest news and gossip site.

The Hunky Hunter of a Missing Indie Taking the UK by Storm! screamed the headline. At some point after that, without anyone really knowing when or how, Joe simply became known as "the indiehunter".

The more he learned, the more uneasy Alex became. The Joe he knew had been helping indies escape the country at great personal cost. But *this* Joe seemed cold and ruthless in tracking them down. Had Peter's murder turned him against all indentured servants? God, he hoped not.

He searched for a glimpse of the Joe he'd met, the sharp, funny man who'd bantered with his husband, but he couldn't see any sign of him. Joe looked cold and brusque, and whenever the press button-holed him, he invariably replied with one of the cutting remarks that were fast becoming his trademark. What if Joe really had become the indiehunter? This kept Alex up at night, fretting, because in every version of his fantasy of bringing Tyler down, it was Joe who was his instrument of justice.

A few days later, when Alex didn't achieve one of the top three positions in an indie show for the first time, Elliot threw a major tantrum.

"It's because you're getting flabby," he accused, pinching a non-existent roll of flesh on Alex's midriff.

Alex was as lean as ever, but it was true he'd lost muscle definition. He never worked out these days, and he hadn't done his yoga for some time.

"That's it," Elliot declared. "I'm taking you to a gym." True to his word, he found one nearby, complete with a gruff personal trainer whose obvious heterosexuality was, Alex was sure, the main reason why he'd been chosen. Elliot had no problem with Alex having sex with other men for *his* enjoyment, but he definitely didn't want it happening behind his back.

D'Angelo Clarke was a burly guy in his thirties who tried to engage Alex in conversation that was almost entirely limited to females he found "sizzling", whether they be girls working out, celebrities, or the virtually naked women who gyrated constantly on the music holovids that played in the gym 24/7.

Alex would have had little enough to say to D'Angelo at the best of times, but as Chris, he knew they had nothing in common, so he kept his replies short and non-committal and never initiated conversations.

He was sure D'Angelo found him unsatisfactory, but that didn't bother him in the slightest. He still found working out tedious, but he welcomed the time away from navigating Elliot's petulant demands and childish behaviour.

For the first few sessions, Elliot drove him to the gym, hung around watching him work out, then drove him back again after. However, Alex could see that was starting to pall, even when there were attractive men working out alongside him for Elliot to ogle.

One morning, Elliot was so excited over breakfast that Alex could tell he had something planned. He even waved aside his morning blow job, which Alex usually delivered while Elliot was eating his toast and reading the holonews.

"No, no, I have something to show you," Elliot announced, grabbing Alex's arm excitedly and dragging him outside. "A present!"

Elliot was still in his bath-robe – he rarely bothered getting dressed before noon. "Close your eyes," he squealed, and Alex obliged, though he didn't trust Elliot to lead him safely across the manicured front lawn, so he did peek a little on the way.

They arrived on the street, and Elliot clapped his hands together. "You can open them now. *Look!*"

Alex did as he was told, and his stomach somersaulted in shock because there, parked by the side of the road, was a sleek, shiny maroon duck, all wrapped up in a giant pink bow. And she wasn't just any duck. She was *his* duck. The Destiny. The one he'd designed, that had got him into all this trouble in the first place. Yet, he couldn't bring himself to hate her. She was beautiful, his first-born child, and he loved her. He ran a finger along her gleaming metal side, remembering all the milestones along the way that had led to her difficult birth.

"It's the Destiny duck," Elliot cooed. "The one everyone's talking about. *The* must-have duck of the year. I bought her for you."

He'd bought her so he didn't have to drive Alex to the gym anymore, but Alex didn't care. He couldn't wait to get inside and drive. Elliot programmed the biokey to his metrics, and they both climbed in.

She travelled beautifully, gliding over the lost zones like a swan, barely touching the surface of the water, cutting journey times in half. She also looked as beautiful as he'd always intended.

"People have money again, and they want to spend it on something luxurious, not some chugging piece of metal," Alex remembered saying to his father once, and here she was. Nobody could ever call the Destiny a chugging piece of metal.

"Don't you love her?" Elliot asked, clapping his hands excitedly. "Isn't she wonderful?"

"I *do* love her," Alex agreed, and then he followed Elliot back indoors and gave him one of his finest blow jobs to say thank you. Along with the duck, Elliot also gave him a nanopad.

"It only makes and receives calls," Elliot warned. "There's no access to the internet. I don't approve of indies spending hours on social media." Whether that was the real reason or whether Tyler had placed certain conditions on his sale, Alex didn't know. "The point is, if you are out and about in the duck, I need to be able to reach you, so you must carry this with you at all times."

The first time he drove to the gym by himself, it felt almost transgressive. It was the most normal he'd felt in a long time, being out by himself, all alone... apart from the ever-present SUAV following on behind. He could ignore that, though, and just enjoy the drive.

Now that he had his freedom, he wondered what to do with it. It took him a few weeks to pluck up the courage, but one day, on his way back from the gym, he decided to drive to Ghost Eye City, to see if he could reach Inquisitus. Would the black SUAV try to stop him, or was it just there to follow him? It was time to find out.

Swinging his duck out across the lost zone, he headed in the direction of Ghost Eye. The Destiny was faster over water than the SUAV, so there was every chance he'd get there before they could stop him. It felt exhilarating, as if he was taking his life in his hands, which he supposed he was.

Looking in the mirror, he saw the black SUAV enter the lost zone behind him, trying valiantly to keep up, and that was when the adrenaline rush hit him. He was really doing this!

Years of fear melted away as he raced across the huge expanse of water. He could see Ghost Eye on the horizon, the massive floating city filling the skyline, dwarfing the remnants of Old London.

Behind him, the SUAV kept up its pursuit doggedly, but he was winning. Soon, he'd be there. He'd drive right up to Inquisitus, run inside, seek out Joe, tell him he was Ben Smith, and beg for his help. Then this nightmare would be over, and he wouldn't have to pretend to be Chris anymore, or wear the blank mask Gideon had taught him. He could be Alex again, whoever the hell that was.

He was so caught up in his own exhilaration that he didn't hear the nanopad at first, but the duck automatically answered it, and Elliot's voice filled the vehicle.

"Christopher Dacre, where are you?" he screamed.

"I've just been to the gym," he replied, one eye on the mirror to see what the SUAV was doing.

"And where are you now?"

Why was he asking? Did he know about his mad dash across the lost zone? If so, how?

"I'm just driving. I wanted to put the duck through her paces. It's no fun if you don't go across a lost zone."

"Well, that's enough fun. Get home right now," Elliot ordered.

"Will do," he lied. Ending the call, he kept right on driving. The black SUAV was so far behind it was almost invisible, and Ghost Eye was straight ahead.

He was almost there when suddenly, out of nowhere, another black SUAV appeared ahead of him. He swerved as it almost knocked him out of the water. Had Elliot called for backup? Or the occupants of the other SUAV? Either way, he had no choice but to swing the Destiny to one side and turn around. It was over. Deflated, he returned home.

Elliot was furious. "You do *not* have my permission to go driving around all over the place, and especially not through lost zones. You'll drive to the gym, then straight back here. Do you understand?" He paced around the living room, his anger somewhat undermined by the fact he was dressed only in a loosely flowing robe that had fallen open to reveal him in all his naked, tubby glory.

"Yes, Elliot," Alex whispered meekly. "But I was just having some fun."

Elliot slapped him hard across the cheek, taking him by surprise. "You worried me! Don't be so selfish. You know how I lost the first Christopher."

Of course. In his excitement, Alex had forgotten how his namesake had drowned in a duck accident, although whether that was the real reason for Elliot's panic or not, he didn't know.

Later that evening, he saw on the news that Joe was in Northampton on the trail of the elusive Bram Janssen, so he wouldn't have been at Inquisitus even if he *had* managed to get there. He could have kicked himself for doing something so impulsive. If he was going to do this, it had to be planned, and he had to be more careful. Just because he wasn't in Tyler's direct custody anymore didn't mean he wasn't under his control.

He took a long look at himself in the mirror that evening. He'd become reckless and lax. What would Gideon say? He could guess. Returning to the gym had imposed a much-needed discipline on his body, much as he disliked it, and his muscles were starting to show some definition again. Well, the brain could be trained the same way. No more slip-ups. It was time to resume his mental training. He moved the rug to the centre of the bedroom and began his yoga practice. His body ached afterwards, but his mind felt better than it had in years.

From that day onwards, he did half an hour of yoga every morning before going downstairs, all the while listening to his song over and over again on repeat. Elliot had given him an old-fashioned media player and allowed him a playlist, and Alex made the most of the gift.

At first, it wasn't easy finding his mask again. His mind rebelled and he could see himself chafing. There was no doubt that life was more complicated now, as he essentially had two masks to wear, juggling Gideon's blank emptiness with Chris's vacuous hedonism. But that was the challenge he set himself, and somehow, he mastered it.

After the Ghost Eye debacle, he lapsed back into caution. He watched, enthralled, as Joe finally arrested someone who turned out not to be Bram Janssen after all, in a thrilling twist to a saga that had kept the nation gripped for weeks.

Elliot's embargo on him driving anywhere except to the gym lasted several months, but he relented eventually and allowed him to drive around by himself for a couple of hours after his gym sessions, provided he had no other plans for him, and as long as he stuck to certain prescribed routes.

Meanwhile, the parties and the shows continued, as did the holophotography. Alex was becoming an old hand at how to pose for the holocam now. He knew precisely what Elliot wanted and was easily able to gaze elusively on command.

One morning, he heard Elliot having a loud argument on holochat and saw him pacing around in his study afterwards, chuntering away to himself under his breath. A door behind him opened, and the housekeeper, Chantal, entered. Alex moved away from the study door quickly, so she wouldn't see that he was eavesdropping, but she shot him a disapproving look all the same. She adored Elliot, but he always felt she didn't like him. Not that he'd made any effort to befriend her. He'd never forgotten Gideon's insistence that he couldn't have any friends. Besides, there was something about her nervous, birdlike energy that reminded him of D at Belvedere, and that was enough to stop him even attempting to engage her in conversation.

In the weeks that followed, it became increasingly clear Elliot was stressed about money. Not that Elliot shared his concerns with Alex, but he overheard snatched snippets of conversations that confirmed his suspicions. Elliot was at the height of his success in his career, feted everywhere, invited to all the best parties, and his works were increasingly being treated as serious on the arts scene, which Alex found vaguely astonishing. Yet, it seemed the more Elliot earned, the more he spent, wasting his cash on ever more lavish costume parties and vast quantities of drugs that he supplied to an increasing number of hangers-on.

Alex wondered if it would have made a difference if Elliot had had a proper partner in his life. If Chris hadn't died, then maybe he'd have had someone who could have stood up to him and told him he was being a fool, although he doubted it. From what he could tell, Chris had been as much of an airhead as Elliot, and if anything, would probably have egged him on.

. . .

Joe was back in the news again a few months later, standing outside Inquisitus, dressed as exquisitely as ever.

"I feel the same sense of shock as the rest of the nation that one of our members of parliament has been murdered," he announced in a grim tone. "This is an attack on our democracy, and I can assure you that, as Inquisitus's senior homicide investigator, I will not rest until the perpetrator has been caught."

"Ooh, it's that sexy detective who wears the fancy suits. He should have his own show," Elliot declared, patting Alex's arm as they sat together on the sofa. "Did you know his husband was murdered a few years back?" He lowered his voice to a dramatic whisper. "They say the husband bled out in his arms. Awful. So tragic." He shook his head sadly, but Alex could see that Joe's tragedy was no more than another interesting titbit of gossip for him to enjoy. The fact that Joe was also gay meant that Elliot viewed him as one of his tribe, and therefore, of special interest.

The murdered politician dominated the news cycle for weeks, and therefore Joe was frequently in the headlines.

"That sexy Raineman is back," Elliot squealed every time Joe made an appearance, his burly frame a familiar sight in their lounge now. "He's become quite the celebrity, hasn't he? I wonder if he'd like to come to one of my parties?"

Alex almost choked on his tea, but then he couldn't stop thinking about it. He was fairly sure that Joe would *not* want to attend any of Elliot's sleazy events, but he fantasised about what it would be like to meet him again, to take his hand and lead him away to a quiet spot, and reveal to him that he was Ben Smith.

The next time Joe appeared in the news, he looked exhausted and dishevelled, which was unusual because he was usually so well groomed. His shirt was ripped and covered in blood, and he had a large purple bruise under his eye.

"I can confirm that, tonight, we've charged Ryan Strutt with Sir John Marcham's murder," he announced.

"Strutt was Marcham's indie, wasn't he?" Elliot said. "Good lord. The Raineman really does hate indies, doesn't he? Not surprising, given what happened to his husband."

Alex leaned forward, gazing at Joe intently. He looked cold and closed off, as if he was suppressing a vast reservoir of anger. There were none of his usual gruff putdowns, which had become legendary. Alex shivered. He wouldn't want to be on the wrong side of *this* Josiah Raine. Was Elliot right? Was Joe conducting some kind of personal vendetta against indentured servants? The media certainly seemed to think so and reported on it gleefully.

Alex was aware of a new mood sweeping the nation. Indies were being reported about more negatively and a few high-profile cases of pilfering, escape, and violence caused big splashes. The IS system, which had once offered a way for both servants and houders alike to benefit, had turned ugly. Houders no longer trusted the people who shared their homes and workplaces, and indies were tired of a system that was becoming more oppressive with each passing day.

As Alex watched an exhausted Joe being interviewed, it suddenly struck him that his fantasies of being helped by this man were childish. He had no way of knowing if Joe would aid him in bringing Tyler down. He barely knew the man. He certainly didn't know *this* icy, wary, unsmiling figure, this... *indiehunter*.

After that, Alex stopped fantasising about meeting Joe again. There would be no more stupid high-speed chases across the lost zone to Inquisitus, no dreams of telling Joe his true identity. He would have to find a different way to bring down Tyler.

One night, at one of his parties, Elliot introduced him to a grey-haired man with a paunch.

"This is Jeffrey Mead," he announced. "Do be kind to him, Chris, darling. He's such a good friend."

"Do be kind" was Elliot's code for "sleep with". Alex wasn't remotely attracted to Mead, but that wasn't important. He hung on to the man's arm, offered him drugs, and then led him to the little bank at the bottom of the garden to follow Elliot's orders.

"So, how do you know Elliot?" Alex asked as they both inhaled some croc.

"He's an old friend," Mead replied with a sly expression. "An old friend who owes me a favour." Mead leaned forward and caressed his cheek.

Alex allowed Mead to push him down on the grassy bank and undress him. He lay back and listened as Mead sucked on his cock, making weird squelching sounds.

Later, Mead held on to him tightly, as if he was frightened he'd disappear, and fucked him. Then they lay back on the grass and snorted some more croc.

"God, that was good. I'm going to ask Elliot if I can have you for a weekend. You're so gorgeous." Mead trailed a finger over Alex's bare chest. "I'd ask to take you home tonight, but I have to work tomorrow. Another time."

"What work do you do?" Alex asked absently, not remotely interested. The croc kicked in and he began to revel in the mellow high.

"I'm an investigator with Results Inc," Mead said, puffing out his chest proudly. Alex felt his heart skip a beat.

"That must be interesting." He snuggled up against Mead, gazing at him sycophantically through his tears. "Do you know that Investigator Raine who's always on the news? The hot bloke in the fancy suits?" It was worth a try. They both worked in the same line of business, after all.

"No, I don't know him," Mead snapped irritably. "But I *do* know he's a bloody great show-off. Wearing those expensive suits and pushing himself into the media all the time." Mead sounded extremely put out that a gay investigator that wasn't *him* had become famous. "That's not what being an investigator is about at all. Josiah Raine just wants the bloody limelight, instead of putting in the hard work that true investigation requires."

"Do you investigate murders and stuff?" Alex asked nonchalantly.

"I have in the past, yes, but mostly I'm involved in tracking down drug gangs," Mead replied, which was rich given the crocodile tears flowing freely down his face.

"How would you report a murder, hypothetically speaking?" Alex asked casually. "I mean, supposing you had information. Would you call the police, or contact an IA? Who would you speak to?"

"Police are first port of call, usually, for murder," Mead replied, looking delighted to be able to show off about his profession. "They make a decision about the most appropriate IA to hand it to. Inquisitus currently holds the government's primary homicide contract, with a remit to investigate a few other areas like fraud and major drug gangs. My firm deals mostly with escaped indies and street drugs, as I said."

"Right. So, you'd call the police?" The chances of him being able to do that were almost non-existent, but he stored the information away in his head.

"Yeah. Why? You got a murder to report?" Mead asked, chuckling.

"Nah. Just been watching a ton of those crime dramas and wondering if they get it right," Alex replied, and then he changed the subject.

Mead became a frequent visitor to the house after that. Elliot never allowed him to take Alex away with him, but the man often stayed over, and it was taken for granted that Alex would sleep with him. Alex toyed with the idea of telling Mead about Solange, but in the end, decided against it. He only had one shot at this so he had to get it right, and he both disliked and distrusted Mead. The man was sleazy, for a start, and corrupt. Alex soon figured out that Mead had been given a tip-off about all the drugs at Elliot's parties and was blackmailing him into giving him Alex for sex.

At first, Alex had the impression that Elliot disliked Mead, but over time, the two seemed to grow close, and their acquaintance morphed into a weird kind of friendship. It wasn't one Alex welcomed, but he had no say in it. They shared a sense of humour, both loved to gossip, and Mead provided Elliot with a degree of protection, against both other blackmailers and other investigation agencies.

Alex had to figure most of this out for himself because, oddly, for a man as indiscreet as Elliot, when he wanted to he could play his cards very close to his chest. He certainly never confided in Alex. He made it clear that he wanted Alex to play a very specific role in his life, and while he expected Alex to look and behave like the dead Christopher, that didn't confer the intimacy one might have expected of a substitute husband. Alex was Chris only as far as Elliot wanted him to be, and no further.

. . .

After one workout session at the gym, Alex returned to the changing room, removed his bag from the locker, and opened it to find a familiar face staring back at him. His knees almost gave way, and he held on to the locker for support.

It was Solange, gazing at him sadly, as if judging him for his failure to bring her killer to justice.

It took him a few moments to pull himself together and realise that it wasn't actually Solange in his bag, but a photo of her. A very familiar photo. It had been so long since he'd seen this picture that it was shocking. He'd almost forgotten the shape of her face, the depth of her brown eyes, and the sweet wistfulness of her expression. How had the picture come to be in his gym bag? It definitely hadn't been there when he'd placed his bag in the locker and locked the door earlier.

He looked around, but nobody else was in the changing room. He knew that only two people had a copy of this photo: Ted and Gideon. Which one of them had left it here? It could be Ted, but he thought it unlikely. It seemed far more likely to be Gideon, but why? Alex's guilty conscience filled in the blanks. Gideon was clearly wondering why he hadn't fulfilled his mission, and so had sought him out and placed it in his bag to remind him.

The photo felt like a reproach. *Look at her. You said you loved her, that she was your best friend, but you've done nothing to bring her killer to justice.*

"I'm sorry," he whispered, gazing at the picture. Did he even want to fulfil his mission now, given all the years that had passed since her death? He sat down, suddenly feeling winded. Did he? Or was he just fooling himself? Yes, it would be difficult, and yes, he was afraid, but how hard was he even trying? Should he give up on it altogether?

"No." The answer was immediate and clear. He still wanted to bring the full force of the law down on George Tyler's head. There was, buried inside him, a thirst for justice that went so deep he knew he'd never give up on it. "I promise," he told the photo. "I promise I'll find a way to make it happen one day."

When he returned home, he ran straight upstairs to his bedroom, took the image of Hudson Brink off the wall, and slipped Solange's photo behind it to keep it safe and hidden from Elliot's view. From then on, whenever he wanted to stiffen his resolve, he would pull out the photo and gaze at it, remembering his vow. He would do this. Somehow, he would find a way, even if it took him years.

After its meteoric rise, Elliot's star began to fall. His holopics, which had once seemed so cutting edge, now seemed cheesy as new photographers emerged with better ideas.

In a desperate attempt to regain his crown, Elliot decided to double down on the homoerotic content of his pictures. There was no doubt he'd always had a primarily gay and female following, who loved the way he captured the male body, and now he embarked on a series of portraits he titled simply "Muse". These consisted largely of a number of nude black-and-white holopics of Alex.

For this series, Elliot stripped away all the drama. There were no ruined castles or dramatic snow scenes, and definitely no ravens. It was simply Alex in various nude poses as the holocam moved around him, drinking in his beauty and somehow managing to capture the mask that made him so tantalisingly elusive.

Elliot created a room decorated entirely in white, placed a black bed in the centre, and bought white satin bedding. Then he applied a light layer of make-up to Alex's back to hide the silvery scars.

"I don't want anything to spoil the perfection of the image, my love," he murmured as he rubbed it in.

He circled Alex for hours, trying to recapture the magic that would reverse his ailing fortunes. Alex knew for sure that he was in financial trouble now, because he'd heard him talking to various banks and pleading his case. It was all very well being a famous holophotographer, but even when it had been going well, it hadn't been bringing in the kind of money that Elliot had been spending. That fact had finally caught up with his houder, who was robbing Peter to pay Paul.

This made Alex increasingly anxious. Supposing Elliot sold him? He had to be the most expensive thing Elliot owned, and he was sure that if he did sell him, Tyler would want a say in who bought him next. The worst-case scenario was that Elliot would sell him back to Tyler; he didn't think he could survive that.

"Okay, Chris, I want you on your front while I move around behind you. When I say the word, look over your shoulder, straight at the holocam," Elliot instructed.

Alex lay on the bed, naked, the cool air from the nearby open window wafting over his bare skin.

"So, sweetie, I have a funny story to tell you," Elliot said as he worked away behind Alex, moving the holocams around. Alex drifted off. Elliot's funny stories invariably involved tedious gossip about his numerous gay friends. "Would you believe, someone offered to buy you? Isn't that a hoot?"

Alex's stomach flipped. Charles. It had to be him. Wonderful, beloved Charles. He'd promised he'd save enough money to buy him, but Alex had never been entirely sure he believed him. Like Elliot, Charles was terrible with money. Alex took a moment to ensure his mask was firmly in place, and then he turned to look straight at the holocam.

"Oh, that's perfect, Chris," Elliot said, snapping away. "Marvellous. Anyway, I gave him short shrift. He ran off with his tail between his legs, I can tell you."

"Who was it?" Alex asked in a nonchalant tone, as if he didn't care.

"Oh, I don't know. Neil somebody. He sent a letter. Can you believe that? How old-fashioned. I thought, at first, that he wanted to buy a portrait of you, but no. He wanted to actually buy your contract."

Alex shivered. Neil? Surely it had to be Neil Grant. But how the hell would he have found enough money to buy his contract?

"Anyway, I thought you'd find that amusing." Elliot laughed, seemingly oblivious to the fact that Alex hadn't smiled once. "Of course, I said no. As if. You are *not* for sale, sweetie. Never ever." He said that very firmly, and Alex had no doubt he meant it. But he also knew that Elliot's whims were so changeable as to make it meaningless. "I promise you that I tore up his letter and threw it away."

He hadn't thought about Neil Grant in years. Maybe it hadn't been Neil, but surely it was too much of a coincidence? Alex returned to his room a little while later and gazed at the *Halo of Fire* picture. Neil Grant and this picture were indelibly linked in his mind, together with all the complexities of that relationship. God, he hoped it wasn't Neil.

The last thing he wanted was his former flatmate gatecrashing back into his life.

He took the picture off the wall and removed the photo of Solange. "Soon," he promised. She stared back at him from those sad, dark eyes. "I haven't given up on you. It's just very hard. I know I overthink it, but if I fuck it up, that'll be it – for you and for me."

The nude series turned out quite beautiful, but it wasn't enough to halt the decline in Elliot's fortunes. As his financial woes increased, he became more and more bad-tempered, and Alex was forced to tiptoe around him. Elliot was never vicious like Tyler. He thought nothing of delivering a sharp slap to Alex's face, but never anything worse than that. Still, Alex had no wish to provoke him.

A few weeks later, Elliot told him about another offer to buy him, sounding just as gleeful as before.

"You see, *I* have the IS that everyone wants," he crowed. "But they can't have you because you belong to me." This all fed into his sexual proclivities, the idea of other men lusting after Alex, and Elliot deciding who could have him and who would be denied – one of Elliot's favourite fantasies.

"Who was it this time?" Alex asked, pretending to glance at the magazine he was reading, so that Elliot wouldn't think he cared that much.

"Not anyone you'd know." Elliot laughed. "Are you imagining it's some handsome movie star, like Hudson Brink? Ooh, you'd like that, wouldn't you?" *Not really.* "Well, it isn't. It's just this man who saw us out one day and took rather a fancy to you. When he noticed me having a latte at The Coffee Cabin while you were at the gym this morning, he approached and made an offer. Isn't that hilarious? I said no, of course, but he was quite serious." Elliot frowned. "I wonder why all these bids are coming in now?"

"Maybe because my sentence was for seven years and that's up soon?" Alex suggested. "So, technically I can be freed, if my houder is willing to take the loss."

"Well, you're not going anywhere," Elliot exclaimed. "It's not about the money. I simply couldn't live without you, darling."

Alex knew it very much *was* about the money, given that Elliot didn't have any. He was sure Elliot would find someone to replace him soon enough, but he obviously couldn't afford to simply free Alex, and he didn't expect him to.

He'd rarely ever thought about his court sentence, but all these offers gave him hope. Was it possible that Charles had somehow come into a large sum of money? Elliot might not want to sell him, but if his financial situation worsened, he'd have no choice.

Now, it made less sense for him to risk everything by going after Tyler. He'd be better off waiting and seeing if Elliot sold him. There was, surely, a possibility that he might soon be free… and then he could decide what to do about Solange.

Chapter Seventeen
NOVEMBER 2096
Josiah

There was a little patch of grass opposite the courtroom, not big enough to be called a park, but there was a bench and a large, shady tree. Josiah sat down and put his hands on his knees, breathing in deeply, trying to regain control of himself.

Why had that hurt so much? He wasn't in a relationship with Alex, but he knew that was semantics. He loved him, whether they were together or not, and it hurt to think that Alex might have been using him all along. Did it change anything, though?

He thought of Alex's kindness to him, the gentle way he'd brought him back from the frozen isolation of his grief and helped him reconnect with the world again. It didn't change that.

He thought of the terrified young man who'd stepped up to fight Lars Driessen, a man twice his size who'd been wielding a knife. It didn't change that, either.

Why hadn't Alex told him how deep his relationship with Tyler had gone? No wonder Tyler felt so hurt and betrayed. It was clear that he'd been as much in love with Alex as Josiah was, and yet, Alex walked through it all untouched by the emotions of others, seemingly impervious.

Josiah wished he understood. He viewed himself as a simple, direct kind of man, but Alex was the opposite. Would he ever understand him? It was possible, of course, that *this* was part of the attraction.

Some time passed as he mulled it over. He was so deep in thought that he was surprised when someone sat next to him. He was even more surprised when he realised it was Tyler.

"Poor Josiah Raine. Did you really think he loved you?" Tyler chuckled. "I did warn you. I told you what he was like."

"He's what you made him," Josiah said quietly. "He was nineteen when you first tried to get your claws into him. Nineteen. You were punching down, George. Whatever he is, whatever he became, he did it to survive you and the nightmare you created for him."

"Ah, still defending him, I see."

"I understand him better than you do." Josiah sat up straight and looked Tyler in the eye.

"You keep telling yourself that. Maybe it'll hurt less." Tyler gave a rueful smile. "I'm glad you're here. I've been looking for an opportunity to talk to you. Privately." He waved his arm at the little park they were sitting in.

"You mean with no opportunity to be recorded or overheard? That's your trick, George, not mine."

"Not entirely. You had that ludicrous dog cam." Tyler chuckled. He sat back and breathed in the warm air. It was a gloriously sunny day, albeit with a distinct chill in the air. "So, it's not going well for you, is it?"

"That's for the jury to decide, not you."

"Oh, I already know what the jury will decide," Tyler told him smugly.

Josiah felt a chill creep up his spine. "You've paid them off?"

"Certainly not." Tyler shrugged. "That's harder than you might think. But no – the next-best thing."

Realisation slowly seeped in. "The media. You've bought them off," Josiah guessed.

"Some of them." Tyler grinned. "The jury were warned against following the trial on the news sites, but that's impossible to police nowadays, so they don't even try. This is a case that comes down entirely to which version of events you believe; there's no conclusive evidence, on either side. If the jury keeps seeing and hearing that the nation's media doesn't believe a word Alex is saying, well, that'll make it harder for *them* to believe it, too."

"Were you that much in love with him?" Josiah asked quietly. "Did he hurt you that much?"

Tyler's expression changed, and for a brief second, Josiah caught a glimpse of a sad and lonely man.

"Yes," Tyler said softly. "And now you know how that feels, too." He put a hand on Josiah's shoulder. "I almost feel sorry for you." He squeezed, gently. "We're both in Alexander Lytton's discarded pile, aren't we?"

"Not really. I ended it with him," Josiah told him, pushing his hand away.

"As did I, but for the same reason, I'd imagine. Because we knew he didn't feel the same."

That stung, to know that he and George Tyler of all people had this in common.

"So, I've been doing some digging on you, Josiah Raine." Tyler stretched out his legs and put his hands behind his head. "With some surprising results. How amusing it was to find out that the great indiehunter is, in fact, a bleeding-heart liberal who scoops up poor, wretched indies and takes them to freedom across the sea."

It wasn't unexpected, but he felt a cold hand grip his heart all the same. He felt like a mouse being played with by a snake. Tyler held the upper hand in every aspect of his life right now.

"I was so angry with you, but seeing you here now, I almost feel sorry for you. You had it all, and you threw it all away because of Alexander Lytton. I was where you are now once, so I know how it feels."

"You came here to tell me this?"

"No, I came here to make a deal. You've lost the case – forget about that. However, I want whatever Jabir gave you. Give it back to me, and I'll keep your secret."

"Who said he gave me anything?" Josiah queried with a cold, hard stare. He could bluff with the best of them.

"Don't fuck with me," Tyler snapped. "I very much doubt it'll be much use to you. There's no way you'll ever find your way into it, but I want it back. Give it to me, and you can rest assured that nobody will ever find out who the indiehunter really is. Otherwise, well..." He leaned forward and spoke softly into Josiah's ear. "You'll be the one eking out the rest of his life in prison, Josiah, not me. Or maybe they'll sentence you into servitude. That would be amusing. To see the mighty fallen. The great, self-righteous Josiah Raine, reduced to wearing someone's ID tag, with a chip in his arm. You know what? I think I might buy you myself. Big guy like you, who knows how to fight. I always need good security officers. Or perhaps I'll find you something more in Alex's line of work. I'm sure I'd have men queuing up to enjoy your services." He grinned and nudged Josiah conspiratorially. "You should have accepted my offer when you had the chance, instead of taking me on. I never lose, Josiah."

Josiah stared straight ahead, feeling the sun soaking into his skin. There was an inevitability to this, like the last act of a carefully choreographed show reaching a foregone conclusion.

"What will you do to him?" he asked. "If you get him back."

"*When* I get him back," Tyler replied sharply. "That's none of your business. You'll be in no position to help him; you'll be under arrest."

"Will you kill him?"

"No. Despite what you and he think, I'm not a killer." Tyler sighed. "Besides, I still care about him."

"Not so much that you won't make his life a living hell," Josiah predicted.

"Well, he has to pay for what he's put me through this past year," Tyler said with a wave of his hand, as if that much was obvious.

Josiah shivered. He could only imagine what it would be like to be this man's prisoner. Alex had already lived through years of it, and it had warped and twisted him almost beyond endurance.

"So, what do you say?" Tyler asked. "Give me those nanodrives, and you, at least, will go free. Not Alex, of course. He's mine. There's no scenario in which you get him. But I'll keep your secret if I get back what's mine."

"No." Josiah stood up. "I won't belong to anyone, George. I'd rather take my chances with the justice system than sell myself out to a snake like you. If I'm sentenced into servitude, so be it, but I won't betray myself in the process."

"You're a fool," Tyler snapped. "When I place my ID tag on you, you'll wish you'd taken this deal."

"*If*," Josiah corrected. "*If*, George. This trial isn't over yet."

"It's as good as, and your data tech won't find his way into those drives if he tries for a hundred years."

"Then you have nothing to worry about, do you?" Josiah gave him a pleasant nod. "Now, lunch recess is nearly over, and I'm due on the witness stand this afternoon, so if you'll excuse me."

He stalked off across the grass, leaving Tyler behind. He'd always known this was a high-stakes game, and he'd gone into it with his eyes open. Had that been a mistake? Maybe. Yet he knew he'd do it all again if he had his time over.

Alex came running to meet him as he entered the courtroom.

"I've been looking all over for you,"

"I was in the park, getting some air," he said tightly.

"Joe, please... we need to talk," Alex said urgently, tugging on his arm.

Josiah glanced around at the various members of the media and public waiting to file back into the courtroom.

"Not now. Later," he growled.

"Okay, I just want you to know it's not as simple as he made it seem. There's so much more to it than that footage suggests."

"I know that. Of course I know that," Josiah said. "Now go and sit down. We'll talk later."

He watched as Alex returned to the courtroom. The thought of Tyler getting his hands on him again, of torturing what was left of his sanity out of him, wringing him dry and leaving him a shattered ruin, was too much to bear. He wouldn't even be able to help or launch a rescue attempt because he'd be behind bars.

Tyler had him backed into a corner, and there was only one thing he knew how to do in that situation, and that was to come out fighting. It might be dirty, and he might have to do things he'd rather not, but he wasn't going down without a fight.

He was called to the stand next as a character witness for Alex.

There weren't many people who could testify on Alex's behalf. Elliot and Solange were dead, and Alex had kept most people at arm's length during his servitude, with good reason.

Josiah knew he himself was generally well liked by the public. They admired his reputation for catching killers, empathised with his tragic personal life, and had loved watching him overcome an intrusive media with his brusque responses to their inane questions over the years. He had that on his side, at least.

Byrne questioned him first, which gave him an easy start. He spoke of how Alex had been a well-behaved indie, good at his self-imposed job.

"The truth is, I didn't want an indentured servant. I've never had one, and I've never wanted one," he said firmly.

"Because your husband was killed by one?" she asked.

"No, because I don't like the system. Pay someone an honest wage for an honest day's work, but don't trap them into a repressive system that's little different from medieval serfdom," he replied. This caused a stir in the media gallery; they'd always supposed they had the measure of the indiehunter.

"So, you found it distasteful to have an indentured servant living under your roof?"

"I did, but that wasn't Alex's fault. He performed his duties perfectly. He prepared meals for me, helped around the house, and polished my shoes, all without me asking."

"You'll forgive me for being surprised. You have quite the reputation for disliking indentured servants and, indeed, for pursuing them and holding them to account for their misdeeds."

"I know that's the popular perception, but it has nothing to do with me. I've never once given an interview or said anything to that effect. Until now, only the people in my life have had any idea what I think or believe. This speaks to a wider truth: none of us really knows public figures, even if we think we do. The media has painted a picture of me that bears only the smallest relation to my reality. In my opinion, having got to know him very well, I would say that the media's impression of Alex is similarly misleading."

"In what way?"

"He's not the pantomime villain he's been painted as, for a start. He's a real person. I find him kind, warm-hearted, and genuine. He's artistic and a little mercurial, prone to moodiness and occasional flashes of temper, but he's also witty, extremely intelligent, and loyal to a fault."

"You have arrested numerous indentured servants in your time," Byrne pointed out.

"I've arrested killers. I might not agree with the system, but I won't give indies a free pass for killing people," Josiah replied firmly. "I've never targeted indies, though. I do my job. I've also arrested dozens of people who aren't indentured servants, but the media is less interested in that."

HMS sallied forth to take over the questioning.

"It sounds like you're more than a little in love with Alexander Lytton," he said, his lips quirking into a knowing grin. He winked at the jury. "I can see why – he's a handsome young man."

"I like Alex a great deal, but when this case is over, he will be returned either to Mr Tyler or, if he's found guilty, to Tyler Tech, who are his proxy houders. That's another reason why I dislike the system. To return an IS to a person or company that has abused him for years is despicable."

"There is no evidence he's been abused for years."

"Jabir Aldaba, Mick Reynolds, Ted Burgis, and Alex himself have all spoken at length about how he was treated."

"If we believe them."

"I do."

"I put it to you that you have been dazzled by Mr Lytton's looks and charm into believing the frankly ludicrous story he concocted."

"The assumption I'd be swayed by his looks is both patronising and simply untrue," Josiah snapped. "I'm not so easily won over, as anyone who knows me will testify."

"So, you were impressed by his virtues as an indentured servant – despite having no time for indentured servants?" HMS raised an eyebrow.

"No, I was struck by his bravery and decency from the moment I first met him," Josiah said stoutly.

"When you first met him, you arrested him on suspicion of murdering his houder." HMS gave the jury a look of frank disbelief.

"That's not when I first met him," Josiah said quietly.

HMS frowned and glanced at his notes. "Forgive me, am I in error? When *did* you first meet him?"

Josiah looked straight at Alex and smiled. Alex put his hands over his heart, his eyes burning with pride, and nodded. Only he knew just how hard it was for Josiah to talk about this.

"I first met Alex the night my husband, Peter, was murdered," he stated firmly, gazing around the courtroom. "Alex had just escaped from Tyler because he was abusing him, and he was first on the scene when Peter was stabbed. He tried to save Peter's life by jumping on his assailant and trying to disarm him. I arrived seconds later and joined in, but for several moments, Alex was alone in that fight. He was considerably shorter and slighter than Lars Driessen, the man who attacked my husband, but he didn't hesitate to try and protect Peter."

There was a stunned silence. HMS looked confused, and Tyler's jaw dropped open in disbelief. The jury looked completely shocked, but the media had lit up like a beacon in a lost zone, clearly excited by this new twist in the story. Alex nodded at Josiah across the courtroom, his eyes shining.

"So, he was on the run, and he just happened to be passing your vehicle at the moment your husband was stabbed?" HMS sounded sceptical. Josiah knew he was only moments away from the Kathleen Line being revealed, but he ploughed on regardless.

"Alex saw Driessen attacking my husband and tried to save Peter's life. It was Alex who called the emergency services. The court can listen to the recording we have on file. It's clearly his voice. He ran off before they arrived because he knew he'd be returned to Tyler if he stayed. This corroborates a key moment in Alex's story, that Tyler was angry with him because he escaped. It also ties in precisely, in terms of dates, with when Solange was killed."

HMS looked angry at having this revelation sprung on him, as well he might. Josiah hadn't intended to speak about Peter's death. It still felt too raw, too personal, and he hated the idea of putting this most private and tragic part of his life on display, but he owed this to Alex. He'd been so brave that night, and the jury deserved to know about it.

"We already knew Mr Lytton had absconded, from Mr Bates's earlier testimony," HMS said testily.

"And I'm corroborating it." Josiah shot him a steely look.

"So, you were inclined to believe Mr Lytton's allegations against Mr Tyler simply because he aided you the night your husband died?"

"*Simply?*" Josiah rounded on him. "What Alex did that night was nothing short of heroic. He was just a scared indie on the run. He had so much to lose, and yet, he tried to save my husband's life. I'm an investigator, and when Alex told me that a young woman was murdered and her killer never brought to justice, I was inclined to believe him. Nothing I've found out subsequently has convinced me that he was lying."

"Did you know that Mr Lytton and Mr Tyler once had a romantic affair?" HMS asked suddenly, wrong-footing him. "You seemed shocked by the footage of them together."

"No," Josiah said shortly. "I didn't know that until recently."

"Does it change your view of Mr Lytton?"

"Not fundamentally, no."

"Surely it must cast doubt on the veracity of his testimony?"

"Tyler didn't mention it when giving evidence, either. Does it cast doubt on the veracity of *his* testimony?" Josiah flung back.

"Why would Mr Lytton have an affair with a man he believed had killed his best friend?" HMS demanded, avoiding the question.

"He had no choice. He was Tyler's prisoner, and Tyler was prostituting him. He'd seen him kill Solange, and had every expectation that Tyler might kill him, too. Why wouldn't he have sex with the man under those circumstances? Why not even pretend to love him? I have no doubt he was doing it to survive. I don't believe he ever really loved George Tyler. He saw, first-hand, what an angry, vengeful man Tyler is. Tyler never got over Isobel Lytton's death and he's been obsessed with pursuing vengeance against the man he believes is responsible ever since."

HMS paused for a moment, frowning. "The person he *believes* is responsible?" he queried.

"Yes. Tyler believes that Alex killed the love of his life, and he can never get over that."

"Your use of the word 'believes' is misleading, surely? Mr Lytton pleaded guilty in court of driving under the influence of the drug crocodile tears. Are you saying that's not the case?" HMS demanded.

Josiah glanced at Alex's white face. They only had this one final roll of the dice to convince the jury that what they knew about Alex was all wrong. It was a risk, because it established that Alex was prepared to lie under oath, but Josiah wasn't just fighting to convince the jury of Alex's essential goodness. He was also fighting for Alex's future in the all too likely event that they lost and he was returned to Tyler. Maybe the hatred between them was now too well established to be changed by this new information, but if it would save Alex even a little suffering at Tyler's hands, then surely it was worth it?

Strategically, this was a curve ball that would also buy Reed more time to crack the encryption on the blackmail footage. All of this went through his mind as he stood on the witness stand with the eyes of the nation upon him. It made sense to speak up, if it wasn't for one thing: he'd promised Alex that he wouldn't.

Alex's eyes were locked on his, agonised and pleading. He'd spent years protecting his secret. Was Josiah really going to betray him by offering it up to the world? He'd be ruining their friendship, possibly forever.

He hesitated. He'd once told Alex he always kept his promises, and he'd always believed that was exactly the kind of man he was, but now he found he was something else, too, something that was even more central to his identity. He was an investigator, and he should never have made that promise. It was time to put his personal feelings to one side and do his damn job.

"Yes," he said, loudly and firmly. "That's exactly what I'm saying. Alex Lytton wasn't driving that duck at the time of the accident that killed his mother."

He saw Charles's look of alarm, saw Noah turning, baffled, to gaze at Alex, saw Tyler's jaw jerk open in stunned surprise.

"Then who was?" HMS asked.

"That's not for me to conjecture in this courtroom," Josiah replied.

The entire room broke out in an uproar, and the judge called both barristers to the bench to discuss this sudden turn of events. Tyler had his arms folded across his chest in stubborn disbelief. Charles looked as if all the blood had drained from his face as he sat frozen in place. Noah was talking to him urgently in a low tone, but Charles was paying him no attention.

HMS returned to his desk. "The judge has allowed continued questioning on this matter as it pertains to the character of the main witness," he said. "Investigator Raine, can you explain why you're so sure that Alexander wasn't driving that day?"

"I watched the court recording of the case, and I was troubled by his conviction for driving under the influence of drugs. Something about that case didn't feel right, so I investigated it. It soon became clear to me that there was no way either of the two people sitting in the front of the duck that day escaped without serious injury. I examined the road and the photos of the duck and spoke to witnesses, and I concluded that Alex had to be sitting in the back at the time of the accident. That explains why he escaped with comparatively minor injuries."

"Why would Alex take the blame for an accident that killed his mother and seriously injured his brother?" HMS demanded.

"Because he's loyal to a fault and would do anything to protect the people he loves."

"Who is he protecting?" HMS demanded.

"You'll have to ask him that. As I said, I won't conjecture."

The judge called Byrne and HMS to her desk for a brief discussion and then adjourned. It was clear she thought there had been quite enough revelations for one day. Josiah assumed that Alex would be called back to the witness stand the following day, and then he'd have to decide whether to lie again under oath or reveal the truth. Well, that was on him. Josiah had done all he could do.

Alex wouldn't even look at him as he stepped down. Now they were both angry with each other, but for different reasons. So be it.

Charles stumbled towards the exit, leaning heavily on his walker, looking dazed, as if in a dream. Alex was beside him, his hand resting protectively on his brother's shoulder. The media surrounded them the second they stepped outside.

"Charles, Charles – was Alex driving the duck that day?"

"Alex – who was driving? Why did you lie?"

Josiah shouldered his way through. "Give them space, let them through," he bellowed.

Charles grabbed hold of his arm and pulled him back, looking terrified. "I want to talk to them," he stammered.

"Charles – no." Alex placed his body between his brother and the media. "Don't say a word," he hissed.

"I want to talk to them," Charles repeated stubbornly.

The media surged forward, scenting blood, and a microphone was thrust under Charles's nose.

Out of the corner of his eye, Josiah saw Tyler, surrounded by his lawyers and bodyguards, joining the throng. He had no idea what Charles was going to say, but Alex's fate hinged on it. He leaned forward and spoke directly into Charles's ear.

"For God's sake, Charles, for once in your life, be a man," he growled.

Charles looked at Alex for a long moment, and something wordless seemed to pass between them. Then Charles looked back at the waiting media. His hand was shaking as he raised the microphone to his lips.

"Investigator Raine is correct. Alex wasn't driving the duck at the time of the accident that killed my mother," he said, his voice barely more than a whisper. "*I* was. It was my fault Mum died. It wasn't Alex, it was me."

The media erupted again, shouting out a thousand questions at the same time.

"Why, Charles? Why?" one of the reporters yelled, his voice ringing out over all the others.

"I asked Alex to take the blame because I was scared my gold medal would be taken away from me," Charles replied. "Alex has always had a kind heart. He did as I asked because he was trying to protect me. He still is. That's who he is."

"Why? Why were you scared you'd lose your medal?" The questions rang out, all clamouring to know the same thing.

"I..." Charles closed his eyes, then opened them again, visibly mustering all his courage. Josiah squeezed his shoulder, lending him his support. "In case I was tested for taking a performance-enhancing substance," he whispered.

Pandemonium broke out once more, but Josiah's gaze was fixed on one man. George Tyler's face had gone grey and he was staring at Charles in disbelief. He'd been able to justify everything he'd done to Alex on the basis of his supposed responsibility for Isobel's death. Would he be able to accept this new reality, or would he try to defend his own version of events?

Alex turned to look at Josiah, and there was an expression on his face that Josiah had never seen before. His eyes were dark with a fury bordering on hatred, and he found himself almost wishing that his maddeningly vacant mask would return.

"I'm sorry," he said softly, but Alex turned away in disgust.

The media surged in, surrounding them, and Josiah looked around in alarm. This was turning ugly.

"Charles, we need to get you away from all this." Josiah forced a pathway through the throng and led Charles back into the courthouse to a private room. Then he called for backup from Inquisitus and a solicitor.

"You'll need legal representation," he explained to Charles. "And thank you," he added, "for finally doing the right thing."

Charles looked petrified, small, and diminished, and Josiah saw him then for the weak, good-natured fool he really was – and finally understood that *this* was who Alex had been protecting all along.

Josiah knew that he'd been instrumental in tarnishing the reputation of a great national hero. Would the nation ever forgive him? It had always been so easy to love Charles and hate Alex. The world wanted its villains and heroes to be entirely black and white, without any messy shades of grey. Charles was the good brother, the golden boy, and Alex was the bad brother, the black sheep. Everyone knew that, so it had to be true. Didn't it?

Alex fought his way into the room a few seconds later. He went straight over to his brother, knelt in front of him, and wrapped his arms around him. The two brothers clung on to each other for several minutes while Charles sobbed into Alex's shirt. Alex swallowed hard, fighting back tears of his own, then he looked up at Josiah, his eyes blazing.

"Are you satisfied now?"

"I'm sorry," Josiah said again, helplessly. He didn't regret what he'd done, but now, in the aftermath, he realised what an incredibly big deal it was. He'd known it would be, of course, but knowing and being confronted by the reality were two different things.

These brothers had a bond he'd never understood and had failed to fully appreciate. He'd never liked Charles, so he hadn't taken into account how much love there was between them. As much as Charles had failed Alex, that wasn't the way Alex viewed it. His promise to his brother had been unbreakable, and he would have gone to his grave with it, as Gideon had warned. He'd endured years of torment because of it, but had never once revealed his secret – until Josiah had blundered in and done it for him. He had the sudden realisation that if his affair with Alex wasn't over before today, it certainly was now.

At that moment, help arrived in the form of Esther and several burly Inquisitus agents.

"You don't do things by halves, do you, Joe?" she said, briskly taking charge. She parked her wheelchair in front of Charles and spoke to him in firm, no-nonsense tones.

"Mr Lytton, you've done the right thing and unburdened your conscience of what I'm sure was a great weight," she told him sternly. "I must warn you that there will be ramifications, but I'll see to it that you have the best legal representation."

"Yes, thank you," he whispered. He was still sobbing, his chest heaving. Alex had a protective arm around his shoulder.

"When you're ready, we'll ensure you're able to leave safely. We can take you to Inquisitus, away from the media, or you can return to your own home. I can provide you with a handful of agents to help you fend off the worst of the intrusion. But I should warn you, it will last some time, and it won't be pleasant."

"I understand," he said, his voice breaking. Josiah saw then what

Alex had always known: Charles wasn't strong enough to handle the consequences of his own actions. He was a good-natured fool, utterly unable to withstand the hostility of the waiting journalists. He'd always loved playing to the crowd when they were on his side, but he'd be utterly flattened by their hatred.

"Where's my father?" Alex asked suddenly, looking around. Noah was nowhere to be seen, and Josiah feared for him in the crush outside.

"I'll find him," he said, grateful to leave the room and the drama he'd unleashed.

He fought his way out of the scrum of people milling around like vultures outside. They all wanted him to talk to them, but he used his large body like a battering ram and bulldozed his way out.

There was no sign of Noah anywhere. A thought occurred to him, and he walked away from the baying mob, back to the calm and safety of the courtroom. It was completely empty now, except for one sad figure sitting exactly where he'd been for the entire trial.

Silently, Josiah sat down next to him. Noah didn't move or speak. He just sat there, his head down, his body trembling. Aware of his poor health, Josiah was wondering if he should call for help when, finally, Noah lifted his head.

"Is it true?" he asked quietly. "Alex wasn't driving?"

"It's true."

"It couldn't have been Isobel because she didn't drive, so..."

"It was Charles."

Noah looked at him with blank incomprehension. "Why the lie?" he asked. "Why lie about this?"

"Charles was taking a banned substance called Flex that almost certainly helped him win the gold medal. He was terrified the medal would be taken away from him if his blood was tested. He asked Alex to take the blame."

Noah stared at him, his face haggard, his eyes bleary with shock. "Did Isobel know?" he asked eventually.

"Yes. It was her idea. She obtained the drug for him. That's partly why she had the affair with Tyler. She wanted him to pay for the drug, so you wouldn't find out."

Noah stared into space for a long time as he processed this. "Did I ever know any of them?" he asked eventually. "Isobel, Charles, Alex? What kind of a fool am I to not truly know any of my own family?"

"Not a fool, a good man," Josiah reassured him. "They hid it from you precisely because they knew you wouldn't approve. You couldn't have guessed because, unlike Tyler, you don't seek out the worst in people."

"I loved them all," Noah said despairingly.

"You still do," Josiah murmured gently. "I'm sorry you had to learn it in this way. I wish things had been different." God, did he ever! He'd never shirked at taking the hard path, at doing the right thing rather than the expedient one, or the kind one, but now he was paying a high price for that, as were the entire Lytton clan.

"All these years of believing Alex was behind the wheel, that his broken promises to me were behind his actions that day, only to find..." Noah shook his head. "Charles. Poor, silly Charles. I don't blame him, not really." He looked at Josiah. "He would have found it hard to say no to Isobel. Most people did."

"I think you're giving Charles too much of a free pass," Josiah said. "He was a grown man and he went along with all this willingly. It was Charles who asked Alex to lie for him. Charles would have done anything to protect that bloody medal."

"Maybe he's more like his mother than I thought." Noah gave a wry smile.

"Just remember that Alex is the one who bore the brunt of your family's mistakes," Josiah told him. "He's the stronger of the two, the braver, and the one who most deserves your love."

"He has it," Noah said. "We've all failed him, but that ends now."

"As for Charles... he'll need you now more than ever. Don't turn your back on him the way you did with Alex. He just stood outside and admitted everything. He's been brave today."

"I'm bitterly ashamed of how I treated Alex. I won't make the same mistake with Charles."

"Good. Now, you can't just leave. The media is like a pack of wolves out there. Esther is making arrangements for Charles. Let me take you to where your sons are, and you can decide what to do from there."

Noah nodded, and Josiah helped him to his feet. He was shaky, and

Josiah had to hold him up as they walked towards the exit. He was worried for his health and greatly relieved when Noah managed to walk safely along the hallway to the room where the rest of his family were.

Charles and Alex were both where he'd left them, Alex still holding his brother protectively. They looked up when Noah entered, and Josiah could see the terrible anxiety on their faces. Noah gathered up all his strength, released his hold on Josiah's arm, and walked purposefully towards his sons.

"It's alright," he said, in a quiet, decisive voice. "It's all out in the open now and we'll deal with it together. As a family." He reached out and put one arm around Alex, while resting his other hand on Charles's shoulder and squeezing firmly. "I love you both," he said. "Nothing else matters. None of it. Understand?"

Alex buried his face in his father's shoulder, while Charles wrapped his arms around his father's waist, and they stood there, sheltering from the storm together, a family united against the world.

Josiah cleared his throat. How could he possibly think he'd done the wrong thing when this was the result? Or was that just self-justification? Yet, he couldn't deny that he was fiercely satisfied by the fact the world would now see Alex as he truly was and not the pantomime villain they'd loved to hate. He hoped so, anyway. It occurred to him that he wasn't so different to Gideon, wanting the truth to surface, no matter who was hurt in the process.

After a family conference, Noah and Charles decided they wanted to return to The Orchard. Esther saw to it that they were transported there with an Inquisitus escort that would stay with them for the foreseeable future.

"I'd like to go with them," Alex said.

"Absolutely not," Esther told him firmly, and Josiah was grateful it was her turning Alex down, not him. "You're in Inquisitus's custody, and I won't risk that with this trial hanging in the balance. You'll remain with Josiah."

Alex shot him a look of pure venom, and he knew that neither of them would be getting much sleep tonight.

Alex climbed into the duck and slammed the door, then rammed his hand to the radio, filling the AV with the gleeful tones of what seemed like every person in the country with an opinion on today's drama.

Neither of them spoke for the entire journey home, but the second they walked into the house, Alex turned on him.

"I begged you! I pleaded with you not to use that information. You didn't have to. It wasn't fucking well relevant."

"Alex, listen to me. You have every right to be angry, but please hear me out," Josiah said urgently. "Tyler found me during the lunch recess. He told me he'd paid off some of the media to ensure they'd write negative stories about you. I wanted to give them something else to write about. The perception of you as the villain of this piece was holding us back. Nobody was going to believe your story because of it."

"Well, now they all know that I lied under oath when I took the blame for the accident. So how does that help us?"

"It was a gamble, but we had nothing left to lose."

"Charles had a great deal to lose."

"Charles is a liar and a cheat. Why do we have to keep protecting him?"

"Because he's my brother, and I love him!"

"Well, you're my friend, and I love you!"

"I don't want your fucking love. I didn't bloody well ask for it." Alex took a running jump and kicked over a nearby footstool. It slammed against the sideboard with a resounding crash. "Some fucking friend."

"I did it for you."

"No, you did it for yourself. You wanted to win at all costs. This was always about you winning because you've never lost a case, and you can't bear the thought you'll lose this one."

"That's not true. I told you at the beginning that I'd do everything it took to get justice. I asked you if you had the fire in your belly for that, and you said you did."

"I didn't know it'd mean this."

"I've never hidden this side of myself, Alex. I'm an investigator – this is who I am."

"You're also hiding a great big fat secret. How would you like it if I blabbed about *that* in court?"

Josiah sighed and threw himself down on the sofa. "Too late. George is going to beat you to it," he said, feeling suddenly completely shattered.

"What?" Alex stared down at him.

"That's one of the things he wanted to talk to me about in the park earlier. He's got a dossier. I'm not sure entirely what's in it, but he knows about the Kathleen Line. His plan is to take me down, too. It always was. He just wants the biggest audience possible for when he drops his bombshell. My guess is HMS was supposed to do it this afternoon when questioning me but events rather slipped away from him. I'm sure he'll pick up where he left off when the court reconvenes."

"So, you gave up *my* secret to protect yours?" Alex accused.

"God, no." Josiah was shocked. "I promise that wasn't the reason I did what I did."

"Oh, well, if you *promise*, then it must be true, because you always keep your fucking promises, don't you?"

"I deserve that." Josiah sighed. "But it's true, nonetheless. This buys me a day at most, so it's definitely not the reason I did it. The truth is we're going to lose, and then Tyler's going to take you back, and he's going to crucify you, and I won't be able to help you or rescue you because I'll be in prison." Josiah's voice broke in despair. "At least now, he can't justify what he does to you by using your mother's death against you. He might go easier on you as a result. I had to do it, Alex, for that reason alone. I had to do something to make it easier for you when you're returned to him. You can see that, can't you?"

"No. You can't really believe this will change how Tyler treats me. There's far too much water under the bridge for that."

"It had to be worth a shot. It also threw a spanner in HMS's carefully planned works, and maybe bought us a few extra hours."

"Bought us a few extra hours for *what*?" Alex demanded.

"I didn't tell you because I didn't want you to get your hopes up. Jabir gave us a whole bunch of nanodrives from Tyler's safe in Spain."

"What?" Alex sat down suddenly, his legs giving way beneath him. "The blackmail footage?"

"Very likely. If, and it's a big if, we can crack the encryption. Reed has been working on it non-stop for days, with no luck so far. So, I was trying to buy us time for that, as well."

"Are you sure?" Alex leaned forward. "Was that really what you were doing, or were you trying to get back at me for that footage of me with Tyler?"

"What?" Josiah blinked, startled. "No."

"You were so furious that you had to leave the court. You couldn't bear to even look at me. I saw it. You were disgusted by that footage."

"I was taken by surprise. I'm not naïve, Alex. I knew you slept with Tyler. Of course you did. I just assumed it wasn't willingly."

"Well, now you know." Alex gave a twisted smile. "You want the truth? The truth is that I wanted him, at first anyway. I can't explain it, but there was always this fire between us. We loathed each other, but we were fascinated by one another, too. I hated him, Joe, I honestly did, but for a while, I craved him. I was his prisoner, and it'd be easy to say I had no choice. But right from the start, he told me that he'd never take me to his bed until I begged him and meant it, and in the end, I did. So there. You wanted to know, and that's the honest bloody truth. I went to his bed willingly. I begged him to fuck me."

"Christ, Alex." Josiah felt the bile rise in the back of his throat. "Were you in love with him?"

"No. God no. But we were in a relationship for some time, however fucked up it might have been. I'd say it wasn't my choice, and in many ways it wasn't, but all the same—" He broke off, shaking his head. "I had to sleep with him to convince him that I wasn't a threat, to encourage him to let his guard down around me. But did I also enjoy it? Yes, I did – at first, anyway."

"I can't begin to understand that."

"No, of course you can't, because you're Josiah fucking Raine," Alex said savagely. "Everything's always black and white for you, isn't it? You're brave, direct, and fearless. You couldn't lie for years like I did with Tyler. You could never have worn that mask Gideon taught me to put on. It isn't in your DNA. Maybe you're just too honourable, or too much *you*. I don't know, but it doesn't make you better than me, or Solange, or anyone else forced into that situation."

"I never said I was."

"You believe it, though. You walk around believing in the great Josiah Raine. So fantastic at your job, so benevolent to escaped indies. So fucking perfect, in fact, compared to the rest of us messy mortals."

"That's not true, and it's not fair."

"Fair? It's not fair that you gave away my secret to protect your own."

"That's not why I did it."

"No, you did it because of what you saw in that footage. You did it because, like Neil and like everyone else, you saw me as the poor, damaged boy who needed you to pick him up and fix him. Then you saw that footage and it ruined the image you had of me, and that made you angry."

"That's not true."

"You wanted to see me as a victim, but instead, there I was, having an affair with the man I'd accused of murder. You couldn't stand it. You hated it. That's the real reason you told the court about Charles."

"I was upset about that, but that's not it. Jesus, is that how you see me? As yet another Neil? One more person who falls for an image of you that isn't true?"

"It's what everyone does. Nobody falls for *me*. Why the hell would they? I'm not very nice. You know that but consistently deny it."

"Because I don't think it's true."

"Then why were you so upset about that footage of me with Tyler?"

"Because..."

"Well?" Alex jumped to his feet and loomed over him, his face twisted with anger. "Come on, say it. We both know why."

"Fine," Josiah snapped. "I was upset because it made me wonder if you'd been any more honest with me than you were with him. You can hide who you are so easily. Is it all fake, Alex? Everything we've been through together? Were you just playing me to get me to take on this case, the way you played Tyler? Is *that* who you really are?"

"And there it is." Alex flopped down on the sofa beside him, all the fight suddenly leaving his body. They sat silently for a long time, and then, finally, Alex turned to him. "For what it's worth, I wasn't playing you, Joe."

"You were a bit at the beginning," Josiah said softly.

"Yeah. I suppose I was in the beginning." Alex sighed. "See, I'm really not very nice."

"Sometimes, I'm not very nice, either," Josiah said wryly. "I betrayed your secret when you begged me not to, and for that, I'm genuinely sorry."

"You were always going to," Alex told him with a wave of his hand. "I knew it, deep down, from the minute you took me back to where it happened. I knew it because that's who you are."

Silence descended again, both of them exhausted by the furious fight.

Then Josiah turned to look at him. "Do we see each other clearly at last, Alex?" he asked quietly. "Do we finally see each other now?"

"I suppose we do." Alex gave a tired smile. "I had a full-blown affair with George Tyler and it wasn't all coercive. He was a fantastic lover, a truly great shag." He bit out the words, meaning them to wound, and they did. "I didn't tell you because I didn't want you to see me as I really am, or to question what we had between us."

"I had to investigate you. I had to keep digging," Josiah said tightly. "I couldn't leave it, and when I uncovered the truth, I couldn't *bear* that Charles got away with it, that he was lionised and adored while you took the rap. That, more than anything else, stuck in my craw."

"*That's* who we are," Alex sighed. "It's not very pretty, but it's true."

Josiah gave a little chuckle. There was a kind of catharsis here. "I'll miss being your knight in shining armour," he murmured. "I liked how it felt."

"And I'll miss being Ben Smith, the poor, broken boy you wanted so much to save."

"I'll miss him, too." Josiah sighed. "I guess I come alive when there's someone to save. Peter always knew that."

"Well, to be fair, I was always attracted to how safe you made me feel."

They didn't speak again for so long that Josiah wondered if he'd dozed off. He came to, glancing at Alex to find him staring into space.

"We should go to bed," he murmured. "Separately."

"Well, yeah," Alex said, rolling his eyes. "That ship has well and truly bloody well sailed."

"Yup." He forced himself to his feet, feeling drained beyond belief.

"What now?" Alex asked.

"Who knows? I guess it all depends on what happens in court."

"I'm still so bloody angry with you."

"I know… and I'm still so bloody hurt by you."

There was nothing more to be said. They exchanged honest, regretful smiles and then dragged themselves off to their separate rooms.

Josiah had barely been asleep for an hour when he was woken by a buzz from his holopad.

"Yeah? What? Raine," he mumbled, in a fog of weariness.

"It's me," said a voice at least as tired as his own but also bursting with excitement.

"Who?" He frowned groggily, trying to wake up.

"Me – Cam. You have to come into the office right now, Joe. I've found something."

Chapter Eighteen
OCTOBER 2095
Alex

The next show Elliot planned to take him to was on Eden Floating City. Alex didn't give a damn about the show, but he was interested in the floating city. It looked as if Tyler's investment in the tech had paid off, because these cities were springing up all over the place.

He was, therefore, disappointed when he saw it. It was grey, utilitarian, and ugly, squatting on the surface of the water like a vast metal spider. He wasn't sure why he'd expected anything different. Tyler had been clear that the future of floating city tech lay in mass-producing them as cheaply as possible. This was no Ghost Eye, all opulence and grandeur, designed and built for the rich. Eden was functional, intended to house as many people as possible on the cheap.

The hotel hosting the show was squalid, but he was used to that. He was given an armband with the number sixteen on it and took his place in a side room with all the other indies. He found these shows tedious and distasteful, but Elliot loved them. He'd often wondered whether he should speak of Solange to one of the houders who won his services for the night, but so far, none of them had been interested in talking, and he'd never felt that any of them were entirely trustworthy. What was he expecting them to do, anyway? Call the police? And say what? "This indie I traded for sex says a girl was killed by a famous businessman a few years ago?"

The longer he kept his mission a secret, the less he felt he'd ever be able to share it with anyone. Maybe he'd end up taking it to his grave. He just hoped Solange wouldn't meet him there full of reproach for his long years of inaction. He hated himself for it, berated himself constantly, but he simply didn't know what to do. Time was dragging by, and he was no closer now than he'd ever been.

Next to him, a sweet-faced blond boy smiled flirtatiously.

"Save it for the houders," Alex said. He looked like the kind of boy Elliot would choose. He always went for the sweet, innocent-looking ones at shows. He liked to pretend they were virgins and he was the kindly older man showing them the ropes.

"They're all old and ugly. You're hot," the boy said, grinning.

"This your first time?"

"At a show? Yeah. Not at sex, though. I've been shagging blokes for years." The boy laughed. "I'm Eric." He held out his hand.

Alex ignored it. "Not here you're not. Here, you're number nine," he said, glancing at the boy's armband.

"So, what are these shows like?" Eric asked.

"Boring. You wait here for ages, then parade around onstage. The houders vote on you, then there's a terrible floor show – usually two blokes in costumes having sex. The votes are counted, but they're really only interested in the top three indies. The houders get to pick an indie they want to sleep with. After that, the whole thing descends into horse-trading, with the houders mainly just desperate to make sure they get their hands on a different indie to the one they came with."

"It sounds hot." Eric grinned.

"It's really not."

"This place is amazing. I've never been on a floating city before." Eric helped himself to a glass of Coke from a big tray on the side, gulping it down in one go. "Free drinks!"

"Oh, trust me, nothing here is free. It's a cattle market."

"It's fun. I like it."

"Where the hell are you from?" Alex asked, frowning.

"Oh, I'm not supposed to say, but…" Eric looked around, then lowered his voice theatrically. "I'm not actually an IS."

"What?" Alex shook his head, bemused. "Then why the hell are you here, if nobody is making you?"

"I'm being paid." Eric looked very pleased with himself. "I usually turn tricks down by the lost zone near the Canary Quarter. This is much more fun."

"You're a rent boy?"

"If you like." Eric shrugged. "Though I spend most of it on croc, not rent." His bright grin faded a little. "I have to hand some of it over to the gang that runs the Quarter I live in," he confided. "Though sometimes they let me suck them off, and then I get to keep it all."

This seemed to fill Eric with glee. Alex felt a little sorry for him; he couldn't have been more than seventeen years old.

"Listen, do you have lube and condoms?" he asked, wanting to impart some wisdom to this stupid kid before he went out there. "Only, these blokes often don't bother with them if you don't bring any. I try to keep a stash in all my pockets now, just in case."

"Sure. Lube, condoms, the works. I'm a pro." Eric winked.

The show started, and Alex watched as Eric sidled out onstage. His earlier excitement had faded and he looked suddenly shy to be onstage, being ogled by all these strange men. Alex felt a pang of sympathy for him.

He was an old hand now, so he knew the drill. He made his entry with as little fanfare as possible, doing just enough that Elliot wouldn't be angry with him later.

He achieved first place, as he often did. He was pleased about that. It'd make his life easier in the coming week if Elliot was able to have his pick of the indies.

Elliot whooped and ran up onstage. "I want number nine," he cried out.

Alex wasn't surprised. Eric was precisely the kind of sweet-looking innocent that Elliot often chose. Despite his profession, Alex hoped that Eric would be able to play along with Elliot's shy-virgin fantasy.

Eric seemed delighted to be chosen by the winning houder and ran up to him, his own houder following on behind. Alex wasn't remotely interested in Eric's houder. He assumed he would be as sleazy and unprepossessing as they always were. He was, therefore, completely taken by surprise when a hand grasped his arm eagerly, swinging him around... and he was face to face with Neil.

"Hello, Alex." Neil grinned, pulling him in close and wrapping him in a tight hug. Over his shoulder, Alex saw Elliot tugging Eric away to his room for the night, eager to unwrap his prize. He didn't so much as glance backwards to see if Alex was okay.

Neil drew away and gazed at him, and Alex stared back, speechless. As a young man, Neil had been mildly attractive, but he was far less so now. He looked prematurely middle-aged, his stocky frame having spread out, giving him a soft appearance. His once floppy dark hair was now receding, so he'd shaved it close to his head, making his face look even rounder. He still had ferociously angry-looking eyebrows, thick and dark, that slanted across his forehead like a canopy.

Alex didn't say a word as Neil took his hand and led him away. They reached the hotel room, a shabby, tiny space, but mercifully clean – they weren't always. Neil shut and locked the door behind them and then turned, and they stared again at each other for what felt like forever. Neil seemed to be drinking him in, studying every detail, while he was still struggling to get his head around what was happening.

"You look good, Alex," Neil said at last. "Still beautiful."

"You look... older," Alex retorted.

Neil's face broke into a pained smile. "Life's not been good to me. I haven't been some rich bloke's pampered pet all these years."

Alex burst out laughing. "Oh, yeah. That's totally what my life has been."

"From where I'm standing it has." Neil shrugged. "That fool Elliot dotes on you, doesn't he? I've seen you in all the magazines and on all the celeb gossip sites. They call you Christopher Dacre now, but I knew it was you the minute I saw you. You're just the same."

"Why are you here, Neil?" Alex demanded. "Do you really want one more night with me that badly? It's not as if you haven't had me many times."

"One night?" Neil scoffed. "Oh no, I don't just want one night with you, Alex. I want so much more."

"What are you talking about?"

"You, me, us." Neil moved towards him, and Alex took a step backwards. "Us, together again, after all this time." Neil put his hands on Alex's shoulders and gazed excitedly into his eyes. "It'll be like the old times."

"The old times were fucking awful," Alex snapped. "And there is no *us*. There never was."

"You know that's not true," Neil said fiercely. "I still love you, Alex. I always have."

"You sold me out to Tyler."

"No, you did that all by yourself." Neil adopted a self-righteous tone. "I think you needed that, though. You needed to fall, to see how the rest of us live."

"You have no idea how most indies live," Alex retorted. "Your life was one of ease by comparison." He thought of Solange, Ted, and Mick. "My father looked after you and your mother. He paid for your education, for fuck's sake."

"Oh, big fucking deal," Neil sneered. "Largesse from the Lyttons. He did it because he loved being the lord of the manor, doling out jobs to those he considered most worthy, and bathing in their gratitude."

"Compared to the houders I've had, he's a bloody saint."

"Well, that's all over for you now," Neil said sweetly. He sat down on the side of the bed and patted the space beside him, inviting Alex to join him.

"How?" Alex asked warily, not moving.

"Because now you've got me on your side. I told you I'd always take care of you, Alex, and I meant it. I tried to buy you, you know."

"Yeah, I know." Alex shrugged. "But Elliot turned you down. Where the hell did you find the money, Neil?"

"That doesn't matter. I just want you to know that I tried to get you legitimately. It didn't work, so I thought I'd try this instead. The point is, I'm not giving up on you. I never did, and I never will. Everything I've done since the day you were sold is to get you back."

"Get me back?" Alex was stunned by Neil's self-delusion. To still be so obsessed, after all these years – it was beyond belief. "Neil, you never *had* me. We were a business arrangement, that's all."

"No, we had something special. Now, stop it, Alex. You're ruining it."

"Ruining what? Our great reunion? Oh, grow up, Neil. That's not what this is."

Neil's face crumpled, but then, finally, he smiled. "That's good. Say what you think, love. You don't have to pretend with me like you do with that Elliot bloke. You and me, it was always fiery, wasn't it? That's why the sex was so fantastic. You knew how to rile me up, and then we'd channel it into the bedroom."

Alex stared at him. How was he still so obtuse? Finally, giving up, he turned and ran towards the door. Whatever Neil had planned, he wanted no part of it. No good would ever come from trusting Neil Grant, he knew that. He reached the door, scrabbling for the lock, turned the handle – and then Neil was on him.

"You're not going anywhere. I won you for the night, fair and square," Neil said, wrestling him back. He was far bigger than him but not in good shape, whereas Alex was honed from hours at the gym. He thought he could take Neil on.

"I'm not fucking sleeping with you," he shouted as Neil tried to drag him back to the bed.

"You have to," Neil yelled back. "I paid my money."

"Oh, for fuck's sake. This is ridiculous. Neil..." Alex stopped fighting and let Neil drag him over to the bed and throw him on it. "What's the plan here, Neil? What do you really want?"

"What I've always wanted. You and me, the way we used to be. I have money. We can get out of this lousy bloody country and be together properly." Neil's eyes had a weird, glazed quality, and Alex wondered if he was quite sane.

"You want to run away with me?" he asked, startled. "Are you for real?"

"Yes. Come with me, Alex. We'll run away together. I've got a duck waiting outside, and I've paid a guy on the coast to take us to France." Neil's face was stupidly hopeful.

Alex ran through the scenario in his head, but he didn't seriously consider it. For a start, he'd just be swapping one form of slavery for another. Even if he could escape from Neil once they got out of the

UK, he'd be looking over his shoulder for the rest of his life because Neil would pursue him – and so would Tyler.

"No," he said.

Neil's face did that strange crumpling thing again.

"I couldn't do that to you," Alex added in a placatory tone. "You see, I'm being followed everywhere I go."

"By the black SUAVs. Yes, I know," Neil said dismissively. "I've been watching you for ages. I've followed you loads of times. Once, I spent hours in that gym, watching you work out."

"Then you know that I'm very heavily guarded. I'm the most expensive IS in the country, Neil. I don't go anywhere without my houder knowing about it."

"But we can cut out your tracker. I've got a knife." Neil produced a blade from under his jacket, and Alex felt his throat go dry. This was starting to feel dangerous.

"It's no good. Tyler's security guards will be here in seconds if I cut it out."

"It's Tyler's men, then?" Neil asked. "They're the ones following you?"

"Yes. He owned me first, then he sold me to Elliot, but he still keeps tabs on me. For good reason." Alex glanced nervously at the knife still in Neil's hand.

"Is he in love with you?" Neil waved the knife menacingly in the air, looking angry. "Is that it?"

"No, it's nothing to do with that. Tyler killed Solange, Neil. She helped me escape once, and he killed her. So, he follows me to make sure I don't tell anyone."

Neil was the first person he'd told since Gideon, and it felt strange to reveal, to him of all people, the secret that he'd guarded for so long. Neil was gazing at him blankly, as if this did not compute. He hadn't factored *this* into his insane escape plan.

"You remember Solange, Neil; she was nice to you," Alex reminded him.

"Yeah, she was. I told her she could do better than you."

"Well, yeah, but you only said that because you wanted me for yourself," Alex riposted with a wink, trying to charm Neil into putting down the knife.

Neil grinned. "See, you're still the same old Alex. He's still in there."

"Yes, I am, but I can't go with you because Tyler's men will chase after us and I'm afraid of what they'll do to you. Listen…" He squeezed Neil's arm affectionately. "I'm only thinking of you. Of course I'd love to run away with you, but Tyler will kill you like he killed Solange, and I can't let that happen, can I?"

Neil looked confused by this new information but also convinced by it.

"But this is what I had planned," he wailed. "I want you back, Alex."

"I know, I know, but this isn't the way," Alex said soothingly. "Look, if you have the money, then why not keep offering to buy me? Elliot has financial worries. At some point, I'm sure he'll crack and sell me to someone."

"Okay. That makes sense." Neil finally put the knife on the nightstand, much to Alex's relief. He didn't relish the idea of ending up as Neil's IS, but he knew there was another bidder out there. If Elliot *did* ever sell his contract, he'd beg him to choose the other bidder over Neil.

"You look good, Alex." Neil's gaze wandered over Alex's body. "At least we have tonight."

Alex glanced at the knife. "Yeah," he said at last, giving in to the inevitable. "Come on, then."

Neil's body was both familiar and unfamiliar, changed and yet the same. Alex knew the taste and feel of him, the way he liked to kiss, lick, and moan. It was easy enough to pleasure him. Then he lay back, hoping that would be it, because even after all this time, Neil still brought out the worst in him.

"You're so gorgeous. You've still got that don't-give-a-fuck attitude," Neil murmured, lying on his side, gazing at him like a lovesick calf.

"Tell me about your life, Neil," Alex deflected. "What have you been up to?"

"It's been shitty, Alex, I won't lie." Neil rested a hand on his thigh. "I missed you every single day and thought about you all the time. I'm sure it was the same for you, about me."

Alex had barely thought of him at all, but he nodded. There was something more intense about *this* Neil, all these years later. He'd always been an oddball, always obsessive, but it was as if the years had baked that into his soul, turning him into a more extreme version of himself.

"You should have used the money Tyler gave you to make a decent life for yourself."

"I was expecting to work at Tyler Tech after he bought you. When Tyler first approached me, he said he'd look after me. He never said how exactly, but he insinuated that he'd be offering me a job. He took me out to dinner and whispered in my ear, suggesting all these possibilities for how he'd repay me."

"Ah, a Tyler seduction. I know how that feels," Alex said wryly.

"He even said I might still be able to see you after he bought you."

"But he lied."

"Yes, and then I couldn't find work and the money eventually ran out. I struggled to survive, and all I could think about was *you*."

"You should have forgotten all about me and moved on. It's not too late. You can still have a decent life, Neil, with this money you've somehow found." Given how deluded Neil was, he wasn't completely convinced that the money was real.

"I tried." Neil's face crumpled again and he actually let out a sob. "I wanted to hate you but I couldn't. I used to hang around outside Tyler's tower, just to see if I could catch a glimpse of you, but I never did. This feeling, this ache to be with you, it never went away. I need you, and you need me. We belong together. I guess you could say we deserve each other." Neil reached out and stroked Alex's hair.

He recoiled. Despite all the bad things he'd done, the idea that he deserved *Neil* made him feel ill.

"What is it?" Neil sat up.

"I can't do this," Alex said abruptly. He felt stifled, smothered, and sickened. Being back with Neil was making his flesh crawl. He literally couldn't bear it. He wanted to lash out, scream, shout, fight... anything but lie here talking to this man. That was when he realised that Neil was the one person he *didn't* have to pretend around. With Neil, he could be himself – no mask, no empty-headed Chris, only raw, unbridled Alex, just like the old days.

He made a sudden lunge for the knife and grabbed it, then ran to the window and threw it out. It landed with a splash in the lost zone outside.

"Fuck it, Alex." Neil jumped over the bed and looked out of the window. "We were having a nice time. Why do you always have to ruin everything?"

"It's who I am." Alex shrugged. "You know that. Listen to me, Neil. I can't stand you. I never could, and I still can't. You make me want to strip off my own skin and throw it in the water. I *loathe* you."

God, it felt intoxicating. All the words he'd squashed down during his time with Tyler, all the pent-up frustration of being Chris, all the years of lying and hiding – it all stopped for this one night.

"I fucking *hate* you," he screamed, and he wasn't just talking about Neil, but everything and everyone in his fucked-up life. He ran around the room in a frenzy, screaming and shouting, yelling his head off. Neil chased after him, cornering him in the bathroom and pressing his hand over Alex's mouth.

"Shut up! Shut up... someone will hear you."

Alex bit his hand, and Neil yelped and let him go. He ran for the door, but Neil caught him before he got there. He wrestled Alex to the floor, but Alex fought him, kicking, scratching, screaming, and shouting.

The release was profound. Every single repressed emotion came to the surface. Years of suppression, of being a good little servant, came to an end, and he was Alex again. Saying no, screaming and protesting, a being of pure emotion. He brought his knee up into Neil's belly, and the other man let him go with a loud "oomph". Alex tried to wriggle towards the door, but Neil recovered and grabbed him. Alex tried to kick back and he heard Neil curse – and then he felt an unbelievable pain in his buttocks. He screamed and looked over his shoulder. Neil had just bitten him.

"You fucking bastard," Alex yelled.

"You bit me first, so I bit you back." Neil dropped his head and bit him again, on his thigh this time. Alex yelped and wriggled, trying to break free.

He didn't remember much about the next hour. He wasn't sure he was entirely present for most of it, lost as he was in a frenzy of emotion. He stopped screaming, not because he didn't want to but because he didn't have the breath for it anymore. He was locked in a deadly battle with Neil, with neither of them prepared to give an inch.

At one point, Neil flung him on the bed, held him face down, and bit, scratched, and slapped him from his shoulders to his thighs, tearing into him repeatedly, while Alex wriggled and writhed and tried to kick him off. When he eventually broke free, he gave as good as he got, going after Neil with his fists and fingernails, biting, scraping, and slapping him. It was an odd kind of fight. No punches were thrown. Instead, it was a strange, intense tussle.

"Is this what you want? Is it? Is it?" Neil hissed into his ear, forcing Alex onto his back and spreading his legs. Alex laughed. This? No. This wasn't what he wanted, but he'd take it, because in a life of make-believe, this, at least, was honest.

"No, Neil, this is what *you* want, because I never let you do it in all the fucked-up years we were together, remember?"

He saw the dark cloud spread across Neil's face and knew he'd hit a nerve.

"I'll have you that way tonight," Neil said. "You can't stop me. I bought you, so I'll fuck you. I'll take what you always denied me." Neil tried to push his legs open further.

Alex laughed, lulling Neil into a false sense of security, then spat in his face. Neil growled in anger, and they had another wrestling match that only ended when Neil managed to force him onto his front and hold him down.

He bit into his pillow, knowing this was going to happen regardless, and pleased that at least he'd lubed himself before the show began, as he always did, just in case.

Neil let out a weird, sobbing sigh as he shoved into him for the first time. "You're mine now and you can't stop me. This is what you owe me for all those years of looking after you," he hissed. Alex's only reply was to push his arse up and surrender to the raw, brutal sensation of Neil pounding into him.

Later, a long time later, he lay on the bed, shivering, the sweat cooling on his body in the draft from the still open window. Beside him lay Neil, covered in bruises, scratches, and bite marks.

"Fuck, that was hot, wasn't it?" Neil whispered, grinning at him. "We've still got it, Alex. We can still make each other crazy."

Alex stared at him hazily. His entire body ached, but he felt good, as if he'd got something out of his system and given himself a reset.

"Yeah," he muttered. "Crazy. That's the right word." Maybe Neil *was* what he deserved. But if he truly believed that, he'd best go and throw himself out of that window.

They slept, after a fashion, both of them exhausted. The next day, as he took a shower, Alex winced the second the water touched his back. Neil had pinned him face down for most of his frenzied attack, so his front was largely untouched, but when he turned around and looked in the mirror, he could see that his back was covered in wounds, from his shoulders to the bottom of his bum. There were livid red teeth marks, angry long scratches, and massive red bruises covering every inch of his skin. No wonder he ached so much.

He dressed slowly, feeling like a deflated balloon. Had it been worth it? He didn't know. He hadn't felt in control of what had happened last night. In a life where he had to closely monitor his every word, gesture, thought, and feeling... to suddenly let rip had felt wonderful, but it'd also left him empty and drained.

Neil was waiting for him in the bedroom, fully dressed.

"I won't give up on you," Neil said as he emerged. "I'll find a way for us to be together."

"I believe you." Alex was too tired to argue.

Neil grasped Alex's chin and tilted it up, then kissed his lips with great tenderness. "I will," he whispered. "I promise."

Alex was silent on the drive home as he tried to process what had happened. What had come over him? He felt as if he'd been possessed. Beside him, Elliot rabbited on about how wonderful Eric had been.

"So shy. Like a little dormouse. Do you know he'd never been touched by a man before? He was the sweetest little creature. I had to be ever so gentle with him."

Alex tuned most of it out, although he was glad that Eric had known precisely what Elliot wanted and clearly gone out of his way to give it to him.

When they reached home, he walked stiffly into the house. It was only then that Elliot finally noticed that something was wrong.

"Are you okay, my sweet?" he cooed. "You're very pale. Was Eric's houder mean to you?"

"It was intense," Alex admitted.

Elliot's expression changed to one of alarm. "Chris, are you well?"

"I'm alright. I think I just need to lie down," Alex whispered, feeling faint. His legs suddenly gave way, and he would have fallen if Elliot hadn't propped him up. His houder helped him into a chair and brought him a glass of water, then hovered over him anxiously.

"What did he do to you?" he demanded. "Show me."

"I'll be fine."

In all honesty, Alex didn't think it was the wounds Neil had inflicted on his body that had caused his collapse. It was the terrible catharsis. He felt washed out and completely devoid of energy, as if someone had sucked out his soul and left him an empty shell.

"Let me see." Elliot reached out to unbutton his shirt. Peeling it off Alex's shoulders, he immediately burst into tears.

"Oh, my poor darling! Oh, my God. Oh, Christopher. I had no idea. What a bad man I am to make you go with someone so cruel. Oh, oh, oh!" Somehow, even though Alex was the one hurting, Elliot had made it all about himself, as usual. Alex struggled to reassure him, but Elliot was having none of it.

"I've been wicked. I'll make it up to you, I promise. I will never, ever take you to another show again. Never!" His eyes blazed as he pressed hundreds of little kisses all over Alex's face.

He insisted that Alex went straight to bed. The next day, he brought him breakfast in bed, then demanded to see his wounded back again.

"Do you need to see a doctor, my sweet?" he asked, dissolving into tears again at the sight. "I could arrange that, although... I'd be terribly worried in case they thought I'd been abusing you and reported me to the IS agency. Supposing they took you away from me? I'd never survive." He clutched his throat dramatically.

"I'm sure I'll be fine," Alex said wearily.

"Okay, my darling. You just rest up, and I'll bring you anything you want. I'll be the servant, and you can be my houder." Elliot looked delighted by this thought. "I'll tell Chantal not to disturb you when she arrives. Just call me if you want anything, only not in the next hour or so, as I have business to attend to."

He went out, returning around midday, by which time Alex was up and dressed. To be honest, he felt fine after resting. His back hurt but not too badly. He was, however, starting to find Elliot's endless fretting and fussing irritating. Elliot was also finding it difficult. He much preferred being the one fussed over, and he was clearly already regretting his rash promise to never show Alex again.

"We can revisit it in a few weeks," he backtracked. "I know you love shows as much as I do, so it wouldn't do to stop you enjoying yourself because of one bad apple."

Alex wasn't remotely surprised by this. Elliot spent the rest of the day alternately threatening to call the show's organisers to complain and wondering whether "my sweet, darling Eric" would be at any future shows.

The following morning, Alex decided to go to the gym just to get away from Elliot's continuously changing moods. It was exhausting being in the house with him.

"Very well, if you're sure you're well enough, my darling," Elliot said over breakfast.

"I'm good." Alex got down on his knees, pushing Elliot's legs apart to deliver his usual breakfast blow job – or the BBJ, as Elliot had christened it.

"Well, take it easy. I've made us dinner reservations at eight at that fancy new place that's opened up in town. It's a special treat to say I'm sorry for what happened, so I don't want you too tired to enjoy it. My poor, lovely boy." Elliot stroked Alex's hair tenderly, then glanced at the news on his holopad as Alex set to work.

Alex drifted off, still trying to process what had happened. What would Neil do next? Should he be worried about it? God, as if his life wasn't complicated enough.

An image of himself rampaging around that hotel room flashed back into his mind, and he winced. He couldn't afford to let that side of himself out again. He must work harder at his yoga. Elliot said something to him, and he drew back from his crotch, looking up blearily.

"Sorry, sir?" he murmured, still lost in thought.

He felt a sharp slap on his jaw. "Don't call me 'sir'," Elliot exclaimed. "Sir? What am I? A customer in a shop? A lord of the realm?" Alex knew why he was upset – he always hated it when Alex did or said anything that drew attention to the fact that he wasn't Christopher.

"Sorry, Elliot," he whispered, and Elliot immediately looked utterly contrite.

"Oh, no, *I'm* sorry. That awful man already hurt you so much, and now I'm being beastly to you, too." He wrapped his arms around Alex and burst into tears. "I'm just so out of sorts because of what happened to you," he whispered into his neck. "I'm so sorry, my sweet."

He calmed down enough to insist that Alex finish the BBJ – "Because I know how much you love doing this for me, darling." Alex leaned back in relief once it was over, worn out by his houder. He couldn't wait to escape to the gym for a few hours' respite.

"Oh!" Elliot squealed suddenly. "It's here. How efficient of Isaac. I was going to give this to you tonight over dinner, but let me show you now to prove how sorry I am for slapping you, my sweet."

He flicked a holodoc up into the air in front of them. Alex glanced at it in surprise.

Last will and testament of Elliot Marvin Dacre

"Look, look, look!" Elliot scrolled down a few pages, pointing. "See. In the event of my death, I'm setting you free."

"Oh." Alex looked at the will and then back at Elliot. Did the man think he was a complete idiot? He knew Elliot's finances were in a terrible state, and if he were to drop dead any time soon, Alex would have to be sold to pay off his debts.

"I did this for you to make up for what happened on Saturday, my love." Elliot took hold of his face and covered it in tiny kisses.

"That's really kind of you, Elliot, thank you," Alex told him gravely, trying to keep a straight face.

"I've left dear Chantal a little bequest, too. I do love helping people."

"How sweet you are," Alex murmured. "Now, I should really get going. D'Angelo hates it when I'm late."

"Of course. Off you go. Remember, don't wear yourself out – we want to have fun later. Lots of fun! Now, run along. Chantal will be here soon, and I really must get on with some tedious admin."

Elliot gave him one last kiss on the lips and then shooed him towards the door. Alex grabbed his gym bag, glancing back into the lounge as he left to see Elliot still scrolling through his new will, looking delighted about all the joy his death would bring people.

The duck felt like a refuge after the madness of the past few days, and Alex was relieved to finally have some peace and quiet. He kept his gym routine light, because his back and arse were so sore, then took a long, hot shower and changed into a pair of skin-tight jeans and a silver shirt, with a neo-glam jacket over the top to complete the ensemble. Then he gazed at himself in the mirror. His mask was fully in place, and his reflection gazed back steadily, showing no sign of the distaste he felt for the over-the-top outfit.

It was a sunny day, and he almost didn't care about the black SUAV as it fell into place behind him. He drove around for a little while, listening to music and enjoying his freedom, following one of the prescribed routes that Elliot allowed him. He tried not to think about Neil because he didn't want to give him space in his head. He chuckled, instead, as he thought about Elliot's ludicrous romantic gesture in showing him his new will. Madness. Yet so very Elliot.

Finally, he knew he'd stayed out for long enough, and he headed home. The street was busier than usual, and he frowned as he saw a big black van parked across the driveway. Was that one of Tyler's fleet? It didn't look the same, but he'd started to associate all big black vehicles with Tyler.

He parked on a neighbour's driveway, as he sometimes did with their permission when the road was busy, and had just started to walk across the street when a pugnacious-looking man with a squashed nose came barrelling out of nowhere.

"Hey! You! Don't move," he yelled, drawing a weapon. He was wearing a black suit that looked very similar to Tyler livery.

Alex didn't consciously decide to run, his legs just took off. He wasn't going back to George Tyler again. He'd rather die. Elliot might not be perfect, but he was a damn sight better than Tyler. Where was Elliot anyway? Would he really let Tyler just waltz in and take him?

He ran down the street and hurtled, full pelt, around a corner into a side street, then slammed straight into what felt like a brick wall. He landed on the pavement, his sore back aching. Looking up, winded, he realised what had caused him to fall down so spectacularly. A huge man was standing there, looking down on him, so massive he blocked out half the sun. For a moment, Alex thought he had to be imagining things because it couldn't be... it really couldn't be, could it?

Josiah Raine was dressed in a beautifully tailored silver-grey suit over a lilac shirt, with a purple silk tie neatly held in place with an elegant silver clip. Framed in the light of the sun, he looked too big, too solid, too much Josiah fucking Raine to be real.

Joe flipped him over, shoved his knee into his back, and snapped a pair of e-cuffs on him. Alex blinked. What was happening? Was this a dream? Had he died in a duck crash and this was somehow the afterlife? An afterlife in which Josiah Raine, of all people, was arresting him? For what?

The stocky man in the black suit huffed around the corner, and Joe called out to him. Alex lay on the ground, trying to think. He was pretty sure this wasn't the afterlife, and he definitely wasn't imagining it, so this *was* actually happening – but what was "this"?

Joe flipped him back over, and Alex stared up at him, still in shock. Joe gazed down on him, looking surprised. Did he recognise him? Did he see that he was looking at Ben Smith again after all these years? Alex began to tremble. The last time he'd been this close to him, Peter had been lying on the side of the road and Joe had been howling like a wild animal, his clothes covered in blood. If Joe was remembering any of this, too, he gave no sign. He hauled Alex to his feet.

"Are you Elliot Dacre's indentured servant?" the man in the black suit demanded, reaching them.

"Yes." Alex moved his head to show them his gold ID tag.

"What's your name?" Joe asked.

So, he definitely didn't recognise him. "Christopher," Alex replied.

"Christopher... Reed, wasn't Christopher the name of the dead husband? The one who died in the AV drowning accident?" Joe asked his sidekick.

"You're right, sir. Bit of a coincidence, isn't it?"

Joe turned back to him. "What's your *real* name?" he demanded.

"That *is* my real name," Alex said firmly. "Elliot had it registered on the IS database, so that's my name."

"What was your name before you were indentured?" Joe pressed. Alex looked at him intently, willing him to recognise him. *It's me,* he felt like screaming. *It's Ben Smith. You must remember me. You can't possibly have forgotten that night.*

"Don't fuck with me," Joe snapped with a sharp jerk of his head.

Alex felt a wave of intense disappointment. Joe definitely didn't recognise him, and now wasn't the time to enlighten him. He hummed his song in his head and summoned up his mask, emptying his face of all expression.

Joe looked startled by the transformation.

"Like I said, I'm just an indentured servant, nobody important. You should speak to Elliot," Alex told him. "He'll answer your questions."

"I'm asking you." Joe showed him his ID. "I'm Senior Investigator Josiah Raine from the Inquisitus Investigation Agency."

"Oh, I know who you are, *indiehunter*," Alex said pointedly.

"And this is Investigator Reed," Joe continued. "Why did you run when he called out to you?"

How on earth could he explain all about Tyler now, standing on the pavement in e-cuffs? That would have to wait for a better time.

"I was startled. I didn't know who you were. Listen, whatever you think I've done, Elliot will be able to clear me."

Joe leaned in close. "Well, that might be a problem. You see, we're here to investigate Elliot Dacre's murder."

What? Of all the things Joe could have said, that was the most unbelievable. Alex stared at him in shock.

"Elliot's been murdered?" he whispered. "Poor Elliot." Then, suddenly, he understood why Joe was here, and what this was all about. Nothing to do with Tyler, or Solange, or any of the terrible things that had preoccupied him for so many years. Something new, yet equally terrible, had happened.

"And you think I did it?" he asked. Of course Joe did – why else had he snapped those cuffs on him? He suddenly realised that he meant nothing to Josiah Raine. This man, who he'd been thinking about for years, didn't have a clue who he was. He was just here to investigate a murder, and Alex was his prime suspect.

"Did you?" Joe demanded.

Alex met his gaze coldly. "No, of course not."

"What time did you leave the house, and where have you been all day?"

"I left at around nine a.m. to visit my personal trainer at the gym."

"And that took you four hours?" Josiah asked, with a glance at his watch.

Alex hesitated. Shit, this wasn't looking good. "No. I left the gym around eleven-forty-five."

"Then where have you been for the rest of the time? Just driving around in that fancy duck?" Reed asked.

"As a matter of fact, yes."

"For over an hour?" Joe sounded like he didn't believe a word he was saying, and Alex suddenly realised he was in big trouble. Of all the times he'd fantasised about meeting Joe again, he could never, *ever* have imagined it happening this way.

"Yes."

"On your own?"

Alex sighed. "Yes."

"Can anyone vouch for your movements?"

Of course they could. A black SUAV followed him everywhere. Alex glanced over Josiah's shoulder just in time to see the SUAV that had been shadowing him all morning slowly crawl off down the street and disappear. He gave a bitter smile.

"No... nobody can vouch for me."

He saw Joe come to a decision. "You're under arrest. We're taking you back to Inquisitus for questioning." He put a big hand on Alex's shoulder. "Now, I'll ask you again. What's your name? Your real name, this time, not the one Dacre gave you. That little charade died with him."

"Alexander," Alex said quietly, unable to hold back a wry smile. The first time he'd met Joe, he'd told him his name was Ben Smith, and today he'd given him the name Christopher Dacre. Now, finally, after all these years, it was time to introduce himself properly. "My real name is Alexander Lytton."

Chapter Nineteen
NOVEMBER 2096
Josiah

When did he and Cam end up on first-name terms? Josiah mused as he drove into the office. Once, they'd had a nice, formal relationship. It had been "Reed" and "Raine", with a side order of "sir", but now it was "Cam" and "Joe"... and he found he liked it. It was almost certainly his fault. He'd kept Reed, and everyone else, at bay for years, barking at them and freezing them out, because he'd never been able to get over losing Peter.

He wasn't sure why he was even ruminating like this, except that he was unbelievably tired but also full of nervous anticipation for whatever it was that Reed had found. He tried not to be too excited. If it turned out to be Tyler's grocery list instead of the blackmail footage, then all his hopes would be dashed.

He turned on the radio in an attempt to keep himself awake. He usually enjoyed nighttime talk radio; it had kept him company during many sleepless nights since Peter's death, as well as at stake-outs and on late-night duck journeys in pursuit of a case.

Amanda and Alan weren't due on for another few hours. Instead, the host was Frankie Lamb, a foul-mouthed, opinionated hothead best suited to the small hours. The callers tended to be equally deranged in their views, as if by expressing them at night, when most people were asleep, nobody would hear.

"Are they having a laugh? So, all in one day, we find out that Josiah Raine has secretly loved indies all along, Alex Lytton is a fucking saint, and Charles – national bloody treasure Charles Lytton – is a lying, scumbag cheat! What the hell? What do you think, callers? What the bloody hell are we to make of what happened today?"

Himesh from Epping wasn't having any of it. "It's all a pack of lies. All of it," he opined. "Raine has been nobbled by the Secret Service."

Well, that was a new one. Himesh ranted for several minutes but had no coherent argument, so Frankie cut him off abruptly.

A worried-sounding Molly from High Wycombe was next on the line. "I wonder what it can all mean?" she asked anxiously. "Is Josiah on drugs?"

"Apparently, Charles Lytton is the one on drugs." Frankie chuckled. "What is it with the Lyttons and pharmaceuticals? Alex loves his croc, and now it turns out Charles has been knocking back some kind of muscle juice."

"They're a disgrace. The whole bloody lot of them," said Jean from Maidenhead. "I won't vote for them again."

Frankie told her to piss off. "And put the bottle down while you're at it," he cackled after her.

The oddly named Slider from St Albans struck a rare note of sanity. "Looks like we was wrong about all of 'em," he ruminated. "I blame the media. Are they even doing their jobs right?"

Josiah managed a wry smile at that. Not that he entirely agreed. He'd met many decent journalists who'd worked hard to get their facts straight and spent long hours running the details of his cases past him before publishing. There was no doubt the media sometimes made his job harder, but they'd also been incredibly useful to him over the years. He'd lied to them consistently during his fake pursuit of Bram Janssen, and that had bought him time to unmask the true perp in the Emma James case.

A distressed Leanne from Bracknell was up next. "I feel sorry for that poor Lytton boy," she murmured tearfully. "Poor Alex. What will become of him now?"

Josiah turned off the radio. What, indeed?

He reached Ghost Eye City, parked his duck outside Inquisitus, and jogged into the SID. Reed looked terrible. His holotie had long since stopped working and was now a sorry-looking grey blob around his neck. His eyes were bloodshot, and he had several days' worth of stubble on his face and dark smudges around his eyes. Yet somehow, despite that, he appeared energised.

"You cracked it?" Josiah asked eagerly.

"Yes!" Reed's face lit up. "It was a bitch of a code, but I did it. I've sent the key to all my techs, who are busy opening each and every single file and cataloguing the material."

"Is it the evidence we need?" Josiah could hardly breathe as he asked that question.

"Oh, yeah." Reed rubbed a weary hand over his eyes. "Brace yourself, Joe. Once you've seen this stuff, it's impossible to unsee it."

Josiah grabbed a chair and drew it up beside him.

"Ready?" Reed asked, fingers poised.

"As I'll ever be."

Reed clicked, and Josiah found himself looking at a nanovid of a room he recognised.

"That's one of the boardrooms at Tyler Tech."

"Yeah. This is one of the worst ones I've found so far, but we've only just started looking. I mean, I hope the others aren't as bad, frankly."

A man Josiah knew, a man he'd interviewed in this very building, came into view.

"Jake Harper."

"Yup," Reed growled. "And isn't he a piece of work?"

Josiah saw Alex, wearing a smart business suit, looking too young to endure what happened to him next. He put his hand over his mouth, willing himself not to look away. It was every bit as bad as Alex had hinted. Worse.

"Christ," he whispered. "Are they all like this?"

"No. Yes. I mean... not the same, but... look. You should see this." Reed clicked, and Josiah pressed his hand to his mouth again, in surprise this time.

"Solange?" he whispered, leaning forward. It was her. Poor, doomed Solange Alajika, the woman Alex had held faith with all these years.

She was stunningly beautiful, wearing a slinky red dress as she danced, cheek to cheek, with a tall, thin man, whose hands wandered all over her body as they moved in time to the music. So, this was the real Solange, not the fake that Tyler had rehearsed to take her place. This was really her, doing the job Tyler had brought her in to do from the outset, the job he said didn't exist.

"Poor Solange." She had about her that combination of practicality, resignation, and inner strength that he recognised immediately. "Oh, yeah, she's a Quarterlands kid. You can tell." He gazed at her sadly. "You can rest easy now, girl." he told her. "I'll see he pays for what he did to you." She rested her head on the man's shoulder, and for a moment, seemed to look straight at him, as if she'd heard him.

"What now?" Reed asked.

Josiah got to his feet, reaching for his holopad. "Catalogue every single vid in these files and make me copies," he said. Then he put in a call to Esther, ignoring her bleary protests about the hour.

"We've got him," was all he needed to say.

Then he returned home, grabbed a box of chocolates from the kitchen, and ran up the stairs to Alex's room.

"I don't have any champagne," he announced to a barely compos mentis Alex, dumping the chocolates on his bed, "so these will have to do."

"What's going on?" Alex asked, rubbing his eyes.

"Reed cracked the code. We have the blackmail footage. It's all exactly as you said." He sat on the side of the bed, gazing at Alex with a combination of triumph and sadness, trying not to think of that footage of him with Harper. Alex always hated being viewed as broken or damaged, someone to be rescued and fixed, but it was very hard not to view him that way after what he'd just seen.

Alex was immediately awake. "You're sure? You've seen it yourself?" he whispered, his eyes suddenly bright. This was the light at the end of a very long tunnel, and Josiah knew how much it meant to him.

"I've seen it – and I saw her," Josiah told him gently. "You're right. She was beautiful. I could see the sweetness in her."

"Solange?" Alex breathed. He looked overwhelmed. So Josiah left him alone to come to terms with what was almost certainly the beginning of the end of his long journey to seek justice for his friend.

Byrne asked for an adjournment while they compiled the new evidence, which was granted. Josiah and Reed worked day and night on the blackmail footage to get it into a coherent shape that could be used in court, and then handed it over to her. She had the complex task of convincing the judge that it was both relevant to the case and admissible in court. There would be arguments over provenance, and the possibility of it being deep-faked, but truth-marking tech was so good these days Josiah was sure the recordings would be ruled admissable. HMS would no doubt fight with all his might to prevent the material being shown to the jury, but Josiah trusted Byrne to prevail.

During the hiatus, Esther finally relented and allowed Alex to be with his family at The Orchard. They were fighting their own battle, and Alex was determined to be by their side. It was actually touching to see this wounded family finally pulling together and putting on a united front. Josiah was happy to leave them to it. He had enough on his plate.

He watched from his sofa as Charles tearfully apologised to the nation, then put his gold medal in a box and sent it back to the International Olympic Committee. Alex and Noah stood on either side of him throughout, supporting him. He offered to return the paralympic medal as well, although he was at pains to point out that he hadn't been taking any banned substances when he won that one. Josiah couldn't help smiling at that. Poor Charles. He did love his medals so. There was every likelihood he'd be charged over the duck crash and the subsequent cover-up.

There was even talk that Alex would be charged, too, for lying in court and taking the blame. At this point, Josiah was sure there was nothing more the system could do to Alex that would hurt him more than he'd already been hurt. He'd been punished out of all proportion to the crimes he'd committed. He just hoped the courts would agree.

A few days later, Josiah drove over to The Orchard after work. Alex opened the door, greeting him awkwardly. Josiah wasn't sure they'd ever return to the easy companionship they'd once shared. They'd hurt each other too much.

"Has something happened?" Alex asked anxiously.

"Nothing new, no."

"So, you haven't heard from Byrne?"

"No. I'll tell you as soon as I hear anything." Josiah had kept him up to date with all the latest developments, but he understood that Alex's entire future rested on the outcome of the judge's decision on whether the blackmail footage was admissible in court. Of course he was anxious.

"Can I come in?" Josiah lifted his rucksack. "I have something for you – for all of you."

Alex showed Josiah to the living room, where Charles and Noah were both reading.

"Joe! What a pleasant surprise." Noah waved him into the room.

"Forgive the intrusion. I wasn't sure I'd be welcome," Josiah said uncertainly.

"Not at all. You did what you felt had to be done, and I, for one, am grateful," Noah said firmly. "It feels like we can finally move on now as a family."

Charles, downcast and gloomy, looked as if he might not share his father's view, but ever affable, he managed a faint smile of welcome.

"We found something in the material Jabir took from Tyler's hacienda," Josiah explained. "And, well... I thought you should have it."

He took the light box from his rucksack, flicked it on, and Isobel Lytton suddenly appeared in the room, looking so real it was as if she was there. Alex gave a stifled gasp of recognition. He'd clearly seen this hologram before. Isobel looked up, seemed to see them, and her face broke into a smile. She walked across the room towards them, still smiling... and then stopped, frozen in place in that last frame.

He looked at Noah to find him staring at his wife, one hand reaching out as if to touch her. Charles was openly sobbing, his shoulders heaving.

"I know she wasn't perfect," Noah said softly. "But we did all love her very much. Thank you, Joe. This means the world to us."

He shuffled forward, took Josiah's hand, and shook it warmly. "Will you stay for dinner?" he asked. "Alex tells me you like hachée."

"Oh, for God's sake, not that," Alex said beseechingly, and they all laughed.

It felt strange to spend the evening with them. They were very welcoming, but Josiah had the feeling he was intruding all the same. They were slowly healing, these broken and battered men, all of them battle-scarred in some way, and he felt like an outsider. It was bittersweet. He was glad that Alex had his family back, but it made him all the more aware that there was nobody waiting for him back at home. Not Alex, not Peter, not even Hattie. When all this was over, if he was free, then he'd do something about that. It was time.

"Past time," he could almost hear Peter say. *"Waaaay past time, Joe."*

A few days later, he and Alex arrived in the courtroom again as the judge reconvened. Josiah was braced for what would come. Even if they won, it was surely inevitable that Tyler would throw him under the bus and reveal the truth about the indiehunter.

Alex had come without Charles and Noah this time, for two very good reasons. In the wake of Charles's bombshell, his presence tended to turn everything into a media scrum, but also because if the blackmail footage was shown in court, Alex had every reason not to want his brother and father to see it.

Josiah looked at Byrne as he entered the court, but she refused to make eye contact. Was that a good sign? She'd always played her cards very close to her chest, even with him.

Josiah glanced at Tyler. He was as stiff and upright as ever, but then Tyler was a man who'd never look defeated, even if he was on the ropes. Was he? Had the judge agreed that the blackmail footage could be shown to the jury?

There was silence, an expectant hum, and then Byrne stepped forward.

"New evidence has come to light that has a significant bearing on this case," she said. "You may remember the testimony of Mr Martin Bagshaw, the director of the IS agency. He said, under oath, that he'd never had sexual relations with Alexander Lytton, so those liaisons couldn't have been taped and used by Mr Tyler to blackmail him into changing the IS database and substituting false information about Solange Alajika. Well, we invite the court to examine *this*."

The court smartwall system displayed a nanovid, the image crystal clear. Martin Bagshaw came into view, holding Alex close. They were alone in a bedroom.

"You're just a poor, misunderstood boy in need of a kind daddy," Bagshaw said.

"Yes," Alex replied.

"Yes, Daddy," Martin corrected.

Alex suddenly looked up, straight at everyone in the court, and rolled his eyes. "Yes, Daddy," he said, in a tone of barely concealed contempt.

"That's good. Now, do you know what Daddy has for you?" Martin asked, nuzzling his neck.

Alex shook his head.

"It's a lovely present, just for you. It's a big lollipop for you to suck and enjoy."

Byrne paused the footage. "There is much more, of a very explicit nature, which the jury will be allowed to examine privately. We've had independent experts verify that this is real footage, not deep-faked or AI-generated. They've been subjected to the most rigorous truth-marking tests using the latest and best technology. The prosecution has also had a chance for their experts to verify them. All the experts agree that they are genuine."

There was a profoundly shocked silence as everyone in the courtroom processed the implication of her words.

"Understandably, there is no footage of the night of November third 2088, although I have no doubt those events were recorded and subsequently destroyed. However, we do have considerable footage of Solange Alajika, the woman who, according to the defence, worked as a designer at Tyler Tech."

A nanovid flashed up on the court smartwall, and Alex gasped as Solange appeared. But instead of reaching for Josiah's hand, he reached for Ted's, who was sitting on the other side of him. Josiah felt the pang of loss, but he had nobody to blame but himself.

This nanovid showed Solange in a bedroom with a view over Ghost Eye City in the background. A man was undressing her, and she was gazing out over the city wistfully. Byrne stopped it before it became too explicit.

"Just as a counterpoint to that, I'd like to show you this footage of Solange Alajika that we obtained from the film crew following Charles Lytton at Alexander's graduation." A new nanovid of Solange appeared on the courtroom smartwall. She was several years younger and full of vitality as she danced happily with a bunch of other young people. Josiah glanced at Alex to find him transfixed by the nanovid, blinking away tears.

"This is Solange," Byrne said fiercely. "Not the woman who George Tyler paid to pretend to be her. This is the real Solange Alajika, and she isn't here because Mr Tyler killed her. It wasn't a premeditated murder. I have no doubt that he didn't mean to kill her, but Mr Tyler is a man given to violent rages, and her death was the inevitable consequence of his actions that night."

Tyler's jaw was clenched so tight it looked as if it might snap, but otherwise, his face was expressionless.

There was no pandemonium this time. No uproar. It seemed as if the circus of the past several weeks was finally over, as everyone in that room watched Solange smiling and dancing in front of them. A woman was dead, and her killer had twisted the story and manipulated an entire nation in order to evade justice.

The trial was over then, in all but name. It limped on a little longer to a chastened audience and a grim-faced jury. Josiah braced himself because he knew George Tyler. He'd go down fighting. He expected Tyler's dossier on the Kathleen Line to be sent to the media, at the very least, and was on tenterhooks, waiting for it... but it never happened.

As the jury filed in to give their verdict, only then did Alex slip his hand into his. The foreman, a weary-looking, middle-aged woman wearing a sensible cardigan, stepped forward. Surely even Tyler couldn't get out of this, could he? Josiah feared, even now, that the jury could have been bought off. That was Tyler's style.

The foreman was asked to give the jury's verdict, and she spoke up, loud and clear. "Guilty."

There was no sense of jubilation. In fact, nobody reacted at all. Alex's hand, resting in his, gave a little squeeze, and that was it. Even Tyler stood completely still, his body stiff but straight, taking it on the chin. There was an odd kind of dignity to the man that Josiah couldn't help but admire.

As Tyler was taken down to the cells to await sentencing, Alex turned to him with a thousand questions.

"Will he go to prison? Or be sold into servitude?" Then, in a quieter voice, "What will happen to me now?"

"He won't be sold. Anyone found guilty of rape, GBH, manslaughter, or murder – any violent crime – goes to prison," Josiah told him. "As for what happens to you: nothing, for now. You still, technically, belong to Tyler, or at least to Tyler Tech, but there's no way that you'll be sent back there given what the court has seen. However..." He paused, sighing. "That doesn't mean you'll go free, Alex. There's a whole system at work here. Tyler Tech might be missing their CEO, but they're still within their rights to demand that you be sold and the company recompensed. Tyler might be about to go to prison, but he can still give orders to his company and expect them to be obeyed. It might not seem fair, but it's the law. "

"Is that what will happen?"

"I don't know. I'll ask Byrne to set up a meeting with an IS judge to discuss it."

Ted and Mick came over, their faces jubilant.

"I really thought the bastard was gonna get away with it," Mick said. "Like he's always done. Maybe there's some justice in this country after all."

"Alex, thank you." Ted wrapped him in a bear hug. "Thank you so much, from her as well as me." There were tears in his eyes as he said that. Alex welled up, too.

"Another win, Joe. You'll be getting big-headed," Esther told him, motoring her way over to him.

"No. I rather think this one humbled me, if anything," Josiah replied with a strained smile. He knew he should be happy, but he felt empty and lost. A hand slipped into his, and he looked down to see Elsie smiling up at him.

"You did us all proud, Joe," she told him. "When the dust settles, why don't you take a long-overdue holiday? Liz would love you to visit, you know."

"That's a good idea," he said numbly.

He watched as Alex left the courtroom with his family, feeling all too keenly his status as an outsider. Then he realised that Sofie was standing on his left, Elsie on his right, and Cam, Mel, and Esther were all clustered around him. He had his family right here. He'd always had them. He just needed to remember to let them in occasionally.

Alex was pale and shaky as they stepped outside into the sunshine a few minutes later to the waiting media. He read a statement he'd prepared and, as always, Charles and Noah were on either side of him, supporting him. Josiah stood over to one side. This wasn't his moment. It belonged entirely to Alex. He'd gone through hell to get here, and he deserved to be the one giving this speech.

Afterwards, Alex returned to The Orchard with his family, and Josiah returned home – alone. Cam and Sofie had invited him for a drink but he wasn't in the mood. Still, it felt strange to be in this house by himself again, although that had been his reality for some time before Alex. It was hard to be here without the case against Tyler consuming his every waking moment. He felt bereft, at a loss, and he missed Peter more than ever. He missed his teasing voice and the sense that Peter was still here. It hurt. Maybe it always would, but at least now he was letting himself feel it, instead of freezing those feelings out.

. . .

Tyler was sentenced to fifteen years in prison for Solange's manslaughter, with further trials pending on his various other crimes. He didn't say a word as the sentence was handed down, but as he was taken away, he did turn to look at Josiah, briefly, and raised one hand to his forehead in a little salute. An acknowledgement of a worthy opponent and a game well played, perhaps? Who knew with Tyler?

He didn't once glance at Alex, so Josiah had no idea what his feelings were towards him now. Did he accept that Charles had been driving the duck that day, or was he too invested in his vendetta against Alex to ever truly relinquish it? They might never know, for Tyler turned down every request for an interview and refused to cooperate with the courts or Inquisitus. He didn't, though, lodge an appeal. Maybe even he knew he'd lost this fight.

As for the matter of Alex's servitude, the courts took the view that he could not be returned to Tyler Tech. Much to Josiah's surprise, Tyler made no attempt to fight that. An IS judge ruled that Alex's contract should be sold for the exact same price Tyler had paid for it in the first place.

The manifest unfairness of this was expressed at some length in the media, but the truth was, as Byrne explained, nobody wanted to rock this particular boat.

"If Alex, the most expensive IS in the land, is freed without full recompense to Tyler Tech, then what's to stop this being a precedent? The government won't let it happen because it'll undermine the entire system," she explained. "I know, I know. You'd think that everything that happened to him at Tyler's hands would be deemed extenuating circumstances, and it should be, but this system is built on a house of cards. Trust me, nobody at the top will risk that it might come tumbling down. It's not just Alex. If people know the government can just step in and release people from their contracts without recompense because they feel sorry for them, everyone will become very nervous."

"But based on Tyler's abusive behaviour…" Josiah protested.

She held up her hand. "I know, and I agree, but it won't fecking happen. You aren't talking about one person here, you're talking about an entire system, and people are afraid that if the IS system fails, war won't be far behind."

She was right. Questions were asked in parliament, but they seemed to be the wrong kind. Mostly there was a lot of hand-wringing about how the IS agency had been corrupted and what to do about abusive houders. Nobody seemed to have the will to tackle the system itself, and while there was some sympathy for Alex, it was tinged with a sense that the privileged Lytton family had behaved very badly and nobody had the time or money to waste on indulging them further.

In desperation, Josiah asked to speak to the IS court judge. It was, funnily enough, the exact same woman who'd sentenced Alex after his trial for embezzlement. She had a thin, patrician nose and a steely air, and he sensed a certain incorruptibility to her. She was clearly upset about the role she'd played in Alex's downfall, even while she continued to uphold and extol the virtues of the system. She didn't – or wouldn't – see how the abuses were baked into a system she valued so much.

"Can I ask one thing," he requested. "If I can, somehow, raise the exact price Tyler paid for Alex originally, will you agree to sell his contract to me?"

"That depends," she said sharply. "What will you do with him?"

"Free him, of course."

"How will you possibly find this sum of money?"

"I don't know, but if I do, will you agree to sell his contract to me, and nobody else?"

"There is likely to be some interest in him because of the circumstances and his notoriety."

"I know, but Tyler Tech isn't allowed to make a profit from him; the court has already established that. Given the role the state has played in what happened to him, and the failure of the IS agency to protect him, I hardly think you should sell him to the highest bidder and allow the government to take the extra profit. That would play very poorly in the media."

She looked at him sharply. "Don't try and manipulate me, Mr Raine."

"I'm sorry. I'm just trying to save him. He's been through enough."

"I do agree that the system has, in this instance, let him down, although we shouldn't forget that he was guilty of stealing all that money in the first place – he says so himself. He also lied about the circumstances of his mother's death. He's not exactly blameless in his own downfall."

"I know, and I concur, but surely you can also agree that he's suffered enough? All I'm asking is that you sell his contract to me, if I can raise sufficient funds."

She looked down her thin nose at him. "I'm afraid that I cannot agree to this, no. It's my job to consider each application on its personal merits. This is an unusual situation in that we are not asking for anyone to bid over the asking price. The outcome will, therefore, be decided purely on the application I consider the best fit for Mr Lytton. You are certainly welcome to put in such an application, if you can raise the appropriate sum. That's the best I can say."

It was better than nothing. At least he stood a chance. Josiah had no idea if he *could* raise the appropriate sum, but he was going to damn well try.

He drove straight to Greenfields after meeting with the judge. He found Gideon more cadaverous than ever, barely more than a skeleton, his skin now a deep yellow and paper thin.

"All hail the conquering hero," he croaked as Josiah entered. He smelled now, too, a strange, sickly-sweet odour that hinted at his imminent death. "I was wondering when you'd come and visit me. I hoped you wouldn't wait too long because, well, as you can see, I don't have much longer."

"Did you watch it?" Josiah asked.

"I did, and I read all about it, too. What drama. Such a roller-coaster. You must be quite exhausted, my dear fellow. Here, come closer, so I can see you. Oh, yes. Still so very handsome." He gave a delighted laugh. Josiah took a seat on the sofa next to his armchair. "It was glorious," Gideon said, patting his knee. "No man could possibly leave this world behind feeling more satisfied than I do. It all came out, didn't it? You even uncovered the secret. Not quite what I imagined it to be; I was so sure it was something about sex. Maybe that's just me. I was brought up to feel nothing but shame about sex. Perhaps I projected that onto Alex."

"You weren't entirely wrong." Josiah explained about Buzzard.

"I'm sure he's feeling some heat now, too." Gideon clapped his hands together delightedly. "After all, that sample tested clean. How, one might ask, is that possible?"

"Questions are being asked. Alex and Charles know, of course, but so far, they're keeping quiet about it. Right now, they just want to put it all behind them. The last thing either of them wants is to hit the headlines again, especially not with this kind of news."

"Quite." Gideon gave a thoughtful nod. "Understandable. So, Josiah, you've come seeking your pound of flesh. I rather fear there's little left on this old carcass, but you're welcome to whatever you want."

"What I want is a confession, so I can take it to Esther. Neil Grant might have been a nasty piece of work, but he didn't kill Elliot Dacre, and it's not right for the blame to be pinned on him, dead or not."

"You do have an interesting sense of justice," Gideon murmured. "I mean, you choose to uphold some laws and completely flout others. It's really quite fascinating. However do you choose?"

"I have my own sense of right and wrong, forged in this very building," Josiah grunted.

"Ah, well, we both know that Quarterlands justice can be a good deal more rough and ready than the kind you're used to doling out on dry land, but by all means go on believing in your own moral compass, Josiah. Of course I'll give you your confession. A deal is a deal, after all, and you gave me the most wonderful trial. All that courtroom drama kept me on the edge of my seat for weeks, which was a great comfort to me, given how very ill I feel these days." Gideon sat back in his armchair, looking every bit as near death as he claimed to be.

"Here." He reached for his holopad and pinged a document over to Josiah's nym. "My confession, as requested. I've been working on it for some time, so you should find it quite thorough. I even took a holopic of myself holding the gun before I sent it off, in case it should be needed." He smiled.

Josiah read it through carefully, but Gideon had been as meticulous about his confession as he was about everything else. Every detail was there, with nothing left out. There could be no doubt as to who had killed Elliot Dacre.

Josiah finished reading then cleared his throat. "So, I've spoken to the IS judge in charge of Alex's case. She won't agree to bend the rules, but I'm welcome to bid on him, if I can raise the money."

"Well, I'll do my bit, as promised. I have no need of it now anyway." Gideon handed him a cash card. "It's a large sum, so it's encrypted." Josiah tapped it against his holopad to find its value... and then gave a bark of laughter.

"What is it?" Gideon demanded.

Josiah raised his eyes heavenward, shaking his head. "It's not enough, Gideon. It's not nearly enough."

"It's all I have. As I said, Miss Madeleine was always generous with her money, if not with herself, but perhaps not quite generous enough to afford the most expensive IS in the land." Gideon gave a rueful smile.

"Oh, shit. I was so hopeful. I thought..." Josiah slammed the cash card down on the table. "I can't do it. I don't have enough to buy him. Even if I sold my house and Peter's car, and used up every single penny of my savings, it still wouldn't be enough."

"That's not all you have to sell, though, is it?" Gideon asked silkily.

Josiah turned his head, slowly, a chill creeping through his body. "What do you mean?"

"Oh, you know what I mean." Gideon smiled. "Come now, Josiah, are you really so much better than the rest of us Quarterlands scum? Isn't this always the fate that awaits us in the end? Why did you think you'd escape it?"

"No," Josiah snapped. "I made a vow to my father. I promised him, Gideon."

"And do you always keep your promises?" Gideon asked, an amused glint in his eyes.

Josiah looked down at his hands. "No," he admitted hoarsely. "I used to think so, but no, I don't."

"It's up to you, Josiah. The money is yours, regardless of what you do with it. Give up your job and go and live somewhere nice and warm, if you wish. I shan't be here to care. Now, you must leave. I'm really feeling very tired."

He looked it, too. He was a living corpse, with his paper thin skin and sunken eyes.

"Do you know how much longer you have left?" Josiah asked bluntly.

"Days, at most, possibly hours. I only hung on to see the culmination of my great plan. I'm happy to die now. There's no point in a funeral given I've already had one." He grinned, his teeth oddly white in his yellowed face. "So, I've asked Seamus to give me the Quarterlands Splash. It seems fitting. I'll be a Quarter rat to the end, just like you. That's who we are, Josiah. Scum. Now go."

Josiah slipped the cash card into his pocket and left. That was the last time he saw Gideon Bart, but the man's words stayed with him, burning a hole in his conscience.

"That's not all you have to sell..."

He went to see Esther the next day.

"I have a signed confession from Elliot Dacre's murderer," he said, pinging it to her. She read it, her face darkening.

"Why didn't you bring him in?"

"He wasn't well enough, and anyway there was no point. I knew he was on his last legs, and he died last night." He'd had a call from Seamus first thing this morning to that effect, and he couldn't say he was sad about it. Regardless of his motives, the man had been a murderer.

"I see. So, you've solved all your cases as usual." She shook her head in admiration. "I might not always like how you keep things from me and charge around the country without backup, but I have to admit, you do always deliver. No wonder those rival investigation agencies are always trying to poach you. Oh, I know about all the offers you've had." She held up her hand, laughing. "I'm grateful for your loyalty, Joe."

"I'm glad to hear it. In which case, how would you like to lock that loyalty in for the next ten years to stop me leaving you for another agency?"

She looked startled. "What do you mean?"

He took a deep breath. "I have a proposition for you, Esther. Please... hear me out."

Chapter Twenty
FEBRUARY 2097
Alex

Alex looked around his room at The Orchard. He'd been here all too briefly, and now it was time to say goodbye. He finished packing his clothes into a suitcase and then paused for one final look around.

"I'll miss you," he whispered. He picked up his mother's scarf, which he still kept under his pillow, and held it to his nose. Would he be allowed to keep it at his new houder's house? He hoped so. He couldn't bear to be parted from it again. Then, with one last look around his bedroom, it was time to leave.

Charles and Noah were waiting for him downstairs, looking glum.

"Josiah says he won't let you be swallowed up into the system again," Noah told him as he escorted Alex to the door. "You'll be allowed to write to us and have a monthly holocall, and he'll insist we're allowed to visit you at least once a year."

"Yes, I know," Alex murmured. He'd been there when Joe had gone through all this with them.

"You're far too famous for anyone to treat you badly this time," Charles said, his eyes full of tears even though he was attempting a smile.

"That's my Charles. Always looking for the positives." He enveloped his brother in a hug. "It's who you are," he whispered in his ear. "Remember that when the press are giving you a hard time. Remember you're a Lytton."

"I'll remember I'm Alex Lytton's brother, and if he could endure all he's been through these past few years and come out the other side, then there's nothing I can't handle, either. I want to do you proud," Charles said bravely. "I never want to let you down again."

"You won't, Charles." He turned to his father. "You'll take care of each other, won't you?"

"We will." Noah's hand was shaking as he reached out to touch the side of Alex's face, stroking gently. "We'll miss you, son. We love you."

"I know." Alex wrapped his arms around his father and held him tight. It had once been so hard to say and show, but now it seemed effortless. "And I love you, too. We'll be together again, one day."

He hoped so. He was worried about how they'd cope without him. Noah wasn't in good health, and Charles was struggling with his change in status from national treasure to national disgrace. Neither of them was strong; he saw now that they never had been. Elliot had been right in that odd, perceptive way he'd sometimes had. Alex was the one who most took after his mother. He had her strength and resilience, her independent spirit. He might have been taken to the limits of his endurance, but he'd survived. He knew instinctively that his brother and father could never have done the same in his position. He suspected he'd known it, on some level, on that day in the country lane, sitting next to Charles with his mother's dead body staring sightlessly at them. She'd gone, and he'd stepped up to be the family protector without even realising that was what he was doing.

"Are you sure you don't want to stay here tonight?" Noah asked. Alex understood – his father was desperate to have him under his roof for one last night.

"No. I'm due at the IS court first thing tomorrow morning. Joe has to take me to hand me over; it's his job as my current houder. It's much further to drive there from here than it is from his house, so it's better that I spend the night there."

His father nodded over and over again, unable to speak. Alex gave him one last hug, then climbed into his duck and drove away. He didn't trust himself to speak to them again. He just waved and forced himself to leave. As he exited the gates, he looked in the mirror to see them still standing there forlornly, waving as he left.

A delicious smell awaited him when he reached Joe's house.

"Hey! Something smells good," he exclaimed as he entered the kitchen.

"Not my cooking, obviously." Joe grinned, opening the oven door.

"What is it?" Alex peered over his shoulder.

"Fish and chips. What else would we have for a final supper?" He took the food from where he'd been keeping it warm in the oven and placed it on trays, then offered Alex an awkward kiss on the cheek.

Things were a little strained between them, a little cooler than they'd once been. Alex was still angry that Joe had broken his promise, and Joe was still hurt that Alex hadn't told him the full truth about his relationship with Tyler. Tonight, however, wasn't the time to rip the scabs off old wounds.

They sat in the dining room to eat, neither of them speaking. Alex looked around the room, which held almost as many memories for him as The Orchard did. It was in here that he'd revealed he was Ben Smith, that he'd played Joe that song, and also that they'd made love for the first time.

"Are Charles and Noah okay?" Joe asked quietly.

"Yes. No." Alex shrugged. "It was hard to leave them."

"You know I'll look after them. I promise, and that's one promise I'll keep."

Alex sighed. "I know you will."

"I'll always protect them to the best of my ability until you're able to come back and do it yourself."

"Thank you." Alex reached across the table and grasped his hand. "For all of it. I know you risked everything for me. I still can't quite believe it's over, that we did it." He ran a trembling hand through his hair. "After all this time, to know it's done, and I don't have to hide or pretend any more."

"I hope it's brought you some peace." Joe gazed at him searchingly.

"I don't know. It's not as if it changes the fact that I'm still an IS, and that tomorrow I'll be handed over to a new houder." Alex managed a shaky smile. "But at least Tyler is behind bars."

"The others will be, too, soon enough," Joe said. "Bagshaw, Harper – all of them, like I promised."

"I only ever cared about Tyler, but thank you." Alex pushed his plate away, his meal only half eaten. "I wonder who my new houder will be, and what they'll want me to do?"

"Maybe it'll be a woman this time."

"That would be a change, at least." Alex gave a wry smile. "I hope they'll buy me as a butler, or a valet or something. I'd hate for all those Belvedere lessons to go to waste."

"Maybe they'll want a promising designer," Joe suggested.

"I would love that. See, it's not all bad. This could be a fantastic new start. The beginning of a new adventure."

He knew he wasn't fooling anyone, least of all himself.

"There's something I must tell you," Joe blurted out suddenly.

"Uh-oh." Alex grimaced. "That doesn't sound good."

Joe gave a strained smile. "I would have told you before, but I was sworn to secrecy, and besides, there never seemed like a good time."

"More secrets?" Alex groaned.

"I worked out who killed Elliot." Joe's expression was serious.

"What?" Alex stared at him. "I thought... I mean, I assumed it was Neil – wasn't it?"

"I did, too, for a while. He was the most likely candidate, but you know me. I couldn't let it rest. So I did some digging."

"Of course you did," Alex sighed. "And?"

"Firstly, I want you to know that it wasn't your fault."

"Joe, you're scaring me. Who was it?"

"It was Gideon," Joe said unexpectedly.

"What?" Alex struggled to take that in. "But he's dead. He died months before Elliot was killed."

"No, that's just what he wanted everyone to believe."

"But why? He didn't even *know* Elliot."

"He was dying, and he wanted to engineer it so that you and I would cross paths, that Tyler would finally get his comeuppance, and you'd get your happy ending – in his mind anyway. He met Elliot and tried to persuade him to sell you to him. He was the mystery bidder. But when Elliot turned him down, he resorted to more desperate measures."

"What the hell?" Alex buried his face in his hands for a long moment. Finally, he looked up to see Joe gazing at him sympathetically. "Poor Elliot. So, it wasn't even about him? He didn't deserve that. Fuck, I should never have told Gideon about Solange."

"I knew that's what you'd think. Like I said, it wasn't your fault, Alex," Joe told him firmly. "You aren't responsible for the decisions other people make. Gideon felt that he had nothing to lose, given that he was dying. For what it's worth, I'm not entirely sure that he was of sound mind; the cancer had spread to his brain."

"Where is he? Can I see him?" Alex asked eagerly.

"He died not long after the trial ended," Joe said, in a gentle tone. "I asked him repeatedly to see you, because I knew you'd want that, but he refused, point blank. I think he knew that he'd done a very wicked thing, and he didn't want to face your judgement."

"*My* judgement?" Alex blinked. "How bizarre that anyone should care about *my* judgement, of all things."

"No, you're usually more on the receiving end of everyone else's judgements." Joe gave a rueful grin.

"I'm glad you solved it. I'm glad we know what happened and why."

"Are you okay?" Joe squeezed his hand.

"Yes. Shocked, but... somehow not surprised, if that makes sense?"

"It does."

"It's a lot to take in, on top of everything else that's happened, and yet it's so very Gideon. He always did love to pull everyone's strings behind the scenes to get the outcomes he wanted. I was devastated when Tyler said he'd died. I know you've never understood why I viewed him as a friend, but he gave me the tools I needed to survive as Tyler's IS, and also... I just really liked him." Alex sighed. "And I know he liked me, too, although I'd never have guessed he'd commit murder for me."

"You were his masterpiece. The ultimate IS that he trained to fool the most despicable of houders. He was delighted by you. No wonder he wanted to see your story play out in full before he died."

"What did you think of him?" Alex asked, leaning forward. Joe had a way of seeing into the soul of a person and understanding precisely who they were.

"Well, I could see why you liked him. He was easy to like. Charming, elegant, and very clever. Yet, he was also..." Joe paused to consider. "I was going to say dangerous, but I don't think that's the right word. Venomous suits him better. I'm not sure any of us ever got to know the real Gideon; he was too manipulative for that. Like you said, he loved pulling everyone's strings, right to the bitter end." Joe gave a little grimace, and Alex wondered what had passed between them. He'd love to have been there, watching these two men who'd played such huge roles in his life, facing off against each other.

"You must be delighted to have finally uncovered the truth. I know how much you hate unsolved mysteries," Alex teased.

"Yeah, it's a huge character flaw." Joe sighed. "So, how do you want to spend our final night together?"

"I know exactly what I want to do." Alex grinned.

"What?"

"Dance!" He jumped to his feet. "Come on, Joe. We only danced once, and that's a crying shame. Let's twist and shout." He grinned, gyrating around the dining room. He asked the sound system to play that song, and the raw sound of the early Beatles filled the room. Joe laughed and joined him, dancing energetically in time to the music.

"Not bad for an old man," Alex taunted, twisting away from him.

"I'm only eight years older than you," Joe protested. He caught up with Alex and grabbed him, making him squeal with laughter.

Joe pulled him in close and danced with him properly. When the song finished, he called for a slower number and they drifted lazily around the room, wrapped up in each other's arms.

They danced for a long time, neither of them wanting the evening to end. Joe's body was so big and solid. He was wearing a pair of pale blue jeans and a white shirt, and looked as crisp and well-groomed as ever, even in casual clothes. The familiar scent of his aftershave was strong and clean.

Alex leaned into him, enjoying the closeness. For years, he'd had a crush on a fantasy image of who Joe was. He could see now that the real man was both less and more – so much more – than his fantasy.

Maybe, if he was free, and they had the time to mend what was broken between them, then maybe... but it was pointless. He wasn't free and unlikely ever to be free again.

He'd always thought he didn't deserve love, and certainly not the love of a man like this, so kind, decent, and strong, but maybe, one day, if he put his head down and worked on himself, he'd be worthy of a man like Joe.

So much had happened since they'd last danced in this room, a lifetime ago. He recalled those early, cautious days when he hadn't been sure he could trust Joe and felt he was making one mistake after another.

"Remember when I put on Peter's clothes and you had a meltdown?" he murmured as they danced.

"Yeah." Joe chuckled.

"I didn't think. Elliot loved me wearing Christopher's clothes." Alex rested his chin on Joe's reassuringly broad shoulder.

"Everyone grieves differently, I suppose."

"Yes." Alex thought of Tyler, channelling his grief into revenge; and Elliot, needing to pretend his husband was still there, magically transformed into someone else... and Joe, frozen in time, unable to move on, locked in the trauma of that terrible night. Then he thought of himself, drowning in guilt for his mother's death, whether misplaced or not, and trying to make up for it by keeping a promise he should never have made in the first place.

"Then I tried to seduce you." Alex winced. "Honestly, I was all over the place. I thought that if you slept with me, I could figure out whether to trust you, and it'd be easier to tell you about Solange." He leaned back to gaze at Joe. "But I can see why you felt it was one more manipulation in a whole pattern of deceit."

"You were led to expect that all anyone wanted of you was sex. It's not surprising that warped your understanding of people and relationships."

"Shall we agree to forgive each other, then?" Alex asked.

"It's already done." Joe smiled.

Alex leaned forwards and pressed a chaste kiss to his lips and then, regretfully, let him go.

"Time for bed," he sighed. "Big day tomorrow."

As he left the room, he paused for a moment to gaze at the vase Liz had given to Peter and Joe as a wedding present. It looked strong and beautiful, with its golden *kintsugi* seams snaking around where he'd mended it.

Joe smiled at him. "I think I like it better that way," he said.

Alex dumped his suitcase in the spare room and prepared for bed. Then he performed some simple yoga poses while listening to his song. Solange's killer might have been brought to justice, but Alex was still an IS. It wouldn't do to let his method of coping with that fact lapse.

He lay in bed for a long time, staring at the ceiling. Tomorrow was the dawn of a new chapter in his life, and he wasn't looking forward to it. He'd have to adjust to the needs and demands of a new houder, and although he was sure Charles was right, and the next one wouldn't dare to treat him badly, it was still a life of servitude.

An hour ticked by, but sleep wouldn't come. He didn't want it to because that would bring the morning closer, and with it, a day he didn't want to face.

Finally, he gave up, climbed out of bed, and padded next door. Joe lifted the duvet the minute he arrived, as if he'd been waiting for him, and Alex slipped in beside him.

"I know we agreed not to do this again, because we didn't want to make it even harder on ourselves, but... this could be my last chance to have sex with someone of my own choosing – someone I genuinely desire and care about," Alex said softly, resting his hands on Joe's chest. "It's been a while, and I'll understand if you don't feel the same way, but I want you, Joe. One last time."

He looked down to see Joe gazing up at him from sad, dark eyes. No words were necessary. Joe's hands slid around his body and pulled him close, and his lips claimed a passionate kiss. Alex knew this was what he wanted – needed – more than anything else in the world right now; to be loved by this strong, steadfast man.

So much water had flowed under the bridge. They'd hurt and disappointed each other too many times, kept too many secrets, but now, finally, in the darkness of their last night together, there was only honesty.

Joe was already naked, and it was the work of seconds for Alex to remove his own tee shirt and boxer shorts and for Joe to retrieve condoms and lube from the bedside table. Then Joe pulled him back into the warm circle of his arms.

"I want it like the first time," Alex whispered.

"I know." Of course he did. Joe knew precisely what he wanted – needed – tonight. He wanted to be overwhelmed, lost in the moment, and completely consumed by passion, as he'd been when they'd first made love downstairs, a lifetime ago.

Joe took charge, and Alex surrendered, losing himself in the sensations. Joe held him down, his hands circling Alex's wrists firmly but gently, holding him in place while he dipped his head and kissed his lips, and his neck, and then nuzzled lower to take a nipple into his mouth. He sucked down hard, making Alex moan, then kissed his way across his chest to the other one and sucked it too. Alex sighed and bucked up against him, loving the sheer, solid weight of the man on top of him.

He revelled in being the focus of all Josiah Raine's laser-sharp attention to detail. Joe's big hands roved over his body, stroking, tweaking, and exciting him. He was soon lost, consumed by one wave of pleasure after another, until they all joined together and he was a mess of quivering bliss.

Joe was relentless, giving him no time to think, or to dwell, even for a second, on what would happen in the morning. He pulled Alex up, moved him around, and explored every single inch of his body, determined in his quest to give Alex exactly what he wanted.

Pushing Alex onto his front, he gently pulled his buttocks apart. Alex sighed as Joe's warm tongue slipped into his hole. He remembered the first time Joe had rimmed him, and how he'd been taken to a state of incoherent ecstasy.

Alex had always prided himself on being good at sex, but in Joe he'd met his match. Joe rimmed him for a long time, until he was boneless with pleasure, then flipped him onto his back.

He leaned over Alex and kissed him deeply on the lips, swallowing his startled gasp as he wrapped a lubed hand around his straining cock. He rubbed it slowly, firmly, kissing Alex all the while, making him pant and moan. He whimpered when Joe pulled back, then cried out when he moved down and took his cock into his mouth, teasing the tip slowly with his tongue.

"Oh God!" He gripped the sheets with his hands. "Please..." He wasn't sure what he was begging for, but it felt so good.

Joe grinned up at him, a wicked, knowing grin that should have warned him, then deep-throated him with one sudden move, and he almost passed out. For the next few minutes he was lost, until he felt himself coming. Joe held him in place and swallowed down every last drop, then licked him clean.

"That was..." Alex trailed off. He had no words. But Joe wasn't done with him yet. He began kissing and caressing Alex all over again, slowly, gently, taking his time, as if mapping every last inch of his body and committing it to memory. "I should do something for you," Alex murmured, waving a hand vaguely, too blissed out to move.

"No. You'll do exactly as I say," Joe said firmly.

Alex sighed happily, delighted to be surrendering so completely to this man, tonight of all nights.

Joe kissed and teased him for a long time, until there were no coherent thoughts left in his brain. Dimly, he was aware of a cool, lubed finger pressing inside his relaxed hole, and then another. He wriggled down, trying to impale himself impatiently on those fingers, but Joe stopped, tapping his thigh.

"Wait for it," he ordered, with another of those wicked grins.

Alex let out a sound halfway between a laugh and a groan. "You bastard!"

"Yup." Joe continued finger fucking him slowly, taking his time, while gently stroking his nipples and occasionally flicking a tongue over his cock until it was, once again, hard and straining.

"Please, please, please..." Alex whimpered mindlessly, until finally Joe took pity on him and settled between his open legs. His big, beautiful cock was hard and glistening as he pressed slowly into Alex's waiting body.

God, he was so ready! He screamed in pleasure as Joe pushed into him, all the way, loving the sensation of fullness as he took Joe's cock inside him.

Joe leaned down and trailed his mouth over his chest, teasing at his nipples, allowing his weight to settle inside him, and then he shifted, making Alex moan. He gazed up, grinning stupidly, as Joe moved his hips back then pushed forward, brushing his prostate and sending him high into the stratosphere.

Joe sped up, moving his hips faster and faster. He looked like some gorgeous Viking warrior, with his muscular arms and broad chest. His normally neat blond hair was tousled, and if Alex had never seen him like this, he'd never have believed that the man in all those buttoned up suits and sharply pressed shirts could be so completely feral in bed.

Joe fucked him like a piston, and Alex loved every second of the wild ride. He wanted it to last forever, to relish the sensation of Joe being inside him until the end of time. He was slick with sweat, his cock was leaking, and he was lost to the world. There was just him and Joe, joined together in this one last intense night before it was all over.

He came in a haze, watching as Joe threw back his head and roared out his own climax. Joe stayed there for a long time, panting, then withdrew and sank down next to him.

They were both exhausted, but neither of them wanted the night to end. Joe wrapped his arms around him and held him tight, kissing the back of his neck, one hand trailing over his body, stroking him gently.

They dozed for a long while, bodies pressed tightly together, trying desperately to hold onto every last precious second, and then they began again.

Alex lost track of the time. Everything was just disjointed moments now. One moment he was on his front, screaming as Joe rimmed him again, and the next Joe had pulled him onto his lap and was holding him in place while he thrust up into him like an animal. It was wild, unrestrained, raw, and full of passion.

Alex was glad that Joe was in control, and he didn't have to think.

He loved how big Joe was, how he could throw him around the bed, guide him into position, hold him up and hold him down, and all the while play those insanely sweet tunes on his body.

They dozed, and fucked, and kissed, and cuddled, needing to be as close as humanly possible for this one final night, before it all went to hell.

As the pale light of dawn crept around the side of the curtains, they simply held each other. There was nothing left to say. They'd said it all with their bodies.

Eventually, Joe pulled away with a reluctant sigh and reached out his hand, wordlessly, to Alex. They walked to the bathroom hand in hand and took one final shower together, taking it in turns to soap each other as they'd done that first night they'd made love. They still didn't say a word; they just kissed and caressed.

Then, finally, it was over. They shared one last deep kiss under the spray of the shower, water streaming over them, tongues pressed deep in each other's mouths, and then they drew apart.

Alex returned to the spare room to shave, brush his teeth, and dress. He took his time, his stomach full of butterflies as he pulled on his smartest suit and tie to face his fate in court.

When he was done, he stood in front of the mirror and smiled at his reflection. He looked immaculate, without a hair out of place – a trick he'd learned from Joe, the poor Quarterlands kid who'd learned how to armour up to face the world.

Joe was waiting for him downstairs, looking as perfectly groomed as Alex, in a maroon herringbone three-piece.

"Ready?" Joe held out his hand to take his suitcase.

"As I'll ever be." It felt strange to be talking again after the silent passion of the past few hours.

"I have a gift for you." Joe handed him a rectangular package, wrapped in brown paper and string. With a questioning glance, Alex tore through the wrapping, and then smiled, his eyes filling with tears.

It was the picture of Solange. But not the crumpled version that had been folded and stuffed behind *Halo of Fire*. This picture was brand new, digitally rendered to look sharp and clean, and it had been professionally framed.

"I asked Gideon for a fresh copy and had it printed up properly," Joe said. "And I checked with Byrne; you're allowed to take a few personal items, so you can keep it with you. You aren't a felon any more, Alex. You've worked out your sentence. That changes how you must be treated."

"Thank you." Alex hugged the photo to his chest, beaming. "It's what I need to see me through."

"And you have your mum's scarf, too?"

"It's in my suitcase."

"Then you're all set." Joe placed his hands on his shoulders. "Whatever happens, I'm so bloody proud of you, Alex."

"Thank you. I have something for you, too." Alex handed him his little silver box. Joe flicked the lid open to reveal the two dark chocolates nestled within. "One last time," Alex said softly. "You'll have to remember to fill it yourself from now on."

"I will, but it won't be the same," Joe said with a tight, sad smile. "Nothing will be the same without you."

"You'll be okay. Remember that promise you made me – that you won't be alone? Now, I know that keeping promises isn't your strong suit, but I expect you to keep that one, okay?"

Joe gave a strangled little chuckle at that.

"You have friends, Joe, tons of them," Alex told him sternly. "Far more than I've ever had. Let them in. Let them take care of you."

"I will – that's a promise I *will* keep." Joe pulled him in for one last hug, and then all that was left was for Alex to depart this house that had been his home and sanctuary for over a year and to face his future with grace.

"Want to drive?" Joe held up the biokey to the duck he'd bought for Alex. "One last time. In case you're not allowed after today?"

"Yes." Alex took the biokey and they set off. "Talking of one last time. Shall we hear what they're saying about us?"

He turned on the radio, and they were greeted by the excitable tones of Amanda and the more measured interjections of Alan.

"So, today is the day Alexander Lytton appears before the IS judge," Alan said. "What are we expecting, Amanda?"

"Well, I have some huge gossip for you," Amanda chirped. "We've heard that someone very impressive and unexpected has bid on Alex's contract."

"Oh! Who can it be? Do tell."

Alex glanced at Joe, who looked back, startled. "Any ideas?" Alex asked.

"Nope." Joe shrugged.

"Impressive *and* unexpected? Aren't I the lucky one?" Alex muttered.

"So, this certain someone has just signed a three-picture deal in the UK and is intending to be based here for the next five years. It's only Hudson Brink!"

Alex pulled over for a second and rested his head on the steering wheel. "Oh, dear God, no."

"Word from the courtroom is that Hud has just arrived, along with the other bidders, to find out if he's been successful."

"Well, he certainly has the money for it," Alan commented cheerfully.

"Hudson Brink? I can't stand the guy," Alex said in despair.

"Money might not be as important as you'd think," Amanda continued. "The court has already made it clear that they're only accepting the price Alex was bought for originally."

"Which is still a small fortune," Alan pointed out.

"Sure, but they've been very clear the success of the bid will rest on the whole application."

"After the mess the IS agency is in right now, I'd imagine the government will want to get this right," Alan reasoned. "So, Hudson Brink would be an excellent choice. He's a major movie star and I'm sure he'll show Alex the high life. Lots of fun, parties, and premieres."

"Oh, yes," enthused Amanda. "I can't think of a better choice for poor Alex. Hud will be the perfect new houder for him. Here's what Hud had to say when we spoke to him earlier."

"Hey, I met Lytton once, and I liked him. I'm relocating here for a few years, and I love your quaint little IS system. I figure I can give him a good home."

"I'm not a bloody dog," Alex spluttered.

"I've never had an IS, but I like the liveries you have and all the ID tags and all," Hud continued. "Listen, that kid could do a lot worse than end up with me."

"Come on," Joe told him, squeezing his shoulder. "It's not a done deal yet."

"No," Alex said shakily. "It'll be fine. Hud is a shit, but he knows the world will be watching how he treats me. I'm sure it'll be okay."

He took a few deep breaths, then continued driving. Another houder and another chapter in his life of servitude, only this time with no mission to sustain him, and no hope at the end of it. He was dreading it.

The IS court was in the same building where he'd first been sentenced and, much to his surprise, the same judge was presiding. Beside him, Joe kept fiddling with his cufflinks, clearly just as anxious as he was, but Alex was grateful for his solid, reassuring presence.

He looked around as he entered. The courtroom was packed with reporters, so he was glad that he'd insisted his father and brother remain behind at The Orchard. They'd both suffered enough from all the public interest. His gaze fell on a familiar face; Hudson Brink was sitting in the front row talking to someone from his entourage, looking impossibly handsome and extremely confident, his eyes hidden behind a pair of dark glasses, his ludicrously white teeth shining whenever he smiled.

The judge called the court to order. "Mr Lytton, you've served out your sentence delivered by this court for the crime you committed," she said sternly, staring down her thin nose at him.

"Yes, Your Honour," he said politely.

"We've all heard about the trials and tribulations you subsequently faced, and I'm sorry for it. This is *not* how the system should work, and we will do our best to remedy it."

"Thank you, Your Honour, but in my opinion, it's not fixable," Alex told her firmly. "When life is cheap, and people are allowed unchecked power over others, there will always be corruption."

She shot him a sharp look, and Joe nudged him with his foot, a gentle warning to keep his mouth shut to avoid getting into any more trouble.

"Well, I can see why you'd think so, but the IS system has kept the peace in this country for decades," she told him. "And such peace is not something we should surrender lightly."

Alex bowed his head meekly. He'd said his piece, even though he knew it wouldn't make any difference. The cameras were on him, so at least his protest would be noted.

"Now, turning to the matter of your future..." She glanced down at her nanopad. "Tyler Tech has acknowledged that you were not treated properly in their care and have surrendered you back into the system. They will likely receive a substantial fine."

Small comfort to him. Byrne had already told him that the fine money would go to the IS agency, not him. The system was always rigged against the indies.

"We've received a good deal of interest in your contract. You're a famous face and your story has attracted widespread attention. However, our view was that Tyler Tech should not profit from your sale, and your contract has therefore been offered at the same price they paid for it. We've received several bids of that sum and have weighed and considered each of them carefully." She peered at him over the top of her spectacles. Beside him, Alex felt Joe stiffen.

"And we've made a decision. Investigator Raine." She turned to Joe.

"Yes, Your Honour." He stood to attention like the old soldier he was.

"You are relieved of your duties and responsibilities as Mr Lytton's temporary houder," she informed him. "You may step down."

"Yes, Your Honour." He gave Alex's hand a firm squeeze and then strode away, taking a seat in the front row. Alex suddenly felt very alone.

"Your new houder has requested anonymity, as is their right," the judge told him. "I therefore transfer your contract into their keeping." She entered her biosig into her nanopad.

There was a restless rustling among the media; this wasn't what they wanted. They wanted to know precisely who Alex's new houder was, so they could run stories about them and dig up whatever dirt there was. Alex understood their disappointment. He'd like to know, too. But he was sure he'd find out soon enough.

"Now... you've been transferred." The judge checked her screen. "And the money has been received, so that's all complete."

She was making too much of a meal of it for Alex's liking, milking her moment in the spotlight. He wished she'd get on with it, so he could find out who owned him and what kind of service he'd be expected to provide.

"Now, as I said, the court examined all the applications. We were not prepared to get into a bidding war, as we felt that was inappropriate in the circumstances. So, the sole consideration was who would be the best houder for you. With that in mind, I can reveal that only one of your prospective purchasers wished to buy your contract with the sole purpose of releasing you." She glanced around at the excited rustle that greeted this announcement. "The paperwork for your release was submitted with the application, in the event that it was successful. I have that paperwork in front of me now, and I can confirm that it is all in order, and that you are now a free man."

Alex blinked. "What?" he whispered.

"Your contract has been paid in full. You're free to go." She gave him an imperious stare. "You're no longer an indentured servant, Mr Lytton. A medic will remove your chip before you leave."

"But..." Alex looked around the court. "I mean... who do I have to thank for this?" He knew how much he was worth. Who on earth could afford to write off that kind of money?

"I'm afraid that information is sealed, by order of the court. Your last houder wishes to remain anonymous, even from you."

That caused a huge buzz to go around the packed room. Alex stood there, bewildered. His legs almost gave way, and he held on to the desk in front of him for support. He was free? After all this time, all these years? Free?

He sought out Joe, looking for reassurance that he wasn't dreaming. Joe gazed back, his eyes shining, a broad grin on his face. It *was* true! He really had been set free. His gaze fell on Hudson Brink – had he bought his contract? If so, why? Hud looked annoyed, though, his face creased into a disappointed frown. Alex doubted he was a man much given to philanthropic gestures, so no, it wasn't him.

"Now, please clear my courtroom. I have other cases to consider," the judge ordered, and there was a sudden dash for the exit.

Alex went slowly, still trying to take it all in. As soon as he stepped outside, he was surrounded by the media. He made a brief, incoherent statement, and then the court medic approached to remove his microchip. The gloomy grey day was suddenly lit up as hundreds of flash bulbs exploded to capture the symbolic moment – that would be the picture that would dominate all the news sites within minutes.

He looked down at the little puncture mark in his arm and found he almost missed the winking red dot of the microchip. Several reporters pressed their nanocards into his hand, promising him huge sums of money for an exclusive interview, and then, finally, the crush died down and the crowd began to drift away.

Now what? Alex looked around for Joe and saw him, standing over to one side, his arms folded across his broad chest, looking on with a sense of quiet satisfaction.

Alex walked over to him, shaking his head in disbelief. "Can you believe it?"

"I'm so happy for you," Joe exclaimed, enveloping him in a warm bear hug.

Alex clung on to his broad shoulders, still reeling.

"Are you okay?" Joe pushed him away, gazing at him searchingly.

"I don't know. I can't take it in."

"You'll get the hang of it."

Alex looked around, still feeling utterly bewildered. "Who would do that for me? All that money!"

"It doesn't matter. Everyone in the country heard your story, and someone obviously felt moved enough to ensure that your future is better than your past. That's all that's important."

"But... what do I do next?" Alex asked. The world suddenly felt too big, and he felt lost in it.

"Whatever you damn well want." Joe grinned. "And to get you started..." He held up the duck biokey. "Take this. I can walk to Inquisitus;

it's only a few blocks away. You keep the duck. You'll need a way to get around."

"I can't... it's too much," Alex stammered, feeling utterly unworthy of all the generosity he was receiving.

"Nonsense. It's the least I can do." Joe put his hands on his shoulders, gazing at him sternly. "Listen to me. I'll always be here, if you need me, but give yourself a chance to discover who you are and what you want. You're a free man now and can do whatever the hell you like."

"I don't know what that is," Alex blurted, suddenly panicked.

"You'll figure it out. In your own time. No obligations. No pressure. Whatever you choose, it's *your* choice. That's what freedom means." He drew back.

"But what about us? You and me?" Alex whispered.

"Figure out Alex first and then we'll see," Joe said firmly. "Sleep with other people if you want. The last thing you need is to be shackled to me right now." His expression was pained as he said that, but his voice rasped with sincerity. "Now, I've got to get back to work." He leaned in and spoke fiercely into Alex's ear. "Go and live, Alex. Go and live." Then he pressed a kiss to Alex's cheek and turned to go, his long coat flapping elegantly around his ankles as he strode away.

Noah and Charles were waiting for him back at The Orchard. They'd already heard the news and were in the driveway with balloons to welcome him home. Alex had thought he was leaving this place for good just a few short hours ago, and yet here he was, reunited with his family again. He felt too choked up to say anything. He just fell into their arms and let them hold him for a very long time.

He was finally home.

Chapter Twenty-One
MARCH 2097
Josiah

Josiah finished packing up another box, then paused for a rest. He'd been working in the garage all morning and he wasn't so much tired as pissed off.

"Most of this is your stuff, Peter," he growled, tipping up a box full of old engine parts and glaring at them. "I say that with some certainty because I've never had the slightest interest in vehicles, as well you know."

A part of him longed for the days when his dead husband would have replied with a snappy comeback, but he knew it was better this way. He'd told Alex to move on, and he had to learn to do the same, somehow.

He wiped his hands on a towel on the workbench and then glanced up as he heard a duck outside. A few seconds later, his heart did a little flip as a familiar figure strolled into his garage.

"Hey, Joe. I saw the door was open and..." Alex looked around at all the packing boxes in surprise. "What are you doing? Having a clear-out?"

"Something like that."

Alex was wearing ripped jeans and a faded tee-shirt that had seen better days and was clearly a remnant from his youth. He looked a bit of a mess, but Josiah suspected that was a reaction to all the years when he'd been dressed up like a prize pony.

"Only you would wear decent clothes to do this kind of work," Alex observed, rolling his eyes as he glanced at Josiah's smart chinos and the long-sleeved blue polo shirt that precisely matched the colour of his eyes.

"Well, one of us has to dress right," Josiah snorted, with a sly tug on Alex's ugly old tee-shirt.

Alex laughed and pressed a kiss to his cheek. "That's my neat freak. How are you doing?"

They texted, and they'd had several holocalls, but Josiah had deliberately kept his distance in the past few weeks, wanting Alex to have the time and space to figure out what to do with his new-found freedom.

The memory of their last night together was always fresh in his mind, but the last thing he wanted was for Alex to feel any obligation towards him, so he'd kept him at arm's length. It would have been all too easy for Alex to rush back to him because he represented safety and convenience, but Josiah didn't want to be anyone's security blanket.

"I'm fine. You?" Josiah put his head on one side and studied him. He looked tired.

"I'm fine," Alex said abruptly.

"No, you're not," Josiah said. "Want to talk about it?"

"No. Yes. No. Oh, it's nothing." He made an exasperated gesture with his hand. "Just Charles and Dad driving me nuts and, well, it turns out freedom isn't all it's cracked up to be. All these decisions! Reporters calling me, the publishers pressing me about the book, and Charles wants me to start doing after-dinner speeches on that god-awful circuit he's on. I'd say no, but neither of them has any money, and the interview money won't last forever," he grumbled. "I know, I know." He held up his hands. "Regular people's problems. But when I was an indie, I didn't have to worry about any of this stuff."

"No, you had other things to worry about," Josiah pointed out. "What can I say? Welcome to your life, Alex. It's difficult, and scary, and sometimes just plain boring, but at least it's yours now, when it wasn't for a very long time."

"True." Alex sprawled down on his workbench. "I'm like a zoo animal; release me back into the wild and I haven't a clue what to do."

Josiah picked up an empty box and started sorting through Peter's massive collection of paint brushes.

Alex sat up suddenly, looking around. "Where's the Jag?" he asked.

"I sold her." Josiah shrugged.

"What?" Alex looked aghast. "You sold Peter's Jag?"

"It was time. I never drove her. Having her here was a reminder I didn't need."

Alex mulled that over, then gave a reluctant nod. "I suppose so. Well done." He looked pained all the same. Poking around in one of the boxes, he took out a piece of metal, gazing at it thoughtfully.

"I have no idea what that is, and I don't want you to tell me," Josiah said. "It's going and that's that."

"Fair enough." Alex chucked it back in the box.

Josiah began throwing other things into the box while Alex sat there frowning. Something was clearly bothering him.

"How's the book going?" Josiah asked.

"Okay. I don't like writing it, but the publishers have sent someone to help me. I told them I'm happy to illustrate it but writing's not my thing. So, it'll have decent pictures in it, if nothing else." He grinned. "They assure me it'll be a runaway best seller, and I hope it bloody well is because there's no money. Charles seems to spend his the second he has any, and Dad has no income. They're both hopeless in their own way," he grumbled.

"Yeah." Josiah grinned. "But they're family, so…" He shrugged.

"I know, and I love them to bits, but I just had to get away. That's why I came here."

"Is it?" Josiah raised an eyebrow.

"No. No, it isn't." Alex stood up and began pacing around. "Look, Joe, I know you want me to find out who I am and all that stuff first, but the truth is, I can't stop thinking about that last night we spent together and how insanely hot it was."

"Right." Josiah threw an old trainer into the box. It wasn't even

Peter's size. Where had it come from? Then he recognised it as the one Hattie used to carry around – she'd found it in a park and proudly brought it home with her. "And so, you came here... for what? Looking for a good time?"

"No! I mean, yes, but not just for that. I want *you*, Joe. I want *us*. I want the snuggling on the sofa and the in-jokes, the banter, and, yes, the sex, too." Alex came over and put his hands on Josiah's shoulders. "What do you say?"

"I'm sorry, Alex, but the answer's no." Josiah pushed him away gently. "Look, it's only been a few weeks. Of course it's hard; you've been through hell. It'll take you a while to adjust, but you must give it time. I'm not your backup option just because you're unhappy with your life."

"I didn't mean it like that." Alex looked contrite. "I'm sorry if it came out that way. I just miss you," he said honestly. "I really do."

"I'm sure you do, but the answer is still no."

"Why? Don't you want me?"

Josiah winced at the raw vulnerability in his eyes.

"I know I'm not good enough for you," Alex admitted. "I know I'm not Peter. I know you must look at me and see that footage from Tyler's smartwalls and all those people I slept with. You must think I'm sleazy and dirty."

"I don't think anything of the sort," Josiah told him firmly. "Alex, I care about you, but you're just finding your feet. I'm familiar and comfortable, but that doesn't mean I'm right for you. Real life is messy and confusing and doesn't necessarily come with a happy ending. That's what having your freedom means. I meant it when I told you to go and live your life because, however difficult and imperfect it might be, it's still yours. Your life was interrupted when you were barely more than a kid. Find out who you are now without that chip in your arm."

"Stop it," Alex said sharply.

"What?"

"Stop telling me who to be and how to feel! I had enough of that when I was an indie. Well, newsflash, Joe, you don't own me any more."

"I know that." Josiah rocked back on his heels, feeling winded.

"No, you don't understand. My feelings are mine, Joe. *Mine*.

Nobody can tell me who to love or not to love any more. Not even you. I know how I feel, and I know that I want you. I'm tired of pretending. What we had was fantastic, and I want it back."

"Well, you can't have it," Josiah said, more harshly than he'd intended.

"But why not?" Alex took a deep breath and calmed down. "Joe, I don't think you ever stopped loving me. I hope not, anyway. And I..." He glanced away, flushing, then looked back again, and ploughed on. "I love you. There, I've said it. I love you, Josiah Raine. I've loved you for years. I love you, and I want you. Not because you're safe, and familiar, and not because you rescued me, but because you're you, and I'm in love with you. I mean it. I love *you*."

Josiah reached out and gently ran the back of his hand over Alex's cheek, then pulled him in close for a sweet whisper of a kiss.

"Thank you," he said softly, his heart breaking as he drew back. "You're right. I do still love you. I always will. But it's over, and it's time for you to move on."

Alex gave him a look of confused dismay.

"I don't understand. Why is it over? You want me, I want you... what the hell is there to stop us from being together?" He stopped suddenly and looked around the garage. "Are you moving out, Joe? All these boxes... the Jag... are you leaving?"

"Yes," Josiah said quietly. "I've sold up. I'm moving out in a few days."

"But this is Peter's house. You can't sell Peter's house."

"Why not? I sold Peter's Jag."

"Is that what you're doing, then?" Alex demanded. "Moving on? Where are you moving to?"

"I've found a place. It's a flat. I don't need a garden, and it's much smaller, so I can't take all this stuff," Josiah explained. "It's time I cleared it all out and went elsewhere. Past time, really."

"Right." Alex glanced around, looking sad and lost. "I suppose I just thought you'd always be here."

"I'll always be here for you, even if not in the way you want," Josiah told him gently. "I said that when you were freed, and I meant it."

Alex stood there, silent and still, but Josiah could see the cogs working. Alex Lytton was many things, but he wasn't stupid.

"Don't overthink it, Alex," he warned.

"It makes no sense," Alex whirled around, looking at all the boxes, then at the empty spot where the Jag had once stood, and finally back at Josiah. "None of this makes sense. I can't forget our last night together. Nobody could make love like that, with such intensity, and then just walk away without good reason. What don't I know, Joe? What's really going on?"

"Nothing. It's just time to move on."

"Is it?" Alex reached out suddenly and grabbed his arm, pushing up the sleeve of his polo shirt before he could stop him. There, winking away under his skin, was the red dot of his microchip. Josiah still couldn't quite get used to seeing it there. Alex stared at it, all the colour draining from his face.

"Joe... what have you done?" he asked hoarsely.

Josiah pulled his arm away. "What I had to do. What had to be done."

"How?" Alex demanded. "You don't have that kind of money. Even if you sold everything."

"No, I don't."

"Then how?"

Josiah opened the garage fridge and took out a Coke. He handed one to Alex.

"I don't want it."

"Well, I do." Josiah opened his and drank half of it straight down. Alex stood there, waiting, his eyes dark. "I didn't want you to know," Josiah told him.

"Obviously."

Josiah sighed. "Okay, but just so you understand that this was my decision, not yours, and you bear no responsibility, okay?" He told him about Gideon's bequest and how he'd agreed to his terms. When he'd finished, Alex sat down on the workbench again, looking completely blind-sided.

"You spent all of Gideon's money on buying my contract," Alex said slowly.

"Yes."

"But it wasn't enough." Alex glanced around the half-empty garage.

"No. So I used all my savings, and I sold Peter's car, and I sold the house – the sale's only just going through now. Esther agreed to give me a loan to offset the price of the house so I could afford your contract. I'll be giving her the money once the sale completes in a couple of days."

"And it still wasn't enough?" Alex looked at the microchip winking in Josiah's arm.

"No."

"So, you sold yourself. You only went and bloody well sold yourself into indentured servitude, and all to save my sorry arse." Alex looked devastated. "Oh, Joe. I'm not worth it."

"Yes, you are," Josiah told him firmly. "You are to me."

"No. I screw up everything I touch, and now I'm free again, I'm doing just that. I lost my temper with the ghost writer. That's why I drove here today. She was driving me nuts. I hate rehashing my stupid fucking story. I'd like to forget it, not relive it. I'm still a shit, Joe. You shouldn't have given up everything for me."

"My decision." Josiah shrugged. "Not yours. There are no strings attached. You can screw up your life to high heaven for all I care. The important thing is that your life is your own, to make as many mistakes as you like."

"While you're someone's indentured servant," Alex whispered, looking devastated.

"It's not as bad as all that," Josiah told him firmly. "To be honest, my life has barely changed. I asked Esther to buy me, and my contract is only for ten years. I'm doing the same job as always, only I wear a microchip and an ID tag while I'm doing it." He pulled open his polo shirt to reveal the plain Inquisitus ID tag on a necklace underneath.

"Esther agreed to this?" Alex asked, in a tone of disbelief.

"She didn't have much choice. She knew I'd sell myself to another investigation agency if Inquisitus didn't buy me, and she wasn't about to let that happen. She told me she wasn't prepared to lose her best investigator, or one of her best friends." He smiled at the memory. "She also told me, and I quote, 'I don't want you coming to me with any stupid indie shit.' She wants me to carry on as normal, so there's not much change. Yes, I'm having to move out, but Esther's putting me in a nice, self-contained flat next to Inquisitus, so I'll be much closer to the office. It's small, but I don't care about that. Honestly, it's not a big deal."

"It will be when your contract ends. You'll have nothing. No house, no savings, nothing. Where will you even live?"

"Well, there's always the Quarterlands." Josiah grinned. "I hear they're not so bad these days."

Alex didn't smile. He just stood there, his eyes awash with unshed tears. "I would never have asked you…"

"I know."

"And I can never thank you enough."

"I don't want your thanks," Josiah said sharply.

"I'll save up. I'm not like Charles. I mean it. I'll save up and find the money to free you."

"You'll do no such bloody thing," Josiah snapped. "I'm not a debt for you to be saddled with. You'll spend any money you make on building a life for yourself and on taking care of your dad and your brother. I'm fine. There's no way you'll make enough to buy me back, anyway. I mean it, Alex. Don't you dare even try."

"I must do something. I can't just let you give up everything you've worked for all your life."

"Like I said, it was my decision," Josiah said firmly. "My choice, not yours. You don't owe me anything, Alex."

"It's wrong. I can't let you—"

"You can and you will," Josiah thundered. Finally, he saw a grudging acceptance creep into Alex's eyes.

"Okay," he whispered.

"But I'm not free to be with you," Josiah told him. "We can't be in a relationship, Alex; not while I've got this chip under my skin."

"You and your stupid bloody pride! You know Esther wouldn't mind, don't you?"

"*I'd* mind," Josiah said fiercely. "I wouldn't be able to pay my way, my time isn't my own, and I always have to account for my whereabouts. It'd eat away at me, Alex, and ruin whatever we had. I can't do it."

"Surely there must be a way..."

"No." Josiah shook his head. "Esther paid way over the odds for me so that I'd have enough money to buy your contract. I have to give her my all. I won't short-change her. I can't have any other demands on my time and attention. You know me: when I'm in, I'm all in."

Alex stood there, staring at him, for a long time, his eyes full of tears. Then, finally, he brushed them away. "I understand," he said, pressing a little kiss to Josiah's cheek. "Thank you, Joe. The words aren't adequate, but I should say them anyway. Thank you."

"You're welcome." Josiah managed a faint smile.

"Can we at least be friends? Can I visit you? See the new flat? Hang out with you occasionally?"

"Sure." Josiah shrugged again. "But don't wait for me, Alex. You've been waiting for your life to start for long enough. Don't wait any more. Please."

Alex gazed at him sadly and then nodded. "Okay, Joe. I won't."

"Good. Now I need to finish up here, and you need to go and get on with your life."

He leaned forward to kiss him goodbye, but Alex flung his arms around him and held on tightly for several long minutes, his chest heaving. Josiah kissed his hair, inhaling the scent of him, longing to keep him there forever.

"The universe doesn't seem to want us to be together," Alex said finally, drawing back. "We never seem to catch a break."

"It does seem that at least one of us is always destined to be an indentured servant at any given time." Josiah gave a wry grunt.

"I can't believe this is how it ends," Alex whispered. "How *we* end, after all we've been through."

"For what it's worth, I still think you need time, love," Josiah told him, holding his face gently between his hands as he gazed at him. "Time to figure out who you are and what you want from a relationship. You've never had that. So maybe it's for the best."

"I know what I want. I've always known. It just all became so confusing and impossible with everything that was going on. I was in such a dark place, but you dragged me out of that, Joe, by never giving up on me or my cause. By reuniting me with my family, by bringing friends to visit, by fighting my corner when I was too shattered to do it myself. You hung on in there, even when I tried so desperately to push you away because I was so sure I destroyed everything I touched and everyone I loved. And it happened anyway." Alex placed his thumb over the winking red dot under Josiah's skin. "It happened anyway, Joe." His voice broke. "I destroyed you the way I destroy everyone I care about."

"No, you didn't." Josiah took firm hold of his shoulders. "I'm not destroyed, and you're not to blame. I don't regret what I did — I'd do it again in a heartbeat." He drew back. "Now go. I'm setting you free a second time, love. Free of obligation and regret. Free to be Alex, whoever he is. That's all I want for you. That's all that matters."

"I won't let you down." Alex pressed one last kiss to Josiah's cheek, then raised his chin and gave a firm nod. "I'll be the best person I can be. I'll make you proud of me."

Josiah shook his head. "Just be you. That's all I ask. Find out who Alex is and never let him go again."

"I can do that," Alex said softly, turning to go. "Thank you, Joe. I know it can never be enough but thank you."

Josiah watched him walk slowly from the garage, his head held high and his shoulders set in a determined line, as if he'd made a vow to himself.

Josiah had never wanted him to find out, but what use had secrets been to either of them? It was for the best.

Everyone at work was careful to treat him exactly the same as always. They knew, of course, even if he kept his shirt sleeves rolled down and his collar always buttoned up. They knew, but they never once mentioned it, and he was grateful for that.

The flat Esther gave him was tiny, but he suspected it was the nicest IS accommodation she could provide. She also gave him a small allowance to live off, which was a relief. He couldn't bear the thought of having to go to her, cap in hand, for every last thing he needed. Not that he needed much. He brought all the clothes he could fit into the cramped wardrobe and little else except his photos of Peter, Hattie's lead, and Liz's vase. He even gave away all Peter's clothes.

The only other thing he brought was the picture Alex had painted for him, which had pride of place on the wall. It reminded him not to spend all his time alone but, much to his surprise, he found he didn't need reminding very often.

Sofie visited the first night he moved in. She lived next door, in the shared IS facility. They cooked and ate together, and it was easy and comfortable, because they were old friends now.

"Will I ever get used to it?" he asked, looking down at the red dot blinking under his skin as he did the washing-up, his sleeves rolled back to the elbow.

"Yes," she replied. "You will. If it helps, don't look at it as a symbol of your servitude but as one of Alex's freedom. It's a badge of honour, Joe, not a stain on your character."

It *did* help. As much as he hated that little red dot, he couldn't be sorry that he'd exchanged his freedom for Alex's.

Elsie came to visit him as well, or more often he visited her, because she was quite frail these days, although still her indomitable self.

"I've always admired you for the way you took up Peter's cause," she told him as they sat drinking tea and eating biscuits in her flat one Saturday. "But I feared for you, too, becoming swallowed up in his crusade. Now, you've done the same for Alex. I hope there's room for Josiah to exist, too. You don't always have to sacrifice yourself for the men you love, you know."

"I couldn't be happy any other way," he told her ruefully.

She sighed and patted his arm. "Yes, I know. You always do throw yourself full pelt into love. You're not just physically brave, you're emotionally brave, too, Joe."

"I don't know if that's a thing, but thanks." He grinned at her.

. . .

Cam and Sarah invited Josiah around to dinner often. Sarah was pregnant, and Cam was ridiculously excited at the thought of becoming a dad, but also a heap of nerves. At Cam's request, Josiah took him to the boxing gym to help him get into shape. Winston took one look at him and rolled his eyes.

"Whatcha bringing me now, Sergeant? A ruddy desk-boy," he complained, chomping down on his cigar. Josiah laughed his head off, and Cam viewed the whole thing as such an ordeal he never went back.

Mel often invited him to the untidy apartment she shared with four well-fed cats. They sat in her kitchen together, a big ginger tom purring happily on Josiah's lap, and discussed the latest advances in DNA extraction, while trying out all the new offerings from a monthly chocolate club she subscribed to.

Esther liked taking him out to fancy restaurants. Eating out was her thing and she had quite the sophisticated palate. He wasn't sure he liked half the things she made him try, but it was an experience.

"You can't bloody well live off that ghastly takeaway hachée stuff," she chided over dinner at a Lost Cuisines restaurant one Saturday evening. Lost Cuisines eateries served a variety of dishes from regions that had completely disappeared during the Rising, and Esther was very fond of them.

"You sound just like Alex," he laughed.

"Do you still see him?" she asked. She'd never pried into the nature of their relationship, but she knew something significant had happened between them.

"Oh, yes. I'm seeing him tomorrow, as a matter of fact."

"I'm glad." She smiled. "I hope he's doing okay."

"He is. It's not easy, but he's trying very hard. He's been seeing a therapist."

"That's good. He must need it after all he's been through."

"Yeah. I tried to persuade him to see someone when he was living with me. Sofie even found him a therapist, but he refused to go. He didn't believe he was worth fixing back then."

"But now he does?"

"Yes. Or at least he's trying. He hates going, but I think it's helping. Can I ask you something personal?"

"Of course."

"I was wondering whether you'd ever considered trying the medical procedure Charles Lytton underwent in order to be able to walk again?" he asked.

"I did consider it, yes, but it's very expensive, and I still have a bullet in my spinal cord which makes it more complicated. Also, I'd need to take several months off work in order to do it, with no guarantee of success. So, on balance, I decided not to bother. I discussed it with Sofie at some length recently."

"I see. I've often wondered, but, well, I didn't like to ask before. Talking of Sofie, I've been meaning to ask about your involvement with government work camp charities. When did that start?"

"Long before Sofie." She smiled. "Did you know she first contacted me when she was fifteen years old? I was so impressed, I agreed to sponsor her education. I was already sponsoring several other intelligent, hard-working children from the camps, but she stood out. She's quite the force of nature."

"Isn't she just. So how did it all start, your interest in conditions in the work camps?" He'd been so busy fighting his battle against the IS system for all these years that he'd never considered others might be involved in battles of their own. Esther had chosen a safer route to help but had been no less dedicated. He'd always admired her, but now he found he liked her even more. She smiled and leaned back.

"It's a long story."

He shrugged. "We have all evening, and many more evenings to come, I'm sure."

The next morning, he walked to his favourite café, a French place on Ghost Eye that served the most amazing pain au chocolat. He sat in his usual chair, reading the news on his holopad and waiting for Alex to arrive. It turned out that when left to his own devices, Alex was habitually late. He was always consumed by a painting he was working on, or an article he was reading, or simply forgot the time.

Josiah sat down, opening the top button of his shirt as it was a warm day. The barista glanced over, his manner changing abruptly.

"Does your houder know you're here? Don't you have work to do?" he snapped, and Josiah realised, too late, that his IS tag was showing. It had been hard getting used to the change in his status. Before, he'd been someone, a senior investigator at Inquisitus no less, but now he was just another IS, and people treated him differently.

"I'm off duty, and I've paid," he pointed out.

"Fine, but I'll be watching you." The man glared at him.

It had taken him some time to understand that there were less salubrious cafés where indies were welcome, and more upmarket ones like this one where they weren't. He'd have thought nothing of entering this place when he was free, but now he realised it wasn't the kind of establishment that wanted indies on its premises.

He had half a mind to leave, but he was waiting for Alex, and he did really like the pain au chocolat here, so he swallowed his pride and stayed. Swallowing his pride was something he'd had to learn to do many times over as an IS, but it still stuck in his craw. The last thing he wanted was to repay Esther's kindness by causing her problems, so he sucked it up. "No indie shit" had been her only condition for buying his contract, and he'd made that his mantra. So, like all other indies, he knew to always stand on the bus even if there were seats, to always go to the back of the queue behind free people, and to put up with being called "serf", and worse. He'd become accustomed to a multitude of daily humiliations and stayed silent, out of respect for Esther.

At that moment the door swung open and Alex walked in. Eighteen months had passed since that day in his garage, and he'd made a huge push in moving on with his life. He seemed to have rediscovered his dress sense, or maybe he simply made an effort when they met up because Josiah was always so immaculately put together. Today, Alex was wearing a pair of dark jeans with a maroon shirt and black leather waistcoat. There was a thin scarf wrapped loosely around his neck, a leather bracelet on his wrist, and a silver ring on his thumb. He looked beautiful, of course, but more than that, he looked like himself. These were his choices, and they suited him.

"Hey!" He rushed over and pressed a kiss to Josiah's cheek. "Sorry I'm late."

"I'm used to it." Josiah rolled his eyes. "I ordered your usual." He gestured at the cup of tea and slice of millefeuille on the table.

Alex took a sip and let out a happy sigh. "Best tea in New London."

"That it is." Josiah held up his cup approvingly. "So, how's it going?"

"Okay." Alex stabbed at his pastry with a fork.

"Book still selling well?"

"Like hot cakes, apparently. Thank God. At least it means I won't have to give any more of those tedious speeches on Charles's ghastly after-dinner circuit for a long time. I hated that." He swallowed down the pastry as if he hadn't eaten for days, which he possibly hadn't; he was hopeless at remembering to eat if he was engaged in his art.

"Definitely not your thing." Josiah grinned.

"Have you read it?" Alex asked, and for all that he professed to hate his own book, there was an endearing anxiety in his eyes. "I wouldn't blame you if you couldn't face it.

"Of course I've read it."

Alex had sent him a copy before it came out, with a self-deprecating note. He'd taken his time and read it slowly, not least because parts of it hurt like hell and he'd had to put it down and walk away every so often.

"And? What did you think?" The hesitant, hopeful look in Alex's eyes made his anxiety even more palpable.

"It was a hard read in places," Josiah admitted. "But necessary. I liked how you tackled the issue of the IS system head-on. That won't win you many fans, but I'm guessing you don't care about that."

"God, no. It had to be said. It took longer to come out than my publishers wanted because I kept firing all the ghost writers they sent." Alex gave a self-deprecating grin. "But they say I still have a bit of momentum for now. It won't last much longer, so I had to make the most of it to get my message across."

"It's a big ask, to dismantle a system that's become embedded in our national life, like a virus."

"I know. People are very scared of the possibility of civil war, and I understand that, I really do." Alex sighed. "But there has to be a better way."

"I completely agree, and I'm incredibly proud of you for starting a national conversation about it."

Alex gazed at him from luminous eyes, and Josiah realised how much it meant to him.

"That's all that matters," he said softly. "That's all I wanted, to make you proud. After all you've done for me, I had to make it count."

"And you did. Although, to my mind, the best bits in the book were the drawings," Josiah said with a grin. Alex let out a whoop of delight and pressed a happy kiss to his cheek.

"Thank you." He beamed, the praise of his art meaning more to him than anything else.

"So, how's Gina?" Josiah asked. Alex had been seeing Gina for a few months now, his first serious relationship since being freed. Josiah had met her and liked her, although it had been strange seeing Alex with a girlfriend.

"We split up." Alex made a face. "She couldn't handle all the hoopla the book created. She said I was very nice, but..." He trailed off with a wave of his hand.

"I'm sorry."

"Don't be. She did the right thing. We really liked each other, but it never moved into love for either of us." Alex leaned forward and stole a bite of Josiah's pain au chocolat.

"Hey!" Josiah pulled it away from him. "Get your own."

"I should. I'm starving today. I think maybe I forgot to eat yesterday."

Josiah caught the barista's eye and called him over. "Another pain au chocolat, please," he ordered.

"Is he your IS?" the barista asked Alex, ignoring Josiah's polite request. "Only, he's been here for nearly an hour and I'm sure he must have work to do. If he's not your IS, I'll report him to his houder."

"Yes, he *is* my IS, as a matter of fact, and his work is buying me pastries and then sitting and eating them with me," Alex said imperiously.

The man strode away, muttering to himself.

"Fucker," Alex growled. "Sorry, Joe." He put a hand on Josiah's arm. "I hate that you get treated like that. You'd think he'd recognise you. I mean, you *are* still the indiehunter."

"It's been a while since I last hit the news. People forget." Josiah shrugged.

"He didn't recognise me, either. Maybe he's new to the country. He's certainly new to here, or he'd definitely recognise us as we're regulars. I feel quite offended." Alex grinned.

"How's therapy going?" Josiah asked, changing the subject.

"Well, I hate it, obviously, but I'm trying to be less boy interrupted and more man on a mission." He sighed. "I can't expect others to look at me and not see that seventeen-year-old boy sitting on the road with his mum's body making that terrible decision if that's how I always feel inside. So, I've been working hard on bringing something else to the table. Finding out who Alex Lytton is when he's not being that boy, or George Tyler's traumatised punchbag."

"I'm pretty sure *I* know who he is, but I'm delighted you're finding out." Josiah smiled at him.

"C – sorry, old habit – Dr Adams is good for me. I know you thought I should go to the therapist Sofie found, but she looked at me with those sad, understanding eyes, and I couldn't bear it. I needed someone who'd be harder on me. Someone who'd treat me more like…"

"An IS?"

"Yeah." Alex made a face. "I guess so. You've obviously noticed how differently people treat you now. When I was an IS, nobody cared about my feelings. Now I'm free, people are falling over themselves to care. And it's the opposite for you." He turned to glare at the barista again.

"I was concerned about you revisiting your Belvedere therapist, but it seems to be working out for you."

"He knows me, and he doesn't ask me to rehash all my old trauma. Between the trial and the book, I'm done with that. I know what happened to me, and I know I can't change any of it. All I can do is find a way of moving forward."

"Which you're doing superbly."

"Yeah, well, as he pointed out, if I want people to stop looking at me and seeing only my damage, then I have to show them something else. He's very good at finding ways to help me focus on who I want to be, and not who I was."

Josiah loved hearing him talk like this, with such energy, determination, and enthusiasm. He'd told him to move on, and he'd meant it. If that meant that he no longer wanted Josiah in his life one day, then so be it. That was a risk you took when you set someone free.

"Now, that's enough about me. What about you?" Alex asked, leaning back in his chair and gazing at him intently. "Is there anyone in your life, Joe?"

"As a matter of fact, there is."

Alex's face fell. His mask was long since gone, and besides, Josiah spoke fluent Alex. He knew Alex still held a torch for him, and his own feelings remained unchanged.

Alex took a long sip of his tea, and when he'd finished, he'd managed to compose himself.

"So, what's he like?" he asked, and Josiah could tell he was trying very hard to sound supportive.

"Gorgeous. Dark, with big brown eyes."

"Sounds like a right shit," Alex commented, grinning. "Who is he?"

"She," Josiah corrected.

"What?" Alex did a double take.

"She's about so high..." Josiah held his hand at around knee height. "Permanently wet nose. Goes by the name of Penny."

"Oh, you bastard!" Alex slapped his arm, and Josiah laughed.

"She's a rescue," Josiah added.

"Of course she is. We all know you can't resist your waifs and strays. Does Esther know?"

"Of course. She's fine with it." In fact, when he'd asked her, she'd fixed him with a glare and reminded him that he'd promised not to bother her with "stupid indie shit" when Inquisitus bought his contract.

"Where is she? Can I meet her?" Alex asked eagerly.

"She's back at the flat. This place won't let dogs in."

"We must find a new café, then," Alex announced, jumping up.

"And not just because of Penny." He shot another dark glare at the barista, then grabbed Josiah's arm. "Come on! I want to meet her."

He practically dragged Josiah out of the café and a few blocks across Ghost Eye to the tiny apartment next to the office where he lived. Alex had been here many times and had never once left without stuffing a handful of cash cards down the side of the sofa or in the cutlery drawer for Josiah to discover later. He'd tried to give them back, but Alex simply hid them all over again, so it was an exercise in futility. They were never huge sums, because Alex knew he'd never accept that, but they were enough to make his life a little more comfortable.

Penny was a black Labrador mix, like Hattie, but unlike Hattie, she hadn't been raised by adoring people, so she was a little nervous with strangers. Alex sat very still by the bathroom door until she warmed up and then spent the next two hours making her love him. It was never hard to love Alex, and Penny seemed to find it as easy as he did. Soon, she was lying in his lap in a state of pure bliss, having her ears stroked.

"How's the course going?" Josiah asked. Alex was doing a degree in art and design.

"Fine. Great, actually. That's why I was late. I'm working on something."

His face came alive when he talked about his art, and Josiah drank it in. *This* was what he'd wanted for him. He knew Alex had resolved to make something of his life when he'd left the garage that day. He was trying to honour that resolution so that Josiah's sacrifice would be worthwhile.

He hoped Alex wasn't putting too much pressure on himself, but he trusted Noah to ensure he ate and slept and didn't push himself too hard. He spoke to Noah often and was delighted by how much he'd stepped up. In fact, it was clear that Noah positively relished being able to be a father to his son again and was doing everything in his power to support and nurture him. It wouldn't last forever. Alex was already making noises about wanting to find his own place and move out, but for now, they were both enjoying each other.

"How about you? How's work?" Alex asked.

"It's good. I've nearly finished working my way through your list."

Jake Harper was behind bars, serving several years for his assault on Alex. Josiah had been grimly satisfied to watch that arrogant piece of shit get his comeuppance. Tyler's major-domo, Drummond, was also in jail.

In Martin Bagshaw's case, the judge had taken the view that a non-custodial sentence was more appropriate, so he was currently serving ten years as an indentured servant. This was a punishment Josiah found ironically fitting.

A few others had court cases pending, but Josiah expected similar outcomes for them, too.

"I bet you're looking forward to getting back to dead bodies after all this," Alex teased.

"I do like a good homicide," Josiah admitted.

Alex left soon after that, and Josiah sat in his tiny apartment with Penny curled up on the sofa next to him, feeling perfectly content.

"It's not working out too badly, Dad," he said. "I'm one of the lucky ones, of course, but it's not as bad as you thought it would be. I'm doing okay."

The next day he received a call, completely out of the blue, that was a blast from the past. A couple of days later, he drove out to Coldharbour Prison, which was situated on a floating city. Like most prefab floating cities, it was squat and ugly, but Josiah didn't have much sympathy for the inhabitants. Only violent offenders lived here – killers, rapists, thugs, and the like. The prison took up the entire city, so nobody else had to live with them.

He was taken through various gates, each one clanging shut behind him, and finally ended up in a metal box of a room. There, sitting behind a table, wearing a prison-issue grey uniform, was his old nemesis.

"Hello, George," he said, taking a seat.

Tyler looked leaner than ever, without a scrap of spare flesh on his bones, but he still had that same sense of energy and drive, despite his confinement.

"Josiah... seeing as we're now clearly on first-name terms." Tyler inclined his head.

"I bet you never thought you'd end up living in one of these ugly metal cities you created," Josiah said, taking a seat opposite him. "I was surprised to receive the call from your lawyers. It's been a while. Why now?"

"I spent some time exploring my options. I wanted to be certain that an appeal would fail."

"It would. Anyone could tell you that."

"I'm not a man who gives up easily."

"Oh, I know that." Josiah chuckled.

There was silence for a moment, then Tyler sighed. "How is he?" he asked.

"He's doing well, George. Making something of his life, despite everything you did to him."

Tyler nodded, his eyes veiled. "I did love him, you know. I'm sure you'll find that hard to believe, but I did. I didn't want to." His hands clenched into fists. "I wanted to hate him, and I hated that I wanted him."

"It was fucked up, George," Josiah told him firmly.

"Yes, but it was real." Tyler ran a hand over his bald head. It was still tanned, even despite his time in prison. "He had feelings for me, too. I know he did."

"He was your prisoner, and you abused him. He was trying to stay alive."

"No. You weren't there." Tyler shook his head. "We got each other, Josiah. In some ways we're alike, he and I. Both single-minded, both strong and smart."

"Yet in other ways quite different," Josiah said curtly. "He's loyal and loving, often thoughtful and kind."

"Well, I'm glad he's doing okay." Tyler shrugged. "Did you bring what I asked for?"

"I did." Josiah took a folder out of his bag and slid it across the table. Tyler wasn't allowed electronics in jail, so he'd brought a printed copy.

Tyler opened the folder and read slowly and intently for a long time. Finally, he looked up. "Are you sure?" he asked. "Are you absolutely sure?"

"Absolutely. One hundred per cent," Josiah said firmly. "Having read the documents, can there really be any doubt?"

"No." Tyler breathed the word as if it was his last. "No. I see that now. I was in denial for a long time because I didn't want to believe it, but now I do. Alex wasn't driving the duck at the time of the accident. Charles was."

"There's no way that either of the people in the front of that duck climbed out of it with only a few cuts, which is all Alex sustained. It's not possible. Charles admits he asked Alex to lie for him, and he's been honest about why."

"Has he been punished for it?"

"Don't turn your wrath on Charles," Josiah snapped. "Both he and Isobel were equally complicit in what happened, so she's as much to blame as he is. Besides, they both paid a high price for their deceit. It's just a shame they dragged Alex into it."

"Were there repercussions for Alex because he lied?"

"No. Charles received a suspended sentence, but they decided not to take any action against Alex. Wisely, I think, given the public mood around the trial and his subsequent book. Talking of which." Josiah reached into his bag again. "I wasn't sure if you'd read it, so here. I should warn you, you don't come out of it very well – and that's an understatement."

He took out the copy he'd brought with him. The front cover showed a picture of Alex as a seventeen-year-old boy, looking impossibly young and innocent. The title *Disgrace* was printed at the top.

The double meaning of the title hit home. Alex might have experienced a fall from grace, but the system that brutalised him wasn't fit for purpose, either.

The book had been scrupulously fair, but it hadn't shied away from making the point that an entire country had enjoyed hating on him, as if he wasn't a real person but the scapegoat upon whom they needed to visit years of anger, fear, and resentment.

His family's wealth and privilege as well as his own perceived sense of entitlement, awkward personality, and good looks had all combined to make him an easy target. He'd acknowledged his many mistakes in typical Alex fashion, but he was just as frank in analysing the mistakes of the society that had vilified him.

"Fair enough." Tyler glanced at the book, a resigned look on his face. "I hope he's making some money out of it."

"He is. Enough to keep him going for a bit, anyway, and to fund the degree he's taking in art and design."

"Good for him. He always was an excellent designer." Tyler leaned back in his chair. "You bought him, didn't you?" he asked suddenly. "You sold yourself to buy him."

Josiah wondered how he'd guessed. It wasn't common knowledge, and he was doing his best to hide his ID tag, even though he was supposed to keep it on display.

"Yes," he admitted curtly.

"If you love someone, set them free?" Tyler raised an eyebrow.

"Something like that." Josiah shrugged.

"I did something similar."

"No, you didn't. You gave him to Dacre and kept tabs on him. That wasn't setting him free."

"I couldn't, not with what he knew, but I did the next-best thing. I had to." Tyler had a pained expression on his face. "It almost destroyed me, but I had to give him away. I was terrified I'd end up killing him if I didn't. That's what he wanted. He kept trying to goad me into it, and I was so afraid I'd do it. It was bad enough having Solange on my conscience, but I couldn't kill Alex. I loved him."

"If you'd really loved him, you'd have freed him and taken the consequences."

"Like you did? Not all of us are as noble as the great Josiah Raine. I hope it was worth it. You're not with him, are you?" As usual, Tyler was able to home in on any perceived weaknesses with laser-sharp precision.

"No."

"All that sacrifice, and for what? He ran out on you the minute he was freed, didn't he?"

"No. I finished it with him, as a matter of fact, and long before he was freed, because I could see he was in no position to be in a relationship with anyone. Not me, or anyone else. He needed the time and space to heal and work out who he really is and what he wants. I didn't tell him I'd sold myself to pay for his freedom. I didn't want him to know."

"But he figured it out, didn't he? He's too smart not to."

"Yes, he figured it out. He's his own man now, and he's turned his life around. It's not been easy for him, after what you did to him, but I'm proud of how far he's come."

Tyler nodded, his eyes dark with an emotion Josiah couldn't read. Was he pleased, proud, even? He had no right to be.

"I have something for you, too." Tyler had a folder of his own, which he pushed across the table.

"What's this?" Josiah opened it, frowning.

"Quid pro quo. You brought me the file on the accident, so I thought you should have something in return. It's the dossier I made on you. I was going to reveal all at the trial, but events rather ran away with us back then, didn't they? I thought I'd hold on to it, in case I ever needed it, but..." He shrugged. "There's no point using it as blackmail, because you won't be blackmailed, and I have no other use for it. I could use it to destroy you anyway, but it seems you've done a good job of that yourself." He gestured at Josiah's shirt, where his hated ID tag was barely visible beneath his collar.

"Seems a little ironic, doesn't it – that the indiehunter loves indies so much that he kept rescuing them, then sold himself to save one." Tyler snorted. "You can keep it. There are no copies. I ordered that all the digital material be destroyed."

Josiah gave him a grudging nod of thanks and slipped the dossier into his bag.

"I didn't know that Isobel was using the money to buy that drug for Charles," Tyler said suddenly. "I just thought that Noah was keeping her short and she wanted it for herself. I didn't mind. I liked spoiling her. I didn't know she was using it that way."

"I believe you," Josiah said quietly.

"Don't get me wrong." Tyler gave him a laser-like stare. "I'm proud of her for hustling to get Charles to the top. That's my Izzy." He grinned.

"Well, lying and cheating to get what you want *is* your style," Josiah grunted.

Tyler laughed. "You're a Quarterlands boy, you should understand. The system is stacked against us. You don't win by playing by their rules." He looked contemptuous. "I'm not going to apologise for having drive and ambition."

"No, that's not what you should apologise for," Josiah said pointedly.

"I'm not going to apologise for any of it." Tyler shrugged, obviously unrepentant. "Sure, I made some mistakes along the way, but I've lived my life gloriously on my own terms. Not many people can say that." His mood changed and he looked suddenly downcast. "Sometimes..." He gazed up at the ceiling, his eyes glittering. "I wonder if she ever really loved me, or was she just using me?"

"We'll never know. For what it's worth, I think she was far better suited to you than to Noah."

"I know that." Tyler gave a bitter little smile. "I wonder if she ever would have left him to live with me, like she promised. I used to be so sure, but I was wrong about Alex, so maybe I'm wrong about that, too."

"She told Alex she was going to spend more time with him. So, maybe she was playing you all along," Josiah said more brutally than he'd intended. "Or maybe she didn't know what she was going to do. She was just winging it, muddling through, like we all do."

"She could have brought Alex with her. I told her that."

"Well, we'll never know." Josiah sat there, gazing at him. "Do you regret any of it, George?" he asked, suddenly needing to know.

"Only that I was wrong about the accident. I refused to believe it for a long time. I turned it around and around in my head. I said to myself that it was a ploy, a way of Alex gaining public sympathy, but it preyed on my mind. Why would you announce it in a courtroom, under oath? Would Charles really go along with it if it was a lie? Would he hand back his medal if it was a lie? I've *wrestled* with it, Josiah. I've had plenty of time to think about little else," he said in a tone of wretched sincerity. "But I had to be absolutely sure. That's why I asked you here."

"Well, that's one thing you *can* be sure of. Alex wasn't driving the duck that day, and you spent years torturing an innocent man." Josiah stood up. "Enjoy the book, George – if you're brave enough to read it."

"Oh, I will. He lived it, so the least I can do is read it," Tyler said with a shrug.

Josiah had a modicum of respect for him for that.

They said goodbye, and then Josiah was happy to walk out of there and leave George Tyler behind in the past, where he belonged.

A week later he was sitting at his desk in the SID when Reed came running into the office from the rec room.

"Have you seen it?" He pinged up a news channel on his holopad and a reporter appeared in mid-air, speaking in sombre tones.

"I'm standing outside Coldharbour Floating Prison, where it has just been announced that George Tyler has committed suicide in his cell," she said. "Tyler is, of course, notorious not only for being one of the most successful businessmen this country has ever produced but also for his subsequent downfall, when he was found guilty of killing one of his own indentured servants."

"What the...?" Josiah put in a holocall to Alex. "Are you watching the news?"

"No, I'm painting. I'll turn it on." There was a long silence as he stared at his screen in disbelief.

"You okay?" Josiah asked.

"Yes. No. Yes." Alex gave a shaky laugh. "Oh, shit. What the hell has he done?"

Josiah jumped into his duck and drove straight to The Orchard. Alex opened the door, looking pale and shocked. They spent the next few hours watching the news together, trying to make sense of it.

"I can't believe he did that," Alex said, his hands shaking as he reached for the cup of tea Josiah had made for him.

"I suppose I'm not surprised," Josiah said. "He was a control freak, which must have made life in prison even harder on him than on most people. Men like him often don't adapt well to being confined. I know he was on suicide watch for the first few months of his sentence. It was stood down when he showed no signs of taking his own life."

"Well, he always was a sneaky bastard. He probably planned it that way. In fact, knowing him, he's been planning it for months." Alex screwed up his face, looking as if he was fighting back tears. "I don't know why I'm upset. I hated him."

"He was a massive part of your life – and he had a huge effect *on* that life. Of course you're having a reaction." Josiah put his arms around him and held him while he gave in to the conflicting emotions coursing through his body. His chest heaving, he alternately sobbed and laughed, as if demented.

"I think it's because it means it's over. Finally, irrevocably, over," Alex said at last, his face still buried in Josiah's shoulder. "He's not out there somewhere, watching me and plotting against me. He's gone." He looked at Josiah in disbelief. "He really has gone, hasn't he?"

"Yes, Alex. He's definitely gone," Josiah reassured him. "You're finally free."

It turned out that Josiah had been the last person Tyler had spoken to, apart from the prison guards. Had he read Alex's book and been unable to live with what he'd done? Josiah wondered. Yet he doubted it had been that simple. Tyler had clearly been struggling with many different issues when Josiah had seen him, not least his relationship with Isobel and whether it had meant more to him than it had to her. Josiah suspected it wasn't the book that had sealed Tyler's fate but the fact he'd been wrong about the accident and tortured an innocent man. Maybe Tyler had thought it was only right that he turn his fiery vengeance on himself for screwing up so spectacularly.

Josiah didn't pretend to understand the man. He was only concerned about Alex, who, after a shaky few weeks when the whole thing was rehashed ad infinitum on the news, recovered enough to continue with his studies. Josiah was proud of him.

Life soon returned to normal, and he saw little of Alex, who was busy preparing for an exam. Then Josiah caught a new homicide case and was rushed off his feet, and eventually several months passed, during which they both weathered the storm caused by Tyler's suicide.

After solving the case, Josiah took a much-needed day off on Esther's insistence.

"You've been underfoot too much lately. Take a break," she'd ordered.

Penny was pleased about this as he took her out for a nice long walk down by the edge of the lost zone, and she barked for some time at the silvery outline of the old London Eye as it shimmered beneath the water.

He'd just settled in back at his flat for a cup of tea and some chocolates that Mel had gifted him when his holopad buzzed.

"Joe, you're needed back in the office," Esther said.

"You said I was getting underfoot," he protested.

"That was this morning. Now I need you."

"Is it a case?"

"No. Something else."

"Can I bring Penny?"

"Yes, of course. We all love seeing her."

That was certainly true. The minute they entered the SID, Penny had admirers lining up to fuss over her. She wasn't at all anxious now, after lots of work from Josiah, and she knew the SID well as he often took her into work with him. A big, soft dog bed had even miraculously appeared next to his desk one day; he couldn't say for sure who'd put it there, but he knew Esther had a soft spot for her. Everyone assumed that Esther had bought her sparkly pink collar, too. Well, who could imagine big, badass Josiah Raine buying such an item for his dog? He had no intention of letting them in on that particular secret.

Penny ran over to Esther's wheelchair the minute they entered her office and snuffled around in her pocket for treats. Esther made the obligatory fuss of her and then turned to Josiah. She looked different somehow, her face glowing excitedly.

"Joe, I must give you this." She pinged him a holodoc, and he gazed at it, confused.

"It's a copy of my contract," he said blankly.

"Look at the bottom. It's been paid out in full."

"What? I don't understand." He peered at it, sure there was some mistake, but she was right. His contract had been stamped as paid up and discharged by the IS agency. "I've got years to serve yet," he protested.

"Well, the paperwork says otherwise. Your contract was redeemed by the IS agency this morning. You're a free man, Joe."

"How?" He stared at her. "Did you do this, Esther? But you don't have the money." Esther was a fantastic director of Inquisitus, but she had to report to her shareholders. There was no way she earned enough to buy out his contract.

"Nothing to do with me." She held her hands up in the air, and Penny sniffed at them hopefully.

"Then who...?" At that moment there was a commotion in the SID outside, and Josiah ran out to find Sofie standing there. She was gazing at a copy of her own contract, her hand over her mouth, her eyes sparkling.

"Someone has bought my contract," she exclaimed, looking up at him. "Not just mine, Sem's, too. We've both been released and our contracts paid out."

"Me too!"

She ran into his arms, both laughing and crying at the same time.

"Not to gatecrash the party, but I just returned from the rec room and found this envelope had appeared mysteriously on my desk," Reed said, holding up a plain white envelope with his name written on it. "I do hope I haven't been freed, because I had no idea I *was* an IS." He grinned as he slid his finger under the flap of the envelope and drew out a biokey.

"What's this for?" he asked, frowning.

"Looks like a duck biokey. Maybe check out the parking area?" Esther suggested, coming up behind them.

"Esther? What do you know that we don't? Has Inquisitus had a windfall or something?" Josiah asked suspiciously.

She just smiled at him infuriatingly and began gliding towards the exit.

They all followed her out, then stopped in surprise. There, parked right outside the front door, was a beautiful duck. Not just *any* duck, but a state-of-the-art, gleaming, bright red Destiny duck.

"For me? But why?" Reed asked, opening the door with the biokey. Inside was a note.

For Cameron Reed, with thanks, to replace the one that was wrecked.

Josiah turned to Esther. "What the hell is going on?"

"You're my top investigator.' She smirked. 'You figure it out."

"Alex..." he said, the penny starting to drop.

She just gave him another maddening smile and opened the duck door.

"Shall we all get in? I believe someone is expecting us."

It only took them a few minutes to drive across Ghost Eye, with Esther directing the route. Reed pulled up outside a tall tower that Josiah knew all too well. He jumped out of the duck and jogged inside, where a smiling doorman escorted him to the elevator and up to the top floor, as if he'd been expecting him.

The elevator door opened, and Josiah found himself in Tyler's old penthouse suite... only this time it was filled with brightly coloured balloons and chattering people. There was a bustling, joyful air about the place, very different to when Tyler had lived here, and there, waiting to greet him, was Alex.

Josiah being Josiah, he couldn't help but notice that Alex was wearing a beautifully cut navy-blue suit, with a purple shirt, silver tie, and matching pocket square. He looked exquisite. Next to him, clad in his off-duty jeans with a polo shirt and sports jacket, Josiah felt underdressed for possibly the first time in his life.

"Alex... what the hell is going on?" he demanded.

"Did you check your bank balance?" Alex grinned. "It's all there. Every penny you paid for me, minus the sum I paid for you. You're a rich man, Joe."

"Tyler left you all his money," Josiah said slowly, finally figuring it out.

"Yup." Alex took hold of his arm and led him to a huge window with beautiful views over the city. "And he died very much on the up, what with the success of the Destiny duck and his floating city scheme. I couldn't believe it when I saw how much he was worth."

"Why all the secrecy?" Josiah demanded. "How long have you known? Why didn't you tell me?"

"Oh, you're a fine one to talk. You didn't tell me you'd bought me, so I thought I'd repay the surprise." Alex laughed. "I found out soon after he died. His lawyers were in touch within a couple of weeks. I made plans to buy up your contract – and a few others – straight away. I held some clandestine meetings with Esther, who was sworn to secrecy."

"Oh, she's very good at keeping secrets." Josiah shook his head ruefully. "I had no idea."

"Tyler had been planning to commit suicide for months, apparently," Alex explained. "His lawyer said he couldn't stand being in prison. Once he knew there was no point in appealing his sentence, he decided to take his own life. The only question in his mind was where to leave his empire. That's where you came in."

"That's why he wanted me to show him the file about the accident?"

"Yes. He had to be absolutely sure I wasn't the one driving. Once he was, that was it. He was all set. He waited a week before doing it for only one reason."

"To read your book," Josiah said quietly. "I left him a copy."

"That's right. He read it and then he was done. Apparently, he was in a great mood the day before he took his own life. He was happy to be checking out."

"I'm glad he'd already decided to do it before I went to visit him. I thought maybe I'd influenced him into it."

"No. He was always going to commit suicide. He just wanted to be sure about who should have his empire."

"He made the right choice. The only real choice."

"He didn't just leave me his money; he left me everything he owned. All the houses, all the businesses… I don't want any of them, of course. I'm only keeping the two things that are rightfully mine."

"The Destiny duck range and Lytton AV?" Josiah guessed.

"You know me too well. I'll sell the rest." Alex shrugged. "I don't want to become like Tyler. I don't even want to become like my father. I just want to design things and be happy."

"You deserve it. Every single penny. Hell, you earned it. Nobody deserves it more than you, after all you went through at his hands."

Alex flushed and looked out over the submerged London Eye that had given the city its name.

"I'm going to use most of the money to set up a foundation to campaign for an end to the IS system. I was hoping…" He looked a little anxious. "I was hoping you'd help me?"

"That's a fantastic idea," Josiah exclaimed, drawing him into a hug. "Of course I'll bloody well help you. I'm not leaving Inquisitus, though," he added, pulling back.

"I'd never ask you to. I thought this could be more of a spare-time thing. I mean, you *do* have a bit more of that since you closed down" – Alex lowered his voice – "the Kathleen Line. I was hoping this would fill that gap."

"I'd be honoured."

"We'll do it, Joe," Alex said in an excited voice. "It might take some time, and maybe all of Tyler's money, but we'll do it. We'll bring the system down."

"The two of us working together? I wouldn't bet against it." Josiah grinned.

At that moment, the elevator door opened, and Reed, Esther, Sofie, and Mel appeared, accompanied by Penny. Penny saw Alex and rushed towards him. She adored him almost as much as she did Josiah, and he didn't think it was only because of all the treats he slipped her when he thought Josiah wasn't looking.

"Who are all these people?" Josiah asked, looking around the crowded room. Then he realised. "Is that Barney Bates over there?" He saw the portly lorry driver, talking to… "Is that Ted?"

"Yeah. I thought I'd throw a massive party to say thank you to everyone before I get rid of this place." Alex beamed.

"Who's that with Barney?" Josiah gestured to a round-faced, brown-haired young man.

"That's his son, Rob. I bought his contract and set him free. Sem's here, too." Alex grabbed his arm. "Come on, let's go and talk to them."

At that moment there was a loud squeal, and Josiah caught a flash of brown hair before a familiar person leapt into his arms.

"Joe! There you are. Alex said you'd be here soon."

"Liz? *Liz?*" He gazed at her in shock. "How are you here?"

"Alex bought my contract, so technically I'm free to return." She grinned at him. "Isn't it amazing, after all this time?"

"Are Carl and the kids here?"

"Yes. Alex has put us up in a hotel. I left them to go sightseeing as they're all being far too excitable, but we're staying for a few weeks, if you'll be around? Little Peter is desperate to meet you. He's the only one of our kids who hasn't, you know, and the others tease him about it."

"I can't wait." He swung her up into his arms, kissing her. "I think this might be the best day of my life," he whispered in her ear.

"Then here's to many more." She grabbed a glass of champagne and raised it in the air.

The next few hours passed in a haze. Waiters handed out canapes and drinks while Josiah did the rounds talking to all the people Alex had met and felt he owed something to on his journey. Jabir was there, with his wife, Maura, and their throng of well-behaved children.

"He gifted me the hacienda," Jabir told Josiah, clearly still reeling. "He told me today. Of course, I said that I couldn't possibly accept, that it was too much, but he insisted."

"You lost your job because of me, and very probably saved my life by bringing those nanodrives over. That evidence changed the course of the trial, so it was the least I could do," Alex demurred. "Besides... I can never go back there." A shadow passed over his face.

Luckily, at that moment, Marlon Baxter made a huge entrance, towing his tall, handsome husband along behind him.

It was overwhelming, so Josiah retreated to a quiet corner and observed the party from a distance. Mick Reynolds was standing in the opposite corner, slowly getting drunk. Sem and Sofie were next to him, chatting excitedly, making plans for the future. Alex had already asked Sem if he'd like to work for his new foundation, while Sofie was hoping

Esther would put her on a regular contract as she loved working at Inquisitus. Robbie Bates was working with his father in the haulage industry; they were spending hours trucking across the country together, catching up on years apart and trying to mend some fences.

Elsie was chatting earnestly to Noah and Ted's wife, Trudy, a bizarre trio that Josiah would never have expected to have anything in common, while Charles was busy trying to do the impossible and charm Big Jen. Mona Byrne was feeding Penny far too many canapes from her plate while laughing with Mel. It was strange to see Byrne laughing so heartily, but when she wasn't being a ferocious attack dog in the courtroom, she was, apparently, the life and soul of the party.

By the fireplace was a bespectacled man who he recognised from Gideon's memorial service, talking to a woman with a very tight ponytail and a tiny, shy-looking woman, and over by the elevator was the flamboyant Lorenzo, flirting outrageously with Andrew... and too many others to count. And there, at the centre of everything, was a happy, smiling Alex.

"Enjoying yourself?" Alex asked, coming over.

"I'm just trying to piece together who all these people are and their place in your story."

"Always the investigator."

"You know me. I think I've figured most of them out, except them." Josiah nodded at an odd trio of men, looking reticent and out of place – a portly, pompous-looking chap, a tall, earnest fellow, and a young redhead.

Alex smiled. "Well, I knew them as Three, Four, and Five, but it turns out they have names. You're looking at Stanley, Rashid, and Duncan."

"Your companions at Belvedere?"

"Yup. I asked Madeleine Selcourt for their details, tracked them down, bought their contracts, and released them from their servitude, with a lump sum to help them on their way. They were good friends to me when I needed it most."

"They must have been very surprised."

"They were, but it's been great. I've had them all to stay at The Orchard, and we reminisced about the good old bad old days. And by the fireplace are the Belvedere contingent. That's Dr Adams, who I knew as C, and who, of course, is now my therapist."

"Ah. He gave the eulogy at Gideon's fake memorial service."

"That's right, although he didn't know it was fake of course. He really believed Gideon was dead. Next to him is Serena, who was my personal trainer, and poor little Dorothy, the waitress, who still looks as frightened as she did back at Belvedere, although I've done my best to ease her circumstances, too."

"You *have* been busy, tracking all these people down."

"It was my absolute pleasure." Alex beamed. "It's been wonderful seeing them all again and being able to help them."

"You're a loyal friend, Alex. That's never changed," Josiah said softly.

Alex tugged on his sleeve. "Come with me. I want to show you something." He led Josiah to the elevator and took him down to a suite a few storeys below.

"This is where I lived when I was Tyler's IS," he said, drawing Josiah out into a hallway.

"How does it feel to be back? Are you okay with it?" Josiah studied him carefully.

"Yes. I've been here a few times now, once with Dr Adams who helped me slay some demons, and I'm doing okay. Come here, I want to show you this." Alex took him into a spacious living room. "I used to sit in here and look out of this window. Can you see it? Look." Josiah saw that he was pointing to the Inquisitus building, far off in the distance. "It kept me going," he said. "Thinking of you, working at your desk just a short walk away. It might as well have been on the moon as I couldn't reach you, but it gave me strength."

"I didn't know. I wish I had."

"Shh. It's fine. I just wanted to show you. Come on." Alex took his hand again and led him down the hallway to another room. "This was Solange's room. After she died, George made me sleep in here. I think it was supposed to freak me out, but it just made me feel closer to her."

They stepped into a room with views over the water. That was when Josiah realised that Alex was still holding his hand.

"Joe, I wanted to ask you something," Alex said softly. He took a deep breath, as if marshalling all his courage. "I still love you," he admitted. Josiah opened his mouth to speak, but Alex pressed a finger over his lips.

"Let me finish. I need to say it, and I need you to hear it. I've loved you for a very long time, but I didn't think I deserved you, and I was terrified of ruining your life more than I had already. After Neil kidnapped me, I was at such a low ebb that I just couldn't cope with my feelings any more. I shut down. You did the right thing to end it with me back then. I wasn't in a fit state to be in any kind of relationship. But I've been seeing Dr Adams for a while now, and I've done a lot of work on myself, and I've almost... *almost* reached the point where I think I'm good enough for you." He grinned.

"Don't be an idiot. Of course you're good enough. You always have been."

"Not really. I know I come with a ton of baggage, and I know I'm not Peter," Alex continued. "But we had a lot of fun together, you and me, and the sex was always ludicrously hot."

Josiah laughed at that.

"You understand me, Joe, and you can cope with me and all my moods. So, I guess what I'm trying to say is..." He took a little box out of his pocket and opened it. "Will you marry me? Now you're free, and I'm free. Will you?"

"Whoa!" Josiah took a step back, reeling. "I was not expecting that."

"You don't need to answer right now. Just think about it? I've tried dating other people and it didn't work, and you still refuse to date anyone else, which gave me a little hope. I talked it through with Dr Adams, at some length." Alex sighed. "But the truth is, it didn't work out for me with anyone else because I'm still in love with you. I've always been in love with you. In fact, you're the only person I've ever been in love with. So... will you marry me, Josiah Raine?"

Josiah looked at the ring Alex was holding up. It was a plain gold band, simple, shining, and elegantly cut. It was perfect, of course, because Alex not only had great taste, but he knew him inside out, and knew what would appeal to him.

"I'm used to doing the proposing," he said, taking a moment to compose himself.

"Well, like I said, I'm not Peter. It'll be a bit different with me," Alex warned. "If you'll have me? You still haven't said?" He looked anxious. "I mean, I know I'm jumping the gun. That we should probably, I don't know, date first or something, but... I've wasted so much time already, and I don't want to waste any more. I also want you to know I'm serious about this. That it's not a mood or a whim. We don't have to get married any time soon. I just want to know we'll be together one day. If I know there's hope, then..."

"Shut up." Josiah pulled him close and kissed him. Alex sighed and melted into him. It had been a long time since they'd last kissed like this, and Josiah felt light-headed, giddy with joy, as if he'd explode. He didn't have any doubts. He loved Alex every bit as much as he knew he was loved in return.

"Yes," he said, when he eventually released Alex. "Yes, yes, yes!"

Alex gave a laugh of relief, then took the ring out of the box and slipped it on his finger.

"Would you like my father's ring?" Josiah asked. "It's belonged to the two men I loved most in my life before I met you, but if you'd prefer something else, it's no problem. You might like a fresh start with something new."

"No, I'd prefer that one. It has so much more meaning," Alex replied with a shy smile.

"Then it's yours. I'll dig it out for you later. In the meantime..." He raised Alex's hand to his lips and kissed his finger.

"Thank God." Alex leaned into him. "I was terrified you'd say no."

"I love you, Alex. I never stopped loving you." Josiah caressed his face. "I just needed to be free to commit to you. I also needed you to feel free to choose me, not because you felt beholden to me, or grateful, or even because you were too scared to go looking for anyone else. I wanted you to want me for me."

"Oh, I do. I really do."

"One thing," Josiah said, feeling a sudden spark of uncertainty. "I can't share you, Alex. It's not who I am. When I'm in, I'm all in, and I expect the same from you. If that's a deal breaker, then—"

"It isn't," Alex interrupted firmly. "I'm done with living that kind of life; it never made me happy. I only want you. Nobody else."

"Good." Josiah felt a wave of relief. "As for dating – I think, in a way, we've been doing that for the past two years. Let's not waste a single second more, my love."

Alex's eyes were shining as Josiah leaned in and kissed him again, a long, deep, passionate kiss. Josiah wasn't sure when he'd last felt this happy. Not since Peter was alive, for sure. He loved Alexander Lytton with every atom of his being, and he knew how completely loved he he was in return.

They wrapped their arms around each other and stood gazing out of the window, unspeaking, for a long time. Finally, Josiah stirred.

"We should go back to your party. They'll be wondering where we are."

"Not yet." Alex held on to him tightly. "I've waited a very long time for this." He glanced up at Josiah. "And so have you."

"Yeah." Josiah chuckled. "It's been a long journey, but we got there in the end." He dropped another kiss on Alex's lips and hugged him close. "You know, I used to hate parties, but this one has been strangely good."

"Maybe you've changed." Alex grinned up at him.

Josiah nodded slowly. "You know, I think I have."

Outside, the sun was setting over Ghost Eye City, bathing the dark water of the lost zone in a soft orange glow.

"You do know I'm only marrying you for your money, right?" Josiah grinned, leaning back to look at Alex.

"Well, obviously." Alex let out a delighted bark of laughter. "And I'm only marrying you because I'm in love with Penny."

"I knew it!"

They laughed, and then they walked back to the party together, hand in hand.

The End

Get Your Exclusive Dark Water Bonus Novella!

I felt this was the perfect place to end the series, but my readers told me they wanted to spend more time with Josiah and Alex being happy. I completely understand—it's hard to say goodbye after going through so much with them.

So I've written **Safe Harbour**, a 21,000-word bonus novella giving a little glimpse into what their 'happily ever after' looks like and telling the story of their wedding (and, ahem, wedding *night*!). I wanted to truly reward you (and Alex and Josiah) with an abundance of happiness, lashings of spice, and just a smidgeon of angst.

Join my FREE Walter's World mailing list to unlock this exclusive bonus story, available only to subscribers. Plus, you'll get access to a treasure trove of subscriber-only content:

📚 **Exclusive Story Content**
- **Dark Water** bonus novella *Safe Harbour* • **Bonus scenes** from across my story universes
- **Exclusive snippets** from upcoming books
- **FREE gay BDSM pirate novella** *A Willing Lad*

🎵 **Multimedia Extras**
- **Curated Spotify playlists** for each book in the series
- **Ashton's complete song** from *Ghost Eye*
- **Alex's photo stash** from *The Lost Zone*
- **Rising Radio** - listen to episodes of *News-Spec*

🗺 **World-Building Deep Dives**
- **Flood map** showing London's lost zones
- ***The Daily Lowdown***- a fully designed news site with headlines from Elliot Dacre's murder
- **Character profiles** and extracts

🎁 **VIP Subscriber Benefits**
- **First access** to cover reveals
- **Behind-the-scenes insights**
- **Special offers and giveaways** for subscribers only
- **Regular surprises** and exclusive goodies

Your privacy matters: I'll never spam your inbox or share your data with anyone.

Sign Me Up to Walter's World!
www.xanthe-walter.com/walters-world

Join thousands of readers already exploring the hidden corners of my fictional worlds.

Thank you for reading!

If you enjoyed this book, I'd be incredibly grateful if you could help others discover it. I'm not well known, and as an independent author every review, social media post, and word-of-mouth recommendation makes a real difference in helping this series reach new readers.

Here's how you can help:
- Leave a quick review on Amazon (even a few words help!)
- Share your thoughts on social media
- Recommend it to a friend who loves MM romance.

Go here to leave a review: https://geni.us/TQ-TQBM Scroll down to 'Write a customer review'.

Your support means the world to me and helps me keep writing stories I love.

Read on for a special letter from Xanthe Walter about the writing of *The Quarterlands* **and the series as a whole.**

HELLO FROM XANTHE WALTER!

Thank you for plunging into *The Quarterlands*.

Want to know a secret? I'm a pantser (meaning I write by the seat-of-the-pants), not a plotter. I never write chapter plans, I barely even write notes – I keep everything in my head, so the story is always in a fluid state, right up until the end. This gives it room to breathe and develop. When I start, I always have a vague idea where I'm going, but the journey is everything and what I most enjoy about the writing process.

This means I had no idea, throughout the entire writing process, whether the amount of material I had for the Alex timeline matched the amount of material I had for the Josiah timeline. I could have reached the end of either timeline midway through book three while the other one still had an entire book to go, and then what would I have done? So you can imagine my amazement and relief when I found the two matched up perfectly and both ended at the same time. I thought I was going to have to do so much more finessing than I actually did.

When I wrote the part in *The Quarterlands* where Alex meets Josiah for the first time since the night Peter died, I felt this intense wave of catharsis. It was *immense*. I went out for a walk after writing it and floated along on a writing-induced high. It all felt so meaningful. FINALLY, we see that meeting from Alex's point of view, after fully understanding the journey he's been on to get there, none of which we knew when we saw that scene from Josiah's point of view all the way back in *Crocodile Tears*.

I hope that now you've finished reading *The Quarterlands*, you'll go back and re-read the whole series again, with a completely different perspective. I've put in lots of Easter Eggs for you to enjoy, little moments that reward the eagle-eyed reader. There are so many lines that hopefully went unnoticed on the first read but take on new significance on the second. Also, I'm sure you spotted my special tribute to my pink sparkly girl, Penny, but you might also like to know that my beloved mum was called Kathleen.

A note about my portrayal of police and legal procedure throughout the series. This isn't a procedural, and while I did my research, I also wanted to hit all the right dramatic notes, and as this is set in a dystopian future that did give me some leeway. I enjoyed creating a new system of policing, with the majority of it being outsourced to investigation agencies, and I hinted at changes elsewhere, too, such as to the legal system. Did that make the justice system less fair? Yes, but as established, this isn't a fair society.

When I was researching the drug part of the story, I read about the doping that went on in cycling as well as some other doping scandals. I considered making the drug fraud high-tech in my story, but I read a couple of quite farcical accounts about how various real life cheats conducted their frauds, hiding samples under raincoats and shinning down drainpipes to avoid WADA (I changed the name slightly on purpose for my book) officials etc. So I thought it made it more relateable, in the end, to come down to good old-fashioned human ingenuity and frailty rather than use some high-tech gizmo to explain it. I also liked how that tied back into Alex's psychology.

Which leads me onto... Alex! I was so worried people would hate him in *Crocodile Tears*, and frankly he does behave very badly at times and some people really didn't like him. But he was always something of a lost soul, destroyed by the accident that killed his mum, reeling from the secret he'd discovered about Charles, and just a kid really, trying to figure it all out. And then the full force of the media wrath came down on him, absolutely destroying him, and he spiralled into self-destruction. I hope you judge him less harshly now you understand his full story. He was always more sinned against than sinning, and he more than pays for the mistakes he makes. I believe his dedication to Solange's cause, and his loyalty to the people he loves make him worthy of Josiah by the end of *The Quarterlands*.

And as for Josiah... he makes mistakes, too. He can be rigid, unbending, and he breaks a promise he swore to keep, but he's a righteous man with so much love to give. He makes his huge sacrifice because he knows in his heart its the right thing – the only thing a man such as him *can* do because he couldn't live with himself if he didn't. And he's always been perhaps a little too happy to sacrifice himself for the men he loves - that's just the way he is.

Can I ask a favour? If you're loving this series, **please help spread the word.** Reviews, social media posts, and/or recommendations to friends—it all helps *Dark Water* find new readers.

If you want to discuss the many twists and turns of this book series, or just to chat with fellow readers, then join my friendly Facebook group, Xanthology.

For a free bonus novella detailing Alex and Josiah's wedding day (and, ahem, night!), exclusive content, and a FREE spicy pirate novella, please subscribe to Walter's World, my newsletter family. You can find it on my website at www.xanthe-walter.com.

You can find lots of *Dark Water* related content on my Facebook, Instagram and TikTok pages - just search for @xanthewalter.

Thank you again for being part of this amazing *Dark Water* journey with me, and, as always, happy reading!

Xanthe

www.xanthe-walter.com

WELCOME TO WALTER'S WORLD!

Become a Xanthe Walter VIP and join an exclusive community of readers who get the inside scoop.

Your FREE membership of my **newsletter mailing list** unlocks a complete multimedia story experience:

📚 **Exclusive Story Content**
• **Dark Water** bonus novella *Safe Harbour* (only read this after finishing the complete series!)
• **Bonus scenes** from across my story universes
• **Exclusive snippets** from upcoming books
• **FREE gay BDSM pirate novella** *A Willing Lad*

🎵 **Multimedia Extras**
• **Curated Spotify playlists** for each book in the series
• **Ashton's complete song** from *Ghost Eye*
• **Alex's photo stash** from *The Lost Zone*
• **Rising Radio** - listen to episodes of *News-Spec*

🗺 **World-Building Deep Dives**
• **Flood map** showing London's lost zones
• ***The Daily Lowdown***- a fully designed news site with headlines from Elliot Dacre's murder
• **Character profiles** and extracts

🎁 **VIP Subscriber Benefits**
• **First access** to cover reveals
• **Behind-the-scenes insights**
• **Special offers and giveaways** for subscribers only
• **Regular surprises** and exclusive goodies

Your privacy matters: I'll never spam your inbox or share your data with anyone.

Sign up to Walter's World and join thousands of readers already exploring the hidden corners of my fictional world. Sign up here - https://geni.us/ww-bm

ABOUT XANTHE WALTER

Xanthe Walter has been crafting MM romances for over thirty years, creating hundreds of tales about love, adventure, and angsty men falling for each other.

Xanthe specialises in genre-bending stories – vampire cops, paranormal pirates, BDSM romcoms... if she can mix up a few genres, she will! Her dystopian murder-mystery series, 'Dark Water', perfectly shows her love for blending genres and exploring emotional complexity.

When she's not gleefully plotting her next cliffhanger, you'll find her singing along to musical theatre hits, obsessing over Tudor history, and eating far too many scones.

She lives between London and Somerset with two cats who are excellent writing assistants, provided your definition of "assistance" includes strategic keyboard-sitting and delivering unwanted wildlife gifts at crucial plot moments.

Xanthe writes epic emotional rollercoasters, but she promises the landing is always worth the journey.

Come and join her on her friendly Facebook group Xanthology.

You can find all her links on Linktree: https://linktr.ee/xanthewalter

ACKNOWLEDGMENTS

First and foremost, to Emma—thank you for living this book alongside me for so many years and patiently waiting to discover the murderer's identity!

To Angela, who devoured every chapter I sent within a day and provided immediate feedback—thank you for the countless hours spent discussing every aspect of this story with such enthusiasm.

An enormous debt of gratitude goes to my trusted team of audiencers and betas who have been with me since my fandom days. Chris, Leslie, and dot—this book wouldn't exist without your unwavering support and guidance. Also to Lauren, a recent addition to my beta team but hugely valuable. Thank you for your laser sharp attention to detail.

To my incredible Team Xanthe—your practical help and support have been invaluable.

My heartfelt thanks to my wonderful friends in Walter's World, Xanthology, and on my personal Facebook page, whose constant encouragement has meant the world to me.

Special thanks to Jacci, my website designer, for creating such a beautiful site and patiently handling my creative manias and OCD suggestions with grace.

To Tessa, my editor—thank you for tidying my language and your invaluable input. And to Toby, my proof-reader—you are truly awesome in every way.

Finally, to my beloved Penny—demon crocheter, Photoshop wizard, and devoted mother to black labradors. Though you didn't live to see book four, I've woven a special tribute into its pages just for you.

Copyright © 2025 by Xanthe Walter

All rights reserved.

No part of this book may be reproduced in any form or by any electronic or mechanical means, including information storage and retrieval systems, without written permission from the author, except for the use of brief quotations in a book review.

This is a work of fiction. Any resemblance to actual persons, living or dead, or actual events is purely coincidental.

Printed in Dunstable, United Kingdom